ECHOES OF THE DANCE

Acclaimed ballerina Mim was forced to give up dancing after a tragic accident. Knowing that her name would attract even more pupils a friend who ran a successful stage school persuaded her to join the business.

Now, nearly twenty-five years later, history is repeating itself. Daisy, Mim's special protégée, is suffering from injuries and she too will have to rethink her career. Mim arranges for Daisy to take a holiday in Cornwall, in the strange and beautiful house on the edge of Bodmin Moor where Mim's brother, Roly Carradine, is living.

Daisy, starting a new love affair, has difficulty in concentrating on her future but her curiosity and devastating self-awareness enable Roly to take a fresh look at his relationship with the newly widowed Kate Porteous. Meanwhile the arrival of Roly's ex-wife forces their son, Nat, to confront some unfinished business.

Roly, Kate, Daisy and Nat must all find resolution in the beauty and peace of the Cornish countryside.

ECHOES OF THE DANCE

Marcia Willett

WINDSOR
PARAGON

First published 2006
by
Bantam Press
This Large Print edition published 2006
by
BBC Audiobooks Ltd by arrangement with
Transworld Publishers

Hardcover ISBN 10: 1 4056 1452 8
ISBN 13: 978 1 405 61452 8
Softcover ISBN 10: 1 4056 1453 6
ISBN 13: 978 1 405 61453 5

British Library Cataloguing in Publication Data available

Printed and bound in Great Britain by
Antony Rowe Ltd., Chippenham, Wiltshire

To Annie Keay

Family Trees

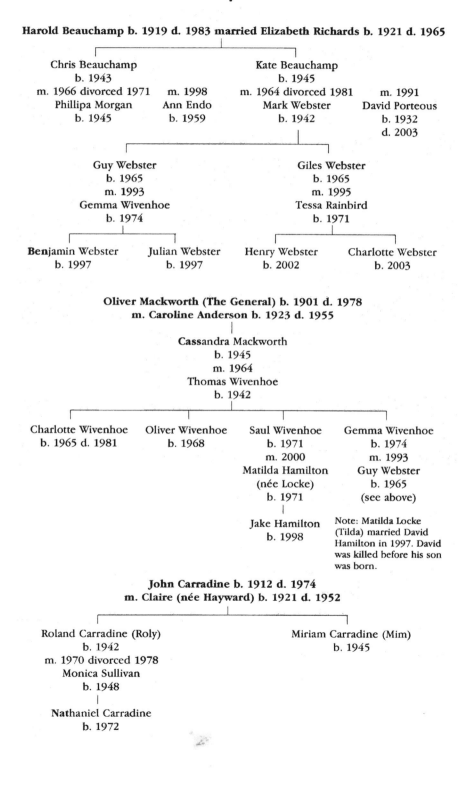

Harold Beauchamp b. 1919 d. 1983 married Elizabeth Richards b. 1921 d. 1965

Chris Beauchamp
b. 1943
m. 1966 divorced 1971
Phillipa Morgan
b. 1945

m. 1998
Ann Endo
b. 1959

Kate Beauchamp
b. 1945
m. 1964 divorced 1981
Mark Webster
b. 1942

m. 1991
David Porteous
b. 1932
d. 2003

Guy Webster
b. 1965
m. 1993
Gemma Wivenhoe
b. 1974

Giles Webster
b. 1965
m. 1995
Tessa Rainbird
b. 1971

Benjamin Webster
b. 1997

Julian Webster
b. 1997

Henry Webster
b. 2002

Charlotte Webster
b. 2003

**Oliver Mackworth (The General) b. 1901 d. 1978
m. Caroline Anderson b. 1923 d. 1955**

Cassandra Mackworth
b. 1945
m. 1964
Thomas Wivenhoe
b. 1942

Charlotte Wivenhoe
b. 1965 d. 1981

Oliver Wivenhoe
b. 1968

Saul Wivenhoe
b. 1971
m. 2000
Matilda Hamilton
(née Locke)
b. 1971

Gemma Wivenhoe
b. 1974
m. 1993
Guy Webster
b. 1965
(see above)

Jake Hamilton
b. 1998

Note: Matilda Locke
(Tilda) married David
Hamilton in 1997. David
was killed before his son
was born.

**John Carradine b. 1912 d. 1974
m. Claire (née Hayward) b. 1921 d. 1952**

Roland Carradine (Roly)
b. 1942
m. 1970 divorced 1978
Monica Sullivan
b. 1948

Miriam Carradine (Mim)
b. 1945

Nathaniel Carradine
b. 1972

PART ONE

CHAPTER ONE

Uncle Bernard was becoming bored with sitting in his drawer. Although he liked to be raised above the other dogs—he considered it to be quite right and proper that a person of his age and infirmity should be granted certain privileges—he was now looking forward to his late morning ritual of a little gentle exercise. He fidgeted irritably. Bevis, stretched out on his side on the flagstones in a puddle of early May sunshine, rolled a sympathetic eye upwards but didn't move until he heard the sound of a car's engine. Both dogs grew alert, ears cocked, listening to familiar sounds: the crunch of tyres, the slam of a door, Roly Carradine's footsteps crossing the yard.

As the door opened, the telephone on the deep-set slate windowsill began to ring. Roly dropped a bulging plastic bag onto a chair, gave Bevis a quick pat and hastened to answer it.

'Mim! How did it go?' His deep flexible voice was warm with interest. 'I didn't dare phone after your description of the dress rehearsal . . . Really? What a relief . . .' Roly sank into a wicker chair, cradling the telephone between his ear and shoulder as he listened to his sister's excited voice, pulling Bevis's ears as the big retriever pushed his head against his outstretched legs. Her voice changed down a gear and Roly's cheerful expression altered to one of frowning concentration. 'Who? Who did you say? Daisy Quin? Yes. Yes, the name is familiar . . . A serious injury? . . . Yes, I don't see why not. How long would she stay? . . . No, that's fine. And you'll be down by then? . . . OK . . . Look, shall we talk again later? I've just got in, Uncle Bernard is whining to go out, and I've just fetched a foster and she's still in the back of the car . . . About five o'clock then? Bye.'

He remained quite still for a moment, his face thoughtful, until Uncle Bernard—indignant at such a disrespectful lack of concern—yelped sharply to remind him of his duties.

'Sorry, old fellow.' Roly pushed Bevis aside and went to the battered pine chest, the top drawer of which was the elderly miniature rough-coated dachshund's sanctuary. 'Out you come.'

He lifted him down and watched him patter importantly—if rather stiffly—out into the yard, followed by Bevis who went to look at the newcomer sitting rather anxiously in the back of Roly's estate car. For the last few years, since he'd announced his early retirement and closed his photographic studio in London, Roly had been fostering dogs for the local retriever rescue society. Bevis and Uncle Bernard were quite accustomed to dealing with a procession of misfits from broken relationships, bewildered puppies abandoned as soon as their charm wore thin a few weeks after Christmas, and faithful companions whose owners had died or been moved into residential accommodation. Here they stayed until homes could be found for them.

The old stone house standing just above the ford, amidst quiet lanes with tracks winding away onto the moor and up to Rough Tor, was a perfect staging post for these confused animals. Bevis, rescued from an acrimonious divorce, was rather

4

like a kindly prefect dealing with nervous new pupils away from home for the first time, whilst Uncle Bernard—loved and cherished from the hour of his birth—adopted the attitude of a confident housemaster given to fits of irascibility at any signs of unsocial behaviour.

Roly raised the tailgate of the car and, ducking his head and hunching his broad shoulders, sat inside close to the small bitch whose tail thumped nervously as she gazed out at this unfamiliar scene. He stroked her trembling body reassuringly and she snuggled in under his arm.

'This is Bevis,' he told her. 'He's a nice person, really. I wish I could say the same for Uncle Bernard, but I wouldn't want to lie to you so early in our relationship.' Bevis advanced his nose, tail wagging, and Roly sighed with relief. 'Good fellow,' he said. 'Make her feel welcome. Her mistress died last week and she's in shock. Her name's Floss.'

He stood up, leaving the tailgate open so that Floss might choose her own time to jump out, and paused for a moment in the sunshine. Across the yard, at right angles to the house, a small stable was set back a little, a short flight of steps climbing to the upper storey and its own front door. It provided excellent—if minimal—guest accommodation and had been a useful source of income as a holiday let in the past. Now, it seemed, holiday-makers required dishwashers, jacuzzis, and wall-to-wall luxury—even on the edge of Bodmin Moor—and these days the flat was used by their own friends, who came with Mim from London at regular intervals to escape from the city. At least it would be available for Daisy Quin.

'Do you remember me telling you about her?' his sister had asked. 'She was one of my favourite pupils. Well, everyone loved Daisy: a real sweetie and such a gifted dancer. She'd just begun to get principal roles with the company she joined last year. Such a blow . . .'

He hadn't asked the nature of Daisy's injury: Mim's words—bringing forcibly to his mind her own terrible accident—were enough to tie his tongue and tense his muscles.

'It's a partly torn muscle in her back and the tissue is badly inflamed,' Mim had added quickly, as if guessing his reaction. 'She did it during rehearsal about six weeks ago and it's pretty serious because it's the third time she's damaged it and each time it takes longer to heal. Anyway, the company has gone on tour without her. She's managing to get about again and I thought a holiday in Cornwall might do her good. Would you mind?'

Of course he didn't mind. It would be good to have some company: human company. He opened the plastic bag that contained Floss's worldly goods and experienced the now familiar pang of compassion: a good-quality leather lead, a green Frisbee, two hard rubber balls and a well-chewed teddy with both ears missing. These were her toys. A clean tartan rug, folded quite small at the bottom of the bag, and a metal feeding bowl completed the inventory. Taking one of the balls he went out to the car. Bevis was watching with benign alertness as Floss hovered uncertainly, making up her mind to jump out.

'Good girl!' said Roly encouragingly. 'Come on, then. Look! What's this?'

6

He bounced the ball several times and Bevis jumped at it, barking excitedly; even Uncle Bernard bustled back to check what was happening lest things were getting out of hand. Floss leaped from the car, chasing the ball with Bevis, and Roly reached for his cap, closed the back door, and led them all out into the lane that descended to the ford.

The clear water trickling down from the high moors barely covered the stony bed of the ford. Nevertheless, Uncle Bernard chose to cross by the old granite bridge as if to disassociate himself from the antics of the two bigger dogs, who rushed gleefully into the stream. Floss drank deeply from the icy water until Bevis barged her playfully and they began a mock fight, splashing and leaping, until Roly threw the ball far beyond the ford and they both raced after it. As he turned up onto the track he could hear the soft clicking call of a stonechat and presently saw the handsome fellow perched high on a clump of bright-flowering gorse. His warning 'tac-tac' cry indicated that he was guarding his mate's mossy nest, hidden out of sight, low down in the bushes.

It was hot: the clear air laden with the rich and exciting scent of the golden flowers. Roly breathed in deeply, joy unexpectedly expanding inside him as he felt the sun's warmth like a blessing on his shoulders. It was at times like these that he remembered the real reason for returning to Cornwall: a determination to cast off guilt and anxiety, or at least to put such destructive powers into proportion, whilst accepting these moments of peace. The dogs were with him again, bringing the ball, jostling to be the first to chase it. It was wet and slimy in his hand as he took it from Bevis's mouth to fling it higher up the path but, even as he grimaced and wiped his hand on his old cords, he laughed to see how they bounded away with their tails waving and paws scrabbling to grip the rocks. Uncle Bernard had picked up the scent of a rabbit and was pursuing his own course, nose to ground, and Roly paused to look around him: the piled granite outcrops of Brown Willy and Rough Tor filled the horizon ahead whilst, below him, hardy villages and farms were rooted into the land; small, scattered fortresses of stone and slate.

A jet plane screamed above his head, trailing vapour, so that the high blue board of the sky looked as if it had been scrawled upon by chalk, shaded thick in places. He watched it dwindle into the west, where smooth white clouds were heaped like pillows and he could see the distant sparkle of the sea. Calling to Uncle Bernard, he began to climb.

*   *   *

It was after a rather late lunch that Roly suddenly remembered that he'd promised to make a telephone call to his ex-wife. He sat back in his chair with a reluctant sigh, folding the newspaper he'd been reading, and then stood up and began to clear the table. He never bothered to use the dishwasher when he was alone and it took very few minutes to stack his lunch things on the draining-board. He knew very well that his decision to wash up immediately was merely a delaying tactic but he turned the tap on and reached for the detergent just the same. He had no wish to speak to Monica;

8

no desire to discuss and review the lack of ambition she attributed to their son, Nat.

'It's not that he lacks ambition,' Roly had pointed out on numerous occasions, 'it's simply that he lacks *your* particular kind of ambition. He rejects your values.'

'Just because you've decided to bury yourself in the wilds of Cornwall . . .'

'No, no! I haven't buried myself at all. I lived in London for years, spending part of the time down here. Now I've reversed that. And I'm very happy, Monica. Would you say that you are happy? And, if you're not, why do you feel able to judge what's best for Nat? He seems to be perfectly content. I've seen some of the gardens he's working on and the pleasure he brings to people. Admit it: if he worked for *Ground Force*, and you could brag to your friends that he was gardening on television, you'd be proud of him.'

These conversations usually ended in acrimonious deadlock and Roly was bored with the endless variations on the same theme. He knew, however, that Monica needed to be in touch with him, required excuses to telephone and to demand that they should meet. His own guilt, his sense of failure, made it impossible to deny her.

'She left you,' Mim would remind him. 'At the first sign of trouble she was off.'

'Oh, shut up,' he'd answer irritably. 'It's just not that simple . . .' And Mim would shrug, unmoved as always by these flashes of temper; always reasonable.

Perhaps it was because they'd relied on each other so much as children that Mim understood him so completely. Just as he'd supported her through the turbulent teenage years when she'd insisted with single-minded implacability that she wanted nothing but to be a dancer, so she had stood by him when things had gone so terribly wrong: when his heavy drinking spiralled downwards into alcoholism and he'd lost his confidence, lost his clients and lost his wife and child . . . Not that Monica was much loss as far as Mim was concerned—they'd never liked each other—but losing the small Nat had been a terrible blow to both of them.

Roly dried the last of the plates, hung the cloth on the Esse rail to dry and wandered over to the French doors that opened into the wilderness spaces of the garden behind the house. Here, as a boy, he had pottered with his mother during the last months of her long illness: here, when he was small, they'd sat beneath the arching boughs of the flowering cherry tree, watching the fish in the big ponds, and here he had first seen the heron in the garden. Until that spring, more than fifty years ago, the overhanging branches had protected the ponds and the heron was only to be seen along the river, but then winter storms had brought down two trees and opened up the wilderness so that the heron could land safely.

He was here now, dammit! Roly made as if to bang on the window but, as usual, some instinct stayed his hand. Instead he stood as immobile as the tall, elegant figure that had alighted on the branching willow some distance beyond the pond: so beautiful, so predatory. Roly moved slightly so as to get a better look and the heron rose at once, soaring with unhurried beats of his great wings, long legs trailing. He would drift downstream now, to the small colony where he and his mate nested year after year.

Turning back into the room, Roly settled himself in the wicker chair and reached reluctantly for the telephone.

CHAPTER TWO

'I'm thinking of coming down,' said Monica—and Roly's heart sank. He readjusted his grip on the telephone, trying to keep calm.

'It's difficult just at the moment,' he said. 'Mim will be home at the weekend and she's invited one of her ex-pupils to stay.'

'Don't worry,'—Monica's pinched voice implied that this was exactly the reaction she'd expected from him: an excuse—'I'm not asking you to put me up.'

Roly resisted the temptation to justify his remark and remained unhelpfully silent.

'I shall stay with Nat,' she said.

'Good,' he answered cheerfully. 'That'll be nice for both of you. In that case you'll see for yourself how he is and you won't need the usual sitrep now. How's Jonathan?'

'Busy.' Her tone was sharp but with a subtle hint of wistfulness. 'I hardly see him. He's started work on this accountancy textbook. And the wretched clients are always wanting something.'

'And to think that you wanted that for Nat.' He couldn't resist the little snipe. 'He's very contented with life. Still, you'll see that for yourself.'

'I only want his happiness, Roly.' Suddenly she

was quiet, dignified. 'It's all I've ever wanted.'

He deliberately hardened his heart against the instinctive compassion that she would immediately exploit as weakness.

'I wonder what it is that makes us all feel that happiness is some kind of divine right,' he answered lightly. 'After all, we only have to look around us to see that it's such a difficult state to achieve. Contentment, possibly, but happiness . . . ? Do you remember those lines by Alexander Pope? "Hope springs eternal in the human breast: Man never Is—but always To be blessed."' He chuckled. 'A bit of a cynic, would you say?'

'I've never understood poetry,' she answered rather coldly. 'I don't think it's cynical to hope that one's child will be happy.'

Roly sighed silently and rolled his eyes.

'Of course not,' he said. 'But it depends on how you define it, doesn't it? Clearly Nat's idea of happiness wasn't bound up in being a junior partner in Jonathan's accountancy firm. Anyway, let's not go along that path. When shall you be down?'

'I shall have to check with Nat. Some time next week, if he can put me up. I'll come over and see you all.'

The wistful note was back in her voice: that familiar intimation that nobody behaved quite fairly towards her and that, in some indefinable way, life owed her.

'That'll be good,' he said. 'We'll wait to hear from you. Must go: the dogs are asking to go out. See you soon.'

He put the telephone back on the windowsill and looked guiltily at the dogs: they lay stretched out, peacefully asleep after their long walk. With Monica—as with the heron—his feelings always tugged in direct opposition: guilt combined with the need to appease her fought against an instinctive requirement to resist her implacable will.

'Deep inside Monica there's an emptiness,' Mim had said once. 'It's terrible. We feel a compulsion to fill it with presents, kindness, ourselves even. And Monica absorbs all of it and wants more because, however much you give, it will never be enough. She's insatiable. Be very careful, Roly.'

He'd tried to laugh it off—it sounded rather dramatic—but part of him knew it to be a truth. Mim had shrugged—she never nagged or hammered home a point—and had gone away as light and graceful as she always was, even after the accident. She had such elegance and style, nothing grasping or possessive about her, driven only by a striving for perfection in her work. She was like their mother: imaginative, impulsive and gifted with the kind of spiritual quality that had made Mim such an outstanding ballet dancer and had drawn people to their mother, Claire.

It was Claire who had seen the potential in the big barn by the ford. John Carradine had saved it, with the stable and the few acres surrounding it, from the sale of his father's farm. His plan had been to knock it down and build a smart little house for his pretty new wife but Claire had been shocked.

'Knock it down, Johnnie?' she'd cried in horror. 'But it's so beautiful. Can't we simply live in it?'

She'd dragged him through the huge doorway, her imagination already seething with ideas, and rather reluctantly he'd gone along with her suggestions: putting in the kitchen at one end, with steps down into a big central dining area that led down in turn to the great slate fireplace at the further end. She'd refused to employ an architect, preferring to spend hours discussing her ideas with the local builder. It had been a long battle with the puzzled workmen but she'd persevered—charming them, inspiring them—and the result was everything she'd dreamed of: a big living space, full of light, but warm and friendly. Her London friends came in a never-ending stream, to sit round the massive rectangular table or on deeply cushioned sofas before the big log fire, and they repaid her hospitality by working in the wild area behind the house: damming the stream to make the big ponds, planting bulbs and shrubs.

Roly had heard the story many times; he could remember 'the chums'—as his parents called them—arriving, sometimes by car, sometimes having to be collected from the train at Bodmin. If they wondered why Claire had given up a promising stage career to settle on the edge of a wild Cornish moor with a young veterinary surgeon they'd ceased to mention it by the time Roly was old enough to understand.

He settled himself more comfortably in the wicker chair, remembering the way she was then.

*　　　*　　　*

If he half-closes his eyes he can see her dancing over the flagged floor with baby Miriam in her arms; he can hear her voice—'Begin the Beguine'; 'These Foolish Things'. Mim leans out from her

14

mother's arms, willing her to go faster, to twirl around, and Roly laughs as he watches them, his crayoning forgotten. He twists round in the Windsor chair to see them as they go waltzing past. Father's fat Clumber spaniel, Claude, barks encouragingly as Mim screams with delight at the movement. The wireless is tuned to the Light Programme and the dance music goes on and on, seamlessly swinging from one tune to the next. Mother sinks down at last, out of breath, her face flushed with exertion, but Mim's mouth turns down at the corners.

'Dance!' she cries imperiously. 'More dance!'

'Tyrant,' says Mother, laughing at Mim. 'I can't manage another step. You must dance on your own if you want to dance,' and she sets Mim down upon the floor, where she stands for a moment, getting her balance, her eyes wide as she listens to the music. Then she is off, staggering a little but turning and hopping, arms held high, her face rapt with the joy of it.

'Don't you want to dance?' Mother leans across the table to him, her fair hair falling all about her face, and he shakes his head.

He doesn't want to dance but he wishes that he could make a picture of her just as she is looking at him now, with her hair anyhow and her eyes glowing. He wants to capture that look and keep it for ever. Instinctively he reaches for his crayon but she smiles and turns away, laughing at Mim's antics, so that he has to try to remember exactly how it was with her face and hair, and the shining look that seems to come from inside her.

*　　　*　　　*

15

Roly jumped awake as Bevis nudged gently at his knee.

'Good grief!' he muttered. 'Sorry, old boy. Was I nodding?'

Floss was watching him from her rug and he felt a pang of sympathy for her. What must it feel like to be suddenly taken from your home and put amongst strangers? It was a fine balance, making fostered dogs feel welcome but not allowing them to bond with him or with his own dogs: they needed to be ready to move on to new homes. He bent to fondle her ears and she sat up, tail wagging hopefully. He glanced at his watch: another hour at least until Mim was due to telephone.

'Come on,' he said. 'We'll take a walk up to the farm and see if they have any cream.'

He picked up Floss's lead, lifted Uncle Bernard from his drawer, and they all went out together into the warm spring sunshine.

*   *   *

Later, after Mim's telephone call, he had a more complete picture of Daisy Quin. It had been clear from the beginning, Mim told him, that Daisy's career was more likely to be bound up in dancing than in acting or singing, yet she'd been the best all-rounder the school had ever had. It was Mim herself, once so single-minded, who had encouraged Daisy to extend her talents: to develop a wide area of expertise to fall back on if something should go wrong. Nobody knew better than Mim how very vital it was to be flexible in the precarious world of dance.

16

After the accident, a friend who ran a successful stage school persuaded Mim to join her. She knew that Mim's name would attract even more pupils and she promised that the dancing classes would be Mim's own special province.

'You can see for yourself,' Jane West had said bluntly, 'how important it is to be versatile.'

Now it seemed that Daisy might have to be versatile too. Roly had said as much to Mim.

'Yes . . .' she'd answered—but she'd sounded vague, as if she was searching for something just below the surface of her thoughts. 'There's an idea—nothing I can quite grasp yet. Daisy was different: rather special. I need to see her again.'

Roly had made no attempt to press her—he knew Mim in this mood—yet the conversation increased his curiosity and he realized that he was looking forward to meeting Daisy Quin.

CHAPTER THREE

Daisy Quin woke early on Friday morning. She could hear the blackbird singing in Henrietta Park—Pavarotti of the Park she called him—and the crying of the gulls as they drifted upriver. As she stretched sleepily, carelessly, the sharp pain knifing in her back and down her leg seized her anew with an awareness of her vulnerability and fear. The physiotherapist was by no means able to reassure her how fast, or even how total, her recovery might be and her short-term contract had expired at the end of the rehearsal period. Now it was the old story for the dancer: no performance, no fee.

She edged stiffly out of bed, sitting for a moment on the side of it and stretching cautiously, and then went into the kitchen to make some tea. They'd been so lucky, she and Suzy and Jill, to find this flat in Henrietta Street. During the last two years she'd made herself very much at home in Bath and the prospect of having to leave it was grim indeed. Especially just now. . .

Daisy took her mug to the window and gazed down into the street. She was by nature an optimist and she struggled valiantly with the twin devils of misery and depression, refusing to dwell on the dismal results of her disastrous fall during rehearsal six weeks earlier. Instead she thought about her forthcoming journey to Cornwall, smiling with gratitude when she remembered Mim's sympathetic reaction. She sipped her tea slowly, watching the splashy patterns of sunlight in the blossom of the trees in the park, and all the while conscious of a small car parked beside the kerb.

She almost missed him when he came out. Suddenly he was there, below her on the pavement: briefcase in one hand, his car-keys in the other. He opened the door, hesitated, and then turned to cast a swift look upwards. She almost ducked out of sight, suddenly fearing that he'd think she was watching out for him—'Well so you are,' she told herself—but, instead, raised her mug as if in salute. He lifted his hand in response, climbed into the car and drove away.

She drew back from the tall sash-window, feeling both elated and slightly foolish. After all, they barely knew each other.

'I'm your new neighbour,' he'd said as they'd arrived in the hall together one evening towards the middle of March. 'Paul Maynard.'

'Daisy Quin,' she'd said, liking him at once. He had very dark hair and his eyes were bright and quick. Everything about him was quick: his gestures, his movements, even the way he talked.

'Hello, Daisy Quin,' he'd said. 'Are you first floor or second floor?'

'First,' she'd answered. 'With Suzy and Jill. We're dancers with the Upstage Dance Company.'

He'd looked so surprised that she'd laughed at his expression.

'Someone has to do it,' she'd joked—and he'd laughed too.

'I love the dance,' he'd said. 'What fun. I'm settling myself in so as to be ready to take over the Art Department at Beechcroft School next term. Lots to do. See you later, Daisy Quin.'

He'd opened his door and vanished inside so quickly that she'd felt oddly bereft. Indeed, had it been anyone else she would have considered it almost ill-mannered, but there was some quality about Paul Maynard that made her certain that no rudeness was intended. She'd gone on her way thoughtfully, unable to put him out of her mind. It was odd, too, that she didn't mention him to Jill or Suzy. She couldn't quite bring herself to make the usual jokey observations about their new neighbour that would have been normal under the circumstances but, instead, waited to see if either of them met him by chance.

Neither of them mentioned him and then, a few days later, she saw him again in Argyle Street. She'd stopped at the florist on Pulteney Bridge and her arms were full of tulips; as she paused at the kerb, waiting to cross, she found him suddenly beside her. He smiled delightedly, as if she were the one person he was hoping to see.

'Daisy,' he said. 'How nice! And what gorgeous flowers.'

'Tulips are my favourites.' She smiled back at him, foolishly glad because he'd remembered her name, confused but so pleased to see him. 'Especially this dark rich purple colour.'

'In that case,' he answered at once, 'I think we should go to Bar Chocolat and have something delicious, don't you? Your flowers will match their décor so perfectly.'

She was surprised at this impulsive invitation but his ease of manner and complete naturalness made refusal seem immature and boorish.

'It's one of my favourite places,' she admitted, 'but I have to ration myself. The toasted coconut fudge ice cream is to die for.'

They crossed the road together, pausing to read the words on the blackboard outside—'Who says only pigs like truffles?'—before going into the little café. Sitting at the small round table, with Daisy's tulips laid carefully on one of the purple and chrome seats, they studied the card that told them that the drink of the month was iced orange and geranium chocolate.

'Well, who could resist that?' asked Daisy contentedly. 'Are you an orange and geranium man, would you say?'

He grinned at her. 'I am now.'

They laughed and suddenly she was seized with an uncharacteristic fit of shyness. Looking at him more closely she could see now that he was probably thirty-five—a good ten years older than she was—and she guessed that his ease of manner was all part of a sense of rightness with himself. He wasn't overbearingly self-confident, he was simply himself and happy to be so. He ordered their drinks and then began to talk about an exhibition he'd seen at the Holburne Museum; he was so unaffected, so utterly natural, that her awkwardness quickly passed and she was able to relax.

Afterwards, they walked back to Henrietta Street and he left her in the hall with the same abruptness she'd witnessed at their first meeting.

He was absent for nearly the whole of April, no sign of him or his car, and she guessed that he was away for the school holidays. Then, early one evening as she was letting herself in after a gruelling session with the massage therapist, he appeared beside her at the front door. As she passed before him into the hall, he saw at once that all was not well.

'What's up?' he asked. 'Been working too hard?'

She grimaced miserably and explained the problem: the accident in rehearsal just after their last meeting, the diagnosis, how she'd been dropped from the company's three months' European tour. Her natural optimism had sustained a grievous blow that she was unable to hide and his sympathy was genuine and wholehearted.

'That's terrible,' he said. 'You must feel absolutely gutted. And I was going to ask you if you'd like to come to the ballet at the Theatre Royal at the end of the month. The last thing you'd want to do now, I should think.'

'Have you got tickets for the Royal New Zealand Ballet?' She was jolted out of her misery. 'Oh, I should love it. I was expecting to be abroad so I never booked and now it's sold out.'

'A friend of mine can't make it and gave me a couple of tickets. *Romeo and Juliet*, isn't it?'

She took a deep, happy breath of delight. 'It's a new production choreographed by Christopher Hampson. He's fantastic and it's had the most amazing reviews . . .'

Words failed her and he smiled at her enthusiasm.

'Then I'll take that as a "yes". I'll let you know which evening it is when I've checked the tickets. And I'm really sorry about the accident and everything.'

He took out his key, gave her a smiling little glance and vanished. Once again she experienced the sensation of being abandoned; the warmth he spread so comfortingly around her twitched away suddenly as if a blanket had been pulled from her shoulders. She slowly climbed the stairs, depression held at bay by the definite prospect of seeing him again, trying to analyse her feelings. He was so . . . friendly? No, that wasn't quite the right word here. He seemed so *accessible*—a sense of real intimacy was so swiftly established—and yet as soon as he was gone she felt that no real progress had been made. It would be impossible, for instance, for her to go back downstairs now, bang on his door and invite him up for a drink. Why? It seemed that, without her being aware of it, Paul Maynard had already laid down certain rules for their relationship: he might invite her to the Bar Chocolat and to the ballet but not into his flat.

This was at the root of her confusion: it would have been so natural to have said, 'Come on in while I look for the tickets,' or something like that. Instead there had been another charming brush-off; the quick smile, the little wave, and he'd disappeared. Perhaps the flat was still in a muddle—after all, he hadn't been in very long—or perhaps he was in a rush to go out again or had work to do.

'Next time,' Daisy promised herself, 'I'll invite him up for a drink.'

She wondered when 'next time' might be, knowing that the Royal New Zealand Ballet was due in Bath at the end of the month: three weeks away. Briefly she wished she hadn't accepted Mim's invitation but common sense soon reasserted its hold. It would be crazy to take it all too seriously.

Two days later she found a note folded small on top of her letters on the shelf in the hall downstairs. It read: 'Friday 28th May at 7.30. How about a 7 o'clock start? Come down and bang on the door when you're ready. P.M.'

She hoped she might see him to confirm the plan but decided to scribble a note in return anyway: 'Seven o'clock is fine. Looking forward to it. Daisy.' After a few moments' thought she added: 'Away in Cornwall for a week from Sunday.'

She reread his note several times, thinking that to sign himself by his initials was rather formal, but all the while she was aware of a deep-down stirring of excitement.

Now, on this bright spring morning, watching his car pull away from the kerb, Daisy wondered if she was falling in love with him.

CHAPTER FOUR

She'd decided to hire a car for the trip to Cornwall. It was an extravagance but she simply couldn't endure the prospect of uncomfortable hours on the train: at least, if she drove herself, she could take regular breaks. This was to be her regime for the foreseeable future: plenty of rest interspersed with gentle stretching exercises to give the torn tissue the chance to heal. Daisy groaned with frustration. Moderation was not something she practised in her daily round; she was generous, enthusiastic, given to impulsive activity. Being careful did not come naturally to her and restraint was boring. Until now, her energizing drive had been channelled into her work: beginning at eight years old at the stage school, continuing amongst other things as a backing dancer for a music video, a stint as one of the six dancers in *Phantom* and for the last two years with the Upstage Dance Company.

She'd been working with a young director and choreographer, Tony Henderson, who was developing his own techniques with modern dance rooted in classical ballet. He'd begun to single her out, working with her on exciting new ideas, and slowly they'd begun to explore the relationship that was developing between them; uncovering the secret core that was an essential part of their joint talent. He'd try to convey the creative process in his head with a gesture—sometimes even a drawing—to which her body would respond with a series of movements. She had no overview, no

24

concept of what potent, inexplicable images he was seeing, but together they would build the piece, always giving and receiving each to the other. Sometimes they'd argue: 'That's not the right step,' she might say, frowning as she searched for some particular movement. 'Like *this* . . .' She'd demonstrate, totally absorbed in finding the perfect expression of the idea, whilst he'd watch critically.

'Who's the choreographer here?' he might ask from time to time—half amused, half irritated—and she'd have to bite her tongue.

Daisy tore her mind away from the thought that Jill would be dancing those roles in Paris and Prague and concentrated instead on the visit to Cornwall. It would be so wonderful to see Mim again. It was two years since Daisy had made a guest appearance at the stage school's celebrated Christmas Charity Matinée and, though she always kept in touch with cards and the occasional telephone call, she was looking forward to spending time with the woman who had been such an inspiration to her. After all, Mim knew what it was like to be in this particular position, although she never talked about it. By the time Daisy started at the stage school the story was already a legend, hidden all about with secrecy and mystery. There were several versions of the cause of Mim's injury. One story was that a taxi driver had run over her foot by accident whilst she was taking her luggage out of the car; another related that the taxi driver had actually dropped a very heavy case on her foot. Either way, the damage was such that Mim could never dance properly afterwards.

The odd thing was that she'd been able to

translate her wonderful gift into inspiring children to dance. Even at eight years old, Daisy had seen at once that Mim wasn't like the other ballet mistresses—she rarely taught a class alone—her magic lay in instilling some kind of ardour, a passion to stretch further, to jump higher, to give that tiny bit extra for her.

Daisy smiled, remembering the tiny pulse of excitement that would shudder through the class when Mim put her head round the studio door. Dressed always in soft, fluid materials of dark, subtle colours—forest green, indigo blue, charcoal grey—and wearing neat leather ankle boots that were supple as dancing slippers, she had a style all her own.

'Come, my darlings,' she'd say with a wicked smile, 'you can do better than that.'

Oh, how true it was: how high they sprang, how they arched their feet and injected some extra grace into their arms. Breathing hard, beaming back at her with delight, they strived to win that special smile or the touch of her hand placing the head, lifting an arm.

'Well done, my darling. Oh, that's perfect . . . now on you go—and one—and two—and three'— and she'd be gone, the door closing quietly behind her.

At the beginning of a dress rehearsal a chair might be placed beside the piano and then a delicious rustle of nervous excitement would ripple around the assembled pupils: 'Madame's coming to watch!'

She'd sit quite still, unobtrusive but potent, and each one of them would drag their performance up a notch, no matter how exhausted they were or

26

how much their muscles ached or their feet hurt. That shining smile and the little gesture she made to indicate approval—hands held high to clap lightly—were worth any amount of pain.

'My darling Daisy! How terrible!' she'd cried, when Daisy had telephoned.

She'd listened carefully to Daisy's troubled story and had immediately suggested the trip to Cornwall.

'I'm going down for a short break and it would do you so much good to have a rest right away from Bath. You simply mustn't sit there moping alone. Anyway, Roly would love to meet you. I'll ask him to send you directions. I'm simply hopeless at that kind of thing and we're rather hidden away.'

He'd done better than that: he'd telephoned.

'I'm so glad that you can get away,' he'd said, as if it were she who was conferring the treat. 'Mim's often spoken of you. Now how would it be if you took down some directions? Got a pencil?'

Getting from the A38 onto the A30 sounded very simple but shortly after he'd talked her past Launceston and onto more local roads she'd begun to laugh.

'Help!' she'd said. 'I'm lost already. I've got it all down but if I could have your telephone number I'll put it into my mobile and then you can rescue me if need be.'

He'd chuckled too. 'If you can get a signal,' he'd warned. 'Don't worry. I'll send you a blow-up of the local map and you'll be fine. Can you manage short walks? . . . You can? Then don't forget your walking boots.'

He'd done just as he'd promised. Each small

road, crossroad and lane along her route was inked with red, leading all the way to the edge of the moor and the ford. Attached to the map was a drawing: an enlarged section of the lane over the ford and the house itself. He'd drawn himself and Mim waiting outside with several dogs in attendance: two retrievers and a small brown person that she'd identified as a dachshund. She'd laughed with pleasure at the little sketch: it captured Mim to the life—elegant, eager—and, if this tall man with a mane of white hair and the small dog in his arms were Roly, then she was very ready to love him too.

She packed her case and gathered her belongings, watching all the time for the return of the little car, listening for a ring at the doorbell. There was no sign of Paul. By Sunday morning the car had not returned and, assuming that he'd gone away for the weekend, she set off for Cornwall feeling oddly disappointed.

*   *   *

On the whole she managed very well, following Roly's instructions, recognizing odd names from their conversation: Kennards House, Pipers Pool, St Clether. Once she'd turned off into the quieter roads she drove slowly, delighted with the variety of the countryside that was unfolding around her. Here, in this tiny village, the sheltered cottage gardens were full of flowers, next moment she was passing over a wild heath where the silently turning sails of a wind farm transformed the landscape into a strange, bizarre world. One minute she glimpsed the sea, the next she'd plunged into a deep narrow lane sunk between high banks of thorn and furze. A board stuck in a hedge advertised a bank holiday fête: the attractions included a flower festival and duck racing.

'*Duck* racing?' Daisy rolled her eyes. How did one race ducks? She had a mental picture of a group of Jemima Puddle-Ducks racing along a track on their yellow webbed feet, quacking madly. She shook her head, dismissing such a crazy idea, and stamped painfully on the brake as a pheasant ran out in front of her. She followed it slowly whilst it zigzagged to and fro along the lane until it rocketed suddenly upwards with a clatter of wings and vanished over the hedge.

She drove on, taking one or two wrong turns but, with the aid of the map, she got herself back on the right route and it was with a sense of triumph that she passed through the ford and pulled into the yard.

Only one dog was waiting for her—one of the retrievers was lying in the sunshine—but it gave her a moment to savour the charm of the old barn and the beauty of its setting. As she climbed rather stiffly out of the car she could hear barking from somewhere inside and almost immediately a man came through the open doorway, the two other dogs at his heels. Daisy recognized him at once from the drawing.

They smiled at each other: his handclasp was warm and firm and she saw a resemblance to Mim in his smile.

'I made it,' she said triumphantly, as if she'd passed some kind of test. 'It's taken much longer than it should but I've stopped every hour to walk about a bit. Thanks for the map. I certainly needed it. What a simply heavenly place this is.'

'We like it.' He gestured towards the dogs. 'This is Uncle Bernard. Don't be fooled by his size. He's top dog here. This is Bevis and this is Floss. Her owner died and I'm fostering her until we find her a home.'

'Oh, poor girl,' cried Daisy, bending down to stroke Floss, who received the caress gratefully. 'How awful for her. She's lucky to have you, though, isn't she?'

'She's settling down very well and I'm hoping that an old friend of mine will be interested in her. She's coming over tomorrow to have a look at her. But I've got some rather disappointing news, I'm afraid. Something's cropped up and Mim won't be down for a day or two. It's nothing too serious, I understand. Someone has twisted an ankle and the understudy has developed tonsillitis. I didn't quite take it all in, but Mim's got to stay until everything's sorted out. I'm so sorry.'

'Well, I'm just so sorry that poor Mim's got problems,' answered Daisy, 'but don't worry on my behalf. Shall I be a nuisance?'

'Of course not. I'll show you the stable flat and you can get settled in. I'll be making some tea if you'd like some but you'll find all that kind of thing in the flat if you simply want to rest.'

'Rest?' Daisy grinned at him. 'How do you spell it? I need some exercise after all that sitting and I'd love some tea.'

His smile was so like Mim's that she felt that she'd known him for ever.

'Tea first,' he agreed, 'and then we'll walk the dogs a little way up on to the moor, if you feel up to it. Let me take that big case.'

He led the way up the flight of stone steps and she followed him, full of eager anticipation, whilst the dogs sat in a semicircle at the foot of the steps and waited patiently for their return.

CHAPTER FIVE

The flat was charming. A tiny lobby, with some pegs and space for gumboots, opened into a square living room that had a window on to the yard and another looking up to the moor behind the stable. The rough stone walls were washed a warm yellow and two comfortable sofas faced each other across the room, one beneath each window. A small wood-burning stove sat on a slate hearth with logs in a big basket to one side.

'This is just so nice,' declared Daisy. 'And you've lit the fire for me.'

'It can be a chilly little place,' admitted Roly, 'and it's not summer yet by any means. We converted the stables in the seventies when our father died and it's a bit rough and ready by modern standards but our friends like it. Through here is the kitchen.'

He led the way beneath an arch to the left of the stone fireplace into a small kitchen and, passing through another tiny lobby, opened the door into the bedroom.

'I hope you'll be comfortable.' He put her case on a chair. 'There are extra blankets in the chest and the bathroom's next door. I'm sorry that Mim isn't here to welcome you. She was so looking forward to it.'

She followed him back through the flat to the front door.

'Honestly, you don't have to apologize. I quite understand. I remember those traumatic moments very clearly. The whole place in an uproar, last-minute rehearsals, costumes being altered and everyone panicking. Everyone except Mim, that is. There's a kind of still centre inside her, isn't there? Something right deep down that nothing can ruffle.'

He stared at her, surprised at her perception.

'That's absolutely true. Even after the accident . . .' He paused, shocked at himself. He never talked about that ghastly moment to anybody.

Daisy was watching him with a kind of compassion.

'How terrible it must have been,' she said gently. 'I'm only now beginning to realize *how* terrible.'

He glanced at her quickly. 'I hope it won't be nearly so final for you,' he said.

'I hope not, too.' She felt a great need to reassure him; to see him smile again. 'I have to be patient. Take things gently.' She grimaced, self-mockingly. 'I can't tell you how dreary that seems. I am so utterly *not* patient.'

She'd succeeded: the smile flashed out and she laughed too.

'I shall keep an eye on you,' he warned her. 'Come over when you're ready.'

He went down the steps and the dogs stood up, tails wagging expectantly.

Daisy looked down at them. 'Will you lend me a dog?' she asked. 'You've got three, after all. Surely you could spare just one of them?'

Roly pretended to consider and then shook his

32

head. 'Can't be done. Uncle Bernard believes the flat to be beneath him socially. It wouldn't be fair to let Floss get too fond of you, she'll be moving on soon, and Bevis has a hang-up about going up stairs. Sorry, Daisy.'

She shrugged philosophically, waved a hand and went back inside to unpack. Roly crossed the yard, feeling surprisingly light-hearted. He'd been anxious about Daisy's arrival since Mim had telephoned, wondering how he'd cope with a girl in her situation. However, one look at that narrow clever face, with its slanting honey-brown eyes, had shown him courage and humour; her ease of manner had done the rest.

It was odd that someone so young had recognized and appreciated Mim's quality of inner serenity. It was their mother's gift. He pushed the kettle on to the hotplate and wandered out through the French doors into the wilderness garden. It was here that he remembered her best; pruning, weeding or simply standing quite still with her hands pressed against her breast—and, just occasionally, her face so full of sadness.

*   *   *

When he is small, he cannot bear to see her look so sad. He shouts to her across the garden, determined to chase away such an unhappy look, and feels a great relief when her eyes brighten and she waves to him.

'Hush,' she says, 'you'll wake Mim. Come and give the fish something to eat.'

He loves to feed the fish: to see the soft blunt mouths sucking at the bread. He watches,

33

fascinated, as those bright shapes that flicker and flash amongst the weed become braver; swimming up, so sinuous, so quick to snatch the food. Others are slower: the huge carp, Old Black and Big Blue, drift slowly upwards and gently mumble the crumbs of food into their mouths. If he moves too suddenly they turn with a great smack of their tails that sends ripples flowing across the pond.

'Look, Mother,' he says, wide-eyed with surprise. 'See the tiny ones,' and he crouches down to watch the cloud of small black fish that cruise in the green and gold depths.

'Babies,' she says, smiling. 'Lots and lots of fishy babies.'

They stand together watching the busy pond skaters who walk on the taut surface skin of the pond, casting fantastic shadows on the floor of it, whilst a dragonfly perches on the edge of a lily pad; its wings vibrate and tremble at such speed that they shimmer like bronze filaments in the sunshine. He is aware of several sensations: the heat under the trees, the feel of her hand on his shoulder, the microscopic world within the shimmering pool and the rich scents all around him.

He wants to hold this moment for ever but he knows that it is already passing: that Mim will wake and it will be time for tea. He can hear the kettle singing on the range.

*   *   *

Roly came in through the French doors as Daisy appeared at the other door. He was so dazzled by the sun and water that he frowned for a moment,

34

wondering who she was.

'I heard the kettle singing,' she was saying cheerfully, 'and Bevis was still waiting for me to show me the way. Wasn't that nice of him?'

'Bevis is a great gentleman.' Roly began to make the tea. 'He is kind and he likes people to be happy.'

Daisy was staring appreciatively around, one hand still on Bevis's head.

'What a fantastic room. And I love that galleried landing at the end. But tell me,' she sat down carefully on one of the chairs at the table, 'why Bevis doesn't like stairs.'

'No-one quite knows why he reacts so strongly but we feel he must have been beaten quite badly when he was a puppy for going upstairs. We didn't have him until he was fifteen months old. When his owners divorced, neither wanted to take him into their new lives. He was very nervous to begin with but he's a much more confident fellow now. Apart from the stairs.'

He put the teapot on the table and saw that Daisy was staring at him, shocked.

'That's terrible,' she said. 'Who would do a thing like that?'

Roly made a little face. 'People lose it, sometimes. And dogs are easy targets.'

She shivered, bending down to give Bevis a hug. 'So you rescued him,' she prompted, as though helping along with a story. 'But how did you know about him in the first place? And what happened then?'

'Some friends of mine knew the couple in question. I thought Uncle Bernard might like a friend so I met Bevis and decided to keep him.

35

We'd just moved back from London, the two of us, and there was plenty of room for another dog. Once he was settled I looked up the local rescue society and agreed to foster other dogs until homes could be found for them.'

'And you haven't been tempted to keep any of the others?'

'Not yet. There has to be a very special rapport.' He passed her a mug of tea. 'We've got lots of decent people ready to give homes to them, I'm glad to say.'

'What about Floss?' asked Daisy.

They both looked at Floss, who was sitting on her rug watching the scene rather wistfully until Roly clicked his fingers and she came to him readily.

'Floss is grieving and she needs someone who understands that,' he said. 'I might be tempted, she's got such a sweet temperament, but I have someone in mind for Floss.'

Watching him, Daisy saw an odd expression— tender and secretive—flicker across his face, and she was seized with curiosity. She thought: It's a woman and he's in love with her.

'And you think this person will understand how Floss feels?' she said. He glanced at her and she grinned back at him. 'Am I asking too many questions?' she asked. 'I don't mean to be intrusive but I'm like the Elephant's Child, I'm afraid.'

He smiled. 'You haven't got the nose for it,' he said lightly. 'But, yes, I think Kate will understand. She's grieving too. She lost her husband recently and then her dear old dog followed suit. I think she and Floss were made for each other. She's coming over tomorrow to meet her. Anyway, enough of dogs for the moment. Tell me about yourself. I know you trained in London with Mim, but what happened after that?'

She accepted his change of direction very readily and made him laugh with descriptions of the jobs she'd taken—especially one as an usher in a theatre when times were really hard—before joining the Upstage Dance Company. He poured more tea whilst she described the flat in Henrietta Street, the glories of Bath and her bitter disappointment at being left behind when the company went on tour.

'And do you have to rush back?' he asked. 'Or can you stay for a while?'

He watched with surprised interest as the narrow, vivid little face was suffused with colour. He thought: There's a man there somewhere and she's in love with him.

'I have to go back for treatment,' she said after a moment. 'For my Pilates class and to see the physio.' She shrugged. 'You know how it is.'

'Oh, yes,' he said. 'I know how it is.'

He stood up and began to remove the tea things whilst Daisy sat in silence, watching him. She was fighting back the most extraordinary desire to tell him all about Paul. Perhaps it was because he was so like Mim that she'd been so immediately at ease with him; whatever it was she must be careful not to go blurting out things like a foolish child.

'Pull yourself together,' she told herself firmly— and, dropping a kiss on Floss's golden head, she got up to help him.

*   *   *

37

Daisy slept late the next morning and took her time over her breakfast. The kitchen had been stocked up with the basic necessities so that she was able to make coffee and toast: she rejected the cereals but found a grapefruit in a bowl amongst some apples and oranges.

'I'm afraid I'm rather slow and uncommunicative much before ten o'clock,' Roly had admitted last evening after a gentle walk on the hill. 'It was those early years in London that set the pattern. Mim and I shared lodgings whilst she was training and I was at art college. She often had late performances or we had friends in—you know the form—and neither of us are early birds. I get up to let the dogs out and then potter very slowly.'

'Sounds perfect,' she'd assured him. 'If I were to have a pre-breakfast stroll, would the dogs come with me?'

'Oh, I should think so. If you follow the route we've just taken they won't let you get lost, and if Uncle Bernard gets bored he'll simply come home by himself. Enjoy yourself. Kate will be here around mid-morning to meet Floss but you'd be back by then. Come and have some coffee with us.'

As it happened she'd slept until nearly nine o'clock. Now, wandering back from washing-up in the kitchen, eating a slice of apple, she caught sight of a woman leaning on the five-bar gate. Daisy moved closer to the window and stared down curiously. She guessed that the woman was in her sixties; she had short, curling grey hair, and her chin rested on her arms that were folded along the top bar of the gate as she watched Bevis and Floss playing together in the yard.

Kate, thought Daisy.

She guessed that she'd left her car down by the ford and had walked up so as to come upon the dogs unannounced. Studying her, Daisy was struck by the look on the woman's face: an odd and touching mixture of tenderness and loss. A little smile lifted the corners of her mouth but her whole expression was one of sadness.

Daisy finished her apple, curbing a desire to go out and give her a hug.

'What are you like?' she asked herself derisively. 'Hugging people you've never met.'

Even as she watched, Roly came out of the house. It was clear that Roly hadn't heard Kate arrive and he gave an exclamation of pleasure that distracted the dogs from their game. They rushed to meet him and, all in a moment, there was great activity. Bevis jumped up at the gate with woofs of welcome and even Floss, losing a little of her reticence, went to claim her share in the greeting. They remained for a moment, Kate leaning on the gate with Roly beside her, discussing the dogs and completely relaxed. Then Roly made some comment that made Kate laugh and a look of great affection—and something more—passed between them.

Quite suddenly, Daisy felt as if she were spying on something infinitely private. She turned away quickly, glancing at her watch: nearly a quarter to eleven. She'd give it half an hour and then go and say hello.

CHAPTER SIX

Kate was sitting at the massive central table, Bevis on one side and Floss by her feet, with Uncle Bernard sleeping peacefully in his drawer when Daisy arrived. Roly placed a huge cafetiere on the table and smiled at her.

'We were hoping you'd turn up,' he said. 'So what happened to that pre-breakfast walk?'

She made a face at him. 'It went the way of all good resolutions,' she answered. 'I slept late.' She paused, her eyes widening with surprise. 'Why is Uncle Bernard sitting in that drawer?'

'Ah,' said Roly. 'Well, it all started when we had two young dogs staying about two years ago. They were litter brothers and their owners simply couldn't cope. We didn't want to split them so I had them here. Poor old Uncle Bernard got tired of being trodden on and generally overlooked so I cleared the drawer out and put him up out of harm's way.'

'It went to his head,' said Kate. 'He looks down on us all now.'

Roly made the introductions. Now that they were face to face Daisy saw that Kate was younger than she'd first judged. The lines around the eyes and mouth indicated that life hadn't always been kind but, looking into the smiling grey eyes and holding Kate's thin brown hand, Daisy's instinct told her that here was someone who generally rejected bitterness and self-pity in favour of the hope of better things to come—but, this time, was finding the battle a difficult one.

40

Realizing that she was staring almost rudely, Daisy turned away and sat down beside her.

'Roly says that you've barely had time to settle in,' Kate was saying. 'Have you been to Cornwall before?'

Daisy shook her head. 'It's my first time. I haven't seen much of it yet but we've been up on the moor for a walk. It's so wild and beautiful, isn't it?'

Kate shrugged. 'It's not bad,' she said, glancing mischievously at Roly. 'But if it's real moorland you want, Daisy, then you need to come and see Dartmoor.'

Roly shook his head warningly. 'Don't start on that one,' he told her. 'We've agreed to differ. Remember?'

Kate gave Daisy a tiny wink. '*He's* agreed to differ,' she said to her, 'but that's because he's a compromising Celt. Between you and me, there's no contest.'

'I gather you don't live round here?' Daisy began to like her very much.

'My family moved from Somerset to West Cornwall when my father took early retirement. But early in my married life I rented a house on Dartmoor and after that I was hooked. I've lived on the moor near Tavistock for nearly thirty years.' She hesitated. 'But perhaps not for too much longer. I was going to tell you earlier, Roly, but Floss distracted me. I've arranged to have the house valued.'

Kate bent down to stroke Floss, as if aware that her remark would have an effect she did not want to see. She murmured to the dog for a moment and then straightened up again to reach for her

41

mug of coffee. Roly was standing quite still, staring at her in surprise.

'You've finally decided then.'

It wasn't really a question but Kate answered anyway.

'I think I have—well, you know all the reasons why.'

Roly sat down and poured himself some coffee. Daisy felt once more as if she were witnessing a private moment between the two of them and, as if she guessed this, Kate smiled ruefully at her.

'Sorry. This is one of these ongoing conversations that Roly and I indulge in at regular intervals. I have this big Victorian semi-detached house. You know the kind of thing? High ceilings, huge rooms, big garden with a paddock that opens on to the moor. Now I'm on my own it's simply crazy to go on living there, even if I could afford to, which I can't. It costs the earth to decorate it and heat it and, anyway, I need to add to my pension fund by downsizing, but even so, I can't quite bring myself to move. Each time I think I've made the decision to leave I lose my nerve about ten minutes afterwards. I'm driving Roly mad with it.'

'Not a bit of it.' He spoke automatically but his eyes were thoughtful. 'You must do what's right for you.'

'If only I knew what that was,' muttered Kate wretchedly.

Despite the fact that it was none of her business, Daisy was now absorbed by the small drama.

'Why is it so difficult?' she asked. Her genuine interest robbed the question of any idle curiosity. 'Can't you find a smaller house in—where did you

42

say?—Tavistock?'

'Kate is thinking that it's time she had a complete change.' Roly answered Daisy whilst Kate hesitated. 'The difficulty is that she can't quite decide what sort of change.'

'Oh, I know,' cried Daisy eagerly. 'Having choices is utter hell, isn't it? Much easier to be told where to live and what to do.'

Kate looked at her in surprise. 'You're absolutely right. For the first time for years I have only myself to plan for. In fact, this is the very first time. Although I'd been alone for a while when I first met David, that's my late husband, the boys—my twin sons—were still young enough to want to come home from university from time to time so there was a point to keeping everything going. Now they're both happily married and not very far away, David's gone, and I just rattle about feeling sorry for myself. Anyway, it's not your problem . . . But you're so right about having choices. It's hell! Now I don't even have the dogs to worry about I ought to change the car for something small and economical.' She shook her head despairingly. 'I can't even manage that. It's crazy. I must be sensible. All I need is a tiny cottage and a tiny car. Should be simple.'

'But what about Floss?' asked Daisy anxiously. Roly and Kate exchanged a glance and she frowned, distressed. 'Am I speaking out of turn? It was just something Roly said—or did I misunderstand? Oh damn . . .'

She groaned with embarrassment as Roly and Kate began to laugh.

'It's OK,' Kate reassured her. 'He didn't say so in so many words but I knew what he was hoping when he asked me to come and see Floss. Dear Roly. He tries to sort us all out, you know. Me, Monica, Mim, Nat . . .'

'Utter rubbish.' Roly shifted uncomfortably. 'I wouldn't have the courage to attempt to interfere in anyone's life.'

Daisy drew breath to ask about Monica and Nat—these were names she hadn't heard before—and then decided that she'd been quite inquisitive enough for the time being.

'I don't remember using the word "interfere",' Kate was saying lightly. She was smiling at Roly. 'And I must admit that I'm very taken with Floss.'

Daisy saw hope leap up in Roly's face. 'She's a very nice person,' he said.

Kate took the dog's head between her hands. 'She's missing her mistress,' she murmured. 'Aren't you, Floss?'

'Shall we give them a walk?' Roly pushed his chair back from the table. 'It would do us all good. Come on, Daisy. What were you saying about rest and gentle exercise? Well, you've had a jolly good rest, by the sound of it.'

Daisy went away to put her boots on, her natural curiosity thoroughly stirred by Kate's dilemma. As she laced up her boots, easing her back carefully, she realized that she hadn't thought about her own problems—or Paul—for almost an hour.

*   *   *

'Sorry,' Roly was saying. 'Actually, I didn't say that you *would* have Floss. Only that you would understand how she was feeling.'

Kate put her hand on his arm.

44

'Don't apologize, for heaven's sake. Good grief, Roly, after all the support you've given me, do you think I'm likely to misunderstand you? You've only ever tried to help me. I can't believe I'm being so stupid. It's just so strange to be alone again after thirteen years. And you know how much I miss the dogs.'

'That's why I wondered about Floss.' Roly nearly covered Kate's hand with his own but couldn't quite manage it. 'She seems almost perfect for you.'

Kate turned away to look at Floss, who had gone back to sit on her bed, watching and waiting patiently.

'She's been well looked after,' she said, assessing her with a professional eye. 'How old is she? Seven? Eight?'

'She's not quite seven. Her owner was elderly so she's very quiet and obedient. She's been very well trained. You can see that she's not used to dashing about but she's certainly enjoying her walks.'

She glanced at him, amused. 'You sound very attached to her already. Are you tempted?'

'A bit. I still think she might be just what you need.'

Kate sighed with frustration. 'I just wish I knew. I'm afraid to make a commitment, you see, and then find I'm moving house.'

He looked at her. 'I expect Floss would be very happy with you even in a tiny cottage and in a tiny car. Well, not too tiny.'

Kate burst out laughing at herself. 'I'm just a crazy woman,' she said. 'There are so many memories, you see, even with the old car. I feel once I make that move I'm cutting myself off from

45

the past and everything I had and loved.' Her face grew sombre. 'But when it gets dark and I'm sitting there alone with all that big empty house around me . . .'

He put his hand out to her and she took it, holding it tightly, not looking at him.

'I'm fine,' she said, almost crossly, daring him to speak. 'Absolutely fine.'

They watched in silence as Daisy appeared in the yard and Floss went out to meet her, tail wagging.

'She's a sweetie, isn't she?' Kate gave his hand a little squeeze and let it go.

'Which one? Daisy or Floss?' asked Roly lightly, putting his hands into his pockets.

Kate chuckled reflectively. 'Both of them,' she said at last. 'To be truthful, I'd like to take them both home with me.'

CHAPTER SEVEN

As she drove back to Tavistock later that afternoon, hurrying along the narrow lanes and through the pretty village of Altarnun, Kate cursed quietly to herself. It had been unfair to announce in front of a third person that she'd arranged to have the house valued. Roly had suggested that she should give herself plenty of time before she made a major change and she'd known that Daisy's presence would prevent another circular discussion in which Roly made sensible suggestions and she was left trying to decide why she couldn't act on them. She'd long ago realized that it was

46

childish to involve other people—however dear, however wise—in her problems. If they gave advice that she couldn't follow she felt guilty and they became irritated. Not that Roly gave advice in that sense: he was far too tactful. All he'd done was to try to double-guess her own needs and guide her into some path that would be the right one for her. Now she felt that she'd cheated in some way: telling him that she'd finally reached the decision in front of a stranger had made it impossible for him to react openly.

She reminded herself that having the house valued was hardly a major step, and that she remained uncommitted to any further move, but deep inside she felt she'd behaved shabbily. The real problem was that she knew that Roly loved her: ever since David had first introduced them in London nearly thirteen years ago, Roly had not quite been able to hide his feelings for her. David had recognized it too, though they'd both agreed that they should spare Roly's pride as far as possible and never let him know that they'd guessed. Roly and Mim were two of David's oldest friends; David was godfather to Roly's son, Nat.

David had been Roly's tutor at art college and it had come as a great surprise to Kate when she'd learned that the brother and sister had been born and brought up in Cornwall. They were so very much a part of David's London circle: that group of actors and artists, dancers and writers to whom—also to her surprise—she'd become so attached. When she'd first met David he was already a well-known artist, an RA; it had been an oddly emotional meeting, tied up as it was with the untimely death of a mutual friend, and within a very short time they'd passed beyond social formalities into an unusual intimacy.

His ability to disarm her had taken her by surprise. Perhaps it was because his arrival in her life had coincided with a time of particular loneliness, with her twin boys grown up and away at university; not that she was a stranger to loneliness, having been a naval wife for ten years until her marriage to Mark Webster had finally collapsed. When her one truly passionate love affair with Alex Gillespie had also come to a disastrous conclusion she'd agreed to sell her cottage and buy the house in Whitchurch with her brother, Chris, who worked abroad and wanted a base in the UK. For the next thirteen years she'd concentrated on bringing up Giles and Guy, managing to avoid any kind of emotional commitment—until she'd met David.

Somehow, he'd managed to break down the barriers of loneliness and fear she'd so carefully erected: not that she'd made it easy for him.

'You must see that we're simply poles apart,' she'd said to him. 'I don't see how it can work. You in London, me here. I hate cities. You'd be bored rigid in the country . . .'

She'd never believed that their relationship could survive, divided between London and Dartmoor, but they'd both worked hard to make it succeed. David had been such a giving, sharing man: optimistic and a lover of life. He'd died after a long illness and she missed him terribly. With David she'd stepped out of her quiet, safe shelter and, for the third time, taken a chance on love. This time, with a much older and experienced man, she'd discovered the real happiness forged within a close companionship that was nevertheless flexible enough to give her new confidence room to grow.

Now, alone again, she was trying to build some kind of a life without him. Swallowing back her grief, Kate drove on through Fivelanes and joined the A30. She was afraid that in her loneliness she might mislead Roly, for she loved him very much, and she was trying to walk a fine line between love and friendship. It was much harder than she'd imagined. Instinctively, as she pressed her foot down on the accelerator, she glanced into her driving mirror as if half expecting to see the noble head of her dear dog and companion, Felix, gazing out at the passing countryside. Even after three months the emptiness of the car still came as a shock to her and she gripped the wheel more tightly, staring resolutely ahead. In the distance the great tors and hills of Dartmoor stretched from east to west across the horizon; powerful and dramatic, dominating the plains to the north, yet peaceful in the afternoon sunshine.

The familiar sight soothed her: all her life the moor had remained her one constant source of comfort. She relaxed, drawing a deep breath, and concentrated on the morning that had passed so happily and on her meeting with Daisy and with Floss.

*   *   *

When she pulled into her drive half an hour later she saw that someone was mowing the long lawn at the back of the house. Her spirits lifted and she went down the garden, waiting until she could make herself heard before she called out.

'Nat,' she cried, as he cut the engine and bent to check the grass-box. 'This is very kind. How nice to see you.'

He straightened up and smiled a welcome; a stocky, well-built young man, strong and tough-looking, with a flair for garden design and a natural knack of being courteous but firm with some of his more misguided clients. 'They think they know what they want,' he'd say, 'but you only have to look at a piece of ground to see its natural shape behind the shrubberies and borders. Luckily, most people are open to suggestion.'

Kate was very fond of him.

'A client cancelled,' he said, 'so I decided to drop by. I hoped you might turn up and I thought I might as well be busy while I waited.'

'Quite right.' She beamed at him. 'I wouldn't have wanted you sitting about doing nothing. I've just been down to see Roly. He's fostering a darling bitch and he's trying to tempt me. He thinks Floss would be good for me.'

Nat shook his head regretfully. 'What a bossy lot we Carradines are. Always telling other people what's best for them.'

'Oh, but it's such a relief sometimes to be told what to do,' Kate said, 'especially when you're a ditherer like me.'

'You're not a ditherer. You've got to take some life-changing decisions and that's the kind of thing that isn't done all in a moment.'

'How comforting you are. How are things? Anything new?'

Nat shrugged. 'Not much.' A slight pause. 'Mum's coming down for a few days.' He looked at

50

her and glanced away again. 'I wondered if you might come over one evening for supper.'

'I'd love to,' said Kate, undeceived by this casual invitation. 'And you could bring her here for lunch or tea or whatever.'

'Thanks. Look, I'll finish the lawn and then I could take the sit-on mower round the paddock. It's time you made the first cut now the grass is really beginning to shoot up.'

'That would be very kind,' answered Kate gratefully. She inhaled appreciatively. 'Doesn't new-mown grass smell heavenly? Come in for a cup of tea when you've done the lawn.'

He turned away, going back to his work, and Kate looked after him compassionately for a moment before finding her keys and letting herself into the house. She knew that Nat found the relationship with his mother difficult to sustain and he had often called upon Kate and David to help out when Monica was visiting. This was never easy. Monica resented the fact that, like Roly, both David and Kate had supported Nat when he'd made his decision to branch out on his own and, after his training, had let him stay with them at Tavistock whilst he found his feet.

Kate had many friends who were willing to give Nat a try and gradually he'd built up a good client base. He'd worked very hard, never turning down a job however small, until he was confident to take the lease on a small terraced cottage in Horrabridge. His gratitude to her and David took the form of looking after their big garden: cutting the grass and the hedges and providing low-level maintenance on the out-buildings. He'd kept an eye on the place when they were in London and had become almost as much a part of the family as her own sons, Giles and Guy.

'And certainly much more useful,' she said to him now, as they drank their tea standing in the warm sunshine in the little paved court behind the house, looking out onto Nat's handiwork whilst she told him the latest family news. 'The garden looks wonderful. I'm afraid I failed with my boys in that area. Neither of them are very practical, although Guy is an expert when it comes to boats.'

'What do they say about you selling up?' asked Nat. 'Do they have any helpful input?'

'They can see that this place is really too big for me now, but they agree with Roly that it would be a mistake to be too hasty in taking a decision. They warn me that I've been used to big rooms and lots of space and that I might feel claustrophobic if I go for something very small, though that's what I feel I'd like to do. The grandchildren like to come for sleepovers but, with Giles and Guy only an hour away, one spare bedroom should be more than enough.'

'And what about dogs? I have to say that you just don't look right without a dog, Kate.'

She laughed softly. 'I don't feel right,' she admitted. 'I can't tell you how much I wish I'd had a puppy before David became ill. The trouble was that my dashes to London put an end to the dog-breeding side of life, though I always meant to have another bitch before Felix was too old, and then it was too late.' She sighed frustratedly. 'To have taken on a puppy with David as ill as he was during that last year would have been crazy but I never thought I'd lose Felix so quickly too.'

Nat put an arm about her shoulders: she felt

thin and frail and he felt an upsurge of concern and affection for her. She'd been such a support during those uncertain, anxious days when his mother, with distressing scenes, tearful pleading and emotional blackmail, had tried to destroy his growing confidence: his brave new world had been a rather cold and scary place. How often he'd sat with Kate at the kitchen table, mulling over his day's work whilst she went through her address book yet again.

'Wait a minute,' she'd say, 'have we tried the Mallinsons? I'm sure their garden needs a makeover. And don't forget that Thea Lampeter said that you must go out and have a look around at her place. She wants some new ideas as to what to do with the stretch of railway track. Let's make a list . . .'

Her enthusiasm and faith in his abilities had been as comforting as a beacon shining out on a dark night and, during the two years he'd stayed at Whitchurch, a unique relationship had sprung up between him and Kate. Friends said that Kate regarded Nat almost as another son but, for Kate, it was precisely because she was *not* his mother— and, for Nat, that he was *not* her child—that this friendship had developed.

'So what about this dog Roly's found?' he asked now. 'Might she be an answer? You have to begin somewhere; why not with this dog? It's a starting point, isn't it? If you have a dog then other requirements follow. It would give you a framework to work within. The trouble with your situation is you have no guidelines. That particular kind of freedom is rather overwhelming.'

'That's what Daisy said.' Kate finished her tea.

'Daisy?'

'I think she's one of Mim's ex-pupils. She's staying in the stable flat for a little holiday. Poor Daisy has injured her back and she's been told to rest. She's great fun. In an odd way she reminds me of Janna.' There was a tiny silence and Kate glanced up at him. 'Have you heard from her?'

He shook his head. 'Not recently. You know Janna. The original free spirit. She was afraid of losing her benefit or something if she stayed on too long.'

Janna was another sore subject as far as Monica was concerned. She was convinced that no decent girl would ever settle down with Nat until he was much more financially viable; equivocal though she was about the flamboyant, new-age Janna, her absence was set to be another area of conflict that would make Monica's visit a difficult one.

'What about you?' Kate suggested gently. 'Perhaps Janna being away is an opportunity for you to be more open with Monica?'

'Perhaps.' His bleak look filled her with a fellow-feeling of confusion and anxiety. 'Why is life so damned complicated?'

'David used to say that it is we who complicate our own lives because we are afraid for all sorts of reasons to be truthful.'

'But surely some of those reasons are good ones? Not hurting people, for instance?'

Kate was silent for a moment. 'Perhaps we underestimate other people's capacity for dealing with the truth,' she ventured at last. 'Perhaps, in trying to protect them, we are actually denying them some form of growth . . . Good grief!' she interrupted herself with a derisive laugh. 'What do

I know?'

'You could be right, though.' He shrugged. 'You could pretend that you're trying to protect someone while all the time you're really trying to protect yourself from the fall-out following the truth telling.'

'Something like that.' She took his empty mug. 'Do you want to stay on for some supper?'

'No, I won't do that, thanks anyway. It's quiz night at the pub and I said I'd be there.' He glanced at his watch. 'Plenty of time to get the paddock done, though. Thanks for the tea.'

She went into the house and, as he started up the mowing machine, he tried to remember who had said that humankind couldn't stand too much reality: his mother was certainly one person who couldn't. He'd spent so much of his time as a little boy trying to make up to her for what she saw as life's unfairness: in her view his father's instability and Mim's selfishness were the two biggest crosses she had to bear. She'd counted on Nat's loyalty and love to redress the balance and when, at last, he'd broken away from her emotional demands the ensuing scenes had been destructive and terrible.

He shook his head, instinctively denying the possibility of being open and truthful with her: the mere prospect of confronting his mother still made him sweat.

CHAPTER EIGHT

Early that same evening, after she'd rested for an hour on her bed, Daisy checked the limited supply of stores she'd brought with her from Bath and made the decision to ask Roly to supper. He'd looked after them all so well that she longed to make some small return for his kindness—and, anyway, she was even more certain now that he was in love with Kate and she felt a foolish longing to comfort him.

' "Comfort me with apples for I am sick of love",' she muttered, taking some rather nice pâté and a small cheese and onion quiche out of the fridge, and trying to remember whether she was quoting from Shakespeare or the Bible. Mim had always been very keen on teaching her students to study both of these great works—'Such beautiful, beautiful language, my darlings!'—and Daisy often became muddled.

'Anyway,' she told herself rather defiantly, 'I haven't got any apples. He'll have to be comforted with pâté and a Waitrose quiche.'

Daisy was already so fond of Roly that she longed for Kate to return his love; she could see Kate's dilemma, but had hardly been able to restrain herself from pointing out to them that, by getting together, all their problems would be solved. Luckily, as she'd grown older, she'd discovered that her somewhat childlike directness was often not the best solution for her friends' troubles and had learned to control her impulse to offer simple solutions to complicated difficulties.

Meanwhile she would comfort Roly with supper.

It had been such a happy day. After a late lunch of cold roast ham, potatoes cooked in their jackets in the Esse and some of the local Davidstow cheddar, they'd all walked with Kate down to the ford to see her off. Daisy had sat on the broken wall of the old bridge with her legs dangling, watching the dogs playing in the transparent, peat-stained water below, whilst Kate and Roly talked privately for a moment. Sitting there in the hot sunshine she'd become unusually aware of the shapes and the spaces all about her: the rounded feathery trees and the humped, dense furze bushes; the stark rocky dome of the high down and the curve of the stony track; all outlined in a swooping scribble against the high roof of a cerulean sky painted with cloudy smudges and white streamers.

Daisy found that she was trying to find a physical movement to describe the glory of it . . . Suddenly, perched there on the bridge, she'd executed a *port de bras*, a swift graceful arm movement, and gasped as the pain rippled in her lower back. She'd waited for a moment, catching her breath. Carefully she'd turned round, edging her feet back onto the bridge and standing up gingerly. Kate had already climbed into her car and Roly was coming back towards the ford.

He'd glanced at her, frowned a little, and suggested that it was time for a rest. She'd nodded, grateful that he wasn't going to make a fuss, and they'd separated in the yard.

Now, feeling much better, she looked over the few delicacies with which she might tempt him and went quietly down the little stone staircase. In the

57

yard she paused: music drifted from the house and a contralto voice was singing.

Daisy went on a few steps, listening intently, strangely attracted to the music. She looked in at the door. Roly was stretched full length on a long sofa beside the fire, legs crossed at the ankles, hands clasped loosely over Uncle Bernard who lay across his chest. She felt certain that he was not asleep but she moved very quietly towards him and sat down opposite, still enchanted by that voice and by the music that made her think of the sea. Bevis came to her, putting a tentative paw upon the cushion. She encouraged him up beside her, his heavy head in her lap, glad of his company whilst she strained to hear the words that filled the quiet room.

As she listened the song changed from a gentle slumber-song, that reminded her of the ebbing tide in a safe harbour, to a passionate and almost religious intensity; and now an evocative, lightly scored quadrille was giving way to a musical storm that was almost Wagnerian in its magnificence. Daisy simply gave herself up to it. Images filled her head: sea-birds lulled by gentle waves; tall grey walls of water, foam-topped, advancing on cold stony shores: the warm, limpid seas of the coral reef; a stormy, livid ocean crested with wild white horses.

When it ceased Daisy was almost breathless. Roly opened one eye and looked at her.

'What was it?' she asked, forgetting everything but the music and the voice that had touched her so deeply.

He smiled and sat up, still clasping Uncle Bernard. 'Elgar's *Sea Pictures*,' he answered. 'The singer is Janet Baker. Wonderful stuff.'

'Sea pictures,' she repeated dreamily. 'You can just see them, can't you? The movement and the rhythm of the tides.'

'They're about love too,' he told her. 'You must read the sleeve. You might know some of the poems. Did you learn much poetry at the school?'

She chuckled. 'I was thinking of that just now,' she admitted. 'Mim was very keen for us to be able to quote great chunks of the stuff. She started us very young and we hated it. There were set pieces for auditions: children's parts from Shakespeare's plays and bits like that. Although the elocution and acting classes weren't really her concern, Madame always had a finger on the pulse.'

'Madame?' he questioned her—and she laughed.

'We all called her that when we were little,' she told him. 'When we got older we had the privilege of calling her Mim. Then we knew we'd really arrived. Sometimes we called her Madame Mim and, just occasionally, we'd call her Mad Madame Mim after the witch in the Walt Disney cartoon film. But don't tell her that. Everyone loved her to bits.'

Roly put Uncle Bernard down on the floor. 'I won't tell her,' he promised.

Daisy suddenly remembered her plan. 'I wondered if you'd have supper with me,' she said. 'You made that wonderful roast dinner last night and lunch again today, it's time I returned your hospitality. It's not what you'd call *haute cuisine* but do say yes.'

'I should like to very much,' he said at once. 'Thank you.'

'Oh, good,' she said. 'Give me half an hour and I'll be ready for you.' She hesitated. 'I noticed that you didn't drink any wine last night or at lunchtime today and I wondered . . . ?'

He shook his head. 'I don't drink alcohol,' he said pleasantly. 'Water is just fine.'

She nodded, her curiosity aroused, but something in his face warned her off.

'Fine,' she said. 'Great. See you about eight o'clock, then.'

When she'd gone he lay down again. Uncle Bernard stood on his hind legs, paws on Roly's arm, and gave a short imperious bark. Roly lifted him up, settling him across his chest, whilst scenes with Mim, with Monica, with Kate, crowded in his mind. An involuntary smile touched his lips as he pictured the increasingly familiar expression of transparent curiosity that lit Daisy's face when she was longing to ask a question.

'There is a directness about Daisy,' Mim had said, 'that you'll find very refreshing.'

'Mad Madame Mim.' He laughed aloud, quite certain that Mim knew her nickname only too well. 'Madame Mim.' The name brought another, more distant, memory and he settled comfortably, trying to pin it down.

*   *   *

He is sitting at the big table, drawing a picture for his mother as a present ready to give her on her return from London. His father sits beside the fire, reading a journal that is to do with his work except that, just occasionally, his head nods forward suddenly so that Roly knows he is falling asleep.

60

Claude, the Clumber spaniel, is stretched before the fire; his long lemon-coloured ear has fallen back, exposing the pink whorls inside. Very quietly, Roly climbs down from his chair and goes to kneel beside Claude; he puts his ear straight and strokes his warm, soft coat. Claude groans in his sleep and his tail thumps lazily. A log crumbles with a hissing sound and his father opens his eyes, tightening his grip on the journal that is slowly sliding to the floor.

Roly smiles at him, kneeling back on his heels, enjoying the heat on his back that comes from the fire.

'Why does Mother have to go to London?' he asks. He makes his voice casual, as if he doesn't really mind; he is very fond of Aunt Mary—Father's elder sister, who comes to look after them when his mother is away—but he likes it better when Mother's at home.

Father seems to find the question a difficult one: he frowns, putting the journal to one side and reaching for his pipe.

'It's all a question of balance,' he says after a moment's thought.

Roly immediately imagines himself balancing: standing on one leg like the heron or doing a handstand and trying to remain upside down, quite still, while his legs are in the air. He can imagine his mother dancing and singing but not doing handstands.

'When you grow up,' his father is saying, 'it's important to balance your life so that your mind as well as your body is . . . happy.'

Roly frowns, still stroking Claude who now rolls onto his back so that his tummy can be rubbed. His

61

front paws flop on his chest and he stretches luxuriously.

'The point is—' his father is trying to make it clearer—'that your mother had a very different life before we got married and you and Mim came along. She was an actress and she had lots of friends who shared that life with her.'

He pauses. Roly nods encouragingly. He knows all 'the chums' and has listened to their conversations about theatres and things called 'digs', which make him think of badgers, and people who were landladies but didn't seem to have anything to do with the kind of land that they have here in Cornwall.

'Well, she gave all that up to come down here to be with me, you see, and sometimes she misses it, just as I should miss Cornwall terribly if I had to go and live in London.'

'But she'd rather be here with us than in London with the chums?' he asks rather anxiously.

'Of course she would! But that's what I mean about a balance. Happy though she is with us here your mother is still interested in the theatre, and what is happening in that world, and it is important for her to keep in touch with it. Depending on who we are and what we do, everyone needs a different kind of balance in their lives. That's why it is essential that when you grow up you choose the right career. I'm lucky to be able to live here and do the job I love.'

'What shall I do when I grow up?' asks Roly, interested now in this question of balance. 'How shall I know about the balance?'

'We shall have to wait and see,' says his father. 'You're rather young yet to take that decision.'

A door opens on the galleried landing and Aunt Mary appears, carrying Mim who has been having her nappy changed. She screams with delight as Aunt Mary leans with her over the banisters.

'Down!' she shouts at once. 'Go down!'

Roly and his father watch as Mim, beaming triumphantly, is carried down the stairs.

'I wonder what Mim will be when she grows up,' says Roly.

His father grins. 'I can answer that one,' he replies confidently. 'Mim will be a proper little madame.'

CHAPTER NINE

The drive back from Camelford, where Daisy had been to stock up her larder, took much longer than was necessary because of the stops. The first of these was so that a tractor could manoeuvre itself across the narrow lane and into a field. The aged driver raised a fraying straw hat in courteous thanks and, as he climbed down to open the gate, she was rather struck by the incongruity of his braces—a bright, smart City red—worn over a faded plaid shirt. Once the tractor had passed into the field she remained to watch a rabbit, which lolloped to and fro amongst the tall buttercups in the ditch beneath the hawthorn hedge. He was clearly enjoying himself: pausing to sit upright in the afternoon sunshine between dashes amongst the campion and mouse-ear that flowered in the grass. His long, delicate, almost transparent ears, twitching to catch the least sound, reminded Daisy of the glistening pink colour of the inside of sea shells.

She drove on slowly, passing up out of the deep, rain-scoured lanes to higher ground. No hedges grew here but the high dry banks were laced through with the knuckly bony roots of ash and oak. Moss as bright as lettuce, soft as tiny cushions, inhabited these roots alongside ferns, whose tender green frondy fingers thrust themselves out from rough brown curled fists. Daisy stopped the car and climbed out to peer into a deep hole: at its entrance a pile of fresh earth indicated recent excavation. A very strong rank smell—one that Uncle Bernard would have recognized at once—made her draw back, wrinkling her nose. As she stood, stretching a little to ease her back, she grew aware of another smell carried towards her on a light warm breeze: a very different, deliciously heady kind of scent.

She walked a little further on·and, rounding a curve in the lane, she gasped aloud with delight. Here, beneath the shelter of a sycamore tree, a fall of bluebells flooded down the bank and into the ditch in a glorious wash of hyacinthine colour. Beyond a field gate several cows lay placidly, taking their ease, their jaws revolving slowly. Daisy leaned on the top bar of the gate and watched them contentedly. Her body felt at ease and her mind refused to dwell on those anxieties and fears that fretted at the edges of her consciousness and kept her awake in the early hours of the morning.

She spoke to the matrons in the field, telling them that she thought that they were very handsome and onto a good thing; they regarded her tolerantly but felt no requirement to return the compliment by getting up to inspect her more closely. Daisy watched them for a little longer, experiencing a satisfying wholeness in the scene and a deep connection with the pulse of the earth. She saw in her mind's eye a series of movements that described the shapes of the cows and the pattern of this green curving meadow that was intersected by thorn hedges and overarched by the shining blue sky.

She repeated the steps in her head, knowing that from henceforward that particular *enchaînement* would describe this pastoral landscape. As she continued her journey she found herself wondering idly—'Not *that* idly,' she told herself sternly, 'be honest!'—whether to send Paul a postcard. She'd bought several in Camelford, rather good ones of Tintagel and the coast, and she sketched out a few casual sentences in her head.

Back home again she saw that Roly's car and the dogs were missing and she carried her shopping up to the flat, still composing some friendly lines.

'So beautiful here. Feeling lots better, back on Monday.' Or: 'Wish you could see the countryside here. Feeling very relaxed. Looking forward to the ballet.'

She made a face: both sounded very trite—and how was she to sign herself? Best wishes? A bit formal. Love? Much too pushy. Daisy finished stowing away her shopping and paused. A car was coming into the yard; the engine cut, a door slammed. She went into her sitting-room and looked down. A tall, elegant figure was stepping from the passenger's door and looking up at the window as if expecting someone to be waiting.

Daisy's heart leaped up with joy.

'Mim!' she cried—and went hurrying out and down the little stone staircase to meet her.

'Darling Daisy!' Mim hugged her warmly, kissed her lightly on each cheek and then held her away so as to study her properly. 'Dark shadows under the eyes and you've lost weight.'

Daisy chuckled. 'Hardly surprising under the circumstances,' she pointed out.

'Typical dancer,' observed Roly, letting the dogs out of the back of the car. 'Eats like ten strong men and stays thin as a reed.'

Mim stooped to embrace the dogs, her long damson-coloured silk jersey coat dragging in the dust, laughing as she suffered the enthusiastic licks of Bevis's greeting.

'Hello, my darlings,' she murmured. 'Hello, Floss. What nice manners you have. Give me your paw. That's right.' She shook hands with Floss and stood up. 'So Kate liked Floss.'

'She did,' agreed Roly. 'And Floss liked Kate. They got on very well together.'

Just for a moment Mim stood still, her eyes closed so as to imagine Kate and Floss together. Daisy and Roly watched her: both of them recognized this characteristic. It was as if Mim were seeing something important that would bring some insight, some special wisdom that guided her thoughts and decisions. It might be to do with a pupil, a relationship, or some creative process in class.

Roly and Daisy waited slightly anxiously until Mim opened her eyes and beamed at them.

'The difficulty is,' she admitted, 'trying to see Kate *without* a dog.'

'Well, I couldn't agree more,' said Roly, 'but she is utterly wumbled at present.'

'Wumbled?' Puzzled, Daisy followed them into the house.

'It means worried and jumbled,' explained Roly. 'It's a word our mother used rather a lot.' He grinned at her. 'So do you like my surprise?'

'I do indeed but you might have told me.'

'I wouldn't let him,' said Mim. 'I was so afraid that something else might go wrong that I decided we wouldn't say a word to you until I was safely home. Oh, what a time it's been. I can stay for only two days. Come and talk to me, Daisy, while I unpack and wash my hands.'

Roly fed the dogs and went out into the yard to fetch some logs, thinking ahead to supper: a rack of lamb with purple sprouting broccoli and leeks in a white sauce. Tomorrow Mim would probably want to go to Padstow and buy fresh fish; she liked to cook when she had the time to think about it. Whistling to the dogs he opened the gate and wandered across the lane onto the path that led along the river bank. Uncle Bernard took his time, investigating a rabbit hole beneath the furze bushes with interest, but the other two barged ahead following a track through the alder and willow trees.

Disturbed from his fishing, the heron rose slowly from the middle of the stream; his great wings spanned the narrow stretch of water, lifting him high above the excited barking of the dogs, who had now plunged into the river. Roly watched him go, delighted as always by the languid grace, remembering how he had seen him for the first time in this very place.

*   *   *

His first impression is not of grace but of his father's old umbrella: it is something to do with the way those long legs hang down like broken spokes and the mackintosh quality of the flapping leathery wings. He sees the long, murderously stabbing beak and the watchful eye and is filled with wonder.

'What is it?' he asks his mother almost fearfully.

'It's a heron,' she answers. Her voice is light with pleasure. 'I've never seen him so far upstream before. Perhaps the heronry is growing and he needs to come further afield to find food for his babies. That's what he was doing: catching fish for his babies.'

Mim has fallen over in her haste to see the heron and she has to be dusted down and comforted.

'It was huge,' Roly tells her importantly. He stretches his arms wide to indicate its wing span. 'It was grey and white with very long legs and a yellow beak.'

Her face is solemn, her eyes round with disbelief, and Roly begins to feel an odd sense of possession over the heron; as if, in describing it to Mim, he has entered into a relationship with it that she cannot share. From now on, he watches eagerly for it when they walk along the stream and, oddly, it is Roly who always sees it first. Gradually it becomes a symbol of the dichotomy of life itself: the rapid swing between delight and gut-twisting fear: the co-existence of beauty alongside violence.

'Balance,' says his father, when the heron arrives

68

in the garden for the first time. 'We have to think about the balance of nature. The heron catches fish and frogs. They are a natural part of its diet.'

'But we put some of the fish in the ponds,' says Roly. He now sees them as trapped in a larder for the heron to raid at will. 'The goldies aren't wild fish.'

'Some of the fish arrived as eggs on the feet of birds,' explains his father. 'And the goldies have had so many babies that the ponds are crammed with fish. The heron will take the slowest, weakest ones and the ponds will keep a balance of healthy fish. That is how nature works. The fish eat frogspawn so as to survive but, even so, there are always plenty of tadpoles. If there were no fish or frogs then soon there would be no herons.'

Roly is confused. The heron gives him pleasure—but so do some of the fish. He realizes—rather ashamed of himself—he might be prepared to sacrifice a few of the smaller specimens but not Old Black and Big Blue. He says as much to his father—who laughs at him.

'Nature doesn't have favourites,' he tells him. 'It's a question of survival. Luckily, the choice is not yours to make. Don't worry too much. The ponds are very big ones and there is plenty of weed to give the fish cover. They'll soon be on the lookout for him. They have to learn to cope with danger just as we all do. There is a fine balance between protecting the weak and teaching them to fend for themselves. I explained to Mim that she couldn't walk on water but she discovered it for herself the hard way and now she is very careful. The heron is part of this landscape, he has a rightful place here, and the fish will adjust to him

69

in time.'

Roly understands what he means about Mim: despite many warnings she tries to walk across the pond, imagining that the dense weed is some kind of carpet, and is rescued, dripping wet and rather cross.

'If only the fish could talk,' he says wistfully. 'We could at least warn them.'

'We'll take a few precautions,' his father promises. 'Herons like to land a little way off and then advance cautiously on foot. We'll put a wire fence round the ponds to make it more difficult.'

Roly feels happier and, as the weeks pass, he is comforted by the fact that the heron is easily frightened away. Even Claude's presence in the wilderness garden keeps it at bay and Roly relaxes, though he still feels a need to protect the fish. It is best to see the heron here, on the banks of the stream, where he can watch it with pleasure that is untinged with anxiety.

*   *   *

Later, when supper was finished and Daisy had gone away to the stable flat, Mim curled up at the end of the sofa nearest to the fire.

'So do you approve of Daisy?' she asked, smiling a little as if she already knew the answer.

'I do.' Roly sat down opposite and lifted Uncle Bernard up beside him. 'She's certainly very direct. You were right to warn me.'

'Daisy has a keen desire to know how people tick.' Mim closed her eyes, the better to see Daisy and be able to explain her motivation. 'It's not a superficial interest, just so that she can gossip or feel superior; she genuinely wants to understand. When we had a pupil with a problem or a secret fear of some kind it was often Daisy in whom they would confide. She has an extraordinary gift for drawing out the most reticent of people.'

'So I've noticed,' he answered drily.

Her eyes opened swiftly, eyebrows raised.

'No.' He shook his head in answer to her unspoken question. 'I held my tongue but there was a moment when I saw how easy it might be to unburden my soul to her. You're right. There's a kind of empathy about her that's dangerous.'

She watched him for a moment, trying to gauge the depth of his seriousness.

'After all,' she said at last, 'it was all so long ago. Would it matter? Who would be interested now in the truth?'

'Monica?' he suggested rather bitterly. 'Nat?'

'Perhaps you're right.' Hearing the tension in his voice she sought to turn the subject. 'How is Kate? Has she managed to come to any decisions?'

She saw his hands relax and, as he began to talk about Kate and the dogs, she was able to sit back comfortably in the corner of the sofa knowing that the difficult moment had passed.

CHAPTER TEN

Mim stood at her bedroom window looking down into the wilderness. She was trying to decide why she hadn't told Roly or Daisy about the real problem she was facing. It was true that there had been several mishaps but these were fairly common in the day-to-day running of a stage school. Something more worrying than a twisted ankle and an understudy with tonsillitis was occupying her thoughts: her American artistic director, Andy Parr, was being tempted back to New York. He was young and lively, inspirational to work with, and the children adored him.

Mim's partner, Jane West, had refused to take the question of his departure seriously and a heated interchange had followed.

'You can't leave us, Andy,' Jane had said flatly at last. 'You've been so happy here. I mean, why?'

He'd raised his hands as if to ward off her angry disbelief, smiling a little.

'It's been great working with these kids, I've loved every second of it, you know that, but this is a chance to really stretch myself. And Martha's kinda homesick.' He'd shrugged. 'She's pregnant and you know how it is? She'd like to be nearer her folks.'

'It's a wonderful opportunity for you.' Mim had spoken for the first time. 'Working with children necessarily has limitations and I can see that a move to a prestigious ballet company opens up all kinds of exciting possibilities.'

He'd turned to her gratefully. 'That's it. That's exactly how it is.'

She'd smiled at him, exerting her charm. 'But you won't leave us in the lurch, I hope? You know the autumn term is going to be such a vital one. Apart from the Charity Matinée there's the discussions about the new television contract. It's an important one for us, Andy. If they hear that you're leaving us we might not get it. Could you wait until the New Year?'

He'd shifted uncomfortably. 'They're pressing me,' he'd admitted. 'Perhaps we can work something out . . . Hey, is that the time? I'm late already. See you guys later.'

He'd hurried away, leaving Mim and Jane in the tiny, overcrowded office where most staff meetings took place.

'Are you trying to let him off the hook?' Jane had demanded.

'I'm trying to buy us time,' Mim had answered. 'Face it, Jane; he's going. Let's try to make certain it's on our terms.'

Now, as she stared down into the garden, she wondered whether she was being wise to attempt to hold him. If Andy's heart was elsewhere then all his inspiration and passion would have gone with it. Mentally she reviewed the few possible substitutes. Andy was going to be very difficult to replace, not only because the children trusted and respected him but also because his reputation had earned the school a certain amount of kudos in the world of television.

The school had produced famous actors, opera singers, dancers and entertainers. It was highly acclaimed and its classes were full. Andy, however, had added a certain glamour; a glitzy lustre, that had opened up new opportunities. A documentary had been made about one of the school's most famous protégées: an actress who amusingly narrated her rise to fame, beginning with her first lessons at the school and finishing with her present, long-running West End success. She and Andy were good friends and Mim knew that the publicity that the school had enjoyed throughout this series was not due simply to the actress's affection for her alma mater.

There had been other high-profile initiatives, the newest being the prospect of a two-year contract for a series of advertisements to be run by an international engineering group well known for its avant-garde equipment. The agency had explained that the television producer would want close collaboration with the school on the series of advertisements that planned to use animation and robotics to promote artificial intelligence products within the domestic scene. They'd seen Andy's work, knew that the children would be professional and keen, and had judged it to be a winning combination.

Would they still be so keen, wondered Mim, once the word got round that Andy was leaving?

A balance was needed here: Andy's continuing goodwill and influence combining with a new artistic director who was willing to be flexible. The children would need to feel confident, as well as excited, and it might be necessary to hold the old and the new together for a short time. It was necessary to find a delicate way forward, balancing very carefully, until her objectives had been achieved.

Mim closed her eyes and took a very deep breath. Gradually the tension flowed away from her and was replaced with a calm readiness to wait for the next move to be made clear. It was a formula she'd learned as a child from her mother.

'Come and sit with me,' she'd say when Mim was fearful or cross. 'Now cup your hands like this; one inside the other, palms upward, and close your eyes. Unclench those fists. That's good. Now take a deep breath. Really deep and slow. Can you feel

74

the air going in? Think about it going all the way down. Now breathe out. Do it all over again. Good. Now get it into a rhythm. What can you hear?'

Something being dropped upstairs; the creaking of the old timbers; Claude snoring—slowly these quiet sounds centred Mim's thoughts and quieted her anxious mind. Other images drifted in her consciousness and an awareness of some kind of waiting presence; a power for good that lifted her and guided her if she could only consent to give herself to it completely.

'Feeling better?' Her mother's face focused again before her dreamy eyes and Mim nodded contentedly. Neither could explain but nor would they deny this gift that enabled them.

Years later, Jane had learned to trust Mim's instinct, though she had soon given up any attempt to analyse it.

'Do you pray?' she'd once asked curiously, seeing Mim sitting quietly in a corner, eyes closed and palms cupped upwards as if ready to receive a blessing.

Mim thought about it. 'Sometimes,' she'd answered. 'If you call it praying.'

'What do you say?'

'I find that the word "Help!" is as good as anything else.'

'You're crazy. Doolally.' Her partner had shaken her head dismissively. 'But keep at it. It's working.'

Now, Mim wondered if Jane would be quite so ready this time to trust the school to an instinct to go forward cautiously but calmly. It would require tact and courage to create a balance between Jane's toughness and Andy's happiness: both were necessary to achieve the school's immediate objectives.

Below the window the dogs appeared in the garden and then Roly emerged, carrying a tray and followed by Daisy. The little procession wound along the path to the paved area beside the larger of the ponds. As Mim watched them setting out the tea things, pausing now and then to talk more intently together, it was as if she could see inside each of them a hard, tight core of unspoken anxieties and fears that weighted their hearts.

'Monica.' She murmured the name aloud, wondering if Roly would ever be able to free himself from the guilt and anger that complicated the relationship with his ex-wife. Was it possible that Daisy might be some kind of agent for good here? Could she use that gift of empathy to enable him to admit the truth and free himself at last?

And Daisy herself? Mim's gaze softened as she watched this dear child that she'd nurtured and encouraged. Daisy was hiding her own terrors very well indeed. Mim knew all about the hazards of strain and accident to dancers and she could guess how Daisy's mind would be fretting and worrying to know the long-term outcome of her own injury. Her love and compassion reached out to both of them as they stood together, unconscious of her scrutiny.

*   *   *

'The hire car has to be back on Saturday,' Daisy was saying to Roly. 'I've got an appointment with the massage therapist on Monday. And there's the Nureyev exhibition beginning next week. I want to see that.'

She fiddled with her long conker-coloured hair, combing it through with her fingers before catching it into a bundle with a scrunchie, thinking: And there's Paul. How is he? What is he doing?

Roly caught that down-turned secret look and wondered who he was: this man that was drawing her back to Bath.

'Come back soon, though, darling.' Mim came out into the garden, folding a long scarf around her neck, stooping to caress the dogs. 'I must go back first thing tomorrow but I shall be down for the half-term week at the beginning of June. Could you manage a few days then? We've got some chums for the bank holiday weekend itself but perhaps from the Tuesday?'

'I'm sure I could. I'd really like that.' Daisy glanced at Roly. 'As long as I shan't be in the way.'

He smiled. 'Wasn't I just trying to persuade you to stay on for a while? Of course you won't be in the way.'

He poured the tea whilst Mim and Daisy talked shop and the dogs sat in a row, yawning but alert, trying not to look towards the cake. Quite suddenly and easily a little silence fell between them all: each, for a moment, was locked in an inward contemplation. The wilderness seemed to be held in a fine web of thick golden light. It glanced between tender green leaves and cloudy pale blossom, striking in shifting patterns through the waters of the pond and polishing the brilliant flowers of the kingcups to a richer yellow. Gleaming shapes darted and fled through rippling, wavering forests of weed, a snail propelled itself gently in the pellucid depths whilst a shadowy newt wriggled swiftly out of sight beneath a stone. The heron's upward soaring flight, which carried him high over the alder trees, brought him into full view of the small group beside the ponds. Gracefully he veered away with strong, measured wing-beats and vanished downstream.

Uncle Bernard began to scratch energetically, breaking the spell, and they turned to each other as if waking from a dream.

CHAPTER ELEVEN

Monica drove carefully along the narrow cobbled lane, passing a row of cottages whose doors opened directly on to this once ancient byway, which now ended in a steep muddy track overgrown with a tangle of brambles. On the opposite side of the lane was the high perimeter wall belonging to a riverside dwelling. None of the neighbours in Nat's row showed any inclination to open up the track or prune back the thicket of holly and thorn.

'It was probably an old droving road but it suits us fine as it is,' Nat said. 'If it were to be tidied up too much we'd have a continuous stream of people trekking past trying to get down to the river.'

His cottage was the last of the row and had a large lean-to garage where he parked his pick-up and kept all his tools. Monica negotiated the car past the garage and tucked it in tight under the small stretch of wall that enclosed the tiny garden. She climbed out and stared critically at the cottage. The wooden window frames were freshly painted and some new terracotta pots stood in a row to the left of the stable-door beside the wooden tub full of herbs.

Janna, she thought at once. Nat would never plant lavender or pansies, or sit on a cushion on the doorstep in the sun as Janna did. Monica's lips compressed a fraction as she remembered last summer and how Janna had sat, all wanton in the sunshine, her skirt rucked above her bare pointed knees, laughing and running her fingers through the herbs.

'Cool,' she'd say. 'Brill. Have a whiff, Moniker.'

Monica would avoid the outstretched hand with its outrageous fingernails—purple or striped and sometimes a different colour for each one—and smile with a wintry disdain. Janna never took offence; she'd sniff her own fingers with a voluptuous delight, eyes closed with the pleasure of it.

'Make yer mum a cuppa, Nat,' she'd say, yawning and pushing her hands through the great curly mane of hair—lion's hair, wild and tangled and the colour of pale marmalade—and Monica would feel a sense of outrage at hearing her son ordered about so casually.

'I can make the tea,' she'd say, stepping pointedly across those bare sunburned legs, lifting her skirt an inch or so. 'Nat's been working all day. I'm sure he's tired.'

'I'm fine, Ma,' he'd answer irritably. 'Quite able to make some tea,' and Monica would feel resentful at his rejection, disliking Janna all the more for being the cause of it. She'd store up the things she'd say later to Roly about her, hoping in some oblique way to wound him by deriding his

79

son's choice of girlfriend. All her disappointments must be laid at Roly's door.

'I'll have the raspberry,' Janna would call, all languid from the doorstep. 'Not that smelly stuff yer Mum likes. Bring a chair.'

'I'd rather have tea in the garden.' Monica's voice would be dangerously sweet. 'I've never really been one for sitting in the street. Yes, the Earl Grey for me if you have it, darling.'

Sometimes, during these tiny verbal battles, Nat's face would break into such a smile: he'd laugh aloud as if quite suddenly the whole scene had simply spiralled out of control and was not worth taking seriously.

'Hardly a street, Mum,' he'd say, 'but why not? We're going into the garden, Janna. Tea's here if you want it.'

Mollified by her victory, Monica would ask questions about his day—trying not to sound critical—until Janna arrived, carrying her mug, hair like a wild springing halo round her small head. Wearing one of her outlandishly printed T-shirts—'Jesus loves you but I'm his favourite'— she'd yawn like a kitten, mouth open to reveal tiny pointed teeth, and pick the flaking black polish from her toenails until Monica wanted to scream.

'And what have you been doing, Janna?' she'd ask, poisonously polite, and Janna would gulp some tea—'Exactly as if she were swigging beer from a bottle,' Monica would tell Roly later, outraged—and begin to talk about the local markets where she and someone called 'Treesa' did face-painting and Indian head massage and sold strange leather objects that—to Monica— could serve no possible useful purpose. Monica would feign a deep interest that disguised the opportunity to ask questions that were deliberately framed to expose all the idle pointlessness of Janna's existence.

The queer thing was, thought Monica, still staring at the terracotta pots, that Nat never made any attempt to defend Janna. He'd listen and watch her with affection, totally unmoved by his mother's contempt. Suddenly, standing there in the little lane, she was reminded of Roly and Mim but, before she could pursue this train of thought, Nat appeared. Framed in the open upper half of the door he looked down at her.

'How long are you going to stand there admiring the pots?' he asked. 'I've just got back and I was changing but I saw you from upstairs. How are you, Mum?'

He opened the lower half of the door and came out to give her a hug. His hair was damp and he smelled of soap but his chin was rough and she drew back a little as it scraped across her cheek.

'Fairly well.' She liked to keep some possible suffering in reserve in case she needed it as a lever—'Well, I've had this ghastly headache all day but I didn't want to make a fuss'—but she smiled at him quite brightly, assessing him carefully. 'Dying for a drink, of course. Jonathan sent a couple of bottles of Merlot, knowing we both like it.'

'I'll get your stuff in,' Nat said, holding out his hand for the car-keys, but she went with him anyway so as to direct the operations and help with a few smaller bags.

She followed him into the cottage, alert to any changes, noting that it was clean and unusually tidy. It was a few moments before she realized that it was Janna's clutter that was missing: no shawl flung on the chair, no shoes kicked off impatiently, no strange iconic pictures stuck up on the shelves or propped against unwashed coffee mugs on the table.

'Janna not here?' she asked casually.

'No,' he answered. 'No, she's off for a few days.'

She noticed a hesitation, as if he were trying to decide what version of the truth to tell her, and her curiosity was roused.

'Off with *Treesa*?' She emphasized the mispronunciation of the name, deliberately mocking Janna and inviting Nat into an amused little conspiracy against her.

Nat frowned—rejecting the move albeit absentmindedly. 'I expect she's with Teresa,' he agreed coolly. 'Shall I pour us a drink? I've made some pasta, not very exciting I'm afraid, but I managed to get into Crebers for a few treats. How's Jonathan?'

She submitted to the putdown for the time being, biding her time, and accepted a glass of wine. Just at the moment she was delighted to know that Janna was not around; later, when they'd eaten, she would find out what it was that Nat was keeping from her.

*   *   *

After supper, however, Nat said that he simply must get his accounts up to date; he cleared the table, spread out his papers and settled down to work. In the tiny kitchen Monica washed up, sipping thoughtfully from time to time from her

82

glass. She noticed the absence of faddy (Monica's word for anything organic or vegetarian) food preparations from the fridge and cupboard and saw that a certain mug—a rather childish Peter Rabbit mug—was missing.

Mentally she raised her eyebrows: surely these were signs of more than just a few days away. She refilled her glass and went to sit on the rather lumpy sofa, refusing the offer of television or radio, staring at the little fire of cones and logs that Nat had made in the iron basket that stood on the hearth. Her reactions to Janna's possible departure were mixed: part relief that the wretched girl was out of Nat's life; part irritation that she, Monica, would be more anxious now that Nat was alone again.

She stirred rather restlessly—the sofa needed reupholstering—and tried to decide what she would say to Roly about it. It was clearly unreasonable to moan about Janna on the one hand and regret her going on the other. Nevertheless, despite her complete lack of practicality, Janna had been company for Nat.

Silently Monica rehearsed a few sentences: 'If he can't keep someone like Janna, how can we expect him ever to find a decent girl?' Or: 'I suppose we might as well accept the fact that he's never going to have the kind of prospects to attract a decent girl.'

She tried to find a substitute for 'decent girl', knowing that this choice of words might lend itself to flippancy on Roly's part—'Surely an indecent girl is much more fun!'—and glanced irritably at Nat's back. With a little shock she realized that the sight of his bent head, the angle of his arm, reminded her of Roly: Roly when young, reading the paper, sketching some silly little cartoon, while she cooked supper and cleared the table, talking about her day. He'd stretch out his long arm to catch her as she flashed past, pulling her down for a casual kiss—except that none of his kisses was casual: his touch simply overwhelmed her senses so that nothing mattered but that they should go on kissing.

Caught off-guard by this evocation of passion that was like a blow to the heart, Monica sat stiffly. She stared unseeingly at Nat's back, conjuring up a quite different scene.

*   *   *

Oh, it's love, she tells herself; no doubt about that. It happens exactly how she knew it would: just as all her magazines and films describe it. One glance across a crowded room and suddenly everything goes kind of dim and hushed and out of focus; everything except this particular face that is special, different, and she knows nothing will ever be quite the same again. Except that he isn't looking back at her across this busy, noisy room, hasn't seen her yet: he's talking to David Porteous, her cousin Sara's husband, and he is utterly unaware of her existence. Well, perhaps not *utterly* unaware . . . David might have said: 'Sara's got this little cousin coming to stay while she finds her feet with her new job. Rather quiet but quite sweet. Make sure you're nice to her.'

He might say something like that. To begin with, David is always very kind to her—too kind sometimes, judging from Sara's steely glances—

but he frightens her. He surrounds himself with writers, artists, dancers and they talk and talk, and she feels gauche and ignorant. And bored.

'Open your mind to new things,' David says impatiently to her one evening when he has seen her sitting silent, unable to join in.

'I don't know anything about art,' she answers, resentful because it sounds as if he's criticizing her.

'But you can learn,' he cries.

His enthusiasm frightens her; it demands a response that she is unwilling to make. Her parents and her school between them have framed a narrow little pattern of beliefs and expectations that is setting nicely into a rigid format by which she can assess life and judge her fellow men. She dimly realizes that any wider experience might disturb these pre-digested opinions—she might be required to think for herself—and something deep down inside her is fearful of smashing this comfortable, undemanding credo.

At the same time there is a neediness; an emptiness waiting to be filled. She waits passively, seeing no requirement to make any effort of her own. Once she meets Roly she knows that he is the answer: it is Love that will answer that aching neediness.

'This is Roly,' says Sara, introducing them. 'This is my cousin Monica. Roly's a photographer . . .'

The way her voice dies away, the tiny lifting of the brows—a kind of mental shrug—implies that Sara has as low opinion of photographers as she does of painters, but she is in thrall too. She loves David as possessively and fiercely as Monica will love Roly.

'Oh, terrible, terrible love!' cries Mim—and

Monica is shocked, for how can love be terrible? Mim frightens her too. When they first meet, Mim looks at her intently. She ignores Monica's polite formalities, as if to say, 'Yes, yes. I can see what you are on the outside but where is the real you?'

Monica fears that Mim might see nothing inside except a reflection of Roly looking out; for it is Roly who is occupying every thought, every plan: nothing but Roly . . .

*   *   *

Nat stirred, as if suddenly conscious of the particular quality of his mother's silence. He turned in his chair, surprised by the expression on her face.

'Are you OK?' he asked. 'Sorry. I got a bit caught up with all this and I didn't notice the time. I'll make the fire up and then we'll have some coffee.'

CHAPTER TWELVE

High on Pew Tor, Kate stood staring across to the rocky mass of Vixen Tor towering above the Walkham valley. Thirty years ago she'd bought a little cottage on the edge of the valley—oh, how she'd loved it—and countless times since then she'd climbed these rocks to gaze in awe at this ancient land stretched in wild splendour below her. Today, away in the west, the hills and tors of Cornwall lay hidden in mist but she could see the silver glint of Plymouth Sound and the sinuous curve of the River Tamar. As a young naval wife she'd walked here, anxious about her deteriorating marriage with Mark Webster, sustained by the moor itself: the subtly changing landscape, combined with its quality of timeless infinity, never failed to calm her restless fears. Each season thrilled her: the sight of a twisty, wind-pruned thorn all newly covered with red may blossom or a hillside flowering with purple, bee-laden heather; the fiery, coppery gold of rusting bracken burning in the late autumn sunshine or a black, stark-etched Tor iced with snow. In all its moods she loved it.

In those early days her twins, Guy and Giles, would have been scrambling below her, playing war games and climbing the rocks, whilst the dogs scattered the grazing ponies as they raced through the bracken. Often her closest friend, Cass Wivenhoe, would have been with them, along with her own brood of children. From shared schooldays and as young naval wives their lives had been so closely linked; indeed it was Cass's father, the General, whose benign presence had held them all steady. Constant as the moor itself, his friendship had supported Kate through those difficult years with Mark, the final break-up of their marriage and her mother's death. Never judgemental, the General's own experiences had marked him deeply with compassion and humility; not odd, then, that she should still miss him.

A lark began its erratic skyward flight, its song spilling down through the soft billowy air. The warm west wind tugged at her clothes and, as she watched the cloud shapes fleeing across the distant slopes of Sharpitor, it seemed as if she heard their voices, the General's and Mark's, in the wind.

'You must be very brave, my darling . . . Your mother died this morning . . .'

'I see no point to children until they're old enough to hold an intelligent conversation.'

'You are stronger than you can possibly imagine and I am here. For the moment that will have to be enough.'

'Children are much more likely to wreck a marriage. You know my views about that.'

'. . . and all shall be well and all manner of thing shall be well.'

Kate pushed her hands deep into her pockets: she felt afraid. The past with its failures and mistakes pressed upon her and, with David gone, she was rootless; there was no framework now to keep her centred. She had her family, of course, and many friends, but it was a mistake to depend too heavily on other people—however close—in an effort to fill this emptiness. During the last terrible year of David's illness there had been hardly any time for anything except the care of him at the London flat; their world had shrunk to the small round of special diets, regular injections and then hospital visits. Oh, back then . . . how she had longed to walk here in the clean air; to hear the sound of clear water bubbling up from the thousand issues that drenched the peaty earth or watch the buzzard suspended high in the milky-blue dome above her head. Now she had all the time in the world, the freedom to do as she pleased, and the knowledge of the empty hours filled her with a kind of panic.

Other voices, human ones, were carried up to her, and the sound of a dog barking. Instinctively she glanced about, ready to call the dogs to her—but she was quite alone: no Megs or Honey; no Oscar or Felix. Pain squeezed her heart and she turned away abruptly as a party of people climbed up towards her. Blinking away tears she stared across Walkhampton Common towards Sharpitor.

There—how many years ago?—she'd stood with Alex Gillespie, shivering under frosty stars, blind with moonlight, taking the first steps away from an empty marriage into her one true love affair.

'. . . I think I love you. I know you're not free. I know there are all sorts of problems. But do you want to try to resolve them . . . ?'

'I'm afraid. If I start, I'm afraid that I shan't know how to stop.'

The climbers were beside her now, exclaiming at the view and beaming at her, including her in their pleasure. She smiled back at them and paused to speak to the dog—a large boisterous person of an indeterminate breeding—before beginning the descent to the car.

*   *   *

Halfway home she remembered that Monica was coming to tea. Kate cursed briefly and glanced at her watch; she'd spent much longer on Pew Tor than she'd realized. Yesterday she'd met Nat and Monica at the pub for Sunday lunch and, hearing that Nat had arranged to keep the following morning free but would be working in the afternoon, she'd invited Monica to tea. The invitation had been accepted readily enough but Kate had noticed a preoccupation that seemed to be exercising an unusual restraint on Monica's typically sharp observations regarding Nat's work or Janna's shortcomings. Only when Kate began to talk about Floss did Monica begin to look more alert; asking how Roly was and saying that she intended to visit him.

'We thought we'd go down one evening,' Nat had agreed, 'if I can finish early . . .'

'Oh, don't worry about that,' Monica had interrupted rather vaguely. 'I'll just pop down on my own. After all, you can see him almost any weekend. I'll go down on Tuesday, perhaps.'

Nat's look of surprise hadn't escaped Kate and she'd turned the conversation away to her own dilemma of whether or not to sell her house, hoping that this would keep them on less controversial subjects until lunch was finished.

As she parked the car and hurried into the house, Kate gave thanks that she'd got into the habit of keeping a few emergency supplies in readiness for the arrival at short notice of Guy and Giles with their young families: scones and cakes in the freezer; baked beans and pasta in the larder. Monica certainly wouldn't want baked beans but perhaps some scones with crab-apple jelly followed by a slice of Victoria sponge might be acceptable. She hurried about, putting out her prettiest china, knowing that Monica would notice—would *expect* a certain amount of effort to be made.

That air of expectation was odd; a belief in some kind of divine right that other people should put themselves out on her behalf.

And the really odd thing, thought Kate, was that this absolute sense of what was due to her was so strong that you found yourself dashing about finding long unused tea-sets and linen napkins. If it had been Cass, say, you wouldn't have hesitated to give her a perfectly ordinary mug and a piece of paper towel. It was even worse than that. You found yourself responding to some deeper need in Monica, an emptiness that was so intense that you actually *wanted* to fill it in some way.

'Which is crazy,' muttered Kate crossly, scooping butter from the carton into a dish. 'What can she possibly need? She has a devoted husband and a villa in Portugal; a lovely son and loads of money. Even Roly can't bear to upset her . . .'

Washing her hands, drying them on the roller towel, she found that her momentary irritation had passed and she was smiling a little. The thought of Roly and Bevis, and Uncle Bernard in his drawer, brought her some measure of calm: imagining them in that strange barn of a house by the ford soothed her. Ever since David had died she was becoming aware of the quality of Roly's undemanding constancy and unconditional friendship. It was this aspect of him that had begun to remind her of Cass's father, the General. He, too, had been unobtrusively available to listen to her woes, to show her a perspective. For her, for Cass, and for their children, he'd been an irreplaceable support and comfort. It was not odd that she should think about him—he'd played such an important role in her young life—but it was unsettling that, just lately, her memories of him had brought along other remembrances that were less happy. It was as if in grieving for David she had opened the floodgates to a more widespread mourning: for the failures and mistakes in her relationships with Mark and Alex, for the death of her mother, and even for the General himself. Oh,

91

how she'd missed him after he'd died: that aching loss for someone who had always been on her side. Roly was just such another. He ignored his private feelings for her so as to be able to give her what she really required at this time.

Kate remembered Monica's expression when she'd mentioned Roly at lunch in the pub: an inward, straining look as if she were attempting to see something just beyond her vision.

'Monica's like the black widow spider,' David had once said. 'She sucks people dry. Luckily Roly got away in time.'

Kate had chuckled at this observation but, once she'd met Jonathan, she'd wondered if David hadn't had the right of it. There was a dried-out, bloodless look to Monica's husband, thin and light as an autumn leaf. It seemed as if one breath of wind would whirl him away.

'I don't like him much,' she'd admitted. 'He's such a stick. It seems so odd, David. I mean how could she, after Roly . . . ?'

He'd made one of his distinctive grimaces, mouth pulled down at the corners. 'He was convenient, d'you see? Solved all the problems.'

'What problems?'

But if David knew why the marriage had broken up he wasn't telling, and Kate still did not know the reason why Monica had left Roly.

Monica's car could be heard coming slowly up the drive. Kate pushed the kettle on to the Rayburn's hotplate and went out to meet her.

CHAPTER THIRTEEN

'I hate Jonathan sometimes,' Monica said. She stared at Kate; her eyes, wide and dark, pleaded for understanding. 'I just hate him.'

The time had marched slowly beyond the hour for tea and was now dragging its feet towards dinner. Since Monica showed no indication to leave, Kate suggested a drink. The idea was a good one. The slight awkwardness that exists between two people who have very little in common was dispelled by the cheerful ceremony of getting two tumblers ready, a panicky hunt for the lemon—'I know I've got one somewhere'—and the comforting sizzle of tonic water. Quite suddenly, halfway through her gin and tonic, Monica kicked off her shoes and became confidential. Kate watched her rather anxiously, fearful lest her measuring of the gin had been too generous. She was not startled by Monica's revelation but rather by the unexpected change from the brittle and sharp-tongued to the emotional and soul-baring. She did not know this side of Monica's character, though Roly and Nat would have recognized it at once, and it caught Kate off balance.

'I've shocked you.' Monica spoke flatly but with just a suggestion that Kate had disappointed her. 'I can't help that. It's the truth. There are moments when I can't bear the sight of Jonathan.'

'I'm not shocked. I should think it's pretty common, isn't it? To tell the truth, I find it amazing that relationships work as well as they do. I've always considered that men and women are two quite different species. Totally incompatible really. How odd.' She frowned, remembering. 'I said that to . . . someone else once.'

Monica watched her eagerly; there was something mesmerizing about her stare. 'To David? Did you feel like that about David? That you hated him sometimes?'

'Oh, no, not David. After all . . .' She paused, confused.

'What?' Monica was as alert as a spider that feels the faintest vibration of its web.

'I was going to say that it wasn't like that with us.' Kate spoke almost reluctantly, thinking it through. 'We'd both been married, made mistakes, but we saw an opportunity for happiness together and decided to try to make it work. Our children were grown up—well, my boys were at university and Miranda was married—so we decided we could concentrate on each other. I loved David very much but it wasn't one of those madly passionate affairs. This was different.'

'Different?' Monica seized greedily upon the word and Kate felt a very slight twinge of revulsion: she sensed that Monica wanted something from her—some intimacy or collusion, perhaps—that Kate was unprepared to give.

'Different,' she said carefully, 'from other love affairs. Anyway, I should think that to feel an emotion as strong as hate for someone really close to you then you'd have to feel an overwhelmingly corresponding depth of love.'

'Oh, no.' Monica shook her head decisively. 'I don't agree. After all, I never loved Jonathan like that either.'

She sat back in the corner of her chair, self-absorbed again, and Kate breathed more freely as if unexpectedly released from a trap.

'I thought . . . well, because you left Roly, I'd imagined . . . Sorry. It's none of my business.'

'You thought I left Roly because I fell madly in love with Jonathan?' Monica laughed with genuine amusement and, just for a brief moment, Kate could see a glimpse of the pretty girl she must have been. 'Oh, no. Jonathan was what we used to call "sound". He was steady and that appealed to me when Roly was drinking so heavily after Mim's accident. Of course, he'd always liked his drink too much—they all did in that crowd—but I hoped that the shock of leaving him, taking Nat away, would make Roly get a grip and we could get back together again but it didn't work out like that. After he'd stopped drinking I allowed him to see Nat but everything was different between us. I tried to show him that we could make it work again but he wasn't having any of it. I decided to stick with Jonathan but I was passionate about Roly. He was the biggest thing that ever happened to me.'

'Well, now you *have* shocked me,' said Kate lightly. It was true: Monica's cold-blooded description of her relationships, both with Roly and with Jonathan, shocked Kate far more than her asseveration of hatred of Jonathan. Suddenly she knew that she didn't want to hear any more. 'Relationships are such private things, aren't they?' she said. 'No-one knows what goes on inside a marriage.'

'I left Roly because he changed.' Monica wasn't taking the hint. Her look was inward, her voice hurt and sad; she'd been the one who'd suffered. 'He was brilliant, you know. You'd be surprised

95

how many photographs that became icons in the sixties were taken by Roly. He'd have been just as great as Bailey or any of them if he hadn't lost it.'

'Lost it?'

Monica sighed. 'Like I said, Roly always drank too much but he'd kept it under some sort of control and it never affected his work. After Mim's accident he became an alcoholic. He was unreliable and his clients couldn't trust him. He'd turn up late or forget about a shoot. It was Mim's fault. She relied on him too much. They'd always been so close, you see, and he felt responsible for her. Of course it was terrible. Ghastly. But he had me and Nat to worry about and I resented the fact that Mim had to come first.' She stared appealingly at Kate. 'That was natural, wasn't it? You'd have felt the same way about your twins. Of course, she was incredibly famous—Fonteyn's natural successor and all that—and the shock of her career being wiped out overnight was cataclysmic. Even so, Roly had other responsibilities. We used to have terrible rows about Mim. It was humiliating having to watch him disintegrate. Shameful.'

There was a little silence.

'I had no idea,' said Kate at last. 'Although I've often wondered why he never touches alcohol.'

'You mean David didn't tell you?'

'Did he know?'

'Of course he knew. It was David who introduced me to Jonathan. He was their accountant, you see: David's, Roly's, Mim's and the rest of them. He specialized in artistic people and he looked after them all. David said, "You'll like Jonathan, Monica. He's much more your sort

96

than the rag, tag and bobtail you meet in my studio." He never wanted me to marry Roly.'

'But you loved Roly—and he loved you.'

Kate tried not to make it a question but Monica's smile was sly and secretive, as if she recognized the doubt in Kate's voice.

'Oh, yes,' she answered confidently. 'Roly loved me. It was the cruellest thing I ever did; leaving him, I mean. He never got over it.'

'I'm sure he didn't.' Kate was profoundly uncomfortable. 'I'm so sorry. Look, I'd better not offer you the other half, had I? Because of you having to drive back.'

'God, no!' Monica glanced at her watch and felt about for her shoes with her toes. 'I must go. Spirits have a terrible effect on me. Usually, I hardly touch them. Gosh! I feel quite tiddly.'

'It was probably a bit strong.' Kate took her glass. 'It's all those years living with sailors. Will you be OK?'

'Of course I will. Though you never did tell me about your great passion.'

'No, I didn't, did I?'

She watched Monica back the car rather erratically down the drive and went inside, thinking about Monica and Jonathan. Monica's brand of hatred sounded as indigestible and weighty as cold porridge, unleavened by the hot-blooded rage and jealousy that often go hand in hand with love. Yet she'd spoken about Roly in much the same chill terms despite her avowed passion for him.

What was odd, thought Kate, trying to work her way through her reaction, was that, repellent though Monica's outburst had been, there was an

97

accompanying emotional undertow that required sympathy; a hypnotic quality that demanded the listener's acquiescence. It was as if Monica lacked the ability to take responsibility for her own actions and the lack of it made her dangerous: she saw herself at the centre of her universe—like a spider in the middle of her web—and used everything that came within its radius as a means of support and survival. How quickly she'd seized on that slip of the tongue.

'You never did tell me about your great passion,' she'd said, as if it were some tasty morsel, enmeshed and waiting to be dealt with another time: as if she and Kate were now ineluctably bound together by sticky strands of revealed intimacies.

Remembering Alex—the joy and anguish, the happiness and the pain—Kate cursed herself for giving any hint of the affair. She'd been caught off guard, reminded of how, years ago, they'd sat together in the May sunshine outside her little cottage at Walkhampton, talking about relationships.

'Men and women are two different species,' she'd said to him. 'We think differently, react differently, require different things. To expect marriage to work is like expecting a fish and a bird to live happily together. Or a bee and a mouse. Totally incompatible, really.'

'Are you trying to tell me something?' he'd asked.

Even now, thirty years later, she could remember the details of their affair: the angle of his head as he played patience and the flick, flick, flick of the tiny cards; the musty, papery smell of

98

second-hand books in the small shop where they'd worked together; his listening face, intent and loving, as she talked out her fears and, afterwards, the physical relief of being held close to him in bed.

She realized that she was standing quite still, her eyes tightly closed, and with an exclamation of impatience at her foolishness she switched on the radio and began to stack the dishwasher.

CHAPTER FOURTEEN

In the chemist's shop on the corner of Argyle Street, Daisy waited patiently whilst a customer talked to the pharmacist, describing his problem with a bloodshot eye. She loved this friendly shop, so full of atmosphere, with its rich dark mahogany counter on which there was a glass display cabinet containing old-fashioned badger-hair shaving brushes, razors and a collection of every type of scissor anyone could possibly desire. On the wall behind the counter were rows of small square mahogany drawers that, way back in the early nineteenth century, had probably contained dried herbs. Daisy gazed with pleasure at the variously shaped jars—rich blue, green and white—that stood on the top shelves that ran the whole length of the shop. She wondered if ancient potions were still stored in them but never asked lest she might be disillusioned by the reply.

Perhaps, mused Daisy, the apothecary who had assisted Queen Charlotte with her purchases might have been able to prescribe some miracle cure for her own torn muscle. She sighed silently, miserably: the physiotherapist had been unable to give a good report and had said that the damage might be worse than they'd feared. Daisy stared down at the packet of arnica tablets she was holding—she had great faith in herbal medicines—and wondered what she would do if the muscle and its surrounding tissue refused to heal.

The customer was finished now, smiling an apology to Daisy for holding her up, and she paid for the tablets and followed him out between the Ionic columns and into Laura Place. The catkins on the pretty silver birch trees were over now and new green leaves fluttered bright and fresh against the ghost-light bark. The sound of the fountain's sparkling water, spilling into the wide shallow bowl, was cool and enticing, and Daisy paused to take in the early afternoon scene. A nurse was pushing an elderly lady in a wheelchair back from the town: the nurse was leaning forward on the handles, talking to the occupant of the chair, whose face was turned eagerly upwards, and they suddenly burst out laughing. On the ledge of the fountain a young couple sat with their bare feet in the shallow water. They leaned together idly, peacefully silent, enjoying the sunshine. The Japanese tourists, standing beside their guide as he pointed out the features of Great Pulteney Street, were not concentrating: they were staring curiously at the young couple with their feet in the fountain as if shocked at such wantonness here in elegant Bath.

Daisy turned into Henrietta Street. She loved these tall, gracious houses, built of warm Bath stone, and the small hotels, so well cared for, with their brightly polished brass work and pretty geraniums and variegated ivy tumbling out of window boxes. The houses were nearly all divided into flats and the street was a busy, cheerful place. The young and the elderly, professional people, students and nine-to-fivers lived here; there was always someone moving out sadly at the end of the tenancy and another arriving full of excitement at the prospect of a new flat.

Through open windows she could hear the sound of a piano being played rather badly mingling with rap music from a student's flat; the smell of cooking wafted up from a basement area, reminding her that she'd eaten very little at lunchtime. Daisy realized that she was peering eagerly ahead, looking for Paul's car although it was far too early to be expecting him. She hadn't seen him since she'd arrived back and was much more disappointed than she liked to admit. Passing her own front door she walked on into the park, not ready to go back to the empty flat: she hated this enforced idleness and she was lonely. She missed the gruelling discipline of work and the company of Jill and Suzy, who would have understood her terror that her dancing career might be over and might have offered sensible advice as well as sympathy.

The park was bustling this afternoon. People were lying on the grass, sunbathing, or sitting more sedately having picnics. A group of students was celebrating a birthday with lots of wine and much laughter. The boys were fooling around with a rugby ball, showing off to the girls who suddenly jumped up and began to join in, much to the consternation of a small girl on a fairy bike. Her

101

young mother, pushing a baby in a buggy, put a comforting hand on the back of the bicycle seat, steering it until they were safely past the jostling gang, but Daisy saw that she was smiling to herself: perhaps it wasn't too long since she'd been a careless, happy girl, fooling with the boys in Henrietta Park on a warm May afternoon.

In the Garden of Remembrance the air was heavy with the scent of roses and wisteria, whose white blossom cascaded over the wood-framed walkways; the laburnum was in full golden flower and the massed pink flowers of the climbing clematis were reflected in the pond's glassy surface. Staring down into the water, Daisy was reminded of Roly: she missed him too. An elderly couple, sitting companionably on a bench, watched her with friendly interest; they leaned as easily and peacefully together as the young couple at the fountain in Laura Place. Couples, families, groups: she felt like an outsider looking in at a world she couldn't possess. With a quick smile for the elderly couple she passed back between the iron gates, up the slope, and out into the street.

Home. She would go home and have some tea, perhaps make a quick telephone call to Cornwall to see how Roly and the dogs were getting on . . . She stifled an exclamation as her heart leaped with surprise and anticipation: Paul's car was parked beside the kerb. Before she could lose her nerve she went quickly into the hall and rang his doorbell. He answered almost at once.

'Daisy.' His smile was so delighted, so genuine, that she felt as if the breath had been knocked from her body. 'I wondered when you'd be home again.'

'I've been walking in the park and suddenly I needed a cup of tea. Why don't you come up and have one?' She didn't want him to vanish back inside with a friendly wave, as in the past, nor was she prepared to wait for an invitation into his flat. 'Or a drink? Is it too early for a drink?'

He didn't hesitate. 'I'd like some tea. Thanks. Give me five minutes and I'll join you.'

Upstairs she paused in the doorway of the sitting-room, wondering how he'd react to the modern influences in this big, elegant room, dominated by the marble fireplace with its central figure of a reclining muse holding a goblet and plucking a grape.

'So wonderfully decadent,' Suzy had observed when they'd first viewed the flat. 'We simply must have it just for the fireplace.'

The noble face of Nureyev, in the role of Albrecht in *Giselle*, gazed indifferently from its framed poster (Daisy's) upon the grotesque papier mâché mask of a pig-faced woman (Jenny's) that hung from a peg. On the bookshelves in the alcove, Shopaholic and Bridget Jones rubbed shoulders with Balanchine, Helpmann and Massine, all piled together in cheerful disorder. A pair of pointe shoes waiting to be darned, their satin ribbons spooling down to the polished floorboards (Daisy's), stood on the window seat alongside a wicker workbasket. Leaflets, photographs, postcards were stuck at random all around the enamel-framed looking-glass (Suzy's) and propped behind the assorted candlesticks that were placed along the mantelshelf above the fire.

'What fun.' Paul was standing behind her, so close that she could feel his breath on her cheek.

103

'Love the mask.'

She turned to look at him so intently that he raised his eyebrows warily as if anticipating a difficult question.

'I suppose this is OK?' she asked. 'Inviting you up, I mean. I've assumed that you're not, you know, *with* anyone. I don't want to cause difficulties. Oh, damn, that makes it all sound serious, doesn't it? It's just that I like to know about people.'

And now, she told herself silently, you've spoiled it all.

She watched him walk further into the room; he touched the snout of the pig-faced woman, readjusted the raised arm of a wooden jointed figure poised in arabesque upon a little table.

'That's fair enough,' he said at last. 'As it happens, I'm married.' He looked at her, noted her expression. 'But not for much longer, it seems. So the answer is, no, not with anyone.'

'I wasn't trying to be nosy,' she muttered—she knew she was blushing—and braced herself to be bright and normal. 'It's none of my business except . . .'

'Except that we like each other,' he assisted her, 'and we want to know each other better. In which case it was a very fair question. I might ask the same of you.'

'No.' She shook her head, encouraged by his reaction, her spirits rising. 'Nobody at the moment.'

'Good.' He took a deep breath. 'Enough to be going on with? Listen, I had an idea on the way up. Why don't we go and have some supper at Clarke's Restaurant later on?'

'I'd like that very much,' she answered.

She was pleased to hear that her voice was well under control but, in the privacy of the small kitchen, she punched the air jubilantly. This was definitely progress.

CHAPTER FIFTEEN

After supper, as she stood at the window of her small bedroom at the back of the flat, Daisy decided that she was in love. It wasn't just the exciting mix of chemistry between them that caused her to laugh one moment and be oddly shy the next; it was much more than a physical attraction. She liked his enthusiasm and his genuine interest in all that was happening around him: he noticed things and she recognized in him her own brand of curiosity. Like her, Paul wanted to know what made things work, what made people tick, and he wasn't afraid to ask questions.

Standing at her window, gazing dreamily beyond the dim, feathery bulk of the plane tree towards Walcot Street, she reflected on the dangers of such a character. She knew from her own bitter experience that a fascination with other people's affairs could give quite the wrong impression and she was resisting the temptation to feel flattered. Paul had encouraged her to tell him about the trip to Cornwall and soon she'd embarked on a description of the great converted barn by the ford, of Roly and of Uncle Bernard in his drawer. This led on to Bevis and Floss and rescue dogs and, after that, it was a natural step to Kate and her dilemma. Fearing that he might become bored with this recital about places and people he'd never seen, she watched him anxiously from time to time, ready at any moment to change the subject.

Paul encouraged her on, clearly riveted by this group of people and their lives. She found that she was telling him about Mim and her tragic accident and then recounting her own experiences at the stage school. He was by no means a passive listener, however; his questions were intelligent, interested, and often led down other little byways as she proceeded with her story.

Daisy sighed with pleasure as she savoured the evening. For a brief time she'd forgotten her own fears and misery—though they'd talked about those too—and had been totally happy. It wouldn't be true to pretend that she hadn't been aware of him close beside her, though. Once, leaning back in his chair, his knee had touched her own and, at one point, he'd brushed the back of her hand very lightly with his fingers; she'd shivered with a kind of suppressed excitement but he'd moved on again, talking about something else, making her laugh.

He'd noticed the point at which her back began to be troublesome and suggested that it was time to go and, when they'd let themselves into the hall, he'd taken her face in his hands and kissed her briefly but with a tenderness that made her want more; much more.

'That was such fun,' he'd said. 'Go to bed, Daisy, you look exhausted. I've been rather selfish, keeping you sitting in that hard chair all evening. Will you be OK?'

And she'd said, 'Yes, of course,' and, 'It has

106

been fun, hasn't it?'—because what else could she say? And she'd come upstairs, feeling exalted yet disappointed; happy but oddly dissatisfied. It occurred to her that she knew very little more about him apart from the fact that he'd accepted the post as head of the Art Department at the well-known public school on the edge of the city when the incumbent had died suddenly halfway through the spring term.

Despite that rare gift of accessibility, he was able to hold her at arm's length. 'We like each other,' he'd said, 'and we want to get to know each other better,' but she realized, now that she was alone again, that the impression of intimacy was based on the atmosphere that he created—and yet again, as on previous occasions, she'd been left in the hall, despite the goodnight kiss. She told herself that his caution simply might be a result of the break-up of his marriage, something they hadn't talked about at all.

A shadowy shape detached itself from an overhanging bush and ran stealthily along the tops of the walls. Daisy recognized the little local fox, with his half-starved look and ragged brush, and, as she watched him making his nightly journey, she decided that she was expecting too much of Paul. He'd suggested that she should pilot him around the Nureyev exhibition and she'd agreed willingly. He said that he could get away early on Thursday afternoon and they'd made a date. Perhaps she'd invite him to go with her to the Walcot Nation Day; he probably wouldn't know about the annual carnival day, full of fun and nonsense, when Walcot Street was closed to the traffic and became an independent nation. Or she might invite him to one of the Peter Hall summer productions at the Theatre Royal as a thank you for the chance to see the Royal New Zealand Ballet.

The fox had long since disappeared; Daisy turned away from the window and began to get ready for bed.

*   *   *

In the flat below, Paul was sitting at his desk in the small study, staring at some framed photographs of his children. Through the open door he could hear the low-level quacking of a television chat-show with the sound turned low. The noise comforted him, reminded him of home: that small terraced house in Clapham where Tom and baby Alice would have been asleep for hours and Ellie would be getting ready for bed. This flat, charming though it was, had none of the atmosphere or vibes of a home, and it was becoming clear to him that he had no inclination for it to be one.

Only the photographs were familiar to him. He'd taken the flat furnished for three months, at the end of which he'd move into the house in the school grounds that went with his job at Beechcroft, and his instinct told him to sit loose to it: no invitations to Henrietta Street; no colleagues asked back for supper or drinks. The flat was neutral ground between the house in London and the house at Beechcroft School; a kind of no man's land where his life could be put on hold for a period of time.

And Daisy? Paul reached out to move the square silver frame a fraction so that he could see Tom beaming out at him. Well, Daisy was a complication he hadn't bargained for and he needed to think about her very carefully.

'You should carry a government health warning,' Ellie had told him more than once—laughing though, not being bitchy about it—and he'd shrugged, indicating that it wasn't really his fault.

It was true that his happy nature and easy friendliness had raised problems before now, mainly with his students, and past experience enabled him to see that Daisy was attracted to him: no point in being modest about it. He was drawn to her too. With her narrow face and pointed chin she reminded him of Modigliani's *Jeanne Hébuterne*, that same foxy-dark red hair and those tilted brown eyes, and she was wonderful company. The trouble was, he hadn't been totally honest with her. It wasn't necessarily true to say that he wouldn't be married for much longer, though that was the impression Ellie was giving, but he really hadn't known how to answer Daisy without going into the kind of details that he wasn't yet ready to talk about with anyone.

Paul picked up the photograph, tilting it under the anglepoise lamp, but as he studied it he began to see a different scene superimposing itself over Tom's happy little face.

*   *   *

'But why are you going away, Daddy?' he asks, taking the small soft toys out of his padded bear house and zipping up the roof. 'Why can't you stay here with us?'

Paul looks across Tom's head to Ellie, who stands beyond him, arms folded across her breast,

109

her eyes narrowed warningly.

'It's a job, Tonks. A really good job.'

'But you've got a job already.'

Paul sees how easy it would be to score points against Ellie, using Tom.

He might say to Tom: 'But if I take this job it means we could live in a bigger house and you could have a playroom for your toys. And a big garden with a slide and a swing. We could even have a dog. You'd like that, wouldn't you?'

The dog would be a very big bargaining counter: it would weigh in very heavily against Ellie's argument about Tom missing his little friends at the Busy Bees playschool. It might even take some of the sting out of his not seeing Rula, the Polish girl who comes to look after Tom and Alice when Ellie is teaching. Three-year-old Tom adores Rula.

But Paul thinks it would be cheating to play Tom off against Ellie.

Of course, he might say: 'This is the job I always wanted and if I turn it down it will be the third time I've rejected this kind of post because your mother puts her friends and her own part-time job before my promotion. If I turn this down I might never get another opportunity. I probably wouldn't have been offered this if they hadn't been in a bit of a jam and needed someone in a hurry.'

He might say that but he knows that it would mean nothing to Tom, although Ellie would know that he was making a point he's made a dozen times already. Tom is now putting all the bears back into the house and Paul tries to think of some way he can show Tom why he wants to take the job in Bath.

'You love going to Busy Bees, don't you,

Tonks?' he asks. 'But I bet you're looking forward to moving up a class next term, aren't you?'

'No,' answers Tom promptly, shaking his head. 'I don't want to leave Mrs Porter's class. I love her.'

For a brief moment Paul and Ellie exchange a glance of pure, spontaneous amusement: she guesses what Paul is trying to do and Tom's reaction makes her smile. Paul's attempt is scuppered before he's started and they are locked in a joint appreciation of the situation.

'Thanks, Tonks,' Paul mutters ruefully. 'Nice one.'

He looks at Ellie's softened expression and wonders if he can take advantage of this reignition of affection sparking between them.

'I don't want to leave you or Mummy or Alice,' he tells Tom, his eyes on Ellie. 'I think we should all go to Bath together. It's a beautiful city. Lots going on.'

'Living on a campus,' says Ellie levelly. 'No privacy. Backbiting and pettiness . . .'

Alice wakes up and begins to cry, and she dashes out.

'What's a campus?' asks Tom.

*   *   *

Paul stood the photograph in its former position, switched off the lamp and went into the sitting-room. A beer and the late night film might distract him from imagining the children asleep, bedclothes flung off, limbs all over the place; or from the thought of Ellie, reading a book, her long dark hair spread across the pillow.

And Daisy? His conscience nagged at him but he refused to think any more about her. In the morning he would decide what he should do about Daisy.

CHAPTER SIXTEEN

When Janna came back to the cottage in Horrabridge, Monica had already driven away to Cornwall to see Roly. Nat was working in his big lean-to garage: cleaning tools, oiling equipment. She came quietly, slipping down the narrow lane in the shadow of the high wall, her quick glance checking out the scene: no cars, no voices. The garage door was propped open, a strimmer leaning against it, which meant that Nat was almost certainly alone.

'Hi, there.' She stood framed in the doorway, smiling.

Nat looked up, frowning against the sunset light that dazzled his eyes after the gloom of the garage.

'Janna.' He felt the familiar affection at the sight of her; thin cotton dress fluttering round her slight frame, marmalade hair curling halo-like against the orange streaky sky. 'Great to see you.'

He came out into the light, wiping his hands on some cotton waste, noting the old canvas tote bag slung over her shoulder.

'Is it?' She grinned at him. 'That's a relief, then. I heard yer mum had been around so I didn't like to leave a message on the answerphone.'

'She still is. She's down in Cornwall today with Roly. I think she's planning to stay the night but, anyway, she won't be back just yet. I suspect she's hoping to wrong-foot him so he has to ask her to stay over.'

Janna made a little sound of amusement. 'Always seems funny, that. Calling yer dad by his name. Why is it?'

'Bloody-mindedness,' answered Nat, after a moment. 'When my mother left him she used to refer to him as "your father", keeping him at arm's length as if he were a criminal or something despicable. I grew to hate the word, so I called him Roly.'

'He didn't mind? Didn't think you were cheeky?'

Nat shook his head. 'I think he knew why. So how are you? Hungry? Cup of tea? I haven't got the stuff you like, of course. You took it all with you.'

'I know.' She made a little face: repentant, wheedling. 'I could do with something, Nat. Nothing fancy. Cheese and some bread, if you've got it.'

He flung away the cotton waste and walked with her to the cottage door.

'Sit in the sun,' he said. 'It'll be gone soon. I'll get you something.' He passed two cushions out to her. 'Relax.'

She arranged the cushions on the step and sat down, curled gratefully, face turned to the sinking sun. When he came out, carrying a tray, he saw that she was asleep with her head drooping sideways against the doorjamb. There were bruise-coloured patches under her eyes, the planes of her face were sharply drawn and her skin was lightly filmed with perspiration. That strong, healthy,

113

sinuous lion-look she'd had all through last summer had gone. Now she looked like an alley cat: thin, bedraggled, poor.

He set the tray on a little stool and pushed her gently with his foot. She came awake with a shock and he passed her a mug of soup.

'You are such a twit, Janna,' he said, not looking at her. 'Where have you been?'

'Around.' She hunched herself defensively. 'You know. Did a few markets, met up with some old mates. Nothing bad, Nat. I promised you, didn't I? We ran out of money, me and Treesa, and then 'twas a bit hand to mouth, that's all. I thought I might stay a night or two. I saw Dave in the village. He thought yer mum had gone.' She glanced sharply at him, hands round the mug, drinking the hot soup as quick as she could. 'Did you tell her?'

'No.' His face was shuttered, bleak. 'No, I didn't.'

'So I could be here, couldn't I? Just for a day or two. Might even be helpful?'

She looked so hopeful that he couldn't help but smile. 'I suppose so.'

She grinned at him. 'Thanks, Nat. You're such a mate.'

'I'm a sucker.' Nat cut a piece of cheese, sawed off a slice of bread and pushed it towards her. 'You look terrible.'

'I know.' She was unresentful, swallowing down the last of the soup, head tilted back to get the last drop. 'What did you tell Moniker?'

'That you'd gone off for a bit. She has no idea for how long but I think she noticed that a few of your bits were missing and jumped to the obvious conclusion. I said you were with Teresa.'

'Well, 'twas true.' She fiddled with the piece of bread, sticking cheese crumbs on it. 'She's got a new bloke.'

'Ah.' Nat was noncommittal.

'Yeah. "Ah" is about right. We don't get on.'

Nat was silent. He rarely asked questions, knowing that sooner or later she'd tell him what had happened. Tiny observations, odd remarks, that was Janna's way. He'd piece together the information, building up a picture, and another section of the jigsaw that was Janna's life would slip into place. He thought about the summer they'd met, four years earlier, when he'd had the job as assistant groundsman at a holiday camp and she'd been working in the bar. It was some time before he understood what it was that he liked about her. She was funny, feisty, sharp, but what he began to recognize in her was a tremendous integrity: her standards of friendship and loyalty were very high.

Piece by piece, during that summer holiday, the picture had grown. 'Dad buggered off before I was born,' she'd said casually once, eating a pickle, taking a swig from his beer glass. 'Here. I saved you a sandwich. Crab mayo OK?' And another time: 'Mum was just a kid herself when she had me. 'Twas hard for her. She loved me, though. Bought me stuff.' It was Teresa who'd told him that Janna's mother had become an alcoholic and that, by the time she was old enough to leave school, Janna had been fostered with four different families, running away from each of them in a determined attempt to be with her mother. In the canvas tote bag were other pieces of Janna's life: a battered copy of Roger Hargreaves' *Little Miss*

115

Sunshine, an Indian shawl with frayed glittering gold threads, and a Peter Rabbit mug. 'My mum bought me these,' she'd said, displaying them with a half-defiant, half-anxious look that smote his heart. 'She always says I'm her Little Miss Sunshine. She really loves me, my mum.'

Now, as Nat watched her cramming the bread and cheese into her mouth, he guessed where she'd been and to whom she'd given her money. She reached to run her fingers through the lavender, sniffing them with the old familiar abandon, giving him her glinting smile.

' 'Tis nice to be home, Nat.' A hesitation. 'I'll go and unpack then, shall I?'

'Yes,' he said. 'Go and unpack.'

She stood up, holding the bag, hesitating half in and half out of the doorway. 'I'll be in with you, shall I? What with Moniker being in the spare room. I won't be a nuisance.'

Her face crumpled suddenly and he pushed her ahead of him into the cottage, threw her bag on the sofa and put his arms round her.

'Come on, old love,' he said, rocking her. 'You're home. Didn't you just say that? So what's this about being a nuisance?'

Her hot tears soaked through the thin stuff of his shirt, her forehead ground against his collar-bone. Words gushed from her suddenly.

'She's really bad, Nat, she can't hardly walk now. 'Twas good to begin with, just like old times when I was little. I got her down on the Hoe in her wheelchair so she could see the ships. She always loved that. Anything that moved, going somewhere else. Then it all broke down again like it always does. I don't know where she's getting it from—

well, it could be any of them though they all swear they're not, and they're all, like, her mates so I feel like some kind of enemy, if you see what I mean. I couldn't find nothing hidden in the usual places, but you could tell she was just waiting for me to go so she could get at it. She lost it in the end, shouting and swearing, so I came away . . .'

He held her calmly, and presently she stopped weeping and leaned against him, worn out.

'Get your things unpacked,' he said. 'Come on. Where's the mug? And the shawl?'

Wearily she reached into the bag: the mug was carefully protected by bubble wrap, the shawl folded in a paper bag. Nat spread the shawl over the back of the chair and took the mug into the kitchen. When he came back she was smiling at him, head up, eyes bright: Little Miss Sunshine.

'Love you, Nat,' she said. It was a formula, a game picked up from a film they'd once seen together, and now she waited for his answer.

'Love you too,' he answered, cheerfully, 'three, four, five. Go and finish unpacking and we'll go down to the pub.'

CHAPTER SEVENTEEN

Monica was drinking her second glass of wine, much more relaxed now that she knew that there was no question of her driving back to Horrabridge, when Nat telephoned to say that Janna was back and they were going down to the pub for supper: he'd leave the key under the flower pot in case Monica arrived back before they did.

'She's decided to stay the night,' Roly told him, trying to inject a note of enthusiasm into his voice. 'Back in the morning. You'll probably be at work so I'll tell her about the key anyway. Enjoy yourselves. Bye.'

' "Yourselves"?' Monica picked up on the word sharply. 'Don't say the wretched Janna is back?'

'She is indeed.'

'Honestly, Roly,' she was delighted with this opportunity to manufacture some kind of intimacy between them, 'how is he going to meet a . . .' she hesitated over the word 'decent' and went on, 'a sensible girl with Janna hanging around him?'

'Perhaps Nat isn't interested in sensible girls.' He went up the steps into the kitchen to check the potatoes, as they'd been on for a while. 'I rather like Janna.' He washed the fillets of sea bass that he would fry in oil and herbs and put them into a frying pan. 'I think Nat is too busy establishing his business to have much time to think about anything else. Anyway, you were saying just now that you worry about him when he's on his own.'

He allowed himself this little dig because he was irritated that she'd forced his hand. Instead of arriving in time for lunch she'd left it so much later that he'd been obliged to offer supper instead. Now, having watched her refill her glass, he suspected that she'd never had any intention of driving back to Nat's this evening.

Monica gave herself a moment to reflect on this remark—one she'd already anticipated—and wondered how to go forward in a way that would bring him on to her side rather than antagonize him.

'Well, I do. Of course I do. When he's on his

own I wonder if he's eating properly, that kind of thing.' She paused, not wishing to irritate him by implying that caring was only attributable to the female sex. 'I expect you do too,' she added generously.

'I expect him to go down to the pub if he's hungry.' Roly avoided any complicity here, noting the tone of motherly wistfulness. 'He's a big boy now. And if there's any looking after to be done in that relationship I suspect it's Nat that's looking after Janna.'

'But that's exactly my point.' Monica was triumphant. 'I really cannot see exactly what Janna has going for her. I suppose she *is* company of a sort for Nat, but really I'm beginning to believe that he's better off alone.'

Roly turned the potatoes and looked at Uncle Bernard in his drawer: he'd curled up neatly, nose on tail, eyes closed. It was odd, Roly thought, that the dogs instinctively avoided Monica. After the initial greeting they'd turn away at once, returning to their beds, as if remembering that this was someone with whom they shared no common ground. Bevis and Floss were stretched out, watching and listening but remaining detached, and Roly wished he had the same ability.

'Whatever we think,' he said calmly, 'it's up to Nat to decide what it is he wants. We must grant him the privilege of allowing him to be an adult. After all, neither of us is in a position to preach.'

The last remark was made in an almost inaudible voice but Monica heard it and her heart lifted: this was exactly the opening for which she'd been hoping, and she got to her feet still holding her glass.

119

'Oh, Roly,' she said, 'it's funny you should say that. I was thinking about us these last few days and how we were all those years ago. I was such a fool, Roly.'

Her voice was tender, thick with emotion and too much wine, and Roly was seized with alarm.

'Wait,' he said. 'Let's not do this, Monica. We're too old for recriminations . . .'

'I don't mean that,' she cried. 'Not recriminations. I mean that I remembered the time I first met you and . . . well, I wished that things had worked out differently.'

Roly tossed the rocket salad in vinaigrette and turned it into a bowl, glad to be busy: it was essential to avoid any eye contact.

'I wish that too. Different for you, for me and for Mim.'

'Oh, Mim!' she cried impatiently—even now Mim was between them as she always had been—and she felt a surge of frustration. 'Well, yes, of course, nobody could wish that on her, but I was thinking of you and me, Roly.'

'Neither of us coped particularly well,' he said. 'You did what you thought was right at the time. Shall we leave it at that? Let's eat.'

She followed him to the table and sat down. Even in her emotionally heightened retrospective state his remark "Neither of us coped particularly well" irked her. After all, it was he who had changed, become unreliable and unable to control his drinking. She wanted to make this point—to defend her own behaviour—yet she knew that it could only cause friction. Slightly irritated she began to pick at her food, wondering how to justify her actions without sounding as if she was

120

accusing him.

Aware of her quandary, relieved that it was deflecting her from a maudlin excursion to the past, Roly began to talk about Janna.

'She's an unusual girl,' he said, helping Monica to salad, refilling her glass, 'but a very genuine one. From the little Nat's told me I gather her mother was a bit of a hippie and now she lives with a group of people in Plymouth in a commune of sorts. It makes it difficult for Janna to make certain that her mother's OK because they all gang up together against the poor girl if she tries to interfere, but she's very loyal.' He talked on, realizing that the subject of Janna was a kind of counter-irritation to Monica's dilemma, until she reluctantly abandoned hope of drawing him into any shared intimacy and concentrated on Janna instead.

'That doesn't mean that she's suitable for Nat,' she began rather sulkily, making it clear that she knew she'd been sidetracked but unable to think her way round it. She'd drunk too much and felt fuddled and slow. 'There's something so . . . flaunting about her.'

'Does it matter, if they love each other?' He was playing devil's advocate, having several theories of his own as to why Nat and Janna were not suited as partners. 'It's a mistake to attempt to judge other people's needs.'

'We're not discussing other people; we're talking about Nat. Nobody knows him better than I do. I happen to love him.'

Anger spurted inside Roly as he remembered how she'd manipulated the young Nat; exploiting his affection for her, controlling him through his sense of guilt and loyalty. He wanted to shout at her, force her to face the truth; yet his own guilt and self-knowledge stayed his hand. To his relief the telephone began to ring and when he heard Jonathan's voice he could have called down blessings upon him.

'Yes, she's here,' he answered. 'No, not bad timing at all. We've just finished eating. Are you well? . . . Good. Yes, I'm fine, thanks. Here she is.'

He passed the telephone to her and began to clear the plates. Uncle Bernard sat up in his drawer, checking to see if there might be some snack for him, and the two other dogs got up, stretching stiff-legged, and strolled out through the open door into the yard. By the time Jonathan had finished speaking, Roly had put cheese and fruit on the table and the atmosphere had splintered and reformed into a different pattern: less charged with frustration and anger but still ominous.

'All well?' asked Roly lightly. 'He sounded in good form.'

'He wanted to be sure that I hadn't forgotten a dinner party on Friday evening.' She still sounded sulky. 'I'll have to go home on Thursday. Well, if Janna's back that won't be much of a hardship.'

Floss came up to Roly, tail wagging, ears flattened. He stroked her and she leaned against his chair.

'Nice, isn't she?' He seized upon the change of subject. 'I'm hoping that Kate might take her. They're both bereaved and grieving and I think they'll do each other good. Poor Kate. She's in such a dilemma as to what she should do now David's gone.'

'Why? What should she do?' Monica frowned. 'I shouldn't think she's got much to worry about, has she? David must have left her pretty well off. That flat in London should be worth a bit.'

'I think David left the flat to his daughter. Do you remember Miranda? I think Kate would find it difficult to afford to stay on in that big house now. She's hoping to downsize and make some money on the way through, but I wasn't really thinking about material considerations, more about where she should live now she's on her own.'

'She didn't say anything about moving when I saw her on Monday.' Her face grew thoughtful and then amused. 'We talked about other much more interesting things. Did *you* know that Kate never really loved David and that she'd had some fantastic affair with someone else?'

He stiffened with dislike and old-fashioned disapproval. 'No, I didn't. Of course she loved David. For goodness sake, Monica . . .'

She shrugged. 'It was she who told me. I just wondered if you knew who it was.'

'*Kate* told you?'

'Well, she sort of let it out of the bag and then she clammed up. It was rather odd, actually. She doesn't seem the type, does she?'

Roly didn't answer and she glanced at him inquiringly and then, seeing his shocked expression, more curiously. He pushed his chair back from the table, going up the steps into the kitchen to fetch the coffee, and she watched him speculatively—her own suspicions growing. The silence lengthened between them.

*　　　*　　　*

In the morning Roly was up early, making

breakfast, walking dogs, explaining that he must hurry away to a dental appointment in Bodmin. He kissed her goodbye, put her firmly into her car and waved her off.

All the way back to Horrabridge, Monica wrestled with frustration: she'd been so certain that she could create an atmosphere between them that would cast a softening glow across the ruins of their shared past and recreate some of that early magic. She'd convinced herself that he must be lonely and, beyond Mim's encroaching presence, ready for some company. Monica had never had any difficulty in persuading herself that his coolness towards her was merely a need to hide his guilt and hurt that she had left him and this was the first time that she'd seen any indication that he might have serious feelings for another woman.

Not that she'd imagined he'd lived for thirty years in a celibate state—that wouldn't be Roly's style at all—but she'd never been jealous. After all, she'd known from the beginning that he was susceptible to pretty women—how else could she have snared him? She'd found that it had given their relationship a bit of an edge, heightened her sexual feelings for him. Monica pulled a face. One of the problems with Jonathan was that he was so boringly faithful; no surprises there, no challenges. It was all of a piece with his reliability. It was so typical of the unfairness of life that the very things she'd first required of him were the things that lately had become so stiflingly dull, especially lately, since he'd started writing his textbook. When Roly had been living in that half-world of alcoholism, beginning to lose clients, she'd found comfort and security in the safety net that

Jonathan was so ready to hold out to her. But back then, she reminded herself quickly, she'd had Nat to consider: naturally she'd put Nat first.

Yet now, reliving those first meetings with Roly, it seemed almost impossible to imagine how she could have ever left him for Jonathan. Listening to his voice on the telephone last night—pedantic, prosy, precise—whilst watching Roly moving about in the kitchen—elegant, exciting, edgy—she'd felt that it was there in that old stone barn that she belonged, not in the smart London house. She'd been cross that she'd been unable to draw Roly into that charmed circle of the past: he'd kept her at arm's length and she'd had a little too much to drink and so lost the chance to weave her web around him.

How odd he'd been after that comment about Kate: surely he couldn't possibly be in love with Kate? Now, on this bright morning, Monica refused to believe it. Much more likely that he felt defensive on David's part. Men were odd like that, and David and Roly had been very close friends; so much so that it had always puzzled her that despite his apparent affection for her, David had never encouraged her relationship with Roly: even her own cousin had discouraged it.

'You'll never have a moment's peace,' Sara had told her, eyes watchful, lips as thin as split slate; every woman was a threat to Sara.

Monica shook her head, remembering: she'd had no such fears. Her one object had been to catch him, to possess him utterly, and it hadn't been too long before she'd seen the way to do it.

CHAPTER EIGHTEEN

Monica plans her own seduction very carefully: Roly must believe that it is his idea and take full responsibility. The timing is important: Mim is away with the ballet company in Holland and David is in Oxford giving a talk at a summer school. She must take a chance with any casual droppers-in, but most of their friends are on holiday and Roly is talking of going down to Cornwall at the weekend. She must act quickly.

She stays on late at the Sales Rooms, saying that she must put in some extra work on one of the catalogues, and it is after seven by the time she arrives in Gloucester Crescent. As she rings the bell she can hear the sound of music—jazz blues: Miles Davis then? She tries to remember the things that Roly likes so that she can use them to bind herself more closely to him. For instance, she knows his predilection for good wine, which is why she has a bottle of claret with her.

'Hello.' She speaks as soon as he opens the door, not allowing any kind of negative reaction on his part to undermine her resolution. 'I've had such a beastly day and I can't quite face Sara yet. Are you very busy?'

He holds the door open wider, as she knew he would, and she goes quickly past him, ignoring the big kitchen where everybody usually congregates— that won't do at all—and runs lightly up the stairs to the comfortable sitting-room on the first floor. She hears him behind her and hopes that he is taking the opportunity to appreciate the shortness

126

of her brief, cotton mini-dress.

Inside the big, light room she turns to him, all embarrassment and shyness.

'I'm being pushy. Sorry.' She indicates the newspaper flung down on the floor, the glass half full of wine, a record still playing: it *is* Miles Davis. 'You were relaxing and I've disturbed you.'

She makes her eyes widen a little, implying that it would be rather fun to disturb him, knowing that some men would pick up on the word and make a joke about it—which would help things along. Roly is never predictable, however, and asks instead: 'Why can't you face Sara?'

She has her answer ready—it was to be part of a later dialogue but she is happy for it to be introduced now—and she sighs, pulling her face into an expression of distress.

'David's away in Oxford for the night and poor old Sara really hates it. All those pretty young students. She'll be out of her tree all evening, waiting for him to phone and when he does she'll snap at him and afterwards she'll cry. God, it must be hell to be jealous.'

She hands him the bottle and he takes it without thinking about it because he's concentrating on what she's just said.

'Is she really that bad? I know they've had rows when David's being a bit overattentive to some dolly bird but I had no idea . . .'

Monica bites her lip; shakes her head regretfully. 'It's terrible. Don't say I said anything. I know how close you and David are so I assumed you knew the scene. It makes me feel so uncomfortable, and I'm very fond of David, but Sara is my cousin. She's just so totally unsuited to

127

the Bohemian life and I don't quite know how to handle it. OK if I stay around for a bit?'

'Of course it is.' She sees him wonder if he is being inhospitable, realizing that he's still holding the bottle and giving himself a mental shake. 'Like a drink?'

She grins at him, just a little touch of cheekiness edging into the winsome waif bit: 'That was the general idea.'

He laughs and, just suddenly, looking at him, she wants him. It's the way he stands there, relaxed, dealing with the bottle: detached and desirable. She sits down in the corner of the long sofa and concentrates her will upon him. She knows he fancies her and her own longing and desire fly out like invisible gossamer threads to draw him to her. When he brings her glass across to her she kicks off her shoes and curls up comfortably, smiling at him.

'Actually, I'm thinking of looking around for my own pad. I was hoping you might be able to give me some ideas. It would have to be very small and cheap.'

She introduces a faintly anxious note here and this time he responds right on cue.

'Would you want to be alone? Can't you find someone else to share with?'

'Like you and Mim? You're lucky to have a sister you get on with so well.' She sounds envious of his good fortune. 'I wish I had a sister or a brother. I don't particularly want to be alone but it's just getting a bit difficult with poor Sara always in a state and I suspect that David's getting a bit fed up with having me around.'

A lightning glance at Roly's unsuspecting face

confirms her suspicions that David has already admitted as much to Roly.

'It isn't easy, playing gooseberry.' She laughs, mustn't get too pathetic, nothing sexy about being pathetic. 'Anyway, I might enjoy being alone.' She makes big flirty eyes at him. 'At least I'll have the chance to do my own thing.'

He laughs too, relaxing now and pouring more wine for them both. 'Sounds good to me.'

'Does it?' Her jokey directness takes him by surprise but she sees that he's pleasantly intrigued. 'That's fab. So.' She shifts closer to him, displaying plenty of bare leg in the process. 'Any ideas about a flat?'

'Gosh, I don't know.' He pretends to consider, entering into the spirit of the thing. 'How about the attic?'

She laughs joyfully, leaning against him, seeing that he's thinking, Actually, she really is fun when you get her on her own, and says: 'Want to show me round?'

'I might just do that,' he answers, looking down at her, and she looks back, eyes widening, so that he has no option but to bend his head to kiss her. She feels his brief shock at her ready response to the kiss but she follows up her advantage very swiftly. After some more wine, and a lot more kissing, she senses that the time is right to turn up the heat a little. She has been clever enough to choose a dress that unbuttons at the front and, since she doesn't wear a bra, the next stage moves along with a nice natural ease. She encourages whilst appearing to be passive. In fact she manages to conduct the entire seduction in a way that makes Roly feel that she is powerless to resist:

overwhelmed by her own emotions and his desire.

Afterwards, when he sees the blood on her thighs, on himself, remembers that moment of resistance and her cry of pain swiftly shut off, he is shocked.

'I had no idea . . . You should have said . . .'

'But I love you.' She smiles shakily up at him, tears on her cheeks—of relief and triumph, but he is not to know the difference—and repeats: 'I love you, Roly. I thought you knew. I'm so glad it was you.'

And Roly feels doubly guilty as he holds her tightly.

During the next few weeks, whilst Mim is still away on tour, Monica makes certain that she and Roly see a great deal of each other and doesn't attempt to hide her ever-growing passion for him. He is flattered, charmed by this blend of sexy innocence, so that when she tells him that she is expecting their child he reacts exactly as she hopes. She is careful not to blame him—no, the fault is all hers, she loves him so much; she weeps with shame and remorse and fear, and his response is to take her in his arms and ask her to marry him.

*   *   *

So strong was this image from the past that it was a shock to see Janna sitting on the step outside the cottage door. Monica parked the car, struggling to regain her composure, and climbed out.

'Hi, Moniker.' Janna's smile was wary. 'Had a good time?'

'Yes, I have. Thank you.'

Today, Janna was wearing frayed denim shorts

130

and a T-shirt printed with the bright, coyly smiling face of a fifties-style girl and bearing the legend: 'I Don't Cook, Clean or Put Icky Things Near my Mouth'. Looking down at her, Monica wondered if Janna was really in love with Nat; if Janna felt that overwhelming passion that she, Monica, had once had for Roly. Almost at once she dismissed the idea: if Janna had those feelings she wouldn't go off for weeks at a time. The brief unsettling sense of kinship flared and died.

'How was *Treesa*?' she asked brightly, stepping past her, not waiting for an answer.

She didn't see Janna's smile fade. She was noticing the shawl draped over the chair and the mug—Peter Rabbit and Mr McGregor, set like flies in amber, eternally following one another round the cucumber frame—back in its place in the kitchen.

I shall go home today, she was thinking. No point in staying now Janna's back. Of course, the fact that she is back gives me a good reason for staying with Roly next time. Lucky that Jonathan is wrapped up in that wretched book. I'll be able to slip away again quite soon . . .

She went upstairs to pack. Through the half-open bedroom door she could see the flung-back sheet, Janna's tote bag with some garment spilling out of it and, just suddenly, she was thinking of Roly again. The physical side of their marriage had been so good; and how proud he'd been of Nat. Standing there, on the tiny landing, she tried to remember when it had begun to go wrong. Of course, there had been whole areas of his life in which she'd never engaged, but she hadn't cared about that. His work was merely something that enabled him to support her and she wasn't jealous of his pretty models: she was his wife, the mother of his son, and she had no intention of antagonizing Roly by behaving as her cousin Sara did towards David.

There was only one woman that she'd resented and that woman was Mim. She'd never been able to influence or affect their relationship: their shared past, mutual friends and the caring they showed for each other was like an irritation on her skin. It wasn't until after Mim's accident, however, that it had been really necessary to apply pressure and to make it very clear to Roly that the time had come to choose between them.

'Want a cuppa, Moniker?'

Janna's voice disturbed Monica's thoughts, recalling her to the present. Trying to shake off her preoccupation, she peered down the narrow staircase at Janna. It would be impossible in this mood, she decided, to sit drinking coffee with Janna. All conversations with this strange girl were fraught with difficulties and she simply didn't have the energy or the patience to expend on her.

'No, I won't, thank you,' she answered. 'I had a call from Jonathan last evening and I have to get back for a dinner party. You'll explain to Nat, won't you? I'll telephone him later.' And she went into her bedroom and began to pack.

CHAPTER NINETEEN

Kate picked up the telephone and put it down again. It was pathetic, this sudden requirement for company—or at the very least to need to hear a friendly voice. She missed David badly: his good-humoured take on life, his instinctive understanding of her character and the comfort he'd given her. She still half expected the telephone to ring and to hear his voice telling her that he was on his way to her or urging her to join him in London.

'There's a party,' he'd cry—or a wonderful new play or an exhibition. 'Do try to find someone for the dogs and come on up.'

She'd enjoyed the variety much more than she'd imagined: rarely in London for more than a few days at a time and always looking forward to the weeks he'd spend with her in Devon, sometimes doing some painting or perhaps getting together a portfolio for an exhibition, but much more likely simply having fun before hurrying away again. She'd been content knowing that he was there in the flat in London: so different from this sense of real aloneness. Bad luck, too, that at this time her closest friend should have recently departed for a three-month visit to friends in America.

'It is utterly bloody,' Cass had cried. 'But what can I *do*? It's been planned since the autumn and I simply can't back out.'

'Don't be a twit, of course you can't. I shall be fine. Good grief, it's not as if I've never been alone before. Send me lots of cards.'

The first of the cards had arrived that morning. Kate picked it up, reread it and put it down again. She simply mustn't do that thing of wandering aimlessly about, staring out of windows, but neither must she give way to this terrible grief that was all stored up inside her. It occurred to her that, in the past, she'd never given herself the opportunity to mourn. There had always been some good reason for not giving way to grief, whether it was for her failed marriage or the death of her mother. It had seemed important to remain strong, either for the sake of the twins or simply because it was a sign of weakness to give way to tears. Now, with David's death, the weight of it was becoming difficult to bear.

Kate looked at the telephone again. It wasn't fair to ring Roly, feeling as she did; he'd guess at once that she was lonely and he'd either invite her down or suggest that he bring the dogs on a visit. Either way, she'd feel guilty; feel that she was using him in some way that wasn't quite fair to him.

It would be good to speak to one or other of her sons, although Giles might be out on some photographic assignment or shut up in his dark room in the converted boat-house in the cove. She was trying not to bother Giles and Tessa just at this time: with baby Charlotte, only a few months old, as well as coping with small Henry, who was not yet two, Giles and Tessa were very busy and very tired. As for Guy, he would certainly be at the chandlery at this time in the afternoon, which would make it impossible to have a satisfactory conversation with him—he had strict ideas about the work ethic—but perhaps Gemma would be at home with Ben and Julian, having fetched them by now from school in South Brent.

Kate thought about Gemma with a faint sense of anxiety. She was such a pretty, happy girl and so very much like her mother, Cass. There had been a moment a few years ago, after a holiday Gemma and Guy had taken up on Exmoor, when she'd wondered if all was well with them. Gemma had been rather subdued for a while and Kate had feared that there had been a clash between Gemma's light-hearted flirtatiousness and Guy's strict sense of propriety. As the time passed, however, Kate had stopped waiting for some kind of explosion to occur and was able to relax again. It would be good to talk to Gemma and perhaps to the children too. Kate dialled and waited. The ringing ceased and was replaced by Guy's voice, sounding rather bored, saying, 'I'm sorry that Guy and Gemma are not here. Please leave a message and your telephone number and we'll get back to you.'

Kate hastily switched off. She couldn't think of a sensible message and she didn't want them to be worrying about her. She imagined Gemma saying: 'Oh, by the way, darling, Kate rang earlier. I wonder if we should ask her over? She must be missing David and with my ma away in America she might be rather lonely.' Kate shook her head. No, no: she didn't want that kind of pitying anxiety and it wasn't fair to them. On the other hand Giles might be taking a break, wandering over to the cottage, having a cup of tea with Tessa. It was worth a try.

This time the telephone was answered at once.

'Hel*lo*, hel*lo*, hel*lo*,' the voice shouted.

'Hello Henry, it's Grannie.' Kate found that she was shouting too. 'Is Mummy there? It's Grannie, darling?'

'Grannie darling, Grannie darling,' the shouting continued enthusiastically. 'Hel*lo*, hel*lo*—'

The voice was abruptly cut short and a loud buzzing followed. Frustrated, Kate switched off again. Henry would have pressed one of the keys, which meant that now she would not be able to reconnect and, meanwhile, Tessa wouldn't realize that nobody could contact her. Kate deliberately blanked out an immediate vision of Giles desperately needing to contact Tessa—a car accident? Sudden illness?—and went to find her mobile telephone. Tessa's answer mail told her brightly that no one was available to take her call but assured her that if she liked to leave a message she could rerecord it at *any* time.

'Sorry, Tessa,' Kate said, after she'd waited for the tone, 'I think Henry's been playing with the telephone. I hope you pick this up soon. Just a quick one to check that you're all OK. Love you lots.'

She tried the telephone again, but it was still buzzing, and she scrolled through the numbers in her mobile, remembering as she did so that she'd agreed with Nat that he and Monica could come to supper one evening. It wasn't fair to bother him while he was working but she might leave a message for him at the cottage. She was surprised to hear Janna's soft West Country voice at the other end of the line.

'How nice to hear you, Janna. How are you?'

'I'm OK, Kate. Nat's not here, though.'

'I didn't expect him to be. I was going to leave a

message. He suggested bringing Monica over for supper before she goes back and I wanted to say that tonight would be fine. I hope you'll come too, Janna.'

'Thanks, Kate, that's really kind. Only Moniker's gone.'

'Gone?'

'She went off back to London just before lunch. Said she had a date.'

'Oh. Well, then . . .'

'Perhaps 'twas me being here. She just arrived back from seeing Nat's dad, packed her case and went. I came back yesterday but she wasn't here then. She was in Cornwall. Nat thought it was OK if I stayed.'

'Well, of course. Are you sure you're OK, Janna?'

'I'm a bit pissed off. My mum and stuff like that. What about you, Kate?'

'I'm a bit pissed off too, to tell you the truth. Missing David and the dogs. Silly, isn't it?'

'Course it isn't silly. Listen, come on over, why don't you?'

'That would be very nice. I was overcome with self-pity and tried to speak to the boys but they're both . . . unavailable.'

'So you tried Nat?'

'Well, I knew he wouldn't be there but I'd promised to help him out with Monica.'

'She doesn't like me. She thinks I'm bad for Nat. She worries about him, or so she says. Do mothers worry more about sons than they do daughters, Kate? Do they love their sons more?'

'No . . . it's different, that's all. They know that one day they will lose their sons to another woman

137

in a way they don't lose their daughters. Have you heard the old saying? "A daughter's a daughter for all of her life. A son is a son till he gets him a wife"? There's some truth in that. Instinctively mothers of boys know it and it colours their behaviour, that's all. I'm lucky with my sons' wives, they generously allow me to still be involved, but some women fear that they might lose their sons altogether.'

'My mum loves me but she doesn't behave like Moniker.'

'I think that you and your mother love each other in an unusually unconditional way. You give each other space. That's very good, very special, but it's not Monica's way. Monica . . . likes to be in control.'

'D'you think I'm bad for Nat, Kate?'

'No. I think you're very good for him. I think you're good for each other, a bit like you and your mum. You love each other but you give each other plenty of room to breathe. That's a very rare quality.'

'I wouldn't want to be in his way . . . Listen, Kate, he's just come in. Hang on . . . he's saying he's off somewhere up on the moor near Cornwood and I can go along for the ride.'

'That's wonderful. Of course you must go . . . I'm perfectly fine and I'll talk to Nat another time . . . I am absolutely sure, Janna. Enjoy.'

Kate pressed the button and put the telephone down, brooding on their conversation. She knew a little of Janna's background; enough, at least, to recognize that her mother's love was very important to her.

'She didn't give me away,' she'd insisted, one

afternoon when she and Kate had been together at the cottage while Nat was at work. 'She loved me. 'Twas just a bit much for her, that's all. My dad going off soon as he knew she was pregnant and not having any money and stuff like that. But she didn't ever think of having me adopted. She loved me. 'Twas the authorities. She'd begun to drink a bit and she was living in a squat, then, and some of the others were, like, seriously off the wall. The authorities didn't ever understand that I'd rather've been with them, like that, than with neat, clean, ordinary people. They were *nice* people, my foster parents—nothing against them—but they weren't *my* people. We didn't speak the same language.'

Now, Kate thought about Janna with a sudden surge of protective anxiety. 'Do mothers love their sons more?' she'd asked wistfully. 'D'you think I'm bad for Nat?'

Kate hoped fervently that her answers had been the right ones. Nat and Janna were like the two babes in the wood: covering each other with leaves in an effort to camouflage themselves from a prying world. She loved them both but knew that there were issues that needed to be resolved. Monica was not necessarily helping that process.

She thought about Monica in Cornwall with Roly, remembering that odd look on her face—as if she were trying to recall something—and hearing her voice saying: 'It was the cruellest thing I ever did, leaving him.' Perhaps, after all, Roly still loved Monica.

And what if he did? Kate stood up, as if to walk away from the question, thinking about the conversation she'd had with Monica and how she'd very nearly betrayed herself by talking about her own long-ago love affair with Alex. Thirty years on, she could still recall their last painful meeting and the words he'd used.

'The point is that the twins come before me. You're prepared to sacrifice me every time rather than upset them . . . If you're not prepared to be open about our relationship then I think we should call it a day . . . No, no. It's not how I want it, Kate. You know what I want. If you're not prepared to acknowledge my position in your life it's your decision not mine.'

Well, she'd made her decision and she'd lost him and, less than a year later, her old friend and close confidant, the General, had died: then, as now, she'd felt very much alone. It was years later that Cass had given her one of his books: Julian of Norwich's *Revelations of Divine Love* in a version entitled simply *Showings*.

'As a keepsake,' she'd said. 'He used to quote from it. D'you remember? "All shall be well and all manner of thing shall be well." Something like that. He'd kept a postcard you sent him in it as a bookmark and I thought you might like to have it.'

From time to time Kate studied Julian's *Showings*, wrestling with the deeper truths of the text, gaining a measure of comfort and hope. Now, she took the book down from the kitchen shelf and opened it at random.

And these words: You will not be overcome, were said very insistently and strongly, for certainty and strength against every tribulation which may come. He did not say: You will not be assailed, you will

140

not be belaboured, you will not be disquieted, but he said: You will not be overcome.

After a moment, Kate closed the book and put it back on the shelf. She took her keys, slipped on a jacket and went out, through the garden and across the paddock towards the moor.

As she reached the furthest gate, well out of earshot, the telephone began to ring.

CHAPTER TWENTY

'This is really cool.' Sitting high up in the pick-up truck, the shawl flung over her shoulders, Janna beamed at Nat. ' 'Tis like being on the road again. I loved the travelling. I get it from Mum. Her favourite song was "Trains and Boats and Planes". Remember it?' She hummed a bar. 'Always going on somewhere else. It's the freedom, isn't it?'

' "Here today—in next week tomorrow! . . . Always somebody else's horizon! Oh bliss! Oh, poop-poop!"' quoted Nat idly as he drove out of Horrabridge, passing the school and crossing the cattle-grid on the road over Knowle Down. 'You sound like Mr Toad.'

Janna smiled tolerantly, knowing from experience his habit to recite bits from books.

The dear of him, she thought affectionately. I sing pop songs and he spouts yards of stuff from books. Isn't that just typical of us? We're so different.

This reminder of the gulf between them had the

141

unexpected power to extinguish her happiness, rousing the old familiar terrors that lurked in the shadows and filling her throat with a choking miasma of fear.

She looked at him for reassurance, fighting off her demons, summoning up Little Miss Sunshine so as to chase away the shadows. As if he understood her need he reached out and touched her knee.

'Look out there,' he said. 'Can you see the church tower amongst the trees? On days like these I think I'd top myself if I worked in an office. Hear the buzzard?'

'We could stop and have an ice cream,' she suggested. 'There's bound to be a van in the car park at Cadover Bridge. And after you've seen your client we could pick up some fish and chips in Ivybridge and eat them on the way home.'

'We could,' he agreed placidly. 'Did you put the flask in?'

Janna nodded, happier now. She had a passion for picnics, impromptu meals and informal celebrations, always ready to make a sandwich or rustle up a 'smackerel', Nat's word for these junkets. She smoothed the shawl, seeing the threadbare patches as evidence of love that rendered it even more valuable in her sight, and dwelled pleasurably on the treats ahead. Humming to herself so as to raise her spirits further, she leaned from the open window to smile down upon an elderly lady with her dog who was standing against a wall to make room for them to pass into the small village of Walkhampton.

'I feel bad about Kate,' she said suddenly. 'She was feeling lonely, Nat. We should've insisted that

142

she came with us.'

'There's only room for two in the pick-up,' he pointed out, 'and I don't think it would be quite her thing but I'll phone her when we get home.'

Janna was silent, thinking about her conversation with Kate.

'Funny,' she observed. 'Moniker going off like that. D'you think 'twas me?'

'No, I don't.' Nat braked at the crossroads by the Burrator Hotel and then drove on through Dousland. 'She'd probably forgotten the dinner party and it was Jonathan's clients. Something like that. Don't give it a thought.'

As they passed over Marchant's Bridge at Meavy, and up onto the open moorland, Janna took his advice and gave herself up to the wild beauty of the landscape: flowing and rolling away to distant folded heaps of rock, it shimmered dense and hazy in the thick, powdery golden light. At Cadover Bridge children and dogs splashed in the shallow waters of the Plym whilst mothers and babies sat on rugs spread along its sandy banks. Nat parked the pick-up alongside the other cars and reached into his pocket. Janna was out of her seat at once, standing in the sunshine and surveying the scene with delight.

'Look at the little one,' she said. 'He'll be in if his mum doesn't hurry up. There he goes.'

She laughed out loud as the staggering child was whisked from the very edge of the bank by his breathless parent, who swung him high into the air. Drawn like a magnet towards the happy family groups, she wandered away and Nat went to buy the ice creams.

As he waited in the queue he watched her. He'd

sensed the plunge into depression that had threatened to darken her day, admiring her courage whilst fearing her growing dependency on him. Janna was a mass of contradictions: a free, wild spirit who yet craved the security of the domestic scene. Her character was defined by her belongings: the tote bag showed that she travelled light yet it contained the images of her childhood. Nat knew that she was beginning to believe that the commitment of motherhood would tame the wild spirit within her and bring her peace and contentment. He was not convinced.

As she wandered lightly amongst the children he was reminded of the English folksong 'She Passed Through the Fair'. She'd changed her shorts for a skirt that wrapped like a sarong around her slight frame and, with her silken shawl and wild-lion hair, she looked as foreign amongst the harassed young women with their offspring as a bird of paradise in a fowl yard.

By the time he'd been served she'd slipped off her sandals and was paddling in the water with the children. He gave her a cone with a Flake stuck in it—her favourite—and moved away, back to the pick-up, where he sat with the door open. She was crouching now, taking the Flake from the ice-cream and offering the end of it to a small boy. He took a bite, catching the chocolate crumbs and sucking his fingers, and now his bigger sister arrived and was immediately offered the Flake. She seemed to hesitate, staring curiously at Janna, before suddenly accepting her share. She drew attention to the now melting ice-cream and Janna hastened to lick up the dribbles, laughing with delight, and the children joined in readily.

144

The small boy was now showing a toy—a boat? A car? Nat couldn't quite see—and Janna was taking it into her own hands so that she could admire it properly whilst his big sister leaned, pointing importantly, to demonstrate the toy's qualities. When the children's mother arrived on the scene, appearing casual but clearly checking out this stranger, Janna's expression was an odd mixture of friendly humility that touched Nat's heart. She seemed to be asking for some kind of acceptance into this woman's world of happy domestic stability, quite unaware of the exotic impression she was creating. They exchanged a few words but clearly it was time for their picnic tea and the children were ushered firmly away, the older girl talking and gesturing whilst the small boy looked back rather wistfully to where Janna stood alone eating the remains of her cone. She wiggled her fingers at him and he copied her gesture before being hauled on more firmly by his mother.

Quite unexpectedly Nat had an image of himself being tugged along in just that same way but twisting to look back at Roly who'd wiggled his fingers and called, 'Write to me, Nat. Send me a picture.' And he'd shouted 'Yes, I will,' and tried to wiggle his fingers too.

His mother's face had been pinched in, mouth tucked down, eyes small, and he'd wanted to ask why they weren't all together any longer because he knew now that the man she'd called 'your father' was so kind and funny and he, Nat, loved him terribly.

He'd forgotten him, this father: the tall person in whom he'd once put his trust had faded and merged into someone called 'your father', who had

145

done bad things and couldn't be with them. Then, suddenly one day, his mother said that they were going to visit him and Nat felt a little cold fist of fear all balled up inside his heart at the thought of it. They travelled on the tube and walked along a street and all the time his throat was dry and his heart banged up and down as if the fist of fear were trying to punch its way right out of his chest. His mother paused for a moment by some iron railings, staring up at a tall, flat-faced house, and then up the steps they went and she reached out and rang at the bell. By the time the door opened Nat could barely breathe and he stared fearfully up at the man who stood there.

'This is "your father", Nat.' The tone in his mother's voice made him feel anxious because it usually meant 'Please be on your best behaviour' or 'You're doing something I don't like' but when the tall man crouched down, so that he was at Nat's level, all Nat could see on his face was love and delight.

'Nat,' he said, with a great sigh, as if Nat were some kind of treat for which he'd been waiting longingly but feared might never happen.

'Hello, Roly,' his mother said, but not as if she were pleased at all to see him, and Roly stood up again and said, 'Hello, Monica.'

Then Nat knew that the man wasn't just 'your father' but also Roly and he didn't have to worry about it any more. He was given a cushion on a chair at a table in a big warm kitchen and after some discussion his mother went away to do some shopping and Roly gave him a picture book with crayons. They had such a lovely time that he hadn't wanted his mother to come back so quickly and when they were out in the street again and Roly said, 'Come again soon, won't you, Nat?' he'd cried, 'Yes, please. May I come tomorrow?'

That's when his mother had taken his hand and hauled him off and he'd twisted round to look back at Roly just the same way the little boy was turning to wave to Janna.

Janna was looking for Nat now, licking her fingers, as she walked back to the pick-up. Looking at her pensive face, Nat felt anxiety rise inside him: he knew what she was thinking. She climbed up into her seat and he started up the engine and drove out of the car park.

'Did you see that little boy?' she asked at last. 'He was an absolute honey.'

He smiled without answering and she stared out of the window broodingly at the man-made cliffs and grass-grown hills of china clay.

'I was thinking about us, Nat,' she said presently. 'You and me. Supposing we had a baby.' She looked at him now, and though he kept his eyes on the winding moorland road he could feel her beseeching him. 'It could solve all sorts of problems, couldn't it?'

He changed gear, pausing at the junction before turning left on to the road to Wotter, seeking for a reply that wouldn't sound as if he were rejecting her. He appealed to her sense of integrity.

'Is it fair to a baby to see it in terms of something to answer our problems?' He spoke gently, as if he were considering the whole aspect of her request rather than dismissing it out of hand. 'It's possible that it might do quite the reverse. We'd need to be utterly committed to one another to risk it and we both know that neither of us is . . . ready for that.'

Out of the corner of his eye he saw her pull the shawl around her, her face down-turned as she mused upon his reply.

'I love kids,' she murmured—but her voice was resigned, as if she accepted his reservation, and he sought for some kind of distraction.

'Did I tell you that I'm working over near Bude tomorrow? Like a day on the coast?'

'Oh, yes, I would.'

She was cheerful at once, Little Miss Sunshine again, but when he glanced quickly at her he saw that her eyes were bright with tears.

CHAPTER TWENTY-ONE

At the same moment, Daisy and Paul were sitting at one of the wooden picnic benches outside the Tea House in the grounds of the Holburne Museum of Art, having visited the Nureyev exhibition.

'I found it fascinating,' Paul was saying, 'to be so close to his belongings. That costume in the glass case, for instance. Did you say that it's the one he's wearing in the photograph you've got?'

Daisy nodded: she couldn't ever remember being so happy. Her sudden tumble into love had the effect of reducing everything else to insignificance; even the physiotherapist's gloomy reports on the damage to the torn muscle in her back no longer had the power to depress her. Just at present Paul was filling her whole world. She'd never felt like this before. She'd been too busy, too obsessed with work, but now, quite suddenly, she'd been translated into a special sphere: the same world, of course, but one seen through a bubble whose protective thin shiny membrane glossed it to an abnormally brilliant clarity.

Paul was talking on. He'd been surprised by the shortness of the jacket Nureyev had worn as Albrecht—he'd expected him to be taller—and wasn't it amazing that his peasant stock could be traced back to Genghis Khan and the Mongols?

She sipped her tea, smiling radiantly, still nodding happily.

'I liked the recreation of his dressing-room best,' she said, getting a grip on herself. She wanted to take and hold on to one of his hands that gesticulated as he spoke but was just managing to control herself. 'Those false ears from *L'Après-midi d'un faune*, and his tights on the make-up table. You expected him to wander in at any minute and start putting on his make-up, didn't you? I'm glad you liked it.'

'Oh, I did.' He was looking with interest at the little single-storey building, with its shuttered windows and latticed porch, and now he took a postcard from his pocket. 'Look at this. I bought it earlier. It's a rather romantic version of the Tea House painted in 1991.' He chuckled. 'It doesn't matter what the artist has done to give it that Regency atmosphere, it still looks like an air-raid warden's hut to me.'

'I hadn't realized that it *was* an air-raid warden's hut,' Daisy admitted, studying the picture. 'I've never been here before. But once you go inside it's like stepping back in time, isn't it? I love the way they cut all the crusts off the sandwiches, and the

149

flapjacks are delicious.'

He looked at her sternly. 'Do I detect that you are more interested in the cakes than in the history of the place?'

'Oh, yes,' she said at once. 'Much more interested. Dancers love their food. I thought you knew that.'

'I'm beginning to believe it. You won't care about this one much either, then, though I bought it especially for you.'

He pushed another postcard across the table. Angelica Kauffmann's portrait of the pretty little Henrietta Laura Pulteney, posing with her basket of flowers, was familiar to Daisy: as she stared at it, however, it was his words 'I bought it specially for you' that filled her mind.

'I thought you ought to have a reminder of the person your street is named after,' he was saying. 'Must be rather good, mustn't it, to have a beautiful city full of your family's names on the streets and bridges?'

Daisy turned the card over. 'But you haven't written on it,' she protested lightly. 'If you're going to send a postcard you ought to write on it first.'

'OK. Give it here.' He took a pen from the inside pocket of the cotton jacket folded on the bench beside him. 'Now then.' He mused for a moment or two and then scribbled. 'There you are.'

It was crazy, she told herself, that her heart should beat quite so loudly at the prospect of his words written on a piece of card. She devoured them eagerly. He'd addressed it: 'To Daisy Quin of Henrietta Street, Bath.' In the space opposite the address he'd written: 'I bought this especially for you.'

She felt foolishly disappointed despite the fact that, only moments earlier, these words had pleased her so much: he might at least have signed his name, she thought. Immediately, however, she reconsidered it, giving the words their full due and extracting the maximum meaning. She was learning to do this: to take a few compliments, an affectionate gesture, a small gift, and weave something of substance out of the meagre sum of them.

It was clear that the breakdown of his marriage had the effect of making him careful: thus far and no further, he seemed to be saying. Yet she was able to tell herself that it was simply a question of giving him the time to recover, to be prepared to wait, and any preconceived ideas she'd had about equality in a relationship had quickly sunk in this flood of longing. She, whose dancing had been the only thing that mattered in the world, had already began to imagine them living together in the house in the school grounds. She saw herself cooking delicious meals and making friends with his pupils, assisting with the school play, perhaps, and suggesting that dancing classes should become part of the curriculum.

The fact that he was withholding himself simply made him all the more desirable. She refused to believe that he was being capricious but guessed that he just wasn't ready yet to make the next big step away from his marriage. He was still adjusting himself to the move to Bath. All she actually knew was that his wife was unable to put Paul's career before her own and that he'd refused to pass up this opportunity, having missed two chances of promotion already. He'd volunteered this information very reluctantly, as if he'd decided that she was entitled to some background colour, and, bursting though she was with questions, she'd controlled her need to know more. Already she was so far gone in love that his happiness must be put before her own and she had no desire to make him uncomfortable or miserable by forcing explanations from him.

Daisy reminded herself that this was not a new situation for her. At twelve years old, after her mother died, she'd had to make exactly the same kind of allowances for her father when he remarried. His new wife was possessive and, when their baby arrived, Daisy's father had explained to her that, though she would always hold a unique place in his affections, his wife and baby needed a special show of love. It was important, he'd told her, that she mustn't misunderstand or be jealous; she must trust him. Daisy, anxious that he should be happy, had gladly received the small tokens of love that he'd managed to spare for her and embraced her new family wholeheartedly. At the stage school in London during term-time, and often working for part of the holidays, her visits to Yorkshire were few and far between so that the new family soon realized that she constituted no threat to them.

Back then, grieving for her mother and missing her father, Daisy had learned to glean the small crumbs and drops of affection left over from her father's new love and take what nourishment she could squeeze from them. Then, her work had filled the empty spaces in her affection, bringing comfort and purpose to her life. Now, when her work had failed her, it seemed that love might be her sustenance. It pressed in on her, leaving no room for depression or anxiety or fear, blossoming like some vital organism and overwhelming her. She tended it carefully, lest it might become bruised or damaged, not wishing to appear demanding or inquisitive.

She was also refusing to give way to an instinct to picture Ellie—she knew Paul's wife's name now—as an archetypal 'harridan wife' figure. Daisy resisted the desire to see her as a selfish woman, ready to put her own ambition before Paul's happiness or their marriage, cold and sharp-tongued. In fact, Daisy tried not to picture Ellie at all and certainly Paul rarely spoke of her. He made no bid for sympathy and behaved as if his marriage had no bearing on his life in Bath. At the same time he continued to withhold some essential part of himself, throwing up those invisible barriers she was powerless to storm and disappearing behind them.

As she finished her flapjack and drank the last drops of her tea, Daisy wondered what alchemy now possessed her: striking her dumb where once she would have asked a thousand questions, and rendering her weak and trembling at the briefest touch of his fingers. It was terribly important to make another date with him before they got back to Henrietta Street so that she had something to which she could look forward and around which she could build her hopes. She was taking his lead, keeping the friendship light whilst gently moving it forward, but she simply couldn't bear another cool farewell or the abrupt withdrawal of his warmth without knowing that they would be together again soon.

She racked her memory for other events they might share: Walcot Nation Day took place in June and the annual French market, that came to Queen Square for a week, wasn't due until the bank holiday at the end of May. Daisy was especially looking forward to this, convinced that Paul would love it as much as she did: the French voices of the stallholders beneath their yellow and white striped canopies, the smell of freshly baked baguettes and croissants, the long queue at the crêpes stall where the experts cooked the delicious pancakes. Visitors would crowd around stalls that sold onions, garlic, artichokes, cheese, pâté and olives, exchanging remarks, often in French, with the stallholders. Yes, Paul would love the French market but it was two weeks away and she needed something much sooner than that.

It was Paul who said: 'Have you ever been on one of the river cruise boats? I only found them a few days ago near Pulteney Bridge. There's a little café halfway down the steps that sells real Cornish crab sandwiches. The cruise company has a landing stage just above the weir.'

'That sounds fun.' She could hardly say the words, so grateful and happy was she at the prospect. 'I'd love to go on a cruise,' she grinned, and mimed smacking her lips, 'not to mention the crab sandwich.'

'You and your inner woman!' He shook his head in pretence reproof. 'Very well, you shall have a crab sandwich. I've got a leaflet back at the flat so I'll check the timetable and let you know. We could take a picnic.'

So relieved and thankful was she that even when

154

he glanced at his watch and said, 'Must go, I'm afraid. There's something on at school and I have to show my face,' she wasn't cast down but was able to smile and say goodbye, watching him walk away across the grounds, his dwindling figure mingling with the visitors until she could see him no longer.

CHAPTER TWENTY-TWO

It was several days before Daisy saw Paul again. Often he arrived back in Henrietta Street late in the evening and she had to remind herself that Beechcroft was a boarding school and his duties would keep him long after ordinary working hours. This was why he would be moving into the house in the school grounds as soon as it was ready for him.

Standing back from the window, heart beating fast, she'd watch him climb out of the car: might this be the evening that he'd come upstairs and knock on her door?

'I've found that leaflet,' he might say. 'How about tomorrow?' Or: 'It's been one of those days. Fancy a drink somewhere?'

She couldn't quite bring herself to picture a scene in which he invited her down to the flat, though she cursed herself for not having the courage simply to go and ring his bell.

'Hi,' she might say, 'I'm just making some supper and wondered if you've eaten yet.' Or: 'It's such a wonderful evening I thought I'd go for a last stroll in the park. Like to come?'

Why should it be so impossible to act naturally with him? She asked Roly this question when he telephoned a few moments later to see how her treatment was progressing. With their friendship so firmly established during her stay in Cornwall, and reinforced through many telephone conversations, Daisy knew that Roly would provide the listening ear and sound advice she so needed with Suzy and Jill away on tour. It was such a relief to talk to someone about Paul that she plunged in almost at once, explaining exactly how she felt so constricted.

'It's not natural for me to be tongue-tied,' she said. 'I like everything out in the open and up for discussion. It isn't good for the soul to hide one's true feelings and especially with those we really love. Why is it so difficult to behave naturally, Roly?'

'It's because we all fear rejection to a greater or lesser degree,' he answered at once. 'And when we fall in love the fear of it is greater than usual because rejection by the beloved is like the end of the world. We become hypersensitive lest by some unconsidered word or action we show ourselves to be unlovable and so we are tongue-tied and utterly helpless.' A pause. 'Does this sound familiar so far?'

She laughed. 'I'm afraid it does.'

'Then you've got it badly. Oh dear, I hope he's worthy of you.'

'He's lovely,' said Daisy promptly. 'He's interested in things and he makes me laugh. And I realize now that all the love songs in the world were written especially for me.'

'Ah, yes. I know that one too. But it sounds as if

156

you're still in the early stages if you can't act naturally with him.'

'Yes.' She became cautious. 'It's . . . a bit tricky. He's just finishing a long-term relationship.'

'Is this modern speak for "he's a married man"?'

'Oh dear.' She began to laugh again. Talking to Roly loosened the tension and she felt more relaxed, rather as if she'd been discussing Paul with Suzy. 'Well, yes, but it's over now. He's moved down to Bath from London to take over the Art Department at a boys' public school and he's living temporarily in the flat downstairs. The previous incumbent died suddenly and Paul will be moving into the school as soon as the widow finds other accommodation. The trouble is his wife won't leave London or her job. She's blocked his last two promotions and he decided to take a stand over this one.'

'I see.'

'He's a really fun person; you'd like him.' Daisy stopped abruptly: she hated people telling her how much she'd like this or that person. She realized that she was feeling the need to defend Paul in some way and reminded herself sharply that there was absolutely no requirement to do so. 'Anyway, like you said, it's very early days but at least it's taking my mind off my other problems.'

'Poor Daisy. I understand that the trouble with badly torn tissue is that even if it heals there will always be an element of risk once you start dancing again.'

'That's exactly right.' Suddenly she was swamped with a terrible depression. 'I don't know what I shall do . . . Hang on, someone at the door.'

Paul stood outside on the landing, leaflet in

157

hand, looking fit and tough in an open-necked shirt and jeans.

'Found it,' he said, brandishing the brochure. 'I wondered about tomorrow afternoon.'

'Come in,' she said, radiant all in a moment, spirits soaring dizzily. 'Just let me finish this call. Come on in . . . Hello, Roly. Sorry, I have to dash. Someone's arrived. Give my love to the dogs. Bye.' She put down the telephone and smiled at Paul, still hovering tactfully in the tiny hall. 'It's OK, we'd finished anyway. Would you like a drink? Or some coffee?'

'I stopped off for a pint on the way back,' he said, 'but some coffee would be good if it isn't a nuisance.' He opened the leaflet, laying it flat on the table. 'This looks like fun. All sorts of things to see including a cave near Brown's Folly with a rare bat population.'

He sat down, pointing to the aerial painting of the river with a bat emerging from its cave and two kingfishers sitting rather grumpily on a branch. She leaned beside him, inhaling the smell of his skin, and was breathless with happiness.

'Look at the dragonflies,' she chuckled. 'They're as big as helicopters compared to the size of the river. And who are these two on the top of the hill?'

She leaned closer, her shoulder pressed against his, his hair touching her cheek; the picture seemed less clear and she closed her eyes for a moment.

'That's an Iron Age fort on Bathampton Down and the scene of the last duel on English soil in 1778,' he was reading, 'between Colonel Rice of Claverton Down and Vicomte Du Barre

158

of France.'

He glanced up at her, amused, and her hand gripped his shoulder for a second as they stared at each other, the amusement dying from his eyes. The silence lasted just too long—she willing him to make a move whilst he seemed incapable of action—and before it could become embarrassing she turned away.

'I'll get that coffee,' she said.

*   *   *

'Is she OK?' Kate was asking Roly. 'Do I gather from your conversation that Daisy is in love?'

'Yes, I think that's a fair deduction.' Roly wondered what had moved him to speak so openly to Daisy about her symptoms in front of Kate. Up until that moment he'd been very careful to avoid the subject, always anxious lest she should suspect how he felt about her, yet Daisy's words—*'It isn't good for the soul to hide one's true feelings . . .'*—had given him a jolt. 'She's got it bad, by the sounds of it, poor darling. Even worse, he's married.'

'Oh, no. Are there children?'

'I didn't ask but she didn't mention children. From what I can gather, the marriage is over and he's on his own. I guessed there was someone special when she was staying here. Well, it's not an easy thing to hide, is it?'

He was surprising himself—going straight at it like this—but Kate merely shook her head almost wistfully; sitting there on the sofa with Bevis and Floss vying for attention, thinking about Daisy. Roly remembered what Monica had said: *'Did you know that Kate never really loved David and that*

159

she'd had some fantastic affair with someone else?'
Impossible to believe that Kate had been
unfaithful to David—and who could the man be?

'Poor Daisy sounds like someone who's been hit
by a truck,' he said, unable to prevent himself
going in even deeper. 'Probably the first time too,
by the way she's speaking about him.'

'Should we be saying "Poor Daisy", though?
Shouldn't we be thinking how wonderful it is for
her to be in love?'

'I think that depends on whether this fellow
loves her in return. She sounds as if she's in the
first throes: agonizing and divine in turns. Can you
remember feeling like that?'

Kate laughed and then frowned, sitting back on
the sofa as if to concentrate better. The dogs lay
down, resigned.

'When I first met Mark it was like that, I
suppose. Obviously you don't marry someone
unless you think you're in love with them . . . do
you?' She glanced at him but he remained silent. 'I
was nineteen and the whole thing was a whirl of
ladies' nights and summer balls and parties. Cass
and Tom, Mark and I. We hardly spent a moment
alone together before the wedding. Wildly
romantic, of course, but no preparation for reality.'

'So you got divorced?' he asked after a lengthy
silence.

'Yes,' she said rather bleakly. 'We got divorced
when the twins were ten years old.'

'Well, you did better than I did.' He hated to see
the expression in her eyes and now wished he
hadn't begun the conversation; yet a new inner
conviction drove him onwards. 'Nat was two when
Monica left me.'

160

'I'm so sorry.' It was Kate's turn to remember Monica's words about Roly: *It was the cruellest thing I ever did; leaving him, I mean. He never got over it.* She thought of the other things that Monica had told her but when she spoke it was as if she knew nothing of his past.

'Personally, though, I find it impossible to believe that she left *you* for that dried-up stick of a man. She must have been out of her mind. I said so to David the first time I met Jonathan.'

'Did you?' He smiled at her partisanship but this same conviction compelled him to be truthful. 'I married Monica because she was pregnant with Nat. We were in lust, but not in love, and she left me because I'd begun to drink too much.' He came to sit beside her on the sofa so that he didn't have to see her face. 'It was just after Mim's accident and I wasn't handling it awfully well.'

'What a terrible time it must have been,' Kate said when Roly fell silent. 'I can understand that it must have been ghastly for both of you. Mim's career in ruins, not to mention the pain she must have been suffering. You knowing what she was going through . . .'

'And knowing, too, that I was the cause of it.'

'*You* were the cause?'

'I met her from the station with the car, you see. Our father was ill and I'd driven down to Cornwall from London to see him. I had an old station wagon in those days and I'd chucked the big metal box that held two of my cameras and some lenses in the back on top of everything else. A heavy old thing it was—you don't see them much nowadays—but it was built to protect the equipment. Mim was arriving next evening by train

161

and I'd arranged to pick her up from Bodmin. I was running late because I'd stopped to have a few pints with a friend of mine. I'd already been drinking before I left home. I drank far too much in those days, but nobody bothered too much about driving while being the worse for wear. I'd had to brake a bit sharply on the way to the station when something ran across the road—a fox or a cat, perhaps—and the box banged back against the tailgate and started sliding about. I hadn't taken the trouble to make it properly secure, you see. Mim was waiting for me so I didn't bother to park; I just pulled in beside her. As she lifted the tailgate, to put her case in the back of the car, the box simply slid out on to her foot and crushed it. I can still remember the noise she made.'

His face was taut with anguish; Kate watched him, unable to think of any single thing to say that might comfort him.

'I drove her straight to the nearest hospital and at some point—I can't remember now—we agreed that nobody would know exactly how it had happened. Rumours began to circulate, of course, but we were a long way off, down here in Cornwall, and by the time we got back to London the myth had already grown of its own accord. Even Monica never guessed the truth. But I couldn't handle it, you see. I couldn't get over the harm I'd done in destroying Mim's career and I simply drank more in an effort to stop going over and over it in my head: if only I'd secured the box properly; if only I hadn't stopped for that drink; if only I'd been on time and had opened the tailgate myself. The truth of it is that I was drunk: I shouldn't have been driving that car. My guilt made my drink problem

162

worse but the odd thing is that you never actually see yourself as an alcoholic. I was never uncontrollably drunk but I was never quite sober either and my work suffered as a result. Monica, understandably, lost patience with me and after a few months she left, taking Nat with her. Losing Nat brought me to my senses. Monica said that I could only see him again if I stopped drinking completely. It took a year. I lost a whole year of him but at the end of that time Monica agreed that he could visit me. God knows what damage I did to him. By then Mim was settling down at the stage school and we were sharing a house again. I managed to pick up some of the pieces of my life but they never fitted together quite the same ever again.'

Kate sat in silence. After such a confession no remark seemed appropriate; every observation must be trite. He passed his hand across his lips and turned to look at her. With a shock he realized that all the romantic emotions he'd cherished about her for so long had vanished along with the weight of his secret guilt. Staring at her he simply saw a very dear, close friend; his old, unhappy passion for her was spent at last, and if he felt a sadness at its passing he was also aware of relief.

'I've never told anyone,' he said. 'I can't imagine why now except for something Daisy said earlier.'

Kate, longing to reassure him, wondered anxiously what might be the next step after such a momentous happening—any reaction must surely be anti-climatic—yet she was conscious of some healing quality of deep-down peace stealing through him. Instinctively she reacted as she always did in such circumstances by suggesting

163

some kind of action, outdoors if possible. Movement through the landscape, connection with the natural world, inevitably brought its own kind of healing.

'Come on,' she said, putting an arm through his. 'Let's go up on the moor. We'll give the dogs a walk. That's what we need right now.'

They smiled at each other, easy with one another, freed at last into uncomplicated friendship. Roly lifted Uncle Bernard from his drawer and they all went out together into the mild spring evening.

CHAPTER TWENTY-THREE

Discovering that Paul was going away for the half-term week had come as a disappointing shock to Daisy—a shock she'd been unable to disguise—and each time she remembered the little scene she felt hot with the shame of her transparency. She'd become too confident, too sure that their friendship was beginning to develop into an intimacy that would allow certain things to be taken for granted. It was not, she told herself firmly, that he was playing hard to get, or deliberately keeping her wrong-footed, but that he simply wasn't ready to let himself relax into complete trust and openness. She believed that he'd been badly hurt and she was determined not to force the pace. At the same time, she reminded herself defensively, they were so happy together that it was difficult to refrain from making certain assumptions about their relationship.

The boat trip on the River Avon, for instance, had been such fun, Paul spotting a kingfisher that he insisted was the grumpy one pictured on the leaflet and, afterwards, buying Cornish crab sandwiches that they'd eaten sitting on a bench by the river just like two carefree holiday-makers. Then, a few days later, they'd met by chance in the town and his expression of delight when he'd first seen her had lifted her heart up into the seventh heaven of joy. She'd been wandering up New Bond Street, pausing to gaze longingly into the windows of Jigsaw and Laura Ashley, and as she'd passed on into Milsom Street she'd seen him coming towards her.

Her answering smile must have been just as pleasing to him because he took her arm, in that wonderfully informal way he had, and said: 'I was thinking about having some lunch. I'm sure you must be hungry, so where shall we go?'

She laughed—her rapacious appetite was now a standing joke between them—and replied: 'Oh, let's go to the Café René in Shires Yard. I just adore their ciabattinas.'

Crossing the road, still arm-in-arm, they turned in, between the flower shop and the wine shop at the entrance of the precinct, and went down the stairs. They paused to look at a display of delicious hand-made chocolates but hurried past some very expensive boutiques, so that Daisy should not be tempted, and out into the yard where Café René's tables stood with their gay red and blue umbrellas.

Paul ordered Provençal mussels served with French bread and Daisy asked for a hot goat cheese ciabattina, and they'd squabbled amicably over the dish of curly fries.

It seemed quite natural and easy for Daisy to say to him: 'Shall we go to the French market next week?' and it was a shock to see the cheerfulness fade so swiftly from his face.

'I shall be away,' he said, almost sharply, as if to imply that she might have guessed as much. 'It's half-term. I'm going down to South Devon to stay with friends at a holiday cottage near Salcombe. It's been booked for ages.'

She tried not to let her disappointment show but the sense of intimacy was utterly shattered and she felt oddly fearful at that veiled look that made his face wary and cool. She managed to pull herself together sufficiently to say quite casually: 'Oh, I'm going away too, back to Cornwall for a few days,' and he, recovering his natural ease and good-humour, said, 'To those people you were telling me about? Roly and Mim, is it, and all the dogs?'

She was foolishly pleased to think that he remembered the conversation, comforted by the fact that at least he wouldn't be spending the week with his wife in London, but, once again, she experienced that same sense of loneliness that pierced her each time he left her abruptly in the hall or, as on this particular occasion after lunch, in Milsom Street.

'Back to the daily round,' he said—but then he hesitated for a moment and, taking her face in his hands, he kissed her on the lips. 'Enjoy your shopping,' he said, and hurried off towards Union Street.

She made some jolly farewell reply and swung away, head high, a smile on those same burning lips, seeing nothing until she found herself on Grand Parade, staring down into the waters of the

166

fast-flowing Avon as it passed under Pulteney Bridge and cascaded noisily over the weir. She tried to control the dark negative thoughts that beat around inside her head like unruly black bats. Paul's volte-face from warm easiness to cool wariness had been so unexpected that she knew he'd seen her unguarded expression of disappointment and surprise. She *had* been surprised that he'd never mentioned that he'd be going away. In fact, so sure had she been that they'd be spending much more time together during the half-term week, she'd half considered cancelling the trip to Cornwall.

Meanwhile, she was constrained to make great efforts to recover her poise and confidence. She had a date with Paul for the Royal New Zealand Ballet on what must be the evening before he left for Devon and she was determined to enjoy it.

It seemed that he too was wondering if he'd been rather abrupt. The day following their lunch in Shires Yard he suggested that, on the evening of the performance, they should have a pre-show supper at the Vaults Restaurant next door to the theatre. She was very ready to fall in with any plan that might restore any intimacy between them and, when he came to collect her, she greeted him with a light-heartedness that completely deceived him; by the time they'd settled down with a bottle of wine at their table to discuss the merits between the braised lamb shank and the seared sea bass, everything had become easy between them again.

While they waited for their food to arrive Paul entertained her with his version of the story of Richard 'Beau' Nash who, having lost the original playhouse to David Garrick as a gambling debt, moved in next door with his mistress, Juliana Popjoy.

'I knew all that, anyway,' she told him airily. 'After the bank holiday I'll take you to supper in Popjoys restaurant. It's very smart.'

'Ah,' he said, not at all put out. 'But did you know that when Nash died Juliana was so affected by his death that she spent the rest of her life in a hollow tree?'

For some reason this seemed so extraordinarily funny to them both that they went off into fits of the giggles. Looking around the vaulted room, revelling in the busy, happy atmosphere and listening to the hum of chatter and laughter, Daisy was thoroughly happy. Paul teased her because she couldn't make up her mind whether she should have sticky toffee pudding or wild berry terrine with mango coulis, encouraging her to have both. At last, they went into the theatre through the stalls bar to find their seats. This time it was Daisy's turn to tell Paul about the huge painted butterfly tied for luck to a rail at the top of the fly tower since the war years and, when he complained because it couldn't be seen from the audience, she went on to describe the theatre's Grey Lady: the ghost of an actress who loved a man who used to sit in one of the boxes but hanged herself in the Garrick's Head pub when her love was unrequited.

'She'd have done better to go and live in a hollow tree with Juliana Popjoy,' he remarked callously—and then the lights dimmed and the music of Prokofiev filled the auditorium.

The performance thrilled Daisy with all the passionate intensity of its choreography and its elegant design. It wasn't until they'd come out into the street and begun to walk home that she realized that she was rather stiff.

'All that sitting,' she said apologetically, as Paul put his arm through hers to help her along. 'I'm fine really. It's been such a wonderful evening.'

He went with her up the stairs but she knew that she'd given him the excuse to cut the evening short and, though she longed for him to stay, he would hurry away as usual. She was quite right: he refused to let her make coffee, insisted that she must take some painkillers and go to bed, said that he had a very early start and needed to do some packing. He kissed her and left her to a sudden declension of spirits: the music and the dance still whirling in her brain along with the terrible sense of loss and fear that she might never dance again.

The feeling was still with her next morning. She watched Paul packing the car, this overwhelming compulsion to see him drawing her back again and again to the window, and when he knocked on her door she had to take a moment to compose herself before she could open it. He looked fresh, alive, and devastatingly attractive.

'Just wanted to say that I'm off now. Have a good time in Cornwall.'

'Oh, I will,' she said gaily. 'It'll be great. Good luck with the traffic . . . Send me a postcard.' She couldn't hold back the words; already she was in despair at the idea of not seeing him for more than a week.

'Oh.' He was clearly disconcerted. 'But you won't be here . . .'

'No,' she said quickly. 'How silly. Wait a minute.' She dashed over to the little bureau and tore a sheet of paper from her writing pad. 'There you are. I'd written it down for someone else but you can have it. No excuses now.'

She kept her voice light, joking, and he took the paper, folded it and put it in the back pocket of his jeans.

'OK,' he answered, just as cheerfully. 'Can't return the compliment, I'm afraid. Haven't a clue what the address of the cottage is until I meet up with my friends. Take care, won't you?'

He'd gone, running down the stairs and out to the car, and she was left to face three empty days before she went to Cornwall. She remembered how she'd considered cancelling her visit and felt ashamed when she recalled how ready she'd been to put Paul before Mim: to set aside Mim's claim on their years-old friendship in preference to someone whom she'd known for such a short time. Paul, it seemed, had no such qualms.

On Tuesday morning, as she drove along a lane flanked and made even narrower by tall cow parsley, whose powdery white flowers brushed against the windows of the car, Daisy's skin prickled hotly with this unhappy thought, and she made an effort to anticipate the approaching reunion with her friends. Driving west, to the house by the ford, Daisy was aware of a sense of homecoming. This time the Cornish names were familiar to her and she greeted them with a pleasurable anticipation that went some way towards ameliorating the tiny pricks of embarrassment she experienced whenever she thought about Paul.

And here she was at last, splashing through the ford, and feeling almost shaky with relief as she

170

saw Roly, playing in the yard with the dogs, and Mim emerging from the house with her arms already stretched wide in welcome.

CHAPTER TWENTY-FOUR

Clearing up from breakfast, a few days after Daisy's arrival, Mim and Roly were discussing her plight.

'Oh, terrible, terrible love,' cried Mim, plates clashing in her hands. 'Poor darling Daisy.'

Roly remembered his conversation with Kate. 'Should we be saying "poor Daisy", though? Shouldn't we be thinking how wonderful it is for her to be in love?'

Mim withered him with a glance. 'Wonderful? You've seen how she is every morning, positively watching for the postman to arrive and then coming over, all bright and brittle while she's trying to see if there's a letter for her. Does she strike you as someone who is happy?'

'No,' Roly admitted. 'No, not happy, exactly, but she did tell me that the affair was in its early stages and . . . and here is the postman.'

He went out and Mim forgot Daisy for a moment as she watched him, leaning on the gate and exchanging pleasantries with the postman. She'd seen the difference as soon as he'd got out of the car at the station: some new freedom in his eyes and in the way he walked towards her. She'd stared at him curiously and he'd smiled down at her. Suddenly it was clear to her and hope leaped in her along with a hundred questions: when? To whom?

'Have you been talking to Nat?' she'd asked.

He'd shaken his head, knowing that she'd guessed the reason for his light-heartedness.

'To Kate,' he'd answered—and she'd nodded, pleased: it would be Kate, of course: non-judgemental, an old friend and someone whom he trusted. Mim had known instinctively that his uncomfortable love for Kate had also been subsumed, along with his confession, into their friendship: he was truly free. Of course, he might miss the passion whose very pain had made him feel alive: freedom carried other burdens, and could bring loneliness in its wake. Nevertheless, she rejoiced to see him look so happy.

'Why *then*?' he'd asked her, bewildered. 'After all these years? Why should it be possible just then?'

'Because that was the right moment,' she'd assured him. 'Life's like that, isn't it? These moments are vouchsafed us and we need to seize them thankfully.'

'After all,' he'd needed to explain it to her properly, 'I knew that you'd forgiven me right from the start and Nat has never reproached me. Yet I clung on to the shame of it for all those years. And why to Kate? I don't see . . .'

'But you had to forgive yourself, not only for the accident, but also for the damage that followed it. That's much harder than forgiving someone else. It's taken all this time for you to work through it and come to this point. Kate being here was simply the catalyst.'

'And it was something Daisy'd said just a few minutes earlier on the telephone: "It isn't good for the soul to hide one's true feelings and especially with those we really love." It seemed to strike right into my heart—especially with Kate sitting there. I'd been doing so much hiding of my feelings, with her and with Nat, and all of a sudden I knew I didn't have to do it any more: I was freed—not from guilt—but from the terrible burden of the need for secrecy. The odd thing is that, once I'd told her the whole story, it was as if my feelings for her had changed too.'

'It was time,' she'd answered gently. 'You fell in love with Kate thirteen years ago and it had become a kind of unhappy habit that you couldn't break. David dying made it even worse, brought it to a head, and made things miserable between you. You can be happy together now: enjoy being the good friends you really are. Much more sensible.' She'd grinned at him. 'And if that makes you feel rather staid and unromantic, well, tough!'

He'd grinned back at her. 'I'll settle for staid for the moment.'

The postman was driving away and Roly returned with a handful of letters. Mim took them from him and began to look through the small pile.

'Ah,' she said. 'Here we are. A postcard for Daisy. A very nice picture of Salcombe.' She turned it over and examined the back of it.

'Mim.' Roly sounded scandalized. 'You're not going to read it?'

She glanced at him briefly. 'How can I see what's going on if I don't read it?'

'Honestly, Mim . . .'

'Roly, this is serious. We've been through it already. Listening to Daisy's account of her injury I don't think she'll be able to dance properly again.

173

The muscle and the tissue aren't healing properly and if she tries to dance to her old standard it will simply cause more damage. I can give her a terrific opportunity in London to reinvent her career but I can't wait too long and I need to know what's going on.'

'I know all that but you can't read people's private correspondence.'

Mim snorted. *'Private correspondence?* Would you write anything personal on a postcard? Nobody sends a postcard if he wants the contents to remain private. Why doesn't he write her a letter? Or why not put the card in an envelope, if he wants it to be private? Anyway, there's nothing here that I wouldn't write to you. Nothing at all. Oh, poor darling Daisy.'

'Mim, you are the absolute limit.'

The sheer inadequacy of his words amused her and she grinned at him, reminded of long-ago years when once she'd borrowed his new white cricket jersey with the school colours and got jam all over it and, on another occasion, had inadvertently sat on his favourite LP and smashed it to pieces.

She mocked him, making a prim face and mimicking him: ' "Mim, you are the absolute limit," ' so that he laughed too and then cried, 'Watch out, Daisy's coming.'

She was crossing the yard, pausing to talk to Bevis and Floss, not hurrying, and by the time she arrived in the kitchen, Roly was loading the dishwasher whilst Mim cleared the table.

'Good morning,' Daisy said, smiling to see Uncle Bernard curled up so comfortably and neatly in his drawer. 'I've decided that I'd better

174

stock up a bit today and I was wondering whether you wanted anything.' Her eyes went hungrily to the small pile of letters. 'I might go to Camelford.'

Mim took pity on her, passing Roly the last of the plates and then picking up the envelopes.

'That might be a good idea. We could go together. One for you, Roly.' She passed him a letter. 'Oh, we have a postcard from Salcombe.' Out of the corner of her eye she saw Daisy tense with expectation. 'Oh, sorry, Daisy. It's for you.'

She passed it across to her at once, pretending to peruse the remaining letters whilst seeing Daisy's shoulders droop a little as her eyes devoured the meagre message. So brief was it that Mim could remember it: 'Very beautiful here and the weather's being kind. Hope all is well in Cornwall. P.'

Her eyes met Roly's briefly across Daisy's bent head: he looked as if he were suffering equally with Daisy. Mim raised her eyebrows, signalling: 'So what now?' and he responded with a tiny shrug of his shoulders and a brief shake of the head. He saw Mim close her eyes, her face stilled and quiet for a moment, as though she were drawing strength from some unseen source.

'Come, Daisy,' she said. 'Sit down.'

Holding her card, Daisy sat obediently at the table across from Mim. Watching Daisy, it occurred to Roly that during those ten years of training at the stage school she'd responded to Mim's authority so naturally that, even seven years later, the old habit held good. He relaxed a little: perhaps this was Daisy's moment for coming to terms with the truth.

'We've talked quite a bit about your injury,' Mim

was saying, 'but we haven't really faced the fact that you might never dance with a top professional company again.'

Daisy dropped her eyes before such a brutal truth, fingering her postcard, and Roly winced at Mim's straight speaking.

'I think I can only say these things because I've been there myself.' Mim's eyes were fixed on Daisy's face. 'I don't think we can pretend that your career can just be picked up where it left off and so the best thing is to look at the alternatives.'

Daisy swallowed, licking dry lips. 'It's not that I want to kid myself,' she said, 'but it's as if I can't seem to think straight at all at the moment. Nothing seems . . . real.'

'But that's because you're in love, my darling, isn't it? Everything dissolves in the face of terrible, terrible love.'

'Is love terrible?' Daisy stared at Mim with such anxiety that Roly longed to defend her in some way from the answer he knew Mim would give.

'Being in *love* is nearly always terrible,' she answered truthfully, 'unless both lovers are always giving to each other—not pulling in opposite directions—so that the love flows freely between them. That way there is no anxiety or fear, no need to score points, each is equal. Generally, this is not the case. You know the saying "There is one who kisses and one who extends the cheek"? That's much more the norm, wouldn't you say? I have known cases where people actually confuse the pain of rejection or betrayal with love. You only have to listen to Ella Fitzgerald singing those blues to begin to believe that suffering is sexy. It isn't.'

'I know that,' protested Daisy. 'I don't do that. It's just . . . I just can't help it. I want to be with him.'

'Oh, my darling, of course you do. We all do. We want to cook them delicious food and have their babies. Clever old Mother Nature has got us well under her thumb, you see. She plays hell with our hormones and makes us blind and insensate to anything but the beloved. I was just the same with Alistair. Oh, how I adored him.'

'Alistair?' Daisy was distracted momentarily from the shock of Mim's blunt observations. 'Who is Alistair?'

'He is my ex-husband. Oh God, how I loved that man.'

'Your ex-*husband*? I had no idea that you'd been married. Nobody ever said anything about it.'

'Probably nobody actually noticed,' said Roly drily. 'It didn't last long. The poor fellow hadn't realized that he was marrying an entire stage school.'

Mim grinned. 'The poor darling. The trouble was that I didn't concentrate on him properly. The sex was terrific but there were other more important things in my life than bed. It was wrong of me to marry him but he was so persistent and I thought I could have it all.'

'But what happened?' Daisy's eyes were round with disbelief. 'When did it start to go wrong?'

'Halfway through the honeymoon,' said Roly, 'when he was told that it would have to be cut short because Mim was going to Bristol to preside over the examination session at the local ballet schools. She didn't break it to him until the day before because she didn't want to upset him.'

'Oh dear.' Mim was laughing guiltily. 'I used to be on the RAD's board of examiners in those days, you see, and I simply couldn't have let them down. He didn't understand at all and I wasn't terribly sympathetic. My work was always so important to me and I wasn't clever about managing him.'

'But what happened?'

'He was very attractive and there were always other women who wanted to comfort him. He liked that: feeling a little sorry for himself and casting me as a heartless career woman. Well, I was. I had so many people to love. My staff and all the children were my family, I suppose, and poor Alistair simply couldn't cope. He went off with an older woman who adored him and made him feel all the things I didn't. He postured about for a while, smirking insufferably and implying that she could appreciate him properly. I was only too grateful to her. *Such* a relief, I can't tell you!'

'But that doesn't mean that love can't work for other people.'

'No, darling, it doesn't, but it does mean that you need to think about it very carefully.'

'But if I can't *have* a dancing career . . . ?'

'Perhaps not the one you had, no, but have you ever thought of choreography?'

Daisy frowned, considering the idea, clearly taken aback. 'No.' She shook her head but her eyes were thoughtful.

'From one or two things you've told me when you were working with Tony, I've been thinking about it quite a lot. Do you remember, in class, you often found it difficult to follow the *enchaînement*? You often got into trouble over it. Once you said to me, "I thought that something else ought to go

178

after the *pas de chat*"—a *pas de bourrée* or a *glissade*, I can't remember—and I realized that you were making up your own sequence of steps in your head and not concentrating on what your teachers were asking you to do.'

'I did that with Tony,' Daisy agreed, 'but then choreography works like that, doesn't it? Bouncing ideas off one another?'

'Of course it does but, listening to you, I had the impression that you often had very clear ideas of your own.'

'Yes, that's true, but even so . . .'

'You know Andy's leaving us? Why don't you come back to us for a while? You could help us in a thousand ways, you'd be so wonderful with the children, and you could choreograph something special for the Charity Matinée. We'd all assist you, of course, but I'd leave it entirely to you to come up with something new.'

Silence: then Daisy began to laugh disbelievingly. 'The *Charity Matinée*? But that's incredibly prestigious. I . . . I couldn't begin to . . . You can't mean it?'

'It demonstrates my trust and absolute faith in you, darling Daisy. Will you think about it? I need to know soon.'

Daisy stared at her with dazed eyes. 'I don't know what to say.'

'Then don't speak now.' Mim got up. 'We'll go to Camelford to get some shopping but I have to do a few things first. Can you give me half an hour?'

She went away from them, up the stairs, and presently Roly put his hand on Daisy's shoulder.

'I have it on good authority that, at moments

179

like these, communication with the Great Outdoors is therapeutic,' he said. 'Shall we take the dogs up on the hill?'

PART TWO

CHAPTER TWENTY-FIVE

The cottage was for sale: the estate agent's post was wedged into the peaty earth of the narrow border, sheltered by the low wall that fronted the lane, and the board was framed by the leaves of the rowan tree whose white blossoms were faded now and drifted down to the grassy verges. Kate, on her way to supper with Nat and Janna, braked sharply and sat staring at the small stone house. Its outward appearance had not changed much since she'd first seen it thirty years ago: the outbuildings had been renovated—work she'd been unable to afford—and the cottage had been given a new slate roof but the whole effect remained one of stability and character. The grey stone walls seemed to have grown out of the earth along with the ancient apple trees and the aquilegias; the robin, hopping upon the flagged path, was surely a descendant of the little family that nested each year in the ivy that clung tenaciously to the holly trees in the hawthorn hedge.

Kate leaned forward, staring up at the board as if it were a portent: a message for which she'd been hoping. How strange that this particular cottage should come on to the market now, at this particular moment when her life was in a state of confusion and grief, when she was considering putting her own house up for sale, though she had no idea where she should go. Thirty years ago she'd fallen in love with this cottage and plunged headlong into the purchase of it with that supreme confidence that comes with the knowledge of absolute rightness. Even now she could remember that first reaction to it and was surprised to discover that she was experiencing those same feelings again: delight, excitement, a sense of a new direction in her life.

Back then the cottage had been a place of shelter through the unhappy months of the breakdown of her marriage: a secure base for her children after the years of moving between the naval bases. Here, away from prying eyes and gossip, she and Alex had made love: such loving as she had never known before. There had been so much to talk about to him, so much to share . . . even now she couldn't understand why their relationship had foundered so disastrously.

The tractor, rumbling round the bend in the lane, caught her unawares; she hastened to pull into the gateway to let it pass and then drove on towards Horrabridge where Nat and Janna were waiting for her.

'You'll never guess,' she said, hugging them and accepting a glass of wine, unable to wait a moment before telling them. 'My old cottage is for sale. I simply can't believe it. It was the first place I ever owned . . .'

The words came tumbling out—the coincidence, the memories—and she laughed and shook her head in turn, unable to contain this wild, new excitement.

Janna caught her infectious exhilaration all in a second. 'Your old home? Where you brought up your boys?'

She entered completely into Kate's delight, easily able to identify with her amazement at the coincidence, as ready as Kate was to believe in signs and portents. To Janna, a home, any home, was a sanctuary and this must be a very special place, she could quite see that.

'Imagine,' she marvelled, 'falling in love with it all those years ago and then finding it again now, just when you've been wondering what to do and where to go. And all those memories of the twins growing up . . .'

'I think it's been a holiday home for the last few years.' Nat was more prosaic. 'I've noticed that through the winter it's often got that shut-up look about it and then at Easter and in the summer you see signs of life.'

'I wonder if it's been changed inside.' Kate tried to imagine it. 'I shall phone the agents in the morning. It's so odd that I should come that way this evening. I'd been for a walk up on King's Tor, you see . . .' She told the story again and then laughed with vexation. 'Sorry. I'm being an absolute twit. Let's forget it. How are you both?'

Bundling away her excitement, containing it in a secret place where she might dwell on it later in private, Kate concentrated on the two of them. Janna had the air of a languorous cat: even the wild lion-hair, springing mane-like around her small head, looked sleek. Her lips curved contentedly upward, even as she leaned to pour the wine, as if she were possessed of some ineffable joy that couldn't be hid. This evening she wore a flame-coloured sarong, knotted round her narrow hips, and a black halter-top that barely concealed her tiny breasts. All her movements were languid and assured, yet there remained something vulnerable in the sharpness of her shoulder-blades and her bare, thin, fragile feet.

185

Kate, glancing at Nat, was aware of tension: there was no joy here. His eyes were inward-looking, his lips compressed, and the heaviness of his spirits was manifested in the tremendous effort he was making to join in with the conversation. Janna seemed unconscious of his gloom, wrapped as she was in her own happiness. Hearing Kate's story about the cottage had given it a kind of lustre, an added brilliance, and she was away into one of her own stories of being on the road. She perched on the arm of Nat's chair, leaning against his shoulder and, as she talked, Kate was shocked into a sharper awareness. There was an unconscious possessiveness in Janna's attitude; she touched Nat's hair and then his arm—such a light, brief caress but with a new, sweet confidence—as she told her light-hearted, amusing tale. And all the while her body language was telling a separate story of its own: its fluid, newly fulfilled grace communicating quite as clearly as any words.

She got up to go back into the kitchen—none of the familiar waif-like hesitation in her movements now; instead the serene certainty of the mistress of the house—and Nat reluctantly raised his eyes at last. He was clearly uncomfortable, unable to meet Kate's gaze openly or to speak out freely, and Kate remained silent out of confusion and politeness.

'So,' he said dully, at last, 'do you think you really might make an offer for the cottage?'

His words, apparently heaved up with an effort from his heavy heart and falling weightily into the silence, filled her with a foreboding that inhibited her and she was relieved when Janna called out that supper was ready.

*　　*　　*

Kate slept badly that night. Thoughts about the cottage distracted her from her anxieties about Janna and Nat but her head seethed with so many other images and ideas that, to begin with, she couldn't sleep at all. She'd resisted the temptation to drive home past the cottage—it would be foolish to go so far out of her way simply to stare at it again—but she simply couldn't prevent herself from thinking about it.

As she let herself into her own house she was seized with a sudden compunction, almost as if she were contemplating infidelity, and she looked around her big, warm kitchen with a kind of placating anxiety. She loved this house, of course she did, but she must try to be rational about it. Now that she was alone it was too big for her and she couldn't afford to maintain it. The cottage, on the other hand, would be perfect: small without being poky, economical to run, secluded but not remote. It seemed surprising, remembering it with the enthusiasm that she felt for it at this moment, that she'd ever been prepared to leave the cottage at all. It had been her brother, she reminded herself as she switched off lights and locked up, who'd broached the idea that they should pool their resources and share a house: her boys were growing up, she was beginning to take the dog-breeding more seriously so as to supplement her income, and Chris needed a base in the UK. This project offered both of them advantages they couldn't supply by themselves. Kate required extra space, both inside and out, and Chris, who was an electrical transmissions engineer and worked abroad a great deal, longed for a proper home to which he could return for holidays.

Lying in bed, staring wakefully into the shadowy spaces, Kate tried to remember if the bitter ending of her affair with Alex had still been raw enough to make her brother's idea even more appealing. Chris's suggestion had certainly come at the time when she'd been trying to come to terms with losing Alex, searching for ways to make a new beginning. Chris understood her dilemma: his own marriage had recently ended in divorce and he'd asked he if might come to stay with Kate for a week's holiday. They'd taken the twins for long walks over the moor, to the coast at Torcross to swim, to Dartmouth to look at the boats, to the cinema in Plymouth. The twins, who had grown up in fear of their father and seen Alex as a threat, had been so responsive to their uncle, so natural and easy with him, that Kate's own tension and anxiety had gently and quietly unravelled. Even now, she could recall the true happiness of that holiday, the blessed absence of stress or strain: uncomplicated and fun. His proposal that they should share a house, coming at the end of that idyllic week, had seemed the answer she'd been seeking. It would be a relief, after her unhappy marriage with Mark and the turbulent affair with Alex, to have a simple, undemanding relationship with her sons and her brother.

It had been the right decision, Kate told herself now. Through the following years, with the twins at Blundell's School and then at university, she and Chris had achieved stability for the boys and a refuge for themselves: a home where the four of them could grow and heal. It had worked for ten

188

years—until Chris, having fallen in love with a delightful Japanese girl in America, had decided to get married again and settle with her in Florida. An unexpected legacy had enabled Kate to buy him out and, a few months later, she'd met David.

Kate stirred restlessly, pushing back the light quilt and sitting on the edge of the bed. These early morning hours were the worst: bringing with them heart-rending memories of the past and terrors of the future. The room was lit with the soft radiance of starlight and from the uncurtained window she could see the distant shoulder of the moor, hunched blackly against the brilliant night sky. No sleeping David, now, to curl up against for comfort: no familiar sound of dogs rustling and snoring in the kitchen below.

'Can't sleep?' he'd ask drowsily. 'Who is it this time? Giles, is it? He's a good fellow, old Giles. Takes his time and likes to know where he is before jumping into things but he's going to be OK, I promise you . . .'

Memories of his warmth and humour crowded at her shoulder and she allowed herself to open her mind to them just a little, peering back half-fearfully at those painful reminders of her loss.

David had come from another world, challenging her to step free from her self-imposed isolation and showing her how to begin to be fully alive again. She still believed that those ten years with the dogs for company, with the twins away at school and Chris's periods of leave infrequent, had been a time of welcome and necessary respite but, even before Chris had remarried, she'd begun to feel lonely. It was so strange that her first meeting with David had been by pure chance; that their

189

connection should be through a mutual friend who had died tragically. Of course, it was precisely because of their sharing in this tragedy that they'd been able to skip swiftly over the usual rules of convention and talk honestly together about their own lives and that of the dead woman, Felicity Mainwaring.

Feeling the milk-warm night air flowing over her bare arms, breathing in the scent of honeysuckle, Kate leaned at the open window remembering how David had talked about his affair with Felicity. He'd admitted that he'd misjudged her, under-estimating how deeply she had loved him, and so had left her with such disastrous results. His grief and guilt had been very real and Kate had comforted him, painting in a wider background and describing their lives as naval wives together, so that he could see Felicity's tragedy in its proper perspective and as a series of events in which his own part was a small one. What had surprised her was exactly how much he had grasped from her word-picture of those past years regarding her own unhappy marriage. As she looked down into the silent, silver-washed garden, Kate recalled his second visit: six months later, on Christmas Day. The twins were away from home—Guy with his father in Canada and Giles with his girlfriend up-country—and she'd been alone for the first time at Christmas. How empty and quiet the house had seemed: how pointless the decorations and the tree. She'd been glad of Cass's invitation to lunch but the houseful of family and guests and the extravagant celebrations had merely underlined her own loneliness. It was strangely ironic to think that it was Felicity, with her characteristic bluntness, who'd once pointed out that she'd been a fool to give up Alex for the sake of the boys.

'The twins will go away and leave you,' she'd said. 'You'll be left alone. You should have thought of that.'

Turning away from the window, resisting the slide into self-pity, Kate remembered David's intuitive sympathy and ready understanding that Christmas Day. How easy it had been to talk to him: how quick he'd been to see through her layers of protective colouring to the essential truth—and how hard she'd fought against him in the following months. He'd forced her from her carefully built shell of fear and made her painfully alive again. Now, curled on her side with her face in her pillow, she regretted how strongly and how long she'd resisted him.

'Love is not enough,' she'd told him fiercely. 'It doesn't overcome all the obstacles and make up for everything. Twice I thought it would. It's taken me years to learn to live alone. To risk it—me— again is a luxury I simply can't afford.'

'You're so certain it won't work? Don't you love me at all?' he'd asked her—but she'd avoided the second question.

'I don't see how it can. You in London, me here. I hate cities. You'd be bored rigid in the country . . .'

Yet he'd persuaded her to confront her fear, to take the opportunity to create a new life with him and, now that he'd gone, it seemed that it was time to do it all over again.

One thing was clear: she must stop thinking about David and resist maudlin excursions to the past. Those paths led only to grieving and inaction,

191

and she must make a real effort to look forward; to take some decisions about her future. In her mind's eye she saw the cottage, snug and homely with its familiar rooms and sheltered garden. Excitement rose within her, banishing grief, warming her. Surely this was the answer for which she'd been hoping? If she were brave enough to take this step then other decisions might automatically fall into place.

Stretched out again on her back she allowed her imagination and memory to lead her, room by room, through the small stone house. Presently she slept.

CHAPTER TWENTY-SIX

When she wakened it was to a sense of anticipation rather than to the familiar gut-clamping panic of recent months. Sometimes she dreamed—vivid, happy dreams in which David was still alive—and afterwards, during those few drowsy moments of waking, continued to believe that her dream was the reality and his dying was simply a nightmare. Then, wide awake to the horror of the truth, it was as if it were all to do again: as if she were hearing the news for the first time. She would scramble out of bed, pulling on a dressing-gown and hurrying downstairs to make coffee, as if she were escaping from the dread shadows of grief and loss that followed at her heels. Oh, then, how she missed the dogs who would have once come wagging to greet her, stretching and yawning, staying for a caress before she opened the door to let them out, across the garden and into the paddock.

This morning, however, she rose up completely focused on what she intended to do: no room here for the passivity of grief. Instead of wandering downstairs in her dressing-gown to make her coffee, which she took out into the garden if the weather permitted, she showered and dressed as if she were girding herself for action. It was not yet half-past seven and she drank her coffee, pacing restlessly, one eye on the kitchen clock. At eight o'clock she pressed the appropriate buttons on her telephone and listened to it ringing in a converted barn high on the moor beneath Cox Tor. Michael Barrett-Thompson's small estate agency had long since amalgamated with a larger local company but Michael was still a partner and one of her oldest friends. It was his wife, Harriet, who answered the telephone.

'Harriet, it's Kate. Sorry to bother you at this ghastly hour but I need a word with Michael. It's rather important or I wouldn't interrupt your breakfast.'

'Hello, Kate. It's not at all a problem. Michael's always up early. Let me call him. Nothing wrong, I hope?'

'No, no. Everything's fine. I just need a quick word of advice and it's not always easy to catch him at the office.'

'Don't I know it. Hang on a moment, Kate.'

She waited impatiently, listening to the sounds of Harriet summoning Michael, and then at last he was there.

'Good morning, Kate. Don't tell me you've made the big decision and you want us to put the

193

house on the market?'

'Oh, Michael, I think I do. The thing is, I was driving over to Horrabridge yesterday and I saw that Horseshoe Cottage is for sale. I couldn't believe it. I expect Harriet's quite forgotten, it was so long ago, but I used to live there.'

'She's never mentioned it but then I probably didn't tell her about it coming on to the market. How strange. But . . . does this mean that you're interested in it?'

'I think I might be. It's such an odd coincidence, isn't it? When I've been wondering what to do?'

'Mmm. It's very small, you know. You might have forgotten that. Quite a change after your place.'

'Yes, I can see that's a consideration, but the whole point is that this house is too big now that . . . now that I'm on my own. How much do they want for it, Michael?'

He told her and she gave a cry of disbelief. '*How* much?' She began to laugh. 'Good grief! I paid four thousand pounds for it thirty years ago. I should have hung on to it, shouldn't I?'

'You won't do badly with your own house,' he reminded her drily. 'Do you want to have a look at it?'

'Yes, I do. Is there much interest in it?'

'Quite a lot. It's in a very good position and it's got all the character that people look for in an old property. It changed hands about eight years ago and it's been a holiday cottage ever since. I wish I'd known that you'd be interested in it. Shall I meet you there later on, say . . . ten thirty? It's empty so we can choose our own time but I have to go into the office first.'

'Ten thirty will be fine. See you there. Thanks, Michael.'

All through breakfast and on the drive to the cottage she was remembering how she'd seen it for the first time: Mark had just begun the long six months of Perisher, the submariners' Commanding Officers' Qualifying Course, and she and the six-year-old twins had been staying with her parents in St Just. Her father, having sold some land, had given each of his children a share of the proceeds, enough for Kate to use as a deposit on a small cottage. She'd driven up from St Just alone, leaving the twins with her mother, and had viewed several properties before she'd seen the cottage. Her first impression had been that she couldn't possibly be lucky enough to be the owner of such a delightful little house.

She'd arrived before the agent and, knowing that the cottage was empty, she'd parked beside the low wall and gone to have a closer look. Peering in at the windows, exploring the small, wild garden, she'd experienced a brief time of pure happiness: everything seemed possible. Mark would surely love it, he would be less irritable and sharp-tongued here. The twins could go to Meavy School and begin to feel more settled; they would make new friends and have a dog at last. Plans for their future as a family had buzzed as busily in her head as the bees buzzed amongst the flowers of the honeysuckle in the hedge.

Here, on the paved terrace behind the cottage, she'd stood looking towards Walkhampton Common and listening to the robin's song with a hopeful, joyful heart—and here, thirty years later, Michael found her.

She stared at him with wide, dreaming eyes and then laughed, embarrassed.

'I was early,' she explained quickly, 'and you said it was empty so I thought I'd take a look around.'

'Why not? You must have passed it a hundred times so I won't ask you what you think of it. Or perhaps it hasn't changed at all?'

'Not much.' She watched him unlocking the door, trying to contain her eagerness. 'They've tarted up the log shed and the garage, and there's a new path, but it looks very much the same.'

'It had a new roof about ten years ago and it's in quite good order. Come on in then, but remember it's been a holiday cottage for eight years and it's clear that the owners had very little money to spare for it.'

He stood aside and let her go through the tiny hall to the sitting-room, leaning against the door jamb and waiting for her reaction, keeping his feelings to himself. Kate paused, gazing about the heavily beamed room, almost shocked at its unexpected strangeness.

'It's smaller than I remember. Of course, there's a lot of furniture packed in, isn't there? We didn't have much. And I'm used to such big rooms now.'

Michael remained silent. It sounded as if she were trying to justify the cottage and he had no intention of encouraging her. Harriet's words prevented him from making the usual encouraging observations at moments like these.

'Don't let her do anything silly, Michael,' his wife had said. 'It's still very early days since David died and she's putting far too good a face on it. She doesn't seem to be grieving. Oh, I know Kate's not the sort of person to break down and weep all over her friends, but even so, I don't feel she should make a drastic change just yet.'

'Hardly a drastic change,' he'd answered. 'It's barely five miles down the road from where she is now and she used to live there once.'

'That's not the point,' she'd answered. 'You know it isn't.'

Watching Kate, unexpectedly moved by her air of vulnerable expectation, he wondered how he was supposed to prevent her from making her own decision about where she should live. She turned to smile at him, as if she were reassuring him as well as herself, and slipped past him across the hall and into the kitchen. She pulled up short and he stopped just behind her, looking over her shoulder.

'They've taken out the Rayburn,' she said blankly. 'Well, I suppose it's not so necessary in a holiday home and it was a solid fuel one. Jolly hard work but it used to keep the cottage aired and warm even in the dampest weather. They've made it rather ugly and modern, haven't they? Terrible tiles and nasty, cheap cupboards. I used to have the dresser against this wall and the table there, under the window. There's another room through here, isn't there? A tiny one but useful as a dining-room.'

The little room had a depressing-looking divan in it and a tacky built-in wardrobe. Michael could feel her distress as if something special had been violated.

'It could all be taken out very easily.' He simply couldn't help himself. 'It's simply superficial stuff. The family used it as a bolt-hole and I gather that they have several young children and didn't think it was worth furnishing it with anything that could be spoiled.'

She smiled at him gratefully. 'It's just rather a shock. Shall we look upstairs?'

The bathroom was fairly inoffensive and, in the smaller of the two bedrooms, there were bunk beds against one of the walls. This time she showed no surprise, rather her face lit with a reminiscent smile.

'That's exactly what we did,' she told him. 'The twins had bunk beds too. How they loved them.'

She moved away and crossed the landing to the larger bedroom, standing in the doorway. He waited for some comment but none came. Instead she turned, her eyes blank with memories, looking about her as though she could see and hear things that were beyond his comprehension. After a moment she went slowly down the stairs and back into the sitting-room.

'It's the same wood-burning stove,' she murmured, as if to herself. 'A Villager. One of the best.'

Michael was unusually tongue-tied: hampered by Harriet's warning and touched by Kate's reactions he felt peculiarly helpless.

'You'll need to think about it,' he muttered. 'No need to rush into anything.'

'But someone else might buy it,' she said anxiously—and he saw that the thought of it strengthened her, bolstering up her courage. 'Have there been any offers?'

'Yes,' he answered reluctantly, 'but it was way below the asking price and it was refused.'

'Even so.' Her eyes widened speculatively. 'Perhaps they'll try to raise the money and try again. How long would it take to sell my house,

Michael?'

'How can I answer that?' He had no intention of telling her that, only this morning, he'd had an offer of the asking price for a Victorian house in Whitchurch that was very similar to her own. 'We haven't done anything beyond give you a valuation guide. I'd need to come and see it again.'

'Will you do that? Could you do it now?'

He glanced at his watch, forestalling her whilst he imagined Harriet's reaction.

'Not now. Perhaps later this afternoon. Can I phone you?'

'Yes, of course. Michael, do you think I could keep the key? I'll give it back this afternoon when you come to see the house. Please?'

'There might be other viewings that I don't know about. It could be embarrassing.'

She smiled gently at his prevarications as if she saw them for what they were. 'I'll drop it in at the office afterwards, if you like. I won't be too long, I promise. Half an hour? Please, Michael.'

He gave in, privately cursing at the situation. 'Don't worry. This afternoon will do when I come to see the house. I'll phone if I've got it wrong and you can meet me here with the key.'

'Thanks,' she said. 'I'm really very grateful. Have you any idea what time I can expect you?'

'Three o'clock. Will that do? I'll see you then.' He hesitated. 'Please don't get carried away just because someone else is interested. Try not to see it in the same terms as you would an item in a sale, for God's sake. It's a big decision, Kate.'

'I know it is. Will you bring a copy of the details when you come? Bless you, Michael. I'll see you in Whitchurch about three, unless you phone.'

It was a polite dismissal and she walked with him to the gate, as if he were her guest, and waved to him as he drove away.

CHAPTER TWENTY-SEVEN

She waited until the sound of the engine had dwindled before she went back into the cottage. Without Michael at her shoulder she hoped to find it easier to reconnect with the past, to conjure up old memories, and as she stood in the sitting-room she tried to ignore the makeshift furniture so as to see it as it had been thirty years before.

*　　　*　　　*

The cottage is empty of furniture, yet it has a welcoming atmosphere and she falls in love with it at once. It is clean, its stone walls whitewashed and the slate-flagged kitchen floor is swept: even the old cream-coloured Rayburn has been polished so as to look its best. As she walks from room to room, noticing the threadbare but serviceable carpets and doing sums in her head, her heart thumps with the excitement that builds inside her at the prospect of owning this perfect little place. Trying to contain her excitement she makes an offer and, as soon as it is accepted, she plunges headlong into mortgages, solicitors, surveyors, and all the other horrors of house-buying, never doubting for one moment that anything can possibly go wrong.

Mark has already begun his submariners'

course, Perisher, and it is left to Kate to complete the purchase. As soon as it is truly hers she scours the Pannier Market and the second-hand shops in Tavistock for bargains, thrilled by the discovery of some threadbare armchairs, a deal table and—a real find—an old Welsh dresser. She spends many happy hours searching for pieces of pretty china to display upon its shelves. The armchairs are surprisingly comfortable, though they need brightly coloured rugs to hide their faded covers, and the deal table and the rickety chairs require much polishing. The final result, however, is all of a piece with the cottage.

During a visit on one of his home leaves, her brother, Chris, puts up shelves in the alcove beside the fireplace. He often comes to her rescue, doing jobs in the cottage and the garden, helped by the twins, who enjoy being his assistants simply because he makes them feel necessary and important, whether it is in the building of a bonfire or measuring up to make some shelves. It seems odd to Kate that Mark never takes any part in creating his home. Neither in his letters nor when he's on leave does he take much interest in it. Rather to the contrary, he coldly points out on numerous occasions that he's a submariner: he is not a carpenter nor is he a gardener nor, indeed as far as she can see—though she never dares to say this aloud—is he useful in any kind of way outside the Navy. In any event, he makes no lasting impression on the cottage.

Despite her expectation that he will reveal himself to her as they grow together, Mark remains self-contained and private. He needs to be in control—using his cruel tongue and cold anger to achieve it—and Kate is unable to persuade him that their marriage could be a partnership in which both are equals. Nevertheless she writes long letters to him, describing her finds in the market and how the cottage is looking and, when he manages a weekend in Devon before going to Faslane to join the submarine chosen to carry out the Perisher running, she is hopeful that he will show some enthusiasm for their new home.

His interest in the cottage and her achievements are cursory, however, and he's not even much interested in how the twins are settling in at Meavy School. He looks strained and pale and is smoking very heavily. His preoccupation with his crucial performance on Perisher is patent. She feels anguish for him, knowing that so much is in the balance here, career-wise, but as usual she is held at arm's length by his inability to trust her love and loyalty. Perhaps he fears that, if he opens himself to her, she might demand more than he is prepared to give in return. Studying this unsettling character mix of vulnerability and cruelty she is beginning to believe that she is the stronger character—yet she fears him.

When she has the telephone call from him telling her that he's passed Perisher she is so relieved that she is unable to speak for a few moments.

'It's wonderful,' she cries at last. 'It's terrific, fantastic! Oh, I'm so proud of you. You deserve it. Well done.'

'There's one thing, though,' he says. 'We've each been told where we're going. It's typical! I've been given a boat in *Dolphin*.'

She is hardly able to contain her dismay: she has

been hoping that, if he passes, he'll be given command of a boat running out of Devonport so that they can stay here in their new home. A boat in the submarine base in *Dolphin* means that they'll have to let the cottage and find a naval quarter or a hiring in Gosport or Alverstoke again. Resolutely she masters her disappointment.

'You've passed,' she tells him, 'and that's all that matters.'

'I knew you'd see it like that,' he says ebulliently. 'I don't care where it is. I've got a boat and that's all that matters to me.'

The turning point in their marriage comes when he refuses to allow her and the twins to join him in Gosport when he takes over his new command. She is unable to believe that he means it. This is the first real reward of his naval career and she wants to share in it—Cass is right when she says that by this stage the wives have earned a bit of glory too—but Mark makes it brutally clear that he doesn't want the distraction of his wife and children. It doesn't occur to him that she has any feelings in the matter.

'After all,' he says cheerfully, 'if I'm driving a boat I'm damned if she's going to spend much time sitting beside the wall.'

'But you'll have to be in sometimes,' she protests. 'Surely it would be fun to be together then? There're bound to be parties and things on the boat and in *Dolphin*.'

His smile vanishes abruptly and she is exposed to the chilling effect of the outward manifestations of his displeasure: the familiar closed expression, the droop of his eyelids over the light grey eyes.

'Not if I can help it. It's not some bloody Sunday

school picnic. When I'm on leave I can come home. It'll be much nicer for me to come here than to be stuck in Gosport in a quarter. If there's anything special on you can come up for it.'

She gives in knowing that, if she insists on going with him, he is more than capable of turning it into a hollow victory. She can easily imagine the tiny public snubs and put-downs of which he is a master, and which are so damaging to her confidence. Anyway, she has no desire to go where she is so obviously not wanted. She puts a brave face on it to her friends, saying that she'll be happier in the cottage, with the twins settled in school, than in some quarter in Gosport with Mark away at sea the whole time. Only Cass and her father, the General, know the real truth.

It is the General who is her greatest comfort during the following months. It is to him she opens her heart and voices her anxieties, knowing that, whilst he is both fair and sensible, nevertheless he is on her side. This is especially comforting during these lonely days when her mother, increasingly unwell, makes the journey up to Devon less often and Kate, frightened by her fragility, is reluctant to burden her with her own problems.

It is the General who breaks the news of her mother's death. He arrives unannounced only moments after she has got home, tired and dispirited, from a weekend in *Dolphin*. It is only on this one occasion that Mark has invited her to a party on the boat and he makes it clear by his behaviour to her that he feels he has been obliged to make the invitation yet he is resentful that she has accepted it. He alternately ignores and humiliates her and only the embarrassed courtesy

204

of the first lieutenant makes the evening bearable.

Glad to be home, waiting for the kettle to boil, she is delighted to see the General. He follows her into the kitchen and takes her hands in his.

'You must be very brave, my darling,' he says. 'Your father telephoned me earlier when he couldn't get an answer from you. Your mother died this morning . . .'

Shocked and uncomprehending, she is unable to contemplate a world that no longer contains her mother or to imagine how she will manage without the solid wall of unconditional love and support that has been at her back since memory began. She recalls to mind the beloved face, worn with pain but still serene, and remembers the feel of her mother's hand holding her own, touching the twins: soothing pain and drying tears. This news, coming so swiftly on the heels of such an unhappy weekend, undermines her strength and courage.

'What shall I do?' she asks helplessly. 'I need her,' and the General puts his arms around her, consoling her as though she is one of the children.

'You are stronger than you can possibly imagine,' he says. 'And I am here. For the moment that will have to be enough.'

*   *   *

Abruptly Kate turned aside and wandered out into the hall. This journey to the past was not going according to plan. She hadn't asked to keep the key of the cottage so that she could brood on the death of her mother or the failure of her marriage to Mark Webster: the cottage had been the refuge to which she'd eventually returned after her

205

separation from Mark and the place where she and Alex had been so happy. It was that year with Alex that she wanted to relive, not the misery of the final period of her marriage. Perhaps, out in the garden, she might find what she was looking for: that golden thread that would connect past and present and future, enabling her to take the next step forward, showing her the way. Hesitating in the doorway, listening to the robin's song, the sun warmed and eased her; she raised her face, eyes closed, remembering. In the heat wave of 1976, a year after her separation from Mark, she'd spent most of her free time in this garden.

She'd met Alex three years earlier, going into his bookshop in the hope of finding an antiquarian print of Plymouth Hoe for Mark's birthday present. It was clear that he'd been attracted to her but clear too that he'd understood that she was married. In the ensuing months she'd seen him from time to time in the Pannier Market and, on one occasion, he'd persuaded her to join him for a cup of coffee in The Galleon, where they'd talked about his trade in antiquarian books and pictures. Though she knew nothing of his work they'd passed a very happy half an hour but the next time they'd met each other she'd had the twins with her and merely exchanged a friendly greeting.

After the final break with Mark, returning to the cottage that had been let for the last year, she'd needed to assess the new situation carefully. Mark had been ready to agree to pay a monthly sum for the twins' upkeep—he had his own reasons for keeping the separation from being made public—and was ready to continue to top up the school fees, two-thirds of which were paid by the Navy.

Kate had no wish to create problems at school for the twins by plunging into divorce proceedings—they were settling down well and their friends were all the children of military families—but she'd needed to feel free. At last she'd persuaded her father to lend her enough money to buy Mark out of the cottage—this far, she could be independent of him—but now she must begin to earn enough to support herself and repay the loan. Then she'd seen Alex's advertisement for an assistant in the *Tavistock Times.*

Even now Kate could recall the trepidation with which she'd answered it and how amazed and delighted she'd been when he'd accepted her application. Six months later she'd begun to fall in love with him.

Sitting on the little bench in the sunshine, Kate took a deep, expectant breath. The tight knot in her heart seemed to loosen a little: this was what she'd hoped for, this unravelling of the events that might help her to understand why something so wonderful had ended so abruptly.

*   *   *

How gently it begins, how kind he is and—oh, what a luxury—how easy to talk to. After the years of silence with Mark, it is Alex's interest in her that is the most seductive element of their relationship. They speak the same language, share the same interests, laugh at the same things and she falls in love with him before she realizes it. She catches herself watching his hands as he touches the old books, looking at his mouth as he talks and smiles, and she begins to experience strange and

207

disturbing emotions.

It becomes clear to her that she hasn't been in love before; that her feelings for Mark have been a romantic reaction to the combination of his darkly handsome looks and the glamour of the whole naval scene of which, elegant in his uniform, he is only a part. The strength of her passion for Alex comes as a shock and she is fearful that rumours of an affair might give Mark grounds for taking the twins away from her: she knows how careful she must be.

Alex goes out of his way to enable her to keep up with the work, taking on part-time assistants so that she can spend the school holidays with the twins, and understanding her problems with balancing the dogs' needs. She is grateful, not only for his kindness but also for his friendship, and she is afraid that he might guess that she is falling in love with him, although it is very clear that he is by no means indifferent to her. Her confusion is made worse, however, by the fact that Alex is divorced and very popular with a number of women—and one woman in particular—who make no secret of their interest in him.

All through that hot summer holiday Kate holds the twins as a shield between her and any possible developments in her relationship with Alex, yet she longs for him dreadfully. His presence has become necessary to her wellbeing and she misses their companionable chats, the shared excitement at the discovery of a valuable old book or print, and those lunch-times when they would shut up shop and stroll over to the Bedford for sandwiches and beer.

Even the moor brings her no comfort. The

drought transforms it into a scorched wasteland: cracks and fissures open in the ground, the streams dry up, and the ponies and sheep crowd into the few remaining areas of shade beneath that shimmering, pitiless glare. Even the skylarks seem to lose heart and only the ravens are in evidence as they strut over the parched grasslands, their stiff-legged gait slow and purposeless, before taking to the airless heights with dispirited wing-beats. Kate is grateful for the coolness provided by the thick-walled cottage. She and the twins, with the dogs, spend a great deal of time lying on the grass beneath the apple trees. It is a relief when the heat wave ends and the heavy rains fall at last.

The evening of Cass's party: that is when the affair truly begins. How fearful Kate is of appearing in public with Alex as her partner, knowing that so many of the guests will be Mark's fellow officers with their wives, and how persuasive Cass is! When Kate opens the cottage door to see Alex waiting for her, elegant, tall and unfamiliar in his dinner jacket, she is panic-stricken, feeling ill-at-ease at being thrust back into the social world as an unattached woman: still fearful that rumours will reach Mark.

When she says lightly: 'You look very dashing,' and he replies thoughtfully: 'And you look just as I thought you would,' she immediately feels gauche and underdressed in her black velvet skirt and silk shirt. She thinks again of his reputation, of those women who pursue him, and wishes that she'd taken Cass up on her offer of a new outfit. It is so easy, she reflects, to carry the hang-ups of a first relationship into the next one. The comradely atmosphere of the shop has fled and she is

209

supersensitive to his glance and touch.

At least, she thinks, there will be plenty of people. Safety in numbers.

She is right: typically of Cass there are plots and counterplots, flirtations and all kinds of subterfuge, and Kate and Alex have no chance to be alone together.

'Well, they certainly know how to give a party,' Alex says afterwards as he drives her home. 'It was so nice to be with you in a non-working situation. May we do it again?'

'It was fun,' Kate admits. Pleasantly relaxed, having had rather more than usual to drink, her emotions are heightened and disturbed by the atmosphere of the party. For a blissful moment she forgets about being married, forgets about her reputation or how gossip or divorce might affect the twins. She touches his knee lightly. 'Thank you for coming.'

He covers her hand with his own and holds it. 'It's a wonderful night,' he says. 'The moon's up. We could take the Princetown road and go up on to the tops. The moor looks so unearthly by moonlight.'

They drive in silence until Alex stops the car on Walkhampton Common and switches off the engine. The flat white disc of the moon bleaches everything of colour: the boulders and the grass, sparkling in the grip of frost, create a silvery white background against which gorse bushes and thorn trees are etched black.

'Shall we get out?' he suggests. 'I've got a rug somewhere. You could wrap yourself in that. The air will be unbelievable.'

They climb out of the car and he folds a rug

about her, holding her close against his side; their breath smokes in the sharp, singing air and the stars glitter with such brilliance that it seems that they too must be touched by the frost.

'I can't imagine a better time or place to tell you that I think I love you,' he says. 'I know you're not free. I know there are all sorts of problems. But do you want to try to resolve them so that we can have a chance? Or is it still too soon for you?'

Her teeth chatter—partly from the cold, partly with excitement—and he holds her closer, turning her chin up with his free hand.

'I'm afraid,' she says, almost inaudibly. 'If I start, I'm afraid I shan't know how to stop.'

'That's what I thought,' he says. He bends to kiss her, and the rug and her shawl fall unheeded to the ground as they hold each other. They are disturbed when a heavy lorry lumbers by on the road below them, the driver banging derisively on his horn, and at last they draw apart. She begins to laugh, her eyes blind with moonlight, shivering in her thin silk shirt, and Alex picks up the shawl and rug, wrapping them around her.

'Come on,' he says. 'I'm going to take you home.'

*   *   *

The insistent double ring announcing a text message on her mobile telephone wrenched Kate out of her daydream and she sat quite still for a moment, resentful at being disturbed at such a moment, just when she'd begun to find her way back into the past. She took her phone from her pocket and read the message. It was from Gemma.

211

'How R U. Wd it b OK 4 U 2 have the twins 4 the w/e.'

Kate stared at the message, frowning a little. It was not unusual for her to look after the twins but such a request was not normally made with such brevity. Anxiety began to crowd out her memories and she put the phone back in her pocket and got to her feet. She would come back later, she decided, after she'd spoken to Gemma and dealt with Michael.

Perhaps she could persuade him to allow her to keep the key for a little while longer. She locked the front door carefully, testing the handle so as to be certain, and paused at the gate to look back at the cottage as though promising herself that she would return soon.

CHAPTER TWENTY-EIGHT

There were three messages on the answerphone. Leaving the kitchen door open to the warm June sunshine, throwing her bag onto a chair, Kate pressed the button and waited. The first message was from Roly.

'Hello, Kate. How are things with you? I've just put Mim on the train to London and Daisy went back to Bath yesterday so the place seems extraordinarily empty. Any chance that you might manage lunch this week? I'll wait to hear from you.'

Michael's was next.

'Just confirming that I'll be with you at three o'clock. No problem with the key for today so I'll pick it up when I see you. Bye.'

The third message was from Gemma: her voice had a breathless, distracted quality, though she was clearly making an effort to sound normal, and Kate tensed as she listened.

'Hi, Kate. It's Gemma. Are you there . . . ? No, probably not. Um, the thing is, I was wondering if you could possibly manage to cope with the twins this weekend. It's just . . . I was hoping that Guy and I could . . . well, you know, have a bit of time on our own. Look, I'll try your mobile, only I need to know soon. Sorry, this sounds a bit crazy. I'll try again later. I hope you're OK?'

This last enquiry was so patently an afterthought that Kate smiled sympathetically, despite her anxiety: poor Gemma sounded too fraught for the usual niceties. Kate hastened to dial her number and Gemma answered almost immediately.

'Oh, Kate, thanks for calling back. Did you get my text message?'

'I did. Both messages, in fact. I'd love to have the twins, you know I would.'

'Oh, that's fantastic. It's just that I think Guy and I need some time on our own. You know what it's like?'

'Oh, yes. I know what it's like. Shall you be going away?'

'No. No, I don't think so. Well, perhaps on the boat if the weather stays fine.'

'That sounds fun. Do you want me to pick the twins up?'

'No! I mean, thanks but I can bring them over. Could you manage from Friday after school until tea-time on Sunday?'

'Of course I can, my darling. It'll be great fun. I'll see you all on Friday, then?'

'It'll probably be just me and the twins. Guy is . . . Guy has rather a lot on this week.'

'Fine. Well, let me know if there's anything special I should get in. About five, then?'

'That'll be great. Thanks, Kate. I'm really grateful.'

Refusing to allow herself to brood over certain aspects of the conversation, Kate telephoned Roly. He took much longer to answer and Kate imagined him hurrying from the yard, wading through the dogs, hoping the caller wouldn't hang up before he could reach the handset. She was just deciding that he must be out when there was a click.

'Hello,' he said rather breathlessly. 'Hello?'

'I'm still here. Is this a bad moment?'

'Hello, Kate. No, of course not. I was just coming back from a walk and I could hear the phone as I crossed the yard. And the dogs would all try to beat me to the door. You know what it's like?'

'Oh, yes. I know what it's like. Thank you for your offer of lunch.'

'Does that mean a "yes"?'

'It does, but I'm going to be pushy and ask if you could manage Gemma's twins too.'

'Of course I can. Splendid idea. In that case, since half-term was last week I imagine it has to be Saturday or Sunday?'

'It does. Whichever is best for you but we'd have more time on Saturday. Gemma's collecting them from me at tea-time on Sunday.'

'Saturday, then. We can all go down to the beach at Rock. They love it there.'

'Shall I bring things to eat? You know, fish fingers or sausages?'

'I can manage fish fingers but I'd be grateful if you could cope with the cake for tea.'

'Bless you, Roly. It's good of you to have us all. They miss the dogs when they come here and I know they'd love to meet Floss.'

'Had any more thoughts about her?'

'Well, to tell you the truth, I was thinking about her earlier. I went to view a cottage, not very far away at Walkhampton. The really odd thing is that I used to live there thirty years ago and I think it could be the answer to all my dithering.'

'Big enough for a dog?'

'Oh, yes. I had my first golden retriever puppy there, Megs. She was so sweet and the twins, my twins, adored her. They were about the same age as Ben and Julian are now. And then I kept a puppy from her first litter. That was Honey. It all came back to me this morning. Rather unsettling, actually.'

'I can imagine it might be. I'd love to see the cottage.'

'Yes, you must. Next week, perhaps. I'll bring the details to show you on Saturday. I'd like you to see it, Roly. I feel very excited and a bit emotional.'

'Well, I'll bring the dogs for a return match next week and perhaps we can take Nat out for supper. And Janna too, if she's around.'

'Yes . . . I mean yes to both. I was there last night, actually.'

'And how is he?'

'Uuh . . . Yes. He's . . . OK.'

'Somehow that doesn't absolutely fill me with reassurance. Is there a problem?'

215

'No. No, not a problem. Janna was with him and they were both fine. Honestly. It's just that the cottage has completely thrown me, if you know what I mean. I saw the For Sale sign last night on my way to Nat's and stayed awake half the night wondering about it and then rushed round first thing this morning. I'm just a crazy woman but it seemed like a sign.'

'Or a portent?'

'Yes, or a portent. Are you laughing at me?'

'Certainly not. Keep me posted.'

'Oh, I will. See you Saturday about midday.'

Kate sat down at the kitchen table, suddenly exhausted. Impressions fluttered and jostled in her head: Gemma's brittle voice and one or two of her comments; Janna's behaviour last night and Nat's wariness; the cottage . . . It was good to be able to talk to Roly with utter freedom, no more worrying about crossing the narrow line between love and friendship. How strange to see that unhappy, stubborn passion of his flow away as he told his story about Mim's accident; but how much easier now, the relationship between them. Perhaps she was foolish to be glad—after all, it was unlikely that she would ever know that kind of love again— yet Roly's friendship was very precious to her and now she could feel secure with him. He felt the same, she was sure of it.

Her thoughts edged anxiously back to Gemma and Nat, to the cottage, and she sighed impatiently. In the past this would have been a time for collecting the dogs and setting off across the moor in an attempt to clear her mind: today, it would be more sensible to have some lunch and prepare for Michael's visit. On an impulse she picked up Dame Julian's *Showings* and opened the book at random:

> If there be anywhere on earth a lover of God who is always kept safe from falling, I know nothing of it—for it was not shown me. But this was shown: that in falling and rising again we are always held close in one love.

It was clear, Kate decided rather bitterly, that despite Julian's own sufferings and the terrible times through which she'd lived—war, the Black Death and national unrest—her unwavering message was one of forgiveness and love. Oh, yes, and joy: Julian had written quite a lot about joy.

Seized by an irrational fit of irritation and frustration Kate slammed the book shut and went upstairs.

CHAPTER TWENTY-NINE

Daisy, too, was suffering a similar mood of disgruntlement. Now that she was back in Bath, the steadily growing determination to accept Mim's offer was already being undermined by the heart-fluttering anticipation of meeting Paul. Here in the flat, in the town, an awareness of his presence informed all her actions and thoughts. This was Paul territory now; the streets and restaurants were overlaid with memories and she was very quickly reduced to a state of nervous hypertension, wondering if she might bump into him or hear his footsteps on the stairs. Mim was quite right to point out that she couldn't think straight because of him: *'We want to cook them delicious food and have their babies. Clever old Mother Nature has got us well under her thumb . . .'*

Surprising herself, Daisy snorted aloud with wry amusement as she suddenly recalled Mim's tale of her marriage. It was quite impossible to imagine Mim being married yet it was clear that she had once been a victim of this terrible malaise.

'It's only terrible,' Daisy reminded herself, 'because it's not reciprocated. If Paul loved me I'd be dancing on cloud nine. Well, perhaps not dancing . . .'

This brought her back to Mim's suggestion: to work with Mim, to teach the children and to choreograph something for the Charity Matinée. It was a fantastic offer, and it was simply stupid of her to hesitate even for a moment; after all, what else was she to do? Her savings were dwindling and soon the old pattern of trying to find temporary work would begin to repeat itself: working as a receptionist for a dance establishment or a dance shop, or as an usher in a theatre. This time there was a difference, however. In the past these jobs would have been merely a filling-in post until a dancing job turned up; now she wasn't certain if she would ever be able to dance properly again.

Down in Cornwall, talking to Mim and Roly, she'd experienced a sense of growing excitement at Mim's plan. Encouraged and enabled by their enthusiasm, with her passion for Paul weakened by distance, this new exhilaration fanned the flame of her real, true love of the dance, of music, of drama and colour. Yet now, back in Bath, her emotional antennae were attuned to him again: she longed to see him so much that the fervour of her new resolution was beginning to dwindle and die down, smothered by the anxious awareness of his proximity.

She wondered if, during the last week, he had missed her. Perhaps, when she saw him again, there might be a difference in his attitude towards her. Watching from the window she tried to imagine her reaction if he were to greet her with real love: which then would she choose? Supposing she were to tell him about Mim's offer; it might open his eyes to the possibility of her moving away. On the other hand, he might encourage her to go, and then what? She shivered a little, imagining how cheerfully brutal he might be, and decided that she wouldn't tell him her news too early. She would play it cool, give herself time to assess his reactions when they met again.

His car sped up Henrietta Street and pulled in beside the kerb. Instinctively Daisy drew back, unwilling to be seen as if she were spying on him. She heard the car door slam and, a few moments later, his front door closed. Waiting, wondering if he would come upstairs to see her, Daisy suddenly remembered Mim's words: *There is one who kisses and one who extends the cheek.'* Galvanized by a quick hot spasm of angry shame, giving herself no chance to recover from it, she picked up her bag and went swiftly out and down the stairs.

It was some minutes before Paul answered the door. He was pulling on his cotton jacket, looking rather preoccupied, and he seemed almost surprised to see her.

219

'Hel*lo*!' he said jovially. 'I thought I heard a knock and wondered if it was Andrew coming to collect me. How are you? How was the holiday, and Mim and Roly and all the dogs?'

All the time he was speaking he was shrugging himself into the jacket, patting the pockets to check for keys, and she was mesmerized, as usual, by his vitality and by the energy that flowed from him. She felt wrong-footed, embarrassed and awkward.

'Are you going out?' she asked foolishly. Once again he'd taken control. Going into his flat clearly wasn't to be an option, and she struggled to hold on to her composure. 'I was going to suggest we had a drink or some supper. Catch up a bit.'

'I've got this meeting on at school.' He made a rueful face. 'I have to say that it's going to be a great deal easier when I'm living on site. Look,' he glanced at his watch, making up his mind, 'I was going to snatch a sandwich on the way. I only arrived back from holiday last night and when I got home from school I remembered that I haven't done any shopping yet. I've decided to grab something *en route* and go to the supermarket later. Since Andrew hasn't turned up we could have a quick bite together, if you like.'

She briefly considered rejecting his offer with a cheerfully unresentful remark—'No, you get on. We'll meet up later when you're not so rushed'— but she was already as helpless as if she had moved within the range of some powerful force of gravity: she wanted to be with him, sharing in the warm radiance of his personality, keeping close to him.

'I could make us something: an omelette.' She chuckled, making light of it. 'To tell you the truth I can't afford to eat out. I've got to start earning some money pretty soon.'

'Poor you.' He slammed the door behind him, looking at her sympathetically. 'Is that going to be easy under the circumstances?'

'It depends. I've had an offer of something.' Reluctantly she made her move simply to hold his interest, to keep him there beside her for a few moments more. 'I thought it might help to talk it through with someone. I miss having Suzy and Jill to help clear my head.' She saw him glance instinctively at his watch and she writhed inwardly from humiliation. 'Look, don't bother. You're clearly in a hurry.'

It was a huge effort to refrain from sounding hurt, to keep smiling brightly as she turned away, but he caught her by the arm in his familiar, easy manner.

'Oh, come on. My treat. Let's have something delicious in Bar Chocolat.'

At the touch of his warm hand her resistance melted and he gave her arm a little friendly squeeze within his own as if to reassure her. She went with him, out into the street, struggling to regain her poise in an effort to match his own sang-froid.

'Tell me about your holiday,' he was saying— and she marvelled that he should recall the tiny details she'd told him about the Carradines and their menagerie of dogs.

As they turned into Argyle Street on their way to the Bar Chocolat she remembered how he'd once met her, further along on the opposite side of the street, standing on the kerb with her arms full of purple tulips.

'I think we should go to Bar Chocolat and have something delicious,' he'd said. 'Your flowers will match their décor so perfectly'—and she'd been unable to refuse him.

Today, written on the board outside were the words: 'I can resist everything but temptation.'

They ordered truffle torte and mugs of hot chocolate, topped with marshmallows, and admired the chocolate-shaped contents of the glass display cabinet: dogs named 'Jess' and 'Shep', boxes of tiny rabbits with pink ears, and the cleverly crafted fish.

As they ate their torte and watched the marshmallows melting into the hot chocolate, Daisy told him why it was that she was running out of funds: explaining that because dancers are always so desperate for work, and the competition is so fierce, they are exploited by the smaller dance companies.

'We're so grateful to get a job that the contract is never our prime concern and we're unlikely to contest the fact that there is no safety net when we suffer injuries. Some companies pay a certain amount for the rehearsal period and then you receive a further fee for each performance. But the bottom line is simple: no performance, no fee. Weeks of sweat and toil all finished in one careless moment by a painful tearing of tissue.'

He was fascinated, asking intelligent questions, completely focused. Under the searchlight of his interest she blossomed and expanded, making him laugh and recoil equally with stories of courage and agony; showing the contradictions of the highly disciplined, finely honed dancers who nevertheless chain-smoke and require regular shots of caffeine: telling amusing tales of petty jealousies and childish bickering and then describing the misery of pulled muscles, bleeding feet and the relentless wear and tear on vulnerable human bodies.

This time, when very reluctantly he glanced at his watch, she felt a triumphant satisfaction. She'd absorbed his attention so totally that he'd forgotten everything else for that short space of time: her pride was restored.

It was only after he'd gone and she was walking home that she realized that she hadn't told him about Mim's offer.

*   *   *

Paul arrived home very late. He'd spent part of the evening with the widow of his predecessor who, to his great relief, was preparing to vacate the house at last. She'd made arrangements to move nearer to her daughter and family in Gloucestershire, she told him, and the house would be available for him by the end of the following week. Paul had already been shown over the house when he'd applied for the post but, so soon after her husband's unexpected death, he hadn't felt able to ask questions or inspect the place too closely. Now, she seemed almost relieved to be going, encouraging him to look about at leisure and explaining the secrets of the rather antiquated central heating.

She'd made coffee and taken it into the garden that looked across the playing fields towards Larkhall village.

'Such a good garden for small children,' she'd

said rather wistfully. 'You have two, I think you said? Will they be able to join you now? I've felt rather guilty to be holding you up from moving in but it's taken a little while to find the right house. My daughter wanted me to stay with her in the interim but I was hoping not to have to put my things into store, you see.'

He'd reassured her that she hadn't inconvenienced him, that Ellie hadn't been able to leave her job at short notice and that he was hoping that his family would join him sometime in the summer holidays.

Well, that was true enough: it was exactly what he was hoping. As he unpacked his shopping he was filled with relief at the prospect of the move. Things were becoming so difficult here with Daisy in such close proximity and he was unwilling to hurt her.

Earlier, when he'd heard the knock at the door, his instinct had been to get out of the flat: this was still neutral ground between the terraced house in Clapham and the school house at Beechcroft. In keeping the flat private it was as if his marriage remained intact within it, in limbo but safe, until he made the final move. He knew that as regards to Daisy he was behaving speciously: that sooner or later he must tell her the truth. Each time he left her he vowed to himself that he would be honest with her on the very next occasion they were together.

It wasn't just that he was being a coward, he told himself, or that he was hedging his bets in case Ellie really pulled the plug on their marriage: it was because he guessed that Daisy was in a vulnerable state, both mentally and physically, and he hesitated to deal her a further blow. The move out to Beechcroft would take the pressure off them both.

He closed the refrigerator door and looked at the clock. He hadn't heard from Ellie apart from a text message yesterday, to say that they were all safely home in London, and he'd texted back telling her the news about the house. As he thought about the holiday, he remembered how Daisy had thanked him earlier for the postcard and he felt a twinge of guilt. Daisy had no idea that Ellie and the children had been at the cottage in Salcombe with him. It wasn't that he wanted to deceive Daisy; it was just that it was simply impossible to discuss his marriage with her. He was very attracted to her and, if Ellie refused to join him in Bath and the marriage ended, he knew that Daisy would become very important to him. He simply wasn't ready, however, to enter into that kind of conversation with her about his private life.

He cursed at the complications of relationships, especially with women, thinking again about the holiday; recalling Ellie's reaction to the postcard.

CHAPTER THIRTY

'Writing postcards?' Ellie pauses beside the table, baby Alice in her arms. 'For heaven's sake send one to your mother. She's only still speaking to me because of the children. Who are you writing to?'

He decides that it would be silly to lie about it: in fact the truth might be valuable here. So far the holiday has been an unhoped-for success. The

225

children are delighted to see him, Tom especially, and Ellie is relaxed. A rather delightfully teasing atmosphere is quickly established between them: an odd combination of familiarity and shyness that lends a frisson of excitement to the normal family scene. This is assisted by the presence of their closest friends, Jo and Ed, who are intent on bringing Ellie and Paul together again. Though they are tactful, Paul senses that they are on his side and it helps that they have already made the move from London, though Ed still commutes in from Kent.

Of the two women Ellie is the younger and more impressionable, and it becomes clear to Paul that she is enjoying being at the centre of the discussions that take place at suppertime when the children are in bed. The foursome gives her the opportunity to make points that, were she and Paul on their own, might simply lead to bitter arguments and angry silences. He begins to suspect that things are less bleak than he feared. Ellie is cross that he has acted without her approval: she wants to punish him for it, to show him that he can't dictate to her, but somehow the situation has spiralled out of control and she needs a mechanism that allows her to back down gracefully.

He says as much to Ed, who is not so patient as Jo with Ellie's behaviour.

'I was beginning to think that she'd met someone,' says Paul, voicing his greatest fear. 'I know all her friends are in London and she loves working at the playschool a couple of mornings a week but I've had difficulty believing that these were more important to her than me and the kids.

I'd begun to believe that either she'd met someone else or she just didn't care. It throws you a bit: makes you wonder whether you've got things wrong and your marriage isn't what you thought it was.'

Ed shakes his head. 'She's painted herself into corner,' he says, 'and you need to offer her a plank so that she can get out. But it has to be an acceptable plank; one that enables her to hang on to her self-respect while she's crawling across it.'

Meanwhile Paul overhears odd snatches of the talks Jo and Ellie have while they are sitting on the beach with their children—Jo and Ed have two small children of their own. Jo's comments are of a practical nature:

'. . . after all, how would you manage to earn a living whilst Alice is so small? Childcare is so expensive . . . Could you afford to continue to live where you are? I suppose you might find a flat if you really can't face the move to Bath . . . Shunting the children between Bath and London will be hell. Paul must miss them terribly. He's so good with them, isn't he, and they absolutely adore him.'

Ellie is beginning to shift from what she has imagined is a position of sassy defiance—a youthful independence flying in the face of the stodgy norm—and is rather envying her friend's placid confidence. Jo is expecting her third child and she is luscious with a sexy fecundity, peacefully maternal with the babies, calm and radiantly happy. As she describes the advantages of the village school with its own playschool, and the network she is already creating with the other mothers, she is aware of the envy she is arousing in Ellie and her descriptions climb to new heights of desirability. Listening to Jo, Paul occasionally detects a tiny note of self-convincing here—perhaps Jo misses the buzz of London more than she cares to admit. Nevertheless, she makes their new life sound idyllic: walking in the woods with the children, strolling down to the local pub, the puppy they intend to buy when they get back after the holiday.

He senses that Ellie is wavering, though he puts no pressure on her. He simply devotes himself to Tom and baby Alice, knowing that Ellie sees how strong the bond is between him and his children.

'Look, I know it's the big one,' Ed says one evening when the children are sound asleep, exhausted after a day of sand and sun. He leans across the table to fill up the glasses with more wine. 'Leaving London is like really accepting that you're not young any more. You've begun to think about the kids and schools and being in the country. London represents our youth: theatres and restaurants and all those things—'

'Even if you never go out any more,' interrupts Jo, 'because you can't get a baby-sitter and anyway you can't afford it. We miss it—of course we do—but the extra space in the house and the peace of being in the country is fantastic.'

'But I just don't feel ready for that,' argues Ellie—but the familiar cry sounds less confident. She is ready to be persuaded. 'All my friends are still in London. I'd miss having everything right on the doorstep.'

'But Bath, Ellie,' says Jo. 'Christ! You've still got everything on your doorstep. It's a fantastic city. We'd kill to be able to live in Bath.'

Paul can see that now Ellie is influenced by *their*

envy and he wisely says nothing to advance his own cause.

Ed is more upfront. 'Anyway,' he says, 'we're talking marriages here. Surely you can't really tell me that living in London is more important than being with Paul, all of you together as a family. It's a bloody good job and a nice big house to go with it. Come on, Ellie. Time to grow up.'

Paul sees Jo's warning frown, guesses that Ed has been told to be sensitive, but, surprisingly, Ellie takes it very well. Of course, they've all had rather a lot to drink, and the holiday mood is helping, but it wouldn't take too much for the whole conversation to swing out of control and Paul decides to intervene.

'Don't bully her, Ed,' he says. 'She's old enough to make her own decisions. Is that someone crying?'

He gets up and goes out into the hall. He hasn't heard anything but feels that it's time to break it up and let the conversation channel off into a different direction.

'You're crazy,' he hears Ed say to Ellie. 'Anyone else would be telling you to stuff it. Perhaps he's found an obliging French mistress.'

'Oh, shut up, Ed,' says Jo. 'Give it a rest. Coffee anybody?'

Paul hears the chair legs squeak as they are pushed back over the slate floor and he hurries a few steps up the stairs. When Ellie appears in the hall he seems to be coming back down. He smiles and shakes his head.

'Hearing things,' he says. She looks rather preoccupied, shaken by Ed's remark perhaps, and he smiles at her. 'How about a stroll on the beach?

Jo will keep an ear open. It's fantastic out there.'

He tucks her arm in his, just as he does with Daisy, and they walk slowly over the sand. He is gratified that she seems to take no interest in the calm beauty of the night but begins to ask questions about his work and his colleagues. He tells her about one or two of them, deliberately sounding rather vague, and her interest sharpens as though she suspects him of hiding something.

So it is that when he sits down at the table to write his postcard to Daisy he decides not to prevaricate.

'Writing postcards?' she asks casually. 'Who are you writing to?'

'It's the girl who lives in the flat upstairs,' he says. 'Daisy Quin. She's a ballet dancer but she's got this serious injury and has been left behind while the company goes on tour. It's really tough on her. She's rather good fun. I took her to the ballet. Remember I told you I'd been given a couple of tickets but you couldn't make the trip down? She was thrilled. It was really interesting to see it from the professional dancer's point of view.'

Careful, he tells himself. Don't overdo it.

He bends more closely over the card so that Ellie can't see the words and he takes it to the post-box himself. After this interchange Ellie is rather quiet but he pretends not to notice, playing a noisy game with the children and then taking them off to swim.

By the time the holiday ends he can see that Ellie has been shocked into a new awareness of the situation and, when they say goodbye, she holds him tightly before she gets into the car and drives away.

*   *   *

Paul finished his beer and put the can in the bin. He thought of Daisy's expression when he'd made some excuse about not going up to her flat and his own reaction to it: he simply hadn't been able to let her walk away with that look of disappointment and embarrassment on her face, yet he knew that it was unfair to give her any kind of encouragement. If only he could get through the next few days without seeing too much of her, then perhaps the move out of Henrietta Street might solve the problem naturally and in its own way.

In his study he paused to look at the photographs of Ellie with Alice and Tom. Perhaps he might have a call from Ellie soon telling him that she and the children would be joining him at the end of term. He'd decided to let her make the next move but, even so, he heaved a great, longing sigh: he missed them all so much.

CHAPTER THIRTY-ONE

When Daisy got out of bed on Thursday morning she knew that she simply couldn't waste time hoping that Paul would appear at her door. On the Wednesday morning, after their visit to Bar Chocolat, he'd gone off to school early and must have returned very late. This happened fairly frequently—when he had evening duties, overseeing prep and bedtime—and she'd become resigned to it, but the prospect of another day spent waiting for him to come back after school to Henrietta Street was too dismal to contemplate.

Instead, once she was showered and had eaten some breakfast, she telephoned Mim. There was the usual sense of chaos at the other end—nobody knew where Madame was, voices were upraised enquiring one to another as to her whereabouts—but presently her voice spoke in Daisy's ear.

'Daisy! I was hoping to hear from you. Have you got good news for me?'

'Oh, Mim. I'm still dithering. I wondered if I could come up and see you. It might be just what I need to help me to decide . . . I know it's crazy even to be doubtful about it and I should be so grateful . . .'

'Darling Daisy, just get on the first train. Can you manage the journey?'

'Oh, yes. I'll be fine. If you're sure?'

'I told you when we were in Cornwall that you should come to see us.'

'I know you did. I'm just so . . . crazy.'

'Terrible, terrible love. Come and see us, darling. Pack a little bag and spend the night. Must rush.'

Daisy did as she was bid, catching the train to Paddington with moments to spare, taking the tube to Holland Park. Outside the tall, gracious house she paused for a moment, seized by an unexpected nostalgia, and then, turning aside from the steps up to the pillared front door, she passed around the side of the building and went down the basement stairs. Once inside the door she stood still, listening. Evocative sounds tugged at her memory: the machine-gun rattle of tap shoes halfway through a routine, the tinkling notes of a piano echoing in a large, mirror-lined studio, and a voice raised above the music shouting, 'Move it *out*. Use the space. That's better. Ready now . . .' and a burst of singing.

As she made her way along the passage, the door of a nearby dressing-room opened suddenly and some older students clad in tights and tunics bundled out and hurried away into the interior of the building. In the lobby Daisy knocked on the office door, turned the handle and looked inside: it was empty. Climbing the stairs, looking up into the spaces of the three storeys above her, she could hear a drama class in progress. Someone was speaking persuasively and at some length: a second voice broke in and a third cried out in anguish, then a short silence before the sound of scattered light clapping broke out.

She hesitated outside the half-open door of one of the studios: through the gap she could see a group of small children standing in rows, heels together, toes turned out, their eyes fixed trustingly upon the slender girl who stood facing them.

'Now watch Miss Nicola, my darlings. Are you ready? And *one* and *two*, now *point* those *toes* . . .'

It was Mim's voice and she appeared suddenly, coming out and closing the door behind her, opening her arms to Daisy.

'How lovely. And you're in time for lunch. We'll have it upstairs in the flat, just the two of us, and you can meet everyone later.' She hesitated, smiling a little. 'And how did you feel when you came in?'

Daisy smiled too. 'I felt as if I'd come home.'

*   *   *

Afterwards, travelling back to Bath on the train, Daisy realized that this was the truth: she'd felt as if she'd been returning home after a long absence. Well, that wasn't surprising. After her mother's death the school had given her the stability she'd so desperately needed, and Mim and the other members of staff had become her family, but this time there was much more to it than that. The children, the atmosphere, the bustle, all these things had injected her with excitement and, as she'd talked to Andy and watched some of the classes, it was as if a new kind of vocation had begun to flower inside her.

'But I still don't know about Paul,' she said uncertainly to Mim. 'When I see him I feel obsessed. He fills up all my vision.'

'Have you talked to him about this feeling?' asked Mim. 'It could simply be sex, of course. That's easily dealt with. You know you did promise me that you would be open with him.'

'I know I did,' said Daisy wretchedly, 'and I meant it, but when I'm with him I feel tongue-tied. Sort of helpless, as if only he can make the running. It's like he's cast a spell over me.'

Mim gave an expressive little shrug, her eyes were compassionate, but she spoke firmly.

'I must know soon, Daisy.'

'I know. I promise I'll have it out with him as soon as I get back. I do want to say "yes", Mim.'

'Good. But we need to be clear. I'm not asking you to choose between us, simply that you must know where you are with Paul before you commit yourself to us.'

She'd carried Daisy off to see *Chicago*, taking her backstage to meet an ex-pupil, and then on to supper at The Ivy.

The following morning Daisy watched a rehearsal for the school's summer show and had another long talk with Andy before catching the train back to Bath.

There was no sign of Paul's car but, this time, she felt a sense of relief at his absence.

Tomorrow morning, she promised herself, she would speak to him: on Saturday mornings he was generally at home and she would go down at about coffee time, tell him about Mim's offer and ask him if he'd ever really considered that they might have a future together. After all, Mim had said that it wasn't necessarily a question of choosing between her and Paul, other people managed to run careers and marriages very satisfactorily, and Bath wasn't very far from London . . .

Daisy turned on the television: she didn't want to think about anything, not Mim nor Paul, until the morning. In the morning everything would be made clear.

*   *   *

By the time Paul arrived home, well after eleven o'clock, she'd switched off the lights and was ready for bed. A tiny part of her was inclined to go down to him now and confront him: perhaps a visit at this late hour, clad in her dressing-gown, might precipitate matters. Surely he'd have to invite her in? She remembered Mim saying: 'It could simply be sex, of course. Well, that's easily dealt with,' and chuckled reluctantly. Mim's prosaic streak always came as a bit of a shock but she might be right. Perhaps this terrible fever might have a simply physical cure and then the torment would be over.

Yet Daisy's rational self shrank from Paul's look of surprise and, possibly, distaste: she simply couldn't risk it. Instead, she took two painkillers and went to bed, only to lie awake rehearsing the next morning's conversation and listening to the distant sounds of late-night revellers. Presently she dozed and dreamed that she was dancing, lifted and supported by a partner whose face was always in shadow. She soared and turned, light as thistledown, until suddenly her partner danced away from her, fleeing down dark corridors and winding passages, whilst she pursued him calling out his name, 'Paul, Paul,' though no sound could be heard. He was far ahead now, disappearing round a corner and, as she rounded the corner in her turn, someone loomed in front of her, blocking her way. She cried out and the person turned to look at her and she saw that it was Mim.

Daisy woke suddenly, bathed in perspiration, her heart banging uncomfortably. She lay quite still, taking deep breaths, schooling herself to be calm. Mim had taught her this trick. When she'd discovered that Daisy was having nightmares following her mother's death Mim had shown her how to breathe deeply, to relax her body, and to concentrate on something else. Because Daisy had difficulty in remembering her lines for her audition pieces they'd agreed that some passage of Shakespeare, or a verse of poetry, would be the best thing to distract her.

'And,' Mim had added smilingly, 'it will almost certainly send you back to sleep.'

Daisy stretched, and then began to relax: what should she try to remember? The Boy's speech from *Henry V*, Act Three had worked well in the past. She began to speak the part inside her head.

'As young as I am I have observed these three swashers. I am boy to them all three; but all they three . . . though they would serve me, could not be man to me . . . for, indeed three such antics do not amount to a man. For Bardolph . . . For Bardolph, he is white-livered and red-faced; by the means whereof . . .' Daisy began to doze again, waking fitfully to cudgel her memory. 'For Pistol, he hath a killing tongue and a quiet sword . . .' By the time she reached Nym she was fast asleep.

She wakened shortly after seven, with a clutching panic in her gut and an ache in her back. Sitting on the side of the bed, drinking some water, she planned her morning. There was no point in attempting to see Paul much before eleven o'clock: four hours to endure. Daisy levered herself up stiffly and went to run a hot bath: she would have a calm morning, she told herself. A long, relaxing bath and a leisurely breakfast would take at least an hour and then she'd have a walk in the park.

As she prepared her breakfast she paused to look across the street at the window boxes filled with striped petunias, pink and white, and blue and white, and with geraniums and trailing ivy. The members of a ladies' jogging club appeared, running down the street, some of them stopping at the entrance to the park, panting and holding on to their sides. An elderly golden Labrador, on an early morning walk with his owner, was much more composed and they too turned into the park.

Slowly Daisy finished her breakfast and cleared

it up, slowly she made her bed and tidied the flat, and by half-past nine she was sitting reading her book on a wooden seat in the Garden of Remembrance. At this time of day there were no students with their textbooks scattered over the grass, studying for their exams; no small children playing hide and seek. A young woman strolled along the path pushing a pram in which a baby was sitting, leaning a little forward, gazing out in a kind of wide-eyed amazement at the antics of the world. Daisy smiled involuntarily at the baby's magisterial expression and gave him a little wave. His mother paused, so that he might return the salute if he wished to, and after a long considering moment he raised his starfish hand in a regal gesture that amused the two women. As he was wheeled away his hand remained, waving majestically from the side of the pram until he was pushed out of sight amongst the mass of white roses that tumbled and cascaded from the wooden pergolas.

Daisy glanced at her watch and closed her book: it was twenty minutes to eleven. Swallowing several times in an oddly dry throat, she put the book into her shoulder bag and with deliberately measured steps walked out of the park and along Henrietta Street, planning how she would go upstairs first and brush her hair, rehearsing her words ready for when Paul opened the door. An unfamiliar car was parked outside and, even before she reached the front door, she could hear the sounds of arrival and excitement: voices were raised above the wailing of a baby and footsteps echoed in the hall. A small boy dashed out of the door, saw Daisy and raced back inside. As Daisy entered she was confronted by an amazing sight: the door to Paul's flat was open and the boy was disappearing through it; in the doorway a pretty dark-haired girl was bending to catch him and, missing, turned away laughing, only to come face to face with Daisy.

Instantly her expression changed. A wary, interested look stilled her face as they stared at each other, the noise seeming to wash and flow around them. The boy ran out again, shouting with excitement, and his mother put out a restraining hand. This time he stopped, holding on to her leg, looking up mistrustfully at Daisy with a finger in his mouth.

'Stop, Tom,' his mother said. 'Do be quiet for a moment. Where's Daddy?' and Paul appeared from behind him, the baby in his arms.

Staring at him, Daisy was unable to conceal her shock. She saw that the girl took note of it as she glanced quickly from Daisy to Paul and it was she who spoke first.

'I'm so sorry about the noise. The children are overexcited. We woke up terribly early, you see, and on the spur of the moment we just piled into the car and drove here. Paul had no idea we were coming.'

'What fun. You must be Ellie.'

Pride just enabled Daisy to control her voice but she couldn't look at Paul. He moved forward now and began to make introductions, gratefully hampered by the baby who'd stopped crying and was patting his face with her hands and putting her fingers into his mouth. He struggled with her, pretending to admonish her, holding her as a barrier between him and the scene that was playing out in front of him.

'Paul told me about you,' Ellie was saying rather too brightly. 'About you being a dancer and going to the ballet together. How nice of you to take pity on him. I'm so sorry to hear about your injury. How ghastly for you. I hope you got your postcard? We had the most fantastic week . . .'

Daisy looked at last at Paul. He looked distressed, embarrassed, thoroughly uncomfortable, and yet he wasn't quite able to hide his natural reactions of relief and happiness at the sight of his family. There was a rightness about him, standing in the doorway holding his baby daughter, his wife and son beside him: even now, in this moment of terrible tension, he still seemed able to control the scene. As usual Daisy felt tongue-tied, submissive to his will, though words that could damage him formed sentences in her head. The little boy was watching her gravely and even the baby was silent, her rosy cheek pressed trustingly against Paul's, as if they sensed a threat.

'I was coming to see you,' Daisy said to him. 'That job I was telling you about. I went to London for the interview yesterday and I've got it. I shall be off any day now so I'll pop in to say goodbye sometime.'

'We're on the move too.' It was clear that he found it difficult to talk with his usual ease of manner with Ellie watching them both so carefully. 'The house is ready at last.'

'I'm going to have a swing in the garden.' Suddenly Tom let go of Ellie's leg. The moment of danger had passed and his fear had evaporated. 'My shoes have got footballs on them.'

He stretched out his foot, pointing his toe, reminding Daisy of the children in the dancing class yesterday. She crouched down, taking his leg in one hand and examining the shoe, whilst Paul and Ellie exchanged a glance that was compounded of relief and a compassionate understanding.

'Here.' Tom twisted his foot, knee bent, showing her the football engraved on the sole of his shoe and clutching on to her shoulder so as to keep his balance.

'Wow!' She was suitably impressed, looking into his glowing little face, sharing his pleasure. His eyes were Paul's eyes: bright, interested, alert. 'Aren't you lucky? I wish I had footballs on *my* shoes.' She stood up again, smiling at them all. 'Have fun,' she said again and turned away.

Daisy didn't see Ellie's involuntary gesture, a hand stretched towards her in friendship, nor Paul's very slight shake of the head. She was already climbing the stairs.

CHAPTER THIRTY-TWO

Roly had just arrived back from Launceston late on Monday morning when Mim telephoned.

'Such a relief, Roly. Daisy has accepted my offer. I can't tell you how thrilled I am. Only, the thing is, I don't want her to be sitting in Bath brooding. Do you think that you could go and get her? Much better for her to be with you and the dogs.'

'She's not coming to London, then?'

'No, no. There's absolutely no point in her being here at the moment. We're just about to plunge into end-of-term exams and it's far too late for her to be involved in the summer show. That would be counterproductive, anyway. No, I need her to be concentrating on the concert and getting herself fit. Lots of work to do. I don't want her being morbid over this wretched man.'

'Do I gather things have come to a head?'

'They've come to three heads. His wife's and two children's. Daisy didn't know anything about the children, poor darling, so it was a terrible shock. Wifie has clearly had second thoughts about separation and simply turned up in Bath with her young, unannounced. Daisy came face to face with them unexpectedly in the hall. The man—Paul, is it?—managed to keep his cool but indicated that they were all moving into the school house very soon.'

'Ah.'

'What does "Ah" mean? I hope you're not having malignant thoughts about him?'

'Not?'

'Certainly not! If you start telling Daisy that he's a cad and a bounder then she'll feel the need to defend him. We don't want any of that nonsense. We need to let her have a good rant and get him out of her system. Your role is simply to listen. Don't get protective. Be rational; see his point of view.'

'Well, to be honest, I *do* feel slightly sorry for him. He was rather between a rock and a hard place. In his situation, with my wife threatening to leave me and Daisy living in the flat above and in love with me, I'd have been terribly tempted to try not to rock the boat until the final decision was made.'

'There you are, then. The vital thing is to make him unimportant in the scheme of things. Daisy needs to concentrate on her work. Jane and Andy are going to take a lot of convincing. Luckily, Jane knows Daisy's work—and Andy was very impressed when he met her—but she's going to have to come up with a lot of good ideas by the beginning of next term. I've put my neck on the block by giving her a chance at choreographing the ballet for the Charity Matinée. She's got to concentrate her mind.'

'Poor Daisy. Is that fair under the circumstances?'

'Fair? I'm not running a counselling service for people who've had their cars broken into, Roly. This is a stage school operating in a very competitive world and she's on the payroll from the end of this month. Make sure she listens to lots of music and uses her eyes. Anything that will trigger off inspiration. Goodness, Roly! You were an artist and then a photographer; you know what I'm talking about. All sorts of things will inspire her. She needs to get into the mood of it, that's all. The other thing I was going to ask you to do is to get hold of Bethany Millar. Do you remember the massage therapist who treated poor Kate when she slipped over on the ice last winter? Kate was full of praise for her and Daisy will continue to need treatment. And *do* telephone and offer to fetch her. The stable flat's all ready. Must dash.'

Daisy answered at the second ring.

'Congratulations!' Roly said. 'Mim's told me the great news. She's thrilled. So does that mean you can give your notice at the flat and come down here for a good rest?'

'That sounds terribly tempting. I was just trying to decide what to do next. I've paid the rent up until the end of the month and Suzy and Jill will be back at the end of next week. I've written to them and to Tony. I expect he'll be relieved that he doesn't have to worry about what to do with me but it'll be a bit of a shock for the girls. I know someone in the company who will be very glad to take over my room so they won't be out of pocket.'

'Splendid. So if I were to drive up with the dogs to fetch you . . . ?'

'Would you really? That would be . . .'

'We'd love it.' He feared that she was crying and was seized by a sense of helplessness. 'When could you be ready? Tea-time?'

She gave a rather watery chuckle. 'It sounds great but I think tomorrow might be more sensible. It'll give me time to pack and clean up. I'll have to take the key round to a friend of mine and sort things out properly. I haven't much in the way of worldly goods but, honestly, Roly, are you sure you can put me up until I go to London?'

'Mim's instructions. I gather that you're on the payroll from the end of the month and she says you have lots of work to do before next term. Getting yourself better and finding inspiration for the Matinée and so on.'

Daisy's laugh, this time, was more natural. 'Sounds like Mim. She's so tough, thank goodness. Just what I need at the moment.'

'If you say so. We'll be with you by late morning. Don't overdo things.'

'Thanks, Roly. I can't tell you how grateful I am.'

'Rubbish. Now I shall need some directions . . .'

The third call was from Kate.

'Just to thank you so much for Saturday, Roly. It was such fun, and Ben and Jules loved it. Don't forget you're coming to have lunch or supper, whatever suits you best, and to see the cottage.'

'Can't wait. I long to see it after reading the details, but there's been a bit of a crisis. Daisy's love affair has crashed and she's giving up the flat in Bath.'

'Oh, poor Daisy.'

'I know. She sounds a bit deflated. Mim's offered her a job starting in the autumn so I'm going to pick her up tomorrow and she's going to spend the summer here.'

'But that sounds wonderful. It will give her time to heal. Mentally and physically.'

'I hope so. Though she's got to get some ideas together for Mim's Charity Matinée.'

'Well, that's good too. It will take her mind off things.'

'How ruthless you women are—but I'm sure you're right. Anyway, perhaps I can bring her with me later in the week and we can all see the cottage?'

'Great. And I'll invite Nat, and Janna too, if she's still around.'

'That sounds fun. I thought that Ben and Julian were rather taken with Floss.'

'We're all rather taken with Floss. It's just . . . I think it would be silly to move her twice.'

'So you've made up your mind about buying the cottage?'

'Probably. Possibly. Oh, I don't know. I took Ben and Jules to see it yesterday and I don't think that they were fearfully impressed. It's rather small after this place; no paddock to play in and no space for a playroom. I've got enough bedrooms here to keep one completely dedicated to the grandchildren's toys. There's room for Giles and Guy's old rocking-horse and they can have the train set left *in situ*, and the fort. They love it, of course, and I was a bit downcast by their lack of enthusiasm for the cottage. But I can't let myself be influenced by two seven-year-olds, can I?'

'No-oo . . .'

'You don't sound terribly positive.'

'There's so much to take into consideration. The upkeep of a house the size of yours, keeping it in good repair, heating it and so on. And you did tell me that you needed to boost your pension. You can't base your decision on your grandchildren's playroom when before too long they'll grow up and lose interest . . . Hello? Kate?'

'Sorry. I was just thinking. Someone said something like that to me before, years ago, when Giles and Guy were young. My marriage had broken up and I was having an affair. The twins saw that it was getting serious and took fright, and in the end I had to choose between Alex and the twins. Damn. Every time I think I've made up my mind something upsets it and I start all over again.'

'Kate, I am so sorry. Hell. Look, why don't you come over and have some lunch? It's so unsatisfactory having this kind of conversation on the telephone.'

'No, no. It's sweet of you, Roly. I'm fine and you've got to get ready to go to Bath tomorrow. We'll speak again soon. My love to Daisy, and thanks again for Saturday. Bye.'

Roly continued to sit on the window seat for

some moments, brooding on these conversations. He was glad that he'd made the decision to return to Cornwall. He was at peace this morning; the dogs stretched out asleep and the old barn lapped and folded in a soft light mist that rolled down from the moor and shrouded familiar landmarks. Foggy-fingered, it reached beneath the thorn trees, silvering the grass with a dewy bloom; it drifted above the stream, smoking and curling between the furze-lined banks, and trailed and folded itself over the stone bridge.

As he stared out of the window, thinking of the three women, Roly wondered if he might be beginning to achieve some measure of balance in his life. He loved to go to London, to visit an exhibition or see a new play and meet old friends, but it was good to return to this quiet place and be alone. He stretched contentedly but he was by no means complacent. Though he was no longer disabled by guilt, the past was not yet done with. He knew that his actions on the night of Mim's accident had had a very negative effect on the lives of Monica and Nat and he suspected that he needed to do much more than simply confess his part in it to Kate.

He still shrank from telling Monica, especially in her latest mood of discontent with Jonathan, but he was beginning to feel that he might make a clean breast of it to Nat. Roly thought of Daisy's words: *It isn't good for the soul to hide one's true feelings and especially with those we really love.*

Confession might be good for the soul but it could sometimes have a devastating effect on the listener. He must be sure that the telling of his story was not simply for his own benefit. Was it possible that, by explaining to Nat just how things had gone so wrong all those years ago, he might be of some assistance to him now? Might it shed some light on Monica's overpossessive behaviour and Nat's own reactions to it? He would be risking the possibility of his son's contempt and resentment in an attempt to tell the truth about the break-up of their family. Part of him desperately wanted the assurance that it would be worth it.

CHAPTER THIRTY-THREE

Kate stood in the playroom, staring at the toys, hoping that Gemma would not be finding the drive across the moor too difficult in the thick mist.

'Can I come and see you, Kate?' she'd asked, phoning on her mobile earlier that morning. 'There's a bit of a problem. Well, you could see that for yourself when we fetched the twins yesterday, couldn't you? They're having tea with a friend after school so I don't have to be back till about six. Will half-past two-ish be OK? Don't worry about waiting lunch.'

Kate picked up a teddy bear and held it for a moment. It was odd that she hadn't wanted to mention Gemma's visit to Roly. Something had prevented her from disclosing her fears about Gemma and Guy when he'd suggested she should go down to lunch; the same instinct made it difficult to discuss Nat with him. Even to such a close friend as Roly, it was impossible to confide completely: a strong sense of loyalty forbade it.

She stroked the teddy's soft fur and straightened

his knitted jacket; a nametape was still attached to the suede pad of his foot: G WEBSTER. Even now she could remember the discussion about which of the teddies should accompany the twins to prep school, although it was Giles who'd found it more difficult to decide which of his furry friends should be selected for the treat: at not quite eight years old he'd had a well-developed sense of loyalty. At length she'd persuaded him that they could take turns and he'd been content to agree with this compromise. Guy had always been tougher, more independent, though his sense of loyalty was just as strong, and his expectation of those same qualities in other people—especially those close to him—was high.

Kate placed the teddy on the bed and stared about the room, remembering her son's face as she'd seen it yesterday when he and Gemma had fetched the twins. There was a severity about Guy, an almost puritanical streak that made him judgemental, and it had been much in evidence this last weekend. When these characteristics were roused his face became expressionless and he withdrew behind a barrier of austerity: it was almost impossible to approach him except on the most formal of levels, difficult to joke or draw him out of it, and it became necessary to rely on his own sense of fairness and the depth of his affection for the person concerned to restore him.

So far Gemma had been able to hold the balance between her light-hearted friendliness and his severity, and the children had done much to soften him, but now something was clearly amiss. Kate guessed that Gemma had intended their weekend together on Guy's boat to be a time of reconciliation after some kind of falling-out—probably Guy had taken exception to a particular display of Gemma's flirtatiousness—but it was evident that this hadn't been achieved. When they'd arrived to fetch the twins Guy was withdrawn and Gemma was nervous: her voice was too high, her laugh too shrill in her attempt to keep the atmosphere jolly, but luckily the twins had been too tired to notice much.

Kate had noticed. One look at Guy's face had transported her back into her own young days when she'd feared to see such an expression on Mark's face and would have gone to almost any lengths to prevent such a mood, which could shatter family peace and destroy a happy atmosphere in moments. Guy had suffered too much from his father's cruel tongue and slighting ways not to have made a very real attempt to control any signs of these traits in his own character, and he loved his family very much, yet she'd experienced that tiny clutch of fear as she'd watched his sealed, unresponsive face.

Now she wondered: Am I afraid of my son?

The answer was probably: Yes. Once, she might have attempted a gentle—a very gentle—teasing approach which, in the past, had drawn a reluctant dawning of humour from him and a faintly apologetic recognition of the chilling effect of his behaviour. Now, she was unwilling to interfere between him and his wife, yet she felt guilty and unhappy that Gemma should be suffering as once she had suffered. Watching them together in the past she'd been relieved to see that they seemed to understand each other: that Guy worked hard to be more broad-minded, less judgemental, and that

250

Gemma's warmth and her fun-loving nature was given stability and a deeper quality by the very nature of his steadiness. They loved each other, and the twins had enriched and expanded that love.

So what had happened that might put it all at risk? Kate had no doubt that Guy and Gemma had had many ups and downs in their ten years of marriage but this was the first time that she'd felt seriously uneasy about them. She was still in the playroom when Gemma arrived and she hastened down the stairs to meet her.

'I was thinking while I was driving across the moor,' said Gemma, following Kate into the kitchen. 'I was thinking that it was odd, you being my mother-in-law when I've known you all my life.'

'True,' agreed Kate, filling the kettle and wondering where this line of thought was leading. 'It's unusual. Of course, you've known Guy all your life too.'

Gemma huddled beside the Rayburn as if she were cold; the sleeves of her pink cotton cardigan hung down over her hands and she folded her arms tightly about herself. Her natural poise had deserted her and she looked frightened. Kate began to make the tea, alert to Gemma's every movement and expression, but without any outward sign of anxiety.

'I think that's why I believed you'd manage him,' continued Kate. 'Because you'd known him for so long, I mean. He's not an easy person.'

Gemma began to laugh; it was a nervous, edgy sound.

'Thanks,' she said. 'For trying to make it easy, I mean. The trouble is, it's not Guy. Well, it is, of

251

course, but I mean it's not his fault. It's my fault.' She went to sit down at the table, her head resting in her hands. 'My past has caught up with me.'

'That sounds exciting.' Kate put the mugs on the table and sat down opposite. 'Since you were married at nineteen and, before that, you were training as a Norland Nanny I can't imagine your past is too sordid.'

Gemma wrapped her hands around the hot mug. Her face was pinched and small, her eyes miserable.

'The really mean thing is that ever since . . . this thing happened, I've been so sensible. It nearly caught me out, you see, and for the first time I realized exactly how much I had to lose. It frightened me and I kind of grew up and stopped playing around.'

Kate watched her. 'So what *did* happen? What is this thing that's come back to haunt you?'

'While I was playing around I made an enemy. The worst kind because up until then Marianne was a good friend right back to schooldays.' Gemma fiddled with her cuff, biting her lip vexatiously, and presently she looked at Kate. 'This is awful for both of us, isn't it? But that's what I meant when I said it was odd, knowing you all my life . . .'

'And Cass is away,' said Kate, puzzled but trying to help her. 'Just when you need her.'

'Oh, no.' Gemma sat up straight, shaking her head. 'You don't understand. Ma wouldn't be much use at the moment. It's because you're Guy's mum that I need you to help me. To tell me how I can reach him and how to handle him. In most cases the last thing you'd do is tell your mother-in-

252

law that you've been unfaithful to her son, isn't it?' She made an uneasy, mirthless sound in an attempt to cover the shocked silence and her anxiety. 'Are you very angry?'

Kate *was* angry: she felt all the hurt and betrayal on Guy's behalf and she longed, just for a second or two, to give Gemma a sound smack. Staring at her across the table it seemed as if time spiralled backwards to just such another crisis and she saw Cass's face, wearing that same guilty, wheedling expression, and heard her voice saying, 'That was a close one. No. No bullet this time but no more Russian roulette . . .' and the moment passed.

'No,' she said rather reluctantly. 'No, not angry. I suppose I'm not terribly surprised either,' she added—and wondered if this might sound offensive.

'Like mother like daughter?' suggested Gemma lightly, and smiled at Kate's reaction. 'Don't worry. Ma hinted once that she'd played the field a bit and warned me against it. I didn't want to know. Well, you don't, do you? It's a bit embarrassing when your parents start telling you how it was for them when they were young, but I guessed that she was trying to give me a hint. I only wish I'd taken it.' She drank some tea, choosing her words carefully. 'The thing is that I had a fling with Marianne's boyfriend, Simon, when Guy and I were on holiday on Exmoor a few years ago. It wasn't just a flirtation but the whole thing, and I was stupidly careless. I was terrified. That's when I knew that I must grow up and that I couldn't bear to lose Guy. Nothing happened and I thought I'd got away with it, though I heard that Marianne was furious. She must have let Simon off the hook

253

because they managed to patch things up eventually and even got married. Then last week it all blew up again.'

'Do you mean you're seeing him again?'

Kate had to make a very real effort to keep any hint of accusation out of her voice but Gemma shook her head, frowning, as if irritated that Kate was missing the point.

'No, of course not. At least, not in that way. I was shopping in Totnes and I went into Effings and there he was, having coffee. I hadn't seen him in all these years, honestly, but it seemed churlish not to have some coffee with him.'

'So? You had coffee . . . ?'

'Yes.' Gemma took a very deep breath. 'And while we were sitting there another mutual friend just happened to come in for some cheese or whatever and she obviously got the wrong end of the stick. The ironic thing is that this time there was simply nothing in it. Nothing.'

Kate stared at her, all her own wrath fading as she saw the misery on Gemma's face.

'And this mutual friend told Marianne?'

Gemma nodded. 'And then she simply wouldn't believe Simon when he told her the truth. She accused him of deceiving her all these years, then she threw him out, and then she wrote to Guy.'

'Oh my God!'

'Yes. That just about sums it up.'

'Did you tell him about what happened on Exmoor?'

'Yes, I did. I felt that he must hear the absolute truth and he believes me when I say that it finished then, I know he does, but he can't forgive me even though it was all that time ago. He can't forgive me

254

and he says that he can't trust me any more.' Her chin shook and tears filled her eyes. 'He looks so . . . so *disgusted* by me.'

'Oh, poor Gemma.' Kate was full of horror. 'Yes. Yes, he would.'

'I don't know what to do, you see. I thought you might be able to help me. I'm really sorry, Kate. You can't be all that thrilled, after all, but I simply don't know what else to do. He can be so . . . upright.'

'You mean he can be a self-righteous prig. What was he doing when you were with Simon?'

'He was off sailing with a man who lived just up the coast. Guy had sold him the boat and he'd offered to take Guy out. Not that I minded. I admit that I wish he wasn't away quite so much, delivering boats, but I'm used to it now.'

'But should you have to be used to it? Guy's always had a need for solitude, ever since he was a small boy, but when he got married he should have been prepared to forego some of his freedom. After all, he's known you all your life; he knows you are a friendly, outgoing girl . . .'

Kate paused, marshalling her thoughts; Gemma raised her eyebrows and the glimmer of a smile touched her lips.

'Are you suggesting that I tell Guy that this is his fault?'

'No. No, not exactly. What I'm suggesting is that Guy should take some share of the responsibility here.'

'You must be joking! And how do I manage that?'

'I think he has to see that you both have needs and that it's time they were catered for more

255

equally. Hang on, I know that sounds a difficult concept to present to him but I'm trying to work it out. I'm not talking about threats: "If you keep going away so much I shall find my own fun." Rather, I'm thinking of a way to appeal to his sense of fair play. I know that Guy often feels a bit guilty about his trips away but it doesn't stop him making them, does it? He doesn't wonder whether you might be lonely or bored. He could quite easily stay in the office and take on someone else to do the delivery part of the work. He's done extraordinarily well with his business; surely he could afford to sit back now and spend some time with you and the twins? I think he needs to see that his own behaviour will have influenced yours and it's time to make a change.'

'And how do we tell him this? Given that he's hardly speaking to me and spending most of his time on his boat?'

'How have you been behaving?'

'Cringingly. Begging for forgiveness. Apologizing and abasing myself.'

'Well, that must stop. You've behaved badly; you've admitted it and you've tried to make up for it since. It's a shock, of course it is, but he can't just think about himself. He must put it behind him, though it might be tricky explaining that to him.'

'Just a tad,' agreed Gemma feelingly.

'It's always difficult,' Kate continued thoughtfully, 'climbing off your high horse. So undignified and terribly easy to fall flat on your face. Best to let him do it on his own. Stop explaining and apologizing and let him make the next move.'

'How ruthless you are,' said Gemma admiringly.

'Is that how you managed Guy's father?'

'Oh, no.' Kate, who had been concentrating, intent, slumped in her chair. She looked sad. 'I didn't manage him at all well. I have no right at all to advise you what to do, Gemma. I never confronted Mark, I was too afraid of him, but with hindsight we might have done better together if I had.'

There was a short silence.

'The trouble with the strong silent type is that they can seem such a challenge.' Gemma shrugged ruefully. 'So exciting and mysterious, like a locked door. We want to know what's behind it. Is that how you saw Mark?'

'Probably. It seems so long ago and he was all so much a part of the naval scene: the Summer Ball at Dartmouth, the Royal Marine Band playing on the quarterdeck and the pretty dresses and the glamorous uniforms. He was like someone on a film set: tall, dark, good-looking, with that strong silent approach and an upright sense of duty and honour. I was overwhelmed by love and high ideals, excited at being allowed a part in it all. It was like being presented with a big, beautiful box except, when the ribbons were undone and the paper torn off, I found that there was nothing inside. It was empty.'

After a moment, Gemma leaned forward and touched Kate's hand. 'It hasn't been like that for me. There's plenty in *my* box, I promise you.'

Kate began to chuckle. 'Oh, darling, I'm so relieved to hear you say that. And, since we're talking genetics, I have to say that I can't help being glad that you are very like your mother after all. Especially as you seem to have more sense than she had at your age. One thing has puzzled me, though. I know that Guy's little cottage in the courtyard was perfect when you were first married and while the twins were small but I've often wondered why you haven't moved into something a bit bigger with a garden. I can't imagine it's a financial decision.'

Gemma looked thoughtful. Kate saw that she appeared happier—the pinched, fearful look had been replaced by a hopeful confidence—and she relaxed a little.

'It's all to do with Guy's being away so much, I suppose. We *have* talked about it but the thought of being on my own doesn't appeal. I like working for Malcolm Bruce at the dental surgery and I love people, Kate, things happening, impromptu gatherings. My neighbours in the courtyard are such mates and there's always someone around for a chat. I'd rather be a bit cramped than be alone.' She grimaced. 'Sounds a bit pathetic, doesn't it? Especially to someone like you, who's been so much alone.'

'I had the naval network to fall back on, remember. I can quite understand what you mean about being alone but if Guy were to be at home more you might feel differently. Anyway, first things first. What will you do?'

'I shall go back but I shan't telephone,' Gemma began, as if reciting lesson. 'I shall stop begging him to come home to supper or asking if he's OK and trying to make conversation. I shall leave the phone on answer. Right so far?'

'Quite right. It's worth a try, anyway. Once he's recovered his pride I think he'll realize that some way forward has to be found. He loves you and the twins far too much to be silly about it.'

'I hope you're right. I love him so much, Kate.'

'So do I,' said Kate.

CHAPTER THIRTY-FOUR

The following morning, across the crowded aisles and piled stalls of the Pannier Market in Tavistock, Kate saw Janna. After a restless evening spent wondering if she'd been mad to speak so frankly to Gemma, and growing more and more fearful of the consequences as the night progressed, Kate had risen early and decided to go shopping: a chat with Brigid Foley in her shop in Paddons Row and the fun of choosing a new outfit for Cass's ruby wedding anniversary party might distract her from imagining Guy's reaction to Gemma's tactics. Eating breakfast, Kate mentally reviewed the morning: coffee in the Bedford, return her library books, buy some of the twins' favourite jam from Crebers, go to Bookstop to see if Natasha had managed to find the book she'd ordered for Roly's birthday.

As she drove into the town Kate decided that she might also look in on Michael to see if there was any movement on the sale of the cottage. Her own house had been advertised for the first time at the weekend so there might be something to report there too. Pulling into a space in the car park of the Bedford Hotel she reflected that it was odd that her grandsons had shaken her confidence by acting so indifferently to the cottage. It was foolish to allow herself to be upset by it. Had she expected

259

that they would behave as Giles and Guy had, all those years before, with cries of delight and excitement? Her own twins had been enchanted at the prospect of sleeping in bunk beds, of having their own home after years of living in married quarters, and their joy had matched her own. Yet on Sunday she'd been unable to recapture that sense of happiness; instead she'd felt a stranger as she'd wandered through the empty rooms, as though the cottage were re fusing to give up its secrets and had closed itself against her.

She went into the hotel and ordered some coffee at the bar, wondering if it had been the presence of her grandchildren that had held the memories at bay: they'd been polite but baffled by this visit, anxious to get back to watch the video of *Shrek 2* that Kate had promised as an after-lunch treat.

'It's a bit like our cottage,' was Julian's verdict. 'I like your house better, Grannie. There's much more room in it.'

'Where would we have our playroom?' asked Ben, the more pragmatic twin. 'Where would you put the rocking horse?'

This was a bit of a facer: she hadn't considered this problem and she had to do some quick thinking.

'Perhaps in here,' she said, showing them the little room off the kitchen. 'We'd have to take the bed and the cupboard out, of course.'

They regarded the room rather glumly, clearly unimpressed.

'There would hardly be room for him,' Ben observed rather judiciously, 'not with all the other toys as well.'

'Don't you like your house any more?' asked Julian kindly. He stared up at her, concerned. 'Are you bored of it?'

'"Bored *with* it." Not really, Jules.' She hesitated, not wishing to sound pathetic. 'It's just a bit big, that's all. You know. Now that I'm on my own.'

'You could have a dog,' suggested Ben cheerfully. 'That would fill it up a bit.'

Julian regarded her hopefully. 'Would a dog do? One like Bevis or Floss would be nice.'

'Yes,' she agreed. 'That would be very nice. Let's go and look at the garden.'

Now, as she drank her coffee, she was frustrated and irritated by her inability to come to a decision and stick with it. It was foolish to be deterred from her plan to buy the cottage simply because two seven-year-old boys weren't enthusiastic about it: she simply couldn't afford to dither. Ever since David's death fear hovered at her shoulder, ready to undermine her confidence, and now, after a brief and happy respite, it was back.

An hour later, entering the Pannier Market from West Street, she paused for a moment in the doorway. Two years after her affair with Alex had ended, unexpectedly seeing him here across the hall, she'd been shocked at how much the memories still had retained their power to hurt. When their affair ended it had come as a blow to her that he'd not only returned to his one-time mistress so quickly but also that he'd flaunted it openly. It was as if their own love, which had seemed so precious and utterly special in Kate's eyes, had been simply another run-of-the-mill affair to him, and she'd been devastated by his

261

callousness. Coming upon him unprepared, two years on, had resurrected memories of the last weeks of the affair: the arguments, justifications, the scenes that needed so much tact, and the terror of losing everything that she loved. How hard it had been to reconcile the Alex of those last painful days with the lover and companion she'd known.

Today it was with something like relief that she saw Janna's tawny lion's-mane hair through the throng of people and Kate threaded her way between the stalls, across the market towards her. Janna greeted her with delight and her smile was full of warmth.

'Look at this,' she said, showing Kate a piece of Mason's Ironstone: a breakfast cup and saucer. 'Don't you think it's pretty? Nat could have his morning tea in it. 'Tis overpriced, of course, seeing it's got a chip in it and the saucer's cracked but I'm getting him down gradually.'

She winked at the stallholder, who gave a shout of laughter.

'Don't know good value when you see it,' he said. 'That's your problem. It's a genuine piece, that is. None of your modern stuff. Six fifty.'

Janna shook her head pityingly. 'What are you like?' she asked him. 'First day out on yer own, is it?'

Kate regarded Janna affectionately: as usual her T-shirt had a slogan: 'I can only please one person each day,' it read. 'TODAY IS NOT YOUR DAY.' Underneath in smaller print were the words: 'Tomorrow doesn't look good either.'

'Oh dear,' said Kate. 'That's bad news. Perhaps I should make an appointment.'

'What's wrong?' Janna looked concerned. So

did the stallholder, who feared he might lose his sale through this new distraction. 'Spent too much money?' Janna indicated the Brigid Foley bag, pulling out an edge of the silky slate-blue garment to have a peek at it. 'Oh, that's *so* cool. Just your colour. So what's up then?'

'Nothing,' answered Kate. 'I was just joking about your T-shirt.' She picked up the tea-cup. 'It's so pretty, isn't it? I love Mason's Ironstone and this pattern, the Fruit Basket, is my favourite. I had a coffee pot in it once. My mother gave it to me and I thought about her every time I used it, especially after she died. I cried buckets when it got broken. So difficult to get it now.'

'Very difficult.' The stallholder saw his opportunity and seized it gratefully. 'Like gold-dust.'

'A fiver,' said Janna firmly. 'Take it or leave it.' She waved the note encouragingly under his nose. ' 'Tis up to you.'

Grumbling, the stallholder wrapped the cup and saucer carefully, and Janna grinned at him saucily as she and Kate turned to go.

'So what's up?' she asked Kate. 'Don't say "nothing". Looks like you've seen a ghost.'

'Good grief! Nothing so terrible. Just trying to make some decisions, that's all.'

They passed down the crowded aisles, jostling between the other shoppers, raising their voices so as to hear each other speak.

'Have you made an offer on your cottage?' Janna cried into Kate's ear.

Kate shook her head, turning her head to shout back. 'I saw Michael just now. He told me that the owners are only prepared to deal with someone who's already had an offer on their own house. I'm nowhere near that yet.' They reached the far end of the market and paused in the doorway. 'Look, would you like some coffee? Or if you're going back to Horrabridge I can give you a lift.'

'Thanks, but I'm going in to Plymouth to see my mum. Nat dropped me off earlier on his way to work, so I thought I'd have a coffee in Duke's and a look at the market, but I've got to get a move on now or I'll miss the bus.'

They walked out together, past the Guildhall and the statue of the seventh Duke of Bedford, into the square.

'Is your mum OK?' asked Kate.

'I think so. I had a text from one of her mates and I thought I'd better go and have a look for myself. First of all she'll grumble because I don't go often enough and then we'll have a laugh and yarn about the old days on the road, then after that she'll get maudlin and last of all she'll start screaming. I don't know why it should be like that. I love her. And she loves me. 'Tis crazy, really. Happens every time the same.' She shrugged. 'You know how 'tis?'

'Oh, yes,' said Kate as they crossed Bedford Square and walked along beside the wall of St Eustachius' churchyard. 'I know how it is. Love and guilt, all bound up so tightly together that we can never quite tell where one begins and the other ends. We can't escape them.'

They paused near the churchyard gate at the crossing outside the hotel: Janna, who was still holding the parcel, suddenly held it out to Kate.

'For you,' she said. ' 'Cos you liked it.'

'But it's for Nat,' protested Kate, taken aback.

264

'It's very sweet of you . . .'

' 'Tis for you,' insisted Janna. She tucked the parcel into the Brigid Foley bag. 'You'll love it, see. Nat won't really think about it, only out of politeness and stuff like that. You'll really use it and when you do then you'll think about me and your mum. All of us sort of tucked in together.'

'Yes,' said Kate, after a moment. 'Yes, I shall do exactly that. Thank you, Janna.'

Driving home she thought about the question of guilt and love: she loved her twins yet inextricable from that love was guilt: that in being unable to sustain her marriage with their father she might have damaged them. Whatever arguments she might employ to justify her actions, deep down lurked the terrible fear that she'd got it wrong: that their problems and character defects were the products of some action of her own. Might that be why a tiny part of her feared to confront them in moments of crisis: that they might reflect back upon her the results of her own inadequacies and lack of foresight?

She knew that Roly had the same misgivings about his relationship with Nat: always conscious of his failure in providing him with a stable home, frustrated by Monica's manipulation of this weakness. Perhaps all parents suffered from this paranoia: realizing their mistakes only when it was too late.

So why should Janna's love for her mother be mixed with that guilty quality? Perhaps Janna believed that it was her fault that her father had gone away. When Janna was born he'd left her mother because he couldn't cope and, not long afterwards, her mother had begun to drink.

Perhaps Janna blamed herself for this series of events and imagined that she saw accusation in her mother's eyes.

'My mum loved me,' she'd said, defending her. 'She bought me things.'

Her whole security was wrapped in those offerings of affection: the shawl, the book, the mug. Instinctively Kate glanced at the bag in the well of the passenger seat, thinking about that earlier offering of love.

'You'll think about me and your mum. All of us sort of tucked in together.'

Vulnerability lurked behind Janna's happy-go-lucky façade; her desperate need to be part of a family, cherished and valued, always at war with some inherent instability that drove her to flee from the very commitment she craved as soon as it began to make demands upon her.

Pierced with a helpless compassion, Kate parked the car in the drive and took her shopping into the house. She went at once to the telephone to see if there was a message from Gemma, and turned away from the red, unwinking light with mixed feelings of anxiety and relief. It was far too early, she told herself, to hope for any results just yet. Nevertheless, she placed her mobile near to hand, just in case Gemma might text, and wondered if Roly and Daisy were on their way home from Bath. Perhaps, too, Michael might telephone to say that someone wanted to view the house: so many things to think about . . .

As she unpacked the delicious cheese and jam she'd bought at Crebers, and shook out the soft silky dress that she and Brigid Foley had selected so carefully together, Kate was conscious that she

266

was waiting.

Waiting was something that had always played a major part in her life: waiting for the boat to come in, waiting for the leave to start, waiting for the shore job. Later, she'd waited for the twins to come home for the holidays: home from boarding school, home from university. Later still she'd waited to hear that the babies were born and that all her children were safe—and so the cycle had begun again. Most recent of all had been the waiting through David's last long illness.

Kate shook her head: best not to think about David. Perhaps she should never have married, never had children; loving people was simply so painful and the worrying never seemed to cease. She picked up the book of *Showings*, still lying on the kitchen table. Maybe Dame Julian might have a word for her.

> Peace and love are always in us, living and working, but we are not always in peace and love; but He wants us to take heed that He is the foundation of our whole life in love and that He is our everlasting protector . . .

Peace and love: Kate sighed longingly. Of course, she might do better if she were to actually sit down and read the book instead of snatching sentences and phrases at random, hoping for a signpost to point her forward. She leafed idly through the pages. Peace and love. Perhaps, after lunch, she'd sit down quietly and concentrate on Julian's *Showings*: rejecting worrying and waiting, learning instead how to exist in love and peace . . .

The telephone bell made her jump.

'Kate, it's Michael. I've got a couple here with me in the office. Mr and Mrs Burns. They'd like to come and see the house. I know it's rather short notice but they're only down for two days. Could you manage it if I were to bring them round at three o'clock?'

'Yes. Yes, of course. Three o'clock? That will give me time to dash round and tidy up.'

'Three o'clock then?'

'Yes,' said Kate. 'Absolutely. I'll be waiting for you.'

PART THREE

CHAPTER THIRTY-FIVE

The dogs sat in a semicircle staring at the newcomer. He bounded to and fro excitedly, pausing to bow down on his front paws with his back end stuck in the air, inviting them to play. At intervals he barked encouragingly, hoping for a reaction. Bevis flattened his ears uneasily, though his tail thumped once or twice, and Floss sat up straight as if poised for flight; only Uncle Bernard barked back. He stood four-square, legs stiff, and told the newcomer exactly what he thought of him. The new arrival, Flynn, sat down abruptly and stared at him in amazement.

Sitting on a bench in the yard, watching the proceedings, Roly laughed out loud.

'Good old Uncle Bernard,' he said to Daisy, who was sitting beside him. 'He reminds me of my regimental sergeant-major: small and dapper but when he opened his mouth, my God, how we jumped to it!'

'It's funny, isn't it, how Flynn knows that though Uncle Bernard is so much smaller he's definitely top dog?'

'He's hardly more than a puppy, poor fellow. Here! Good boy then, Flynn.' He closed his eyes, bracing himself as Flynn, whining with excitement, licked his face enthusiastically. 'You'll have to watch yourself with this one, Daisy. We don't want any more accidents. Luckily we've got someone very interested in him. They'll be over later to see him. I don't think he'll be with us for very long.'

'Poor Flynn.' Daisy watched his antics

compassionately. 'It must be horrid to be taken away from your family, however unsatisfactory it's been. Terribly unsettling for everyone. It was rather different for Floss, with her owner dying, although I suppose she doesn't know the difference.'

'Flynn's been brought up in a very small flat with only a tiny yard and his owners at work all day. They admitted they simply had no idea how much work a puppy would involve or that he'd get so lonely. They're very sad to lose him but they want what's best for him and we all think that he's young enough to settle down with a new owner.'

Flynn dashed away again, circling the yard several times before sitting down suddenly, panting with exertion. Ears cocked and tongue hanging out, he stared hopefully at his audience as though awaiting their approval. Uncle Bernard yawned contemptuously and strutted away into the house but Bevis wagged his tail tolerantly as if he understood Flynn's boisterous behaviour: he'd been young once. Floss stood up and came to lean against Daisy's knee, as if seeking reassurance, and Daisy put an arm around her neck.

'You'll find it difficult to part with her if she stays much longer,' she said to Roly. 'Do you think Kate will take her?'

'Oh, I shall keep Floss if Kate doesn't have her but it's such an obvious solution,' he answered almost impatiently. 'The whole situation is very frustrating. I wish Kate could see her problems as two separate issues. Where she lives is one thing and having a dog is another but I think that she's using them so as to postpone facing her real grief. She needs unwumbling.'

Daisy laughed. 'You used that word before but it was about me, then. Wumbled. Worried and jumbled, I think you said. I'm looking forward to seeing Kate's cottage, aren't you?'

'Yes. Yes, I am.'

'You don't sound too sure.'

'I just don't want her to make a mistake, that's all. Is it a good idea to buy a cottage simply because you were happy in it when you were young? Isn't it going backwards instead of forwards? I simply don't know.'

'But you've come back here,' Daisy pointed out. 'This is where you lived when you were a child. What's the difference?'

'I'm not sure there is a difference.' Roly frowned, thinking about it. 'Except that we never really left here. Not completely. When our father died we kept the house as a retreat and let the stable flat to holiday-makers. We'd come down with friends at regular intervals and for holidays so, you see, it's always been a part of our lives; a kind of continuum. I think that Kate is trying to recreate some kind of happiness that happened years ago. She's relying on building a new life around a memory, probably not even a very reliable one, to assuage her loneliness. I'm not sure it's going to work.'

'And you think that having Floss would unwumble her?'

'She's been in a state of shock, losing David and then Felix so quickly afterwards. First of all she was too numb to think too much or do anything apart from surviving day to day. Now she's in that state where she feels that she's got to do something: anything to prevent her from

273

contemplating the loneliness and grief. Moving house is such a tempting option, isn't it? Lots to think about, lots to do: a new life opening up and so on. Floss would keep her busy but give her time to grieve properly.'

'So you think she's in denial about David?'

'Something like that. It's as if suddenly she's remembering people and things much further back in time, as if he didn't exist.' He paused, as if hesitating whether to speak his thoughts. 'Monica said something once. She said that Kate had hinted at a passionate affair and implied that she'd never loved David and he was, well, very second-best.'

'She said Kate said that? I don't believe it. I don't know her very well but you have an instinct about people, don't you? I can't imagine Kate marrying someone she didn't love.'

'Can't you?' He sounded relieved. 'I must admit I had difficulty with it too. They were always very happy and easy together. I think Monica misunderstood and Kate was talking about an affair she had way back before she met David. She was alone for a long time after her marriage broke up.'

'But that doesn't mean she didn't love David, does it? You can fall in love more than once. Actually . . .' she cast a quick sideways glance at him, 'I wondered if you and Kate might have a future together.'

He smiled. 'I wondered that too. I had a private passion for Kate for a very long time, and she was very tactful and patient about it, but I'm glad to say that the fever has passed and we can be very close friends, which is a great deal more comfortable if slightly less exciting.'

There was a short silence whilst they watched Bevis and Flynn indulging in a wrestling match.

'I envy you,' Daisy said at last, rather bitterly. 'I think I'm still infectious.'

'It's early days,' Roly said comfortingly. 'Poor old Bevis is getting rather the worst of it, isn't he? He's showing his age. Come on. Let's take this lot for a walk.'

*   *   *

Later, sitting by the pond, half hidden by the graceful branches of the weeping almond, he watched the fish as they surfaced: first one and then another with soft, gaping mouths snatching at the food. They swirled in an ever-changing pattern of gold whilst, deep down amongst the drifting weed, the shadowy carp waited their chance. In the muddy shallows, sheltering beneath the crimped-leaved ferns, a frog hopped. Roly smiled to see him.

'A frog he would a-wooing go. "Heigh-ho," says Rowley.' He could remember his mother singing the rhyme and his own delight in it: possibly because he and the frog shared the same name. 'The Rowleys' his mother named them. Each spring the frogs came to do their wooing in the pond and, during the chill, lengthening evenings of February, he listened for the sound of their urgent, thrumming serenade as eagerly as he waited for the cuckoo-call in April.

*   *   *

'Listen,' says his mother, lingering at the open

275

window one cold, sweet spring evening. 'Can you hear them?'

She watches his face, laughing at his puzzlement, and his father gets up and joins her at the window.

'Frogs,' he says. 'Incredible sound, isn't it?'

It is indeed an incredible sound: a deep, throaty, rhythmical purring that fills the quiet dusk.

'Where are they?' asks Roly. 'What are they doing?' and his mother laughs again.

'Wooing,' she answers. 'You know the nursery rhyme. "A frog he would a-wooing go. 'Heigh-ho,' says Rowley. Whether his mother would let him or no . . ."'

She sings the first verse and he nods, saying some of the words with her, but he is not concentrating properly because he is impatient to have a proper answer.

'But what does it mean? Wooing?'

'Come and see.' She holds out her hand to him. 'But you must walk very carefully. They can hear your footsteps vibrating through the ground. Bring the torch, Johnnie. Softly, now.'

They creep quietly, the three of them, across the grass, where the first crocuses are flowering, and beneath the arching branches of the cherry tree. As they approach the edge of the pond his mother's hand restrains him and he stops, peering into the darkness, straining his eyes. Suddenly the torchlight flashes over the surface of the water and there, caught in its beam, are the frogs: supported by the weed their heads emerge from the oily blackness and all the while their croaking song ripples through the garden.

'See them?' She bends down to him. 'Lots of

276

Rowleys come to do their wooing.'

'I can see them.' He is enchanted. Some pop their heads out of the water whilst others simply sit, their hooded protuberant eyes glassy in the sudden brightness. 'And look, that one is having a piggyback. And so is that one. Is that what wooing is?'

'It's love.' She chuckles again. 'That's what it is. They're calling to the lady frogs because they want to make love and have lots of dear little babies.'

'Honestly, Claire.' His father's voice is shocked. 'You are the limit. The boy's far too young.'

'Too young for the truth?' She is teasing his father, and Roly sees her slide her arm around him, but he is too fascinated by the scene in the pond to take much notice. 'Don't you think this is a rather nice way to show him, Johnnie? Much better than all those birds and bees! The Rowleys are having lovely fun and in the morning there will be babies.'

The Rowleys *do* seem to be having lots of fun: apart from the singing they embrace each other with thin arms and clutching, slippery fingers and, here and there, a long leg extends languorously from an amorphous, fleshy bundle. It's fun but, somehow, odd and frightening and fascinating too, as if there is something more than fun happening: something that he cannot understand but which is slightly threatening. He holds her hand more tightly and she bends down to him.

'This is the way the Rowleys do it,' she says. 'Nothing to be worried about. Wait until the morning and you'll see the babies.'

And, in the morning, all over the pond is the evidence of the wooing: a glistening, gelatinous,

277

slippery, wobbling mass.

'Lots and lots of jelly babies,' says his mother triumphantly. 'They'll grow up into tadpoles and then they'll become frogs. It's a Rowley nursery.'

*   *   *

Roly stirred. She'd died when he was ten and Mim was eight yet his mother's capacity for love, her ready humour and particular grace had already informed their lives. He wished he could have thanked her, acknowledging her vital presence that hovered even now so many years later. He'd been reminded of her earlier, whilst talking to Daisy in the yard. Something had ignited an idea that had flared up briefly and then vanished before he could catch its spark; something that was tied up with Daisy. Frustrated, he cudgelled his memory.

His attention was caught by a flash of light, a heavy wing-beat. The great bird was flying slowly, watchfully, upstream, attracted perhaps by the flashes of gold in the water of the pond below. It was the heron.

CHAPTER THIRTY-SIX

Daisy was watching the heron's flight from the banks of the stream. Camouflaged by bushes of dense, prickly furze and the close-growing small, shrubby salix trees, she stared upwards. Long neck drawn back, broad wings arched, spindle legs extended, the heron soared majestically. Soon he disappeared from sight towards the open moor, where bulrushes and reeds grew along the grassy banks.

She walked on a little way, waiting in vain for the inspiration she'd found in the wild beauty of this landscape on her earlier visit. Those moments of sharp awareness that translated themselves into a sense of shape and movement and harmony had seemed pleasant diversions. Now, she would give much to recapture just one of those creative images or be vouchsafed a tiny spark of that earlier inspiration. Her imagination and inventiveness lay dormant: any real attempt to breathe them back to life seemed merely to weigh them down further into sluggish torpor. The more she beat them the less they responded.

'I never thought it would be easy,' she'd cried to Roly, 'but I never thought I could feel so . . . so *paralysed.*'

'You're trying too hard. Don't think about anything in particular; just walk and read and dream. I've found some more CDs: Rachmaninov's *Rhapsody on a Theme of Paganini* and some of his preludes. And this one is Grieg's *Holberg Suite* and his *Lyric Pieces*. They might just spark something off.'

He allowed her a free run of his music library and never questioned her; she was grateful for that. Knowing that anxiety made her irritable— which in turn made her feel guilty—she tried not to be too glum when they were together. It was a relief to play silly games with the dogs, as far as her injury allowed, and she was looking forward to the visit to Kate at the weekend. The proposed meeting with Nat was rather more worrying. She couldn't decide whether it was simply a figment of her own overwrought state of mind or whether she'd actually detected a sense of collusion here: that she and Nat would hit it off, be great friends—and perhaps more than that.

Daisy genuinely wanted to meet Nat—her natural curiosity had not abated along with her creative ability—but she didn't want to be set up for a relationship or pitied because of Paul.

'Will I meet Janna too?' she'd asked—but Roly had frowned, as if perplexed, and said that Janna would be away at a market helping a friend with a stall.

'She's the original free spirit,' he'd answered, 'but she and Nat are great friends.'

He hadn't added 'You'll like Nat', which was good. Some perversity in her disliked being told whom she would or wouldn't like. She preferred to make up her own mind. If he were to be like Roly then she would like him very much indeed. Perhaps he might even distract her from her misery about Paul.

Paul: at the thought of him she cradled her arms about her body as if to ward off the pain. She hadn't seen him again since the scene in the hall: she'd been unable to face any of the possible ways of parting. He might have managed some explanation as to why it was that he'd believed his marriage was finished, though it would have been deeply embarrassing for both of them, but she could think of no good reason why he hadn't told her that his wife and children were at the cottage in Salcombe. After that meeting with his family in the hall she'd imagined various farewell scenarios with a kind of shrinking horror. He might have felt that an apology was in order, which implied that she was the injured party and that he pitied her; or he might have remained cheerfully detached, waving her off and brutally slamming the door on her and everything they'd shared. Either way she'd known she simply couldn't bear it.

He'd made no attempt to seek her out, hadn't even left her a note, and still she couldn't decide whether she was relieved or deeply hurt. She knew exactly what Roly meant when he talked about the fever passing. *'A great deal more comfortable if slightly less exciting.'* Being in love made it quite impossible to be natural: it placed constraints upon the tongue and distorted everything that came into contact with the beloved. At the same time, life was strangely empty without it. Each day stretched ahead, a dull and characterless plain with no landmark or feature to redeem it. Work must be her salvation.

Roly seemed to understand this and was doing everything he could to enable her: if anyone were an unwumbler then it was Roly. She smiled a little at the word he used; he was intent on sustaining her through this difficult time. This afternoon he was taking her to meet a friend of his who lived on the north Cornish coast at a place called St Meriadoc.

'Bruno understands the value of work,' Roly told her. 'He'll know just how frustrated you're feeling.'

She'd been impressed when she'd understood that he was talking about the well-known writer Bruno Trevannion, and now, as she turned back towards the ford, she realized how very much she was looking forward to meeting him. Perhaps he might be able to inspire her: galvanize her into some kind of action.

*   *   *

St Meriadoc was a perfect little valley and she was immediately drawn to the strange stone house, a kind of Victorian folly perched on the side of the cliff.

Bruno greeted them wearing an open-necked shirt with jeans and bare feet, his dog, Nellie, at his heels. Roly introduced Daisy. He'd already explained the circumstances surrounding her accident and her present dilemma and Bruno grasped her outstretched hand with a friendly compassion.

'I know all about writer's block,' he said sympathetically. 'But I'm not sure of the correct term for it when it comes to dancers. Come on in and have a drink.'

She felt comfortable at once, going to stare out at the silky-blue sea from the large outflung window. She turned, pausing before the big black-and-white framed photograph which hung over the sideboard opposite the wide granite hearth. It was well known to her: an icon of the sixties. It showed a Paris boulevard, passers-by stepping round the pavement café, a Citroën parked at the kerb. The girl's head was turned a little aside, chin up, but the long, narrow eyes looked straight at the camera: indifferent yet provocative. Her elbow rested on the small wrought-iron table, a cigarette between the fingers of the drooping hand, whilst her companion, just out of focus, was bending towards her, holding a coffee cup.

Bruno, coming in from the kitchen carrying a

dish of delicious-smelling cassoulet, saw the direction of her gaze and smiled.

'Recognize it?'

'Of course I do. It's a brilliant piece of photography, isn't it? Utterly evocative: you can almost catch the scent of the coffee and cigarette smoke.'

'Sobranies,' said Bruno, putting down the dish. 'She always smokes Sobranies.'

'Do you know her?' Daisy was awed.

'In a manner of speaking. Even in the biblical sense.' Bruno laughed. 'Reader, I married her. And he,' Bruno tipped his head at Roly, 'was the man who took the photograph.'

'This is amazing,' said Daisy at last. 'I had no idea. You never said anything, Roly.' She looked again at the photograph: it vividly evoked a whole era. 'You must have had such fun back then in the sixties,' she said rather wistfully.

'Oh, we did,' agreed Roly. 'I'm sure we did, didn't we, Bruno? Can you remember it? You were in the Navy, if I remember, and I was struggling to make money. Who was it said that if you can remember the sixties you weren't there?'

They began to reminisce, roaring with laughter and bandying famous names about, but drawing Daisy along with them so that suddenly, joyfully, she felt a part of the whole wonderful fraternity of creative artists. After a while Bruno began to ask her about her own career, and the prospects before her, listening intelligently and discussing the possibilities of the brief Mim had given her for the Charity Matinée.

By the time she and Roly set out on the journey back Daisy felt energized and excited.

283

'He's so nice,' she said, sighing with satisfaction, reading the signposts with pleasure: St Agnes, St Tudy, St Mabyn. 'He's rather like you, Roly. An enabler. An unwumbler.'

She glanced at him in surprise as he struck the wheel lightly, exclaiming: 'That was it! That's what I was trying to remember.'

'What?' she demanded. 'What is?'

'*The Starlight Express*,' he answered. 'No, no,' seeing her expression and laughing, 'not Lloyd Webber's creation. Sir Edward Elgar's. It's something that's been nagging away at my subconscious for the last few days. That's where the unwumbling comes from: the play called *The Starlight Express*. Elgar wrote the incidental music for it. It's delightful. My mother loved it so Mim and I know it rather well. I only hope I can find my recording of it. It could be just the thing to unwumble your ideas.'

CHAPTER THIRTY-SEVEN

As they drove home from St Meriadoc, Roly told her as much as he could remember about the play: about the three children who were trying to unwumble their parents and to reintroduce compassion into their troubled lives with the aid of stardust and a band of sprites.

'I expect it would seem rather fanciful now,' he said, 'but then, during the First World War, the world must have seemed a dark and troubled place. The gist of it is that the children belong to a Star Society and their aim is to get as many people

284

as possible out of their selves—their small locked-up wumbled lives, that is—and into the Star Cave where they are transformed by stardust. Metaphorically speaking, of course. It was hoped that the play might have the success of *Peter Pan* but it never quite caught on. The music wasn't to blame, though. I remember that one reviewer wrote something like, "Whosoever is wumbled let him listen to Sir Edward Elgar." I hope you'll like it.'

As soon as they were home Roly went straight into his study and began to search for the tape. Even as he did so his earlier confidence began to leak away: he could see how desperate Daisy was becoming for any kind of inspiration and now feared that he had raised her hopes in vain. He almost wished that he wouldn't find it but there it was, tucked in next to an early recording of Elgar's *Sea Pictures*. Roly reminded himself that Daisy had loved the *Sea Pictures*, took the tape out and went downstairs.

'Here,' he said, giving it to her. 'Don't worry if it's not what you're after. It's just something to think about. You can play it in here if you want to. I'm going to give the dogs a walk before supper.'

He simply couldn't hang about, wondering if his instinct had been a good one. It was like recommending a film to a friend and then sitting through it with them, wondering what it was you'd ever liked about it and feeling hot with embarrassment. As he crossed the ford he wondered why he'd ever imagined that this particular music should be different from anything else he'd selected for her. Perhaps it was just a silly nonsense, tied up with being wumbled and the memories of his mother's dancing, joyful grace.

It eased his tension to walk, the dogs racing ahead, barging and jostling in their delight at being out again after the long hours of confinement. He took the track up the hill, letting anxiety drain away from him as he climbed. The high moors, rising and flowing with bleak grandeur, looked like a dun-coloured sea from which the bony outline of Rough Tor cut sharp and clear against a dazzling sky where gold and scarlet ribbons, frayed into long curling cloudy banners, were blown across the evening sky. Hushed and still now, as long, mysterious shadows came creeping over turf and rock, the moors seemed to retreat, shrouded with an insubstantial secrecy.

Calling to the dogs, turning for home, Roly paused for a moment, giving delighted homage to a thin cockleshell moon, rocking her way up into the eastern sky, a bright star following in her wake like a little dory. The sweet air drifted up from the deep valleys and enclosed lanes, releasing its midsummer scent—honeysuckle, new-mown grass—into the warm evening. Silvery slate roofs and golden thatch nestled together in the gathering dusk, thick-walled granite and stone cottages leaning quiet and close, as the sun began to slip away beyond the western shore.

As Roly crossed the ford he could hear the waltzing, dancing music pouring from the open windows, and Daisy came to the door, her face bright with pleasure and excitement.

'Oh, Roly, I love it,' she cried. 'My head is in a terrible jumble of ideas at the moment but, even so, I just know it's what I've been waiting for.'

He wanted to shout with relief but managed to

contain himself. 'Don't try to think about anything in particular yet. Just listen to it. Get a sense of it. There's no rush.'

She stared at him, her eyes full of visions, and he went to prepare the supper whilst the music played on and Daisy moved about as if dazed, concentrating intently. As he listened to the final duet between the Laugher and the Organ-Grinder, instinctively waiting for the heart-jumping orchestral slide into the opening bars of 'The First Nowell', the chiming bells and the final triumphant clash of cymbals, Roly glanced at Daisy.

She stood quite still, hands clasped, and now her eyes were full of tears.

'Silly, isn't it?' he said into the following silence. 'But there's something very moving about it. I don't quite know how Elgar manages to combine nobility and spirituality in a popular and accessible way but that's how it is for me.'

'I love it,' she said again, quietly this time. 'I want to know more about it and I want to listen to it again. I seem to know bits of it.'

'We'll find out if there's a CD,' he said. 'I'll telephone Sheila or Nola at Opus first thing in the morning. They'll know.'

'What's Opus?'

'A wonderful classical music shop in Exeter. They'll send us anything we need.'

'I want to know more about the play and the characters. The music has masses of scope.' She hesitated. 'You don't think Elgar might be a bit old-fashioned?'

'I seem to remember that Ashton created a ballet to the *Enigma Variations*,' he answered lightly. 'Isn't this Ashton's centenary year? If Elgar

287

was good enough for him he's good enough for us.'

Daisy grinned at him, confidence restored, and he smiled back at her, full of thankfulness.

'Go down to the ford and watch the moon rising,' he said. 'It's a perfect evening, full of magic.'

She went to him and hugged him.

'Thanks, Roly. Really, really, thanks. Can we listen to it again while we have supper?'

'As often as you like. You've got twenty minutes. I'll send Bevis down for you when supper's ready.'

*   *   *

When Mim telephoned a few moments after Daisy had disappeared it seemed the most perfect timing.

'Something good has happened,' Roly told her jubilantly. 'Things are beginning to move but I don't want to give any secrets away. I expect she'll want to tell you herself.'

'I expect she will but I want to know what direction she's taking. Don't worry about being disloyal, Roly. You can rely on me to say all the right things when I speak to Daisy.'

'She did say something about being old-fashioned,' hedged Roly. He could feel Mim willing him to tell her the truth but had misgivings about whether it was his to tell. 'She was a bit anxious about it. That's probably a clue to the way her mind is working.'

'It depends whether she's muddling the sense of the word "old-fashioned" with "classical". Some people might say that *Swan Lake* is old-fashioned but look what Matthew Bourne has done with it.

Or what about *The Nutcracker*? There are often three productions of that in London each Christmas running at the same time. We did a very modern piece for the Charity Matinée last year so I shall be happy with something different. So is that all we know? Come on, Roly. Forewarned is forearmed. If Daisy is going down the wrong path I can let her down more lightly if I'm prepared for it.'

Roly gave in. 'She's been listening to Elgar's incidental music for *The Starlight Express*. She loves it but she's only heard it right through once. She says she needs to listen to it lots more . . . Are you there, Mim?'

'Oh, yes.' She gave a little reminiscent chuckle. ' "The Waltz of the Blue-Eyes Fairy" and the dear old Organ-Grinder. It's years since I heard that music. It was one of Mother's favourites, wasn't it? I remember her dancing, whirling me round in her arms.'

'That's what made me think about it. But nothing's set in stone yet, I wouldn't want you to think that, and I know Daisy will want to talk it over with you.'

'Don't panic. It was mean of me to ask you but I've got Jane and Andy breathing down my neck and I thought I'd sound you out. I think it's promising, Roly.'

'Do you?' For the second time in an hour he felt quite weak with relief. 'Thank God for that.'

She laughed. 'Are you feeling like Piggy in the Middle?'

'Just a tad. But it was wonderful to see her come alive, Mim. She's been so . . . locked up inside herself.'

'And now she's being unwumbled. It was clever of you to think of *The Starlight Express*. Quite the unwumbler yourself, aren't you? You can take the part of . . . who was he, who came to see the children and sorted everyone out? Cousin somebody or other. You can make your stage debut at last!'

'Oh, shut up,' he said. 'Go away! I'm trying to cook supper.'

'I'll phone in a day or two. No need to say we've talked.'

She rang off and Roly went back to his pots. The dogs lay stretched on the cool slate, eyes unclosing from time to time to see if any morsel should be on offer. Uncle Bernard, curled up comfortably in his drawer, knew that he was perfectly placed to receive a titbit without having to worry about it.

Down by the ford Daisy was sitting on the bridge. The moon was netted and cradled in the branches of the hawthorn and, as she watched, she suddenly saw the evening star glittering below the moon's horn. She was filled with a fizzing, bubbling excitement: rinsed clean of fear and doubt, light-hearted with expectation. Some deep-down instinct assured her that this thing that she sought to create was within her grasp and she welcomed the work that would shape it into a reality.

She gave a startled cry as a cold wet nose thrust in under her arm, nearly knocking her from her perch.

'Bevis,' she said with relief. She bent to press her cheek against his warm coat. 'Good boy, then. Is it supper-time?'

As they walked back to the house together she

glanced over her shoulder at the star; music was running in her head like wine and, recalling some little bygone rite from childhood, she crossed her fingers and made a wish.

CHAPTER THIRTY-EIGHT

Gemma telephoned Kate late on Saturday morning.

'A breakthrough! Well, the beginnings of one. Goodness, Kate, it's been really tough.'

It was twelve days since their conversation, during which time there had been no communication from Gemma, and Kate was in that interesting state that combines a sense of anxiety with hurt feelings and irritation. She felt that Gemma could have at least kept in touch, even if there was little or no progress to report, and she'd had to resist the urge to text or telephone by reminding herself that Gemma and Guy were adults and that she had no right to interfere. As the days passed so it became more and more difficult to be natural about telephoning or texting, and every time she rehearsed what she might say it sounded stilted and overmotherly, or as if she was nagging.

Now Gemma's opening remark made her want to be snappish, to say something childish like, 'Well, what did you expect? Of course it's tough,' and she was obliged to pull herself together.

'Ah,' she answered, striving to sound non-committal; but Gemma, always her mother's child and true to form, picked up on it at once.

'Oh, Kate,' she said repentantly, 'I know I should have been in touch. Don't do that thing of being po-faced. Not on the telephone. Honestly, it's been hell.'

'Oh, darling, I'm not a bit upset.' Kate unbent at once, reminded, as so often was the case with Gemma, of Cass making similar appeals over the years. 'I've just been worried about you, that's all. And I've got Roly and Daisy coming to see the cottage and I'm so afraid they won't approve. Crazy, isn't it? Never mind that. Tell me all.'

'To begin with, your advice was spot on. I stopped crawling and begging for forgiveness and backed right off. It took several days—which was awful, I can tell you—but then Guy began to thaw out a bit. The first sign was when I found a message from him on the answerphone and then a few days after that, when I got back from work, he was here. I reminded him that we were invited to supper with Giles and Tessa the following Friday and he agreed, rather reluctantly, to go. I warned Tessa, in fact I told her the whole truth, and when we got there she and I made sure that Guy and Giles were left together for a bit. The journey over to the cove was rather awful, like sitting in the car with an iceberg, but Tessa and Giles were brilliant. It helped just being with them. They are so easy and happy with each other, none of that Tom Tiddler's ground stuff that I have with Guy, and we just relaxed. Giles is so much more laid-back than Guy, but he's calm and rational too.'

'Giles was always the peacemaker,' said Kate, when Gemma seemed to have run out of breath. 'I am so glad that Guy talked to him. He could always make Guy see sense. At least, I imagine that's what happened?'

'Yes. Yes, we gave them time to talk while we put Henry to bed and by the time we got downstairs Guy was looking much more human. Giles was brilliant. He was making us laugh and keeping the conversation going along so easily; I don't know quite how he did it. He made certain that Guy was having lots to drink and really unwinding, and by the time we came home I could see that it was going to be OK. I drove, and Guy was pretty quiet, but that terrible iciness was gone and . . . well, he stayed last night for the first time since he found out.'

'Oh, darling, I am so glad.'

'So am I! Oh God, it's been so awful. He's gone to the office today but he's coming home to lunch and I really think the worst is over. I even managed to touch very slightly on the subject of my being on my own so much. He looked grim but I decided to give it a little try, like you said. He made a couple of sarcastic remarks but I could see he was thinking about it.' A tiny pause. 'Kate, I'm really, really sorry I haven't been in touch. I've been totally tunnel-visioned, I will admit. You know, pretending to the twins that everything's OK and that Daddy's working away and I'm trying to be jolly so they don't suspect. It's so tiring and I miss him so much. And you were so good about everything . . .'

'It's fine,' said Kate quickly. 'Honestly. It's just that I couldn't help worrying but I didn't want to interfere.'

'I know. It was mean, to dump on you like that and then leave you in the air about what was going on. The point was, nothing much *was* going on. It's different now. When he went off this morning, he said that there were *things to discuss*.'

'Oh.'

'Exactly. But I think I can handle it. I feel so much better about everything now. Look, I'd better go but I'll let you know how we go on. Honestly, I will. What's all this about the cottage?'

'Oh, just that I'm taking Roly and Daisy to see it this afternoon. Your twins weren't terribly impressed so I've got the jitters.'

'But if *you* love it does it matter what the twins think? Would you like Guy and me to come and see it? I've remembered now; this is where you and the boys lived when they were little, isn't it? Sorry, Kate, I've been so fixated on my own problems I haven't thought about yours.'

'It doesn't matter at all. Get yourselves sorted out first, that's the important thing. There's no rush for me to be doing anything.'

'Thanks, Kate. I really mean it. And I'll text or phone.'

'You do that,' said Kate. 'Good luck, my darling.'

She put the phone down thoughtfully: the trouble was that it wasn't absolutely true that there was no rush to be doing anything. Earlier that morning Michael Barrett-Thompson had telephoned.

'The good news is that we've got an offer on your house, Kate. It's a really good one: only a thousand under the asking price. The bad news is that this means it's make-up-your-mind time. It's that first couple who saw it, Mr and Mrs Burns, and they've absolutely set their hearts on it. He's being moved by his company so there's no chain,

294

no problems.'

She'd been unable to speak to begin with; shock, excitement, terror, all seethed inside her.

'I don't quite know what to say,' she'd managed at last. 'I'm still dithering about the cottage. I'm taking a very good friend of mine to see it this afternoon.'

'Yes, I remember now. Jackie said you'd been in for the key. OK. Then the best thing is for me to hang fire with the Burnses over the weekend. After all, I might not have been able to contact you this morning so I think that's fair enough. I shall need to know by Monday, Kate.'

Now, as she waited for Roly and Daisy, she tried to force herself to think clearly, to imagine herself living again at the cottage.

'Of course I remember it,' Giles had said when she'd phoned him to talk it over. 'And of course we were happy there. But you need to think forwards as well as backwards. I can understand that the idea of moving to the cottage gives you a sense of security, it's not like going somewhere utterly strange, but it needs to be right for all sorts of reasons. If you can't decide because you're in a muddle emotionally then take a different tack and write down all the pros and cons. It helps to clear the mind. What would David have advised?'

'I can't seem to think about David,' she'd answered wretchedly.

'Perhaps you need to do that,' he'd suggested gently, 'before you go any further?'

Kate glanced at the kitchen clock: Daisy and Roly should be arriving at any moment. Later, once they'd seen the cottage, she would make her decision.

*　　*　　*

It was stupid, Kate told herself as she parked in the driveway, to feel so nervous: it was as if the cottage were a beloved child being shown off before a critical audience. Beside her, sitting in the passenger seat, Daisy was already making encouraging noises, but it was clear to Kate that Daisy was in such a euphoric state that she would have found it difficult to be negative about anything, let alone such a charming scene. The cottage drowsed peacefully in the afternoon sunshine, the hawthorn blossom was beginning to rust along the hedge and the scent of the philadelphus was heavy in the air.

As she switched off the engine Roly leaned forward and touched her on the shoulder.

'*Courage, ma brave,*' he murmured in her ear—and she felt a rush of affection for him. It was such a relief that he wasn't in love with her any more: no more of the 'pleasing plague' to muddle the issue and complicate their relationship. She guessed that he knew exactly what she was feeling and, as she went to unlock the door, she felt comforted. Daisy bounded inside at once and stopped short at the sitting-room door. Kate watched her anxiously: despite Daisy's sense of personal wellbeing Kate knew that she would speak out honestly.

'What's wrong?' she asked, standing at her shoulder.

'Nothing's wrong.' Daisy hastened to reassure her. 'It's sweet. I was just surprised that it's so small. Coming from your big house, and the barn being open plan, it's just such a difference. I love the inglenook and the stove.'

'It's easy to heat,' said Kate lamely.

She stared round the room as if she hadn't seen it before, trying to conjure up her own first excited reactions, whilst Daisy disappeared into the kitchen. Roly went right into the sitting-room, ducking his head to avoid the low beams. He looked about him, thinking of the young Kate and how it must have seemed to her.

'I can see why you fell in love with it,' he said. 'It's absolutely delightful.'

'It was different,' she murmured. 'I had no furniture, only books and a few pictures, and I chose everything to fit it. It was such fun.'

'Yes,' he said, after a moment. 'I can well imagine it would have been. It's like one's first car, isn't it? Nothing ever quite beats that first exciting moment of ownership.'

She glanced at him quickly. 'Do you mean that it wouldn't be the same again?'

'It can't be the same again. But that doesn't mean that it's wrong to buy it.'

'No, no, of course not.' She turned away, following Daisy into the kitchen. 'You can't imagine how this looked back then. There was an old solid-fuel Rayburn and I had a dresser against this wall.'

Daisy appeared from the small room beyond the kitchen.

'They haven't cared about it, have they?' she asked, distressed. 'They've just put in any old bits and pieces.'

'Perhaps they couldn't afford anything else,' suggested Kate. 'It's a second home so it probably took everything they had just to buy it.'

'I suppose so.' Daisy didn't sound convinced. 'It must have been so different when you had it, Kate.'

'Well, it was. You like it, then?'

'Oh, yes. It's sweet. And there's plenty of room for Floss.' She hurried past them and up the stairs.

Roly grimaced almost apologetically. 'Very single-minded girl, our Daisy.'

Kate laughed. 'Ever since we first met she's been determined that Floss and I were made for each other. And so have you. Well,' she looked about her, 'there's plenty of room for Floss here.'

Roly looked at her curiously. 'You sound a bit flat about it. Not about Floss but about the cottage. Disappointed or frustrated in some way.'

'That's rather clever of you, Roly. Frustrated describes it rather well. When I saw the cottage again, once Michael had left me on my own here, it all came back to me. I relived it all again. You know? Seeing it for the first time and buying bits and pieces for it, and how the twins loved it, and other things too: the awful early years with Mark and then my mother dying. It was odd that I'd always remembered it as a place where I was very happy but I realized that it hadn't been quite like that. And then there was Alex. I relived it all then, as I walked about and sat in the sun in the garden. But when I brought Gemma's twins to see it and now, today, with you and Daisy it's as if the cottage is closed against me. It has nothing to say to me. The magic has gone.'

Daisy was calling from the top of the stairs and Kate went out into the little hall and looked up at her.

'At least the bunk beds are here,' she said. 'I remember you saying that you had them for Giles and Guy. The main bedroom isn't too bad at all, either.'

Roly waited downstairs, hearing their footsteps passing overhead and their voices in a kind of question and answer duet: Daisy's raised enquiringly, Kate's lower, slower. They came down again and Daisy went outside, still eager and interested in it all.

'Perhaps,' Roly said quietly, 'you need to see the cottage as a place where you were happy once so that you can believe that you could be happy here again. I think it's a positive thing to remember happy times. Human nature has a way of blotting out the things we find painful—how else could we go forward?—but I don't believe that you should put all your hopes for future happiness in a cottage. It isn't shutting you out, Kate, there's nothing mysterious here. It's just being what it is: a building, and a very nice one, of stone and slate. If you buy it you'll find your life will continue much as it is now, or as it was then, with periods of joy and sadness. Stop seeing it as a solution: there are no guarantees against pain.'

She stared at him almost fearfully. 'What shall I do, then?'

'If you love this cottage and it fits in with all your present requirements and solves your financial difficulties, then buy it. But don't see it through rose-coloured spectacles, Kate. Don't envisage yourself sitting here dreaming about a time when your life was perfect or you'll be brutally disillusioned. You've talked about Mark, and the twins when they were small, and your mother and even Alex, but you don't talk about David. Why is that? What would David be saying to you now?'

'Giles asked that question.'

'And what did you tell him?'

'I told him that I can't think about David. It's too . . . painful. Too lonely.'

Daisy appeared suddenly in the doorway.

'What a heavenly little garden. The apple trees are so old.' She stared at them. 'You both look very serious. Is something wrong?'

'Of course not.' Kate went out into the sunshine. 'Just the eternal question: shall I buy it or not? Is the fruit beginning to set?'

Roly followed them more slowly, cursing himself for being unnecessarily brutal. Daisy was telling Kate something, gesticulating wildly, and quite suddenly they both began to laugh. As they came back towards him he felt an inexplicable lightening of his own spirits, as if something had been resolved, some prayer answered.

Kate smiled at him. 'We must go home,' she said, 'or Nat will wonder where we are. He's coming to tea, remember. Let me just lock the door and we'll be on our way.'

CHAPTER THIRTY-NINE

Nat picked up his jacket and his keys and had got as far as the door when the telephone rang. He hesitated, glancing at his watch, but went back to answer it: it might be the client he was going on to after tea with Kate. It would be damned annoying if he went all that way and they weren't in.

It was Monica.

'What a miracle to catch you,' she said brightly, immediately making him feel guilty, as if he'd been avoiding her. 'How are you?'

'To be honest I'm just going out.' Tactless to tell her where. 'I only dashed in to grab something and then I'm going over towards Callington way. Everything OK?'

'Oh well, the usual.' Her voice held that familiar, faintly martyred tone, and he tensed, shivered through with irritation and wariness. 'I'm thinking of coming down to see you.'

'Oh.' He tried to make it sound a welcoming response; pleasantly surprised. 'That's nice. When?'

'Next week. Friday? Just for a few nights. I can't get hold of Roly but I might spend a night or two down with him.'

'He's got someone staying at the moment.'

'Oh?' Her voice was sharp at once. 'Who?'

'Girl called Daisy. One of Mim's protégées. She's beginning work at the school with her next term and meanwhile she's working on something down in Cornwall.'

'But why? Why does she have to be with Roly? Honestly, Mim is the last straw.'

'I've no idea.' He bristled with impatience—why shouldn't the girl stay with Roly?—but he managed to keep his voice calm. 'Perhaps she hasn't anywhere else to go. Look, Mum, I've got a client waiting. Shall we fix this up now? Friday, did you say?'

'Is Janna with you?'

'Yes. Yes, she is. Well, not today. She's helping

301

Teresa with a stall in Totnes.'

'Oh, she's with *Treesa*, is she?'

As usual she invited him to mock Janna with her and, as usual, he felt dislike and condemnation at her tactics.

'Yes, with Teresa.' His voice was cool. 'Is that a problem for you?'

'What? What do you mean?'

'That Janna will be here next week. Does that make a difference to you wanting to come down?'

'No, I suppose not.' There was a weight of hurt disappointment in her sighed response. 'It's nice to see you by yourself sometimes, that's all.'

He refused to allow his ingrained guilt to trap him into any kind of apology.

'I expect we'll manage a moment here and there. Friday, then. I'll be home about the usual time but you know where the key is. Jonathan OK? . . . Great. See you on Friday.'

He switched off the phone and slammed it back on its stand. His fingers crisped into the palms of his hands, balling into fists. How would they manage, the three of them together? Janna was in such an odd mood just lately, so certain he and she could make some kind of closer relationship work, and he could envisage his mother's glance probing into the delicate structure of their friendship, summing it all up, weighing the pros and cons, throwing in a damaging remark. Dammit, why hadn't he just said at once that it wasn't possible, that he had friends staying? It wasn't necessary to feel responsible for her; that it was up to him to make her happy. That was Jonathan's job.

Nat snatched up his keys and his jacket and went out, locking up behind him, checking that the

302

spare key was under the flowerpot for Janna—she hated carrying keys, always losing them. He drove the road to Whitchurch as slowly as he dared, determined to keep this tea-party as short as possible. It wasn't that he didn't want to see Kate or Roly; it was just this girl, Daisy, who was the unknown quantity. He was tired of friends setting up girls for him, trying to detach him from Janna. Why couldn't they just accept that Janna was the only woman he could possibly live with: someone who had as many hang-ups as he did? Perhaps it was his mother's legacy, those teenage years of trying to placate and support her and, later on, the ghastly scenes when he decided to leave the business and live his own life, that made him so wary and defensive of forming any close relationships.

Kate's garden gate was shut. Roly had brought the dogs: that would be the reason for it. He was glad about the dogs. They gave one a bit of protective camouflage. He left the pick-up outside and walked up the drive. They were grouped round the big wooden table in the garden, putting out plates and mugs, whilst the dogs danced around. Kate saw him first and waved to him. Roly and the girl turned, and Roly came towards him, calling a greeting, drawing the girl along with him. She looked nice: very graceful and open-faced. He instinctively toughened himself against that eager, interested, lancing stare, smiling back and holding out his hand as Roly introduced them. And then he saw her gaze widen, change, and she took his hand with a strong, friendly grip, and he knew quite certainly that it would be OK and was foolishly overwhelmed with relief.

Nat and Daisy carried the afternoon: jokes and conversation rolling like a ball between them to be scooped up and passed back before bouncing off on another topic. Watching his son, Roly felt the kind of happiness that comes when it is clear that a beloved child is peacefully having fun. He laughed as he listened and watched, remembering other happy times when Nat was much younger: a cheerful, careless undergraduate who dropped in for an impromptu chat or a drink, and who was enjoying the first tastes of freedom.

Every now and again Roly glanced at Kate as if to invite her to share in his pleasure; but Kate, though ready to join in the conversation, was so preoccupied with her own thoughts that he began to believe that his earlier sense of relief, that certainty that she'd finally made the decision about the cottage, had been premature. He could see that something was bothering her. It was she who suggested that the dogs should have a run in the paddock before the trip back to Cornwall and it was Daisy and Nat who volunteered to take them.

'That went well,' said Roly, helping to carry the tea-things into the kitchen. 'They've really hit it off, haven't they?'

Kate smiled, nodded, but was unwilling to be drawn further and Roly wondered if he'd been too outspoken when he'd tackled her about David. Before he could think of any satisfactory way of reintroducing the subject, Daisy and Nat returned. Nat was in a hurry to be away.

'I've just realized the time and I'm going to be

late,' he said. 'Great tea, Kate. Thanks.'

They went out with him, waving him off, wandering back indoors together. Daisy swept her hair back and began to secure it with a scrunchie, still smiling to herself.

'He's just so nice,' she said to nobody in particular.

'You like him?' Roly was clearly pleased.

'Of course I do. He's great. But why didn't you tell me he's gay?'

She looked up into the shocked silence, still knotting up her hair, her smile fading as she stared from one to the other.

'My God,' she said blankly. Crimson washed into her face. 'Oh my God.' She covered her face with her hands whilst Roly stood stiffly, his eyes blank with shock. 'I'm so sorry,' whispered Daisy. 'I can't believe you didn't know. I am so sorry.'

'I did know.' Kate was obliged to speak up at last; it wasn't fair to let Daisy bear all of the burden. 'I've known for a while.'

She glanced compassionately at Roly, and looked away again from the expression on his face.

'Did he tell you?' he asked painfully.

'No,' she answered quickly. 'No, of course not. It was Gemma, actually. After she'd met him a few times she more or less did exactly what Daisy's just done. After that I saw things more clearly and somehow the awareness evolved between us. I don't know how to explain it properly but it was as if he guessed that I knew and I somehow conveyed that it was OK. We've never talked outright about it, only obliquely. Please don't be too upset, Daisy. Perhaps I should have spoken up.'

'I can't believe that I can be so crass.' Daisy was

305

almost in tears. 'You've all been so kind to me and I just stroll in and spoil everything.'

'It's nobody's fault,' said Roly almost angrily. 'Nobody's. I might have seen it for myself if I'd really thought it through but there were smokescreens. Janna, for instance . . .'

'I've always thought that Nat and Janna are like the babes in the wood,' said Kate, 'covering each other with leaves so as to camouflage themselves from the world.'

'But why should it matter?' cried Daisy. 'Nat's a terrific guy. Who cares whether he's gay or not?'

Kate glanced at Roly: he still looked bleak.

'I agree with you, Daisy,' she said. 'But until Nat believes that nobody cares he's going to hide it. He hasn't the confidence to speak out and so he's like somebody bearing a load too heavy for him. What do you think, Roly? You agree, don't you, that having secrets can be a burden? It's better to shed them if you can.'

Watching them Daisy felt that there was some other meaning hidden in Kate's words but she remained silent, feeling that she'd said quite enough.

'That's quite true,' Roly was saying. 'Much better. But the moment for the telling has to be right. You can't force it.'

'Even so, I think that it should be soon for Nat.'

Roly turned his head to stare at Kate whilst Daisy slipped away into the garden feeling that she'd already heard more than she should. Roly moved so that he was facing Kate across the kitchen table.

'Why do you say that?'

'I think that their efforts at camouflage are

306

moving into a new stage. A dangerous one. Janna longs to be in a stable relationship, to have a baby, to be like other girls of her age. Nat knows that this is . . . wrong for them. He is intelligent enough to realize that marrying Janna and starting a family won't make him different or her more stable. On the contrary, it could be quite disastrous. At the same time it's tempting, and Janna is becoming more persuasive. Up until now they've just been very good friends but the last time I had supper with them I saw a change. I think they'd been making love and Janna had begun to believe that the dream could come true.'

'Making love? But if Nat's gay . . . ?'

'Oh, Roly.' Kate sighed with an impatience laced with sympathy as she saw the tiny hope flicker in his eyes. 'That doesn't mean that he can't perform with a woman. You know what comfort the warmth of another human body can bring. Don't be so dense. Nat's torn between making Janna happy and holding to his own principles. It's especially difficult because part of him knows that even those things—a home, marriage, a baby— wouldn't necessarily make Janna a balanced, peaceful person. She's been damaged and hurt and she fears commitment. Yet there's that doubt nagging at the back of his mind: is it worth the risk? What will happen to Janna if he refuses? And what will happen to him?'

'Oh God, poor Nat.'

'Yes, indeed. Poor Nat. He needs all the help he can get at the moment. You saw how he was with Daisy: so happy and easy. He's the same with Gemma and he used to be like that with Janna until it got complicated. You could help him, Roly.

Goodness knows, amongst all your friends in London there are plenty of gays. You have no problems about them.'

'It's different,' he said with difficulty, 'when it's your own son.'

'Of course it is.'

'And I don't know how to start. When I told you about Mim's accident it followed on naturally after something Daisy said on the telephone. You were there and it all just . . . happened.'

'Perhaps you should look at this the other way round. Perhaps it's time you told Nat the truth about the accident. After all, it had a catastrophic effect on his life, if you think about it. Doesn't he deserve an explanation?'

He looked grim. 'You mean Nat might be gay because of the way Monica and I behaved?'

'I'm not saying anything of the kind. Can't we forget about guilt and blame and just think about Nat? We love him because he's Nat. We don't want him to ruin his life and Janna's because he hasn't anyone to talk to about his problems. Whenever Janna throws a wobbly about commitment she rushes away to Teresa and her mum and all the mates down there in Plymouth. Poor old Nat just toughs it out on his own. He was managing fine until Janna got broody but now he's vulnerable. You can help him, Roly. He loves you and he knows you love him, up to a point. He needs to know you love him whatever he is. If you start by admitting your part in Mim's accident it might follow on naturally for him to be open about himself. Surely it's worth a try?'

'Yes,' he answered with some difficulty. 'Yes, of course it is.'

Daisy appeared in the doorway. She looked anxious and unhappy, all her earlier joyful happiness gone.

'Shall I take the dogs for a walk?' she suggested tentatively.

'No, we must be getting back.' Roly stretched out a hand to her. 'It's OK, Daisy. Really it is.'

'I can't say how sorry I am.'

Kate went to her and gave her a hug. 'Sometimes we need people who don't pull any punches,' she said consolingly. 'They make things happen. I think good will come out of this, I really do.'

CHAPTER FORTY

When Nat got home there were two messages waiting for him. The first was from his father.

'It was good to see you, Nat. I was hoping for a bit of a chat. Just something I wanted to talk over with you. What about coming down tomorrow for lunch? Anyway, perhaps you'll ring me?'

He raised his eyebrows, wondering what it might be about, and listened to the second message: Janna this time.

'I shan't be back tonight, Nat. 'Tis a bit late now to start checking the buses and I'm bushed after a day on the stall. I'll stay with Treesa and go and see Mum tomorrow. See you later. Love you, Nat.'

She sounded sleepy, vague, and he had the usual fear that she might be experimenting with drugs. Nevertheless his overriding feeling was one of relief. It was rather a luxury to have nobody to worry over or to feel guilty about; nobody making demands he couldn't fulfil. He decided that he couldn't be bothered to cook. He'd have a bath and then go down to the pub. He took the phone upstairs with him, turned on the taps in the bath and dialled Roly's number: engaged.

He found a clean pair of jeans and a shirt, stripped off, flung his clothes in the wicker laundry basket and climbed into the bath. It was good, very good, to relax; to allow worries and weariness to slide gently away down the waste pipe with the overflow of hot water. Images and fragments of conversation jostled behind his closed eyes: the plans for the garden in Callington, Kate's preoccupation whilst Daisy had been making them laugh with a story about dancing in *The Phantom*, and Roly's affectionate smile when he'd said, 'Nat. Great to see you.' How good it would be if he could believe that Roly knew exactly how things were: if he could believe that his father saw beyond the smokescreens and the camouflage and quite simply loved him as he was. What comfort there would be if only he could be certain that his father's love was absolutely unconditional, that it was unimportant to Roly whether or not he, Nat, fell in love, got married or had children.

Nat took the soap and squeezed it in his hands, making a lather. Maybe his father had long since guessed the truth and, like Kate, simply accepted it without making any fuss or discussion about it. He closed his eyes, taking a deep longing breath at the mere idea of such good fortune. Could it be possible? He knew that there was no hope at all of such acceptance with his mother: his stomach muscles tightened at the prospect of confronting her and his heart sank as he suddenly remembered that she was coming to see him again. How odd that she'd been so cross on hearing that Daisy was staying with Roly.

'I might spend a night or two with him,' she'd said.

Nat plunged his head under the water, sat up again, gasping, and began to wash his hair, still thinking about his mother. Why this sudden desire to stay with Roly, and why that sharp reaction when he'd mentioned Daisy? It seemed that she still looked upon Roly as her own possession: she behaved as though Roly had no right to a relationship with any other woman. She might leave him and marry another man but he must remain unattached, devoted, penitent. It wasn't as though she took exception to his casual girlfriends—she seemed to look upon them with the kind of friendly contempt a confident senior wife might show to a lesser concubine—but if one of them seemed to be making any ground with Roly then Monica became unreasonably possessive. It was an attitude that Nat had never understood.

Sophie Klein—the name came from nowhere and, with it, a little cameo. The tiny flashback showed him the morning-room in his stepfather's London house: the breakfast table, on the second or third day of the Christmas holidays, and his mother holding the newspaper.

*   *   *

'Oh, for God's sake,' she is saying distastefully, 'your father is making a fool of himself in public

311

again,' and immediately his gut churns and clenches in preparation for the scene to come.

'What's the matter?'

He tries to sound unconcerned, hoping that a show of disinterest will deflect her messy emotional demands, but he feels despair too. He's had such a good term—he's been made captain of the second fifteen and become a member of his House's rifle team—which made it possible to shelve all the problems he has to deal with at home. Now it all begins again. She flaps the paper down beside him, folded open at a photograph of Roly in evening dress with an elegant, pretty woman holding on to his arm and laughing up at him.

The caption reads: 'The photographer Roly Carradine with the model Sophie Klein at the premiere of a West End production.'

'So what?' He is deliberately cool. 'She looks quite nice.'

He is aware of his mother, tense and focused beside him, staring at the picture.

'After all,' he adds reasonably, 'it's not the first time Roly's had his pic in the paper.'

'It's certainly not the first time with her,' she answers, and the curl of her lip implies that Roly's behaviour and taste are in some way questionable. 'They're being seen everywhere together.'

'What if they are? Does it matter? You left him years ago, so why should it bother you?'

She sits down again and her face takes on a consciously gentle expression. Here is a brave, generous woman, says the look, who has been terribly hurt but continues to love.

'I still care about him, Nat. He's very susceptible

312

to a pretty face and I don't want him to be hurt by a silly chit of a girl.'

For the first time Nat is sickened by her hypocrisy. He is old enough to know that she blackens his father's character so as to win sympathy, to keep Nat on her side, and he is beginning to be unwilling to go along with it. His school life—tough, vigorous, straightforward—has made him less able to identify with her devious, complicated personality and he is not so sympathetic to her needs.

'Well then,' he says lightly, 'if you still care about him you must be pleased to see him looking so happy.'

There is a faint narrowing about the eyes as she looks across the table at him but she holds on to her temper.

'It wasn't easy to leave him, you know. I did what I thought was best for you. Your father let us down so badly, drinking, destroying our security . . .'

'You've told me before.' He simply cannot bear to hear it all over again: having to protect himself from the damage she inflicts whilst trying to hold a balanced idea of each of them in his head so he can love them both. 'Isn't it time to forget it now?'

Her look of patient suffering indicates that she can expect no more from a callow boy, yet she allows it to be clear that he has disappointed her.

'I hadn't thought that you could be quite so insensitive,' she murmurs.

'I don't think it's insensitive to want Roly to be happy. You've got Jonathan, after all. I don't see why Roly shouldn't be happy with . . .' he glances sideways again at the paper, 'with Sophie Klein.

313

She looks very nice.'

'Let's hope you continue to think so if she becomes your stepmother.'

He takes a deep breath. 'Is that likely, after all this time? Roly's always said that he'll never marry again.'

'I know I hurt him terribly.' His remark is clearly to be taken as a compliment. 'I didn't want to, you know, but I simply had no alternative. *You* were my sole concern, Nat. You mustn't imagine that I'd stopped loving your father. It wasn't easy, you know, just to walk away.'

She looks distressed and needy, and he pushes the paper aside almost violently as if subconsciously rejecting Roly and Sophie so as to be able to meet his mother's emotional requirements.

'I know it wasn't. Don't think I'm ungrateful. Look, have some more coffee.'

He gets up, talking to her, comforting her, making plans for the day ahead, in his attempt to feed her terrible emptiness.

*　　　*　　　*

The bath water was cool. Nat climbed out, seizing a towel, rubbing his hair dry. He needed a pint and something to eat but, first of all, he'd phone Roly and accept his invitation to Sunday lunch.

*　　　*　　　*

Kate sat in the evening sunshine, watching long shadows stealing across the grass and wishing vaguely that she'd kept Floss with her. She felt

314

terribly tired. The tensions of the day—Gemma first, then the cottage, and lastly Nat—all culminating in that last emotional outburst had left her without energy or will.

Earlier, standing beneath the apple trees with Daisy, she'd known quite suddenly and clearly that she would not buy the cottage. Roly was right to say that she was trying to invest it with some sense of happiness and security from the past. She'd faced the truth—that she'd been trying to airbrush David out of the picture so that she needn't face the emptiness of life without him—and, at that very moment of acknowledgement, all her panic had vanished and she'd begun dimly to see her way forward.

The first step was to resist the temptation to look back to the past for a solution to her loneliness. Before she'd gone much further than formulating that thought, another tempest had begun to break and, in her anxiety about Nat, she'd not had time to think about herself. All through tea-time she'd been aware that something was going to happen: it weighed on her spirits though she'd tried hard to disguise it.

Poor Roly. His expression when Daisy had lightly made her earth-shattering remark had been terrible to see. It was as if she'd been looking at him during an intensely private moment, seeing him naked and unprotected, and she'd had to look away quickly, pierced with pity and distress.

Kate straightened her back, leaning her head against the high stone wall behind the bench. The sparrows kept up a continuous twittering in the ivy and the scent of the climbing, tangling roses, pretty pink Albertine, lingered in the cooler air. The shadows crept closer as the sun sank, touching her foot, her knee.

She realized that she'd cherished a deep-down hope that Roly had long ago guessed that Nat, by some genetic accident or perhaps because of the emotional battering he'd suffered, was unable to connect in the normal sexual way with women. He simply wasn't interested. He had plenty of friends of both sexes but had no desire to advance these friendships. He was content to work hard, to see his friends, and remain unattached. At university he'd moved in the usual group of girls and boys, happy and casual, the perfect camouflage. More recently he'd found the cottage at Horrabridge, and Janna had become a regular visitor: another smokescreen.

Kate wondered whether Nat was, in fact, one of those people who had very little interest in the physical forms of love. He enjoyed his work, played rugby and cricket, and that was enough. Janna and he had connected in a particular way and it was sad that even this relationship should be edging into peril. It *was* perilous, she felt certain of it; to attempt to stabilize two lives at the possible expense of a third shouldn't be attempted.

She longed, suddenly and achingly, for David's company beside her on the bench, to hear his comforting—and often cynical and amusing—words of advice and to feel the solid bulk of his physical presence. This time, instead of denying it, instead of getting up and walking away from it, she continued to sit where she was, simply allowing herself to miss him. She let the tears come too, falling on her hands and into her lap: falling not only for David but also for other people she'd loved and lost, and for the failures and mistakes of the past.

The shadows had engulfed her, the birds had fallen silent, and at last she saw the real truth: that each one of us is alone. It seemed, after all, something she had always known but perhaps, now, it could be accepted without fear.

CHAPTER FORTY-ONE

From her window after Sunday lunch, Daisy could see Roly and Nat setting off with the dogs: she looked anxiously for any sign of tension between them, checking their body-language, but they seemed to be at ease with one another, rounding the dogs up, closing the gate, disappearing towards the ford. She turned back into the room, still not quite at peace with herself, longing to know how Nat had reacted to Roly's confession and remembering her own shock when he'd told her about Mim's accident.

'Don't crucify yourself,' he'd said, driving home yesterday evening. 'I think Kate's right and good will come out of all this. It has to. I must come to terms with it and somehow let Nat know that it doesn't matter.'

'How will you do that?' She'd felt heavy-hearted with guilt, huddling in the seat beside him. 'God, I'm just so *stupid*.'

'I'm the stupid one for not seeing for myself. Stop it, Daisy. If anyone should be feeling guilty it's me. It's my fault that my marriage split up. Because of my weakness Nat was exposed to a great deal of emotional blackmail. He had to try to hold the balance between Monica and me, and nobody can tell what effect that might have had on him. It's possible that, now I know, things might be easier for him. I just need to let him know that I know.'

'But how? I don't see how you can possibly begin that kind of conversation.'

'I think I shall start by telling him why Monica left me. Kate pointed out, quite rightly, that it had a catastrophic effect on his life and it might be fair to give him an explanation.'

'He doesn't know why Monica left you?'

'He knows it was because I started drinking even more heavily so that I began to lose clients but he doesn't know why. Nobody except Mim knew until a few weeks ago. Then I told Kate: it was the most wonderful catharsis.'

'That's what she meant when she talked about having secrets?'

'Yes. Having a secret is a burden and it was a huge relief to shed it after all these years. That was thanks to you.'

'To me?'

'Yes. You said much the same thing during a telephone conversation; that not being open and honest, especially with people one loves, is bad for the soul. Kate was with me at the time and quite suddenly I was able to talk about it. It didn't absolve me—it's not that simple—but it's freed me from keeping such a shameful secret of it. Now it's time that I told Nat that my carelessness, due to the fact that I'd been drinking heavily, was the cause of Mim's accident.'

There was a short shocked silence before Roly

318

recounted the scene almost exactly as he'd told it to Kate.

'I shan't tell anyone.' It was the only thing Daisy could think of to say when he'd finished. 'How awful . . . for all of you.'

'Yes. And now it's time Nat knows the truth. That's how I shall begin, by telling him the truth about the accident. I shall ask him to lunch tomorrow and take it from there.'

'I'll keep right out of the way,' Daisy promised— but Roly shook his head.

'No, don't do that. Join us for lunch but find some good reason for leaving us together afterwards. I hope he'll be able to come down; I might lose my nerve if I can't do this quickly.'

Nat had accepted the invitation and the lunch had been fun. Afterwards Daisy merely said that she'd got a few ideas she wanted to get down on paper and, back in the stable flat, she'd played *The Starlight Express* CD, recently arrived from Opus, and tried not to wonder how the conversation was going between Roly and Nat. It was a relief to see them come out together, clearly at peace with one another, but she still longed to know if Roly's objective had been achieved.

The thought of his part in Mim's accident horrified her, and she'd tried to comfort him by pointing out that Mim's international contribution to the world of theatre and dance had been far greater than if she'd simply remained a famous ballerina.

'She's inspired so many artists,' she'd said, 'and touched so many lives through them.'

'That's true,' he'd agreed. 'Perhaps you should think about that aspect of it yourself.'

319

'Oh!' She'd been disconcerted. 'But then I was never going to be a famous ballerina.'

'All the more reason, then, to think about it.'

Daisy couldn't help smiling to herself as she remembered this riposte. Roly was right, of course. She might do far more good encouraging other people's talent than trying to force herself on beyond these injuries into third-rate jobs: an offer like Mim's was a once-in-a-lifetime opportunity.

Suddenly the music swept her back into the creative world that had begun to construct itself in her mind: she saw shapes and images, characters and *enchaînements*. Who would sing the parts of the Laugher and the Organ-Grinder? Should they be dancers too, or set apart as narrators? Who would dance the roles of the children: Monkey, Jimbo and Jane Anne? She allowed herself to be drawn into the music and it seemed hours later that she heard the sound of the gate closing and Uncle Bernard barking.

She got up quickly, unable to wait a second before seeing how they looked. Nat was talking, describing something with gestures, and Roly was listening, amused. They both broke suddenly into great shouts of laughter and Daisy felt as if she might fall apart with relief. Roly glanced up towards the window, as if guessing that she'd be waiting on tenterhooks, and beckoned to her.

'Tea,' he called. 'Come and have some tea before Nat goes.'

Nat glanced up. His face was freed from that tight wariness and she knew at once that, somehow, his private burden was a secret no longer and that Roly had succeeded in his mission. Full of hope she went down the steps to meet

320

them.

*   *   *

'Did you do it? You must have done. He looks so . . . carefree.' Daisy could barely wait until Nat's car was splashing off through the ford before she asked the question. 'Gosh, I've never been so strung-up in all my life, and that's saying something.'

'I managed it.' Roly sat down on the bench and the dogs came to him, tails wagging, tongues lolling. He murmured to them mechanically, stroking them with hands that very slightly trembled. 'I told him about the accident. He was very generous.'

Daisy sat down beside him. 'He didn't blame you?'

'No. No, he seemed much more concerned with how it had affected me than how it had damaged him. He was . . .'

'Compassionate?' suggested Daisy as Roly cast about for an adequate description of Nat's reaction.

'Yes, that's a good word. Compassionate. It made it very easy for me to take the same line with him.'

'But what did you *say*? How did you let him know that you knew?'

'I cheated,' admitted Roly. 'I remembered how Kate had said that, once she knew, she allowed Nat to *see* that she knew and that a kind of complicit understanding began to exist between them. I decided not to be brutally honest but to imply that this was something I'd always suspected.'

321

'But how?'

'My confession led on to talking about Monica and her reaction, the difficulties that Nat had had to contend with always being between the two of us, and I said that it must be quite a relief to have someone like Janna who understood the truth and made no demands on him. He went rather quiet, and he coloured up, but after a moment he muttered something about him and Janna having a very particular kind of relationship that helped to cover up for him. Something like that. So I said I thought that was splendid and I only hoped that she didn't begin to think that he might be able to change. He asked me what I meant exactly and I said that, though I could well imagine the temptation it might be for both of them, it would be dishonest for him to commit himself to the role of husband and father. Not only that, but it would be wrong for him to pretend to be other than the person he is. He looked a bit shocked but I could see that he was struggling to come to terms with the fact that I actually knew the truth about him and it didn't affect the way I cared. He said that Janna was beginning to think they could make it together as a couple and that a baby would be the glue to help them stick to it. I'm afraid I *was* rather brutal at that point but it seemed to give him confidence to hear me speak out so strongly against such an idea. He mumbled something like, "I wasn't sure you knew," and I just clapped him on the shoulder and said, "It couldn't matter less to me as long as you're happy," or words to that effect, and then he did an odd thing.'

'What?' asked Daisy breathlessly into the sudden silence. 'What did he do?'

322

'He began to run. He shouted to the dogs and he ran, jumping from rock to rock and waving his arms like when he was a little boy, and the dogs jumped up at him and barked and they all went quite berserk for about five minutes. It was extraordinarily moving.'

'How utterly perfect.' Daisy let out a great breath of contentment. 'You can imagine how he felt, can't you? All that relief and happiness just *spurting* out of him. Oh God, Roly. I think I might cry.'

'Oh, no,' said Roly at once. 'None of that. I can't cope with weeping women. I'll pour you a drink. That'll do the trick.'

They got up and went inside, the dogs prancing at their heels, and Daisy watched as Roly fetched a bottle of wine.

'Wouldn't you like one too?' she asked curiously.

'Oh my God, I'd kill for one just at this moment.' His face was suddenly bleak and she put her hand to her mouth in distress at her own tactlessness. 'I daren't, you see. I daren't trust myself. It caused so much damage and it was so hard to control it once I started down that road. Don't look like that. I shall be fine with a glass of apple juice. It's just occasionally that it hits me. This was one of those moments.'

He passed the glass of wine to her, poured some juice into a tumbler and held it up as if toasting her.

'Remember what Kate said? Good *has* come out of it.' He touched his glass against hers. 'To Daisy, the fearless.'

She laughed. 'And to Nat,' she said.

323

CHAPTER FORTY-TWO

On Monday morning Kate telephoned Michael Barrett-Thompson.

'This is very embarrassing, Michael,' she began quickly, 'but I've made up my mind not to buy the cottage. When I was there yesterday I realized that it was a sentimental thing, to do with the past, and I've decided that it's not right after all.'

'I see. Well, that's fine, Kate. We only want what's best for you. Do you want to have some other details to look at?'

'Oh.' She was taken aback, having got no further than getting up her courage to tell him about the cottage. 'I don't know, to be honest.'

'It's just that these people, Mr and Mrs Burns, need to know about their offer.'

'I thought I might wait a bit, Michael. The cottage has confused me, if you see what I mean.'

'Yes, I can see that it's disorientated you, but you need to be clear about this, Kate. You've explained to me that it's not only that you think your house is too big for you now but also that you can't afford to maintain it and you need to make some money to add to your savings. That's right, isn't it? The market is very buoyant at present but I don't think it will last much beyond late summer. That's not to say there will be some kind of property crash, but if you can sell now and buy a smaller place you'll have done very well.'

A pause.

'I don't quite know what to say, Michael. The cottage was one thing, coming out of the blue with all its associations, but to find somewhere else might take quite a while.'

'True. Have you thought of renting?'

'Renting?'

'You could sell and then go into rented accommodation while you look around. That way you sell at the top of the market and can wait until you find exactly what you want when prices will certainly have levelled out, if not dropped. To be honest that would be my best advice to you just now.'

'But what would I do with my things?'

'You might find an unfurnished place. Or you could put them into store. If you downsize you'll have to get rid of some of your stuff anyway.'

'I'm sorry, Michael, I simply don't know what to say. I need time to think.'

'OK. I'll explain to the Burnses that you can't go ahead with the cottage and we'll take it from there.'

'Thanks. I'm really sorry . . .'

'Don't be silly. You can't do this kind of thing in a rush. I'll be in touch—and I'll send you some details of other properties.'

'Fine. Thanks, Michael.'

Kate put down the telephone in a state of confusion. It was a reflection of her present state of mind that she'd got no further than her decision not to buy the cottage: that effort of will seemed to have taken all her energy. Since Saturday evening, waves of terrible grief washed over her at unexpected moments. She allowed them to come, almost welcoming them, hoping that the sharp pain of loss and loneliness might be rinsed away. At the very least it might become bearable and she would learn how to deal with it without denying it. Meanwhile it was clear that she must decide on the next step. Briefly she longed for Cass to come dashing in, putting the kettle on the hotplate, sitting down at the table, full of plans and helpful words of comfort.

Tom's retirement last year, however, had made a very great difference to that easy age-old companionship. He and Cass had become great travellers: off to see old naval chums who had settled in Australia and America and Italy, trawling the Internet for cheap holidays in France, and talking of buying a little place in Tuscany. Now, it was less easy for Cass to spend time with Kate, unless Tom came too, and this increased her need to be even more self-sufficient.

Her glance fell upon a little colour-washed sketch that stood upon the dresser: a bridge over the River Dart and a group of foxgloves on the bank glowing against the sun-warmed stone. The light danced on the water, which seemed to flow and splash even as she looked at it. David had painted it and given it to Felicity Mainwaring as a present and, when Felicity died, Kate had put it there on the dresser.

'The twins will grow up and leave you. You'll be left alone . . .'

Felicity's words weren't quite true: the twins had grown up and left home but they'd brought their wives and children into a new, extended relationship and this had given Kate such great joy. Nevertheless, she knew that it was necessary to look to her own resources to solve her present problems. She filled the kettle, pushed it on to the hotplate and picked up the cup and saucer Janna had given her. Already it was special, carrying a tiny network of tender associations, and, as she poured out the coffee, Kate wondered what effect Roly's meeting with his son would have upon Nat's relationship with Janna.

Roly had telephoned on Sunday evening, jubilant with relief, and confident that Nat had been reassured. He'd talked at length, describing the whole conversation and Nat's reactions, and Kate, too, had been filled with thankfulness. It was only now, as she picked up the cup and studied its pattern, that she began to wonder how it would affect Janna. Kate could remember that evening at the cottage in Horrabridge—Janna relaxed and languorous, perhaps believing that she and Nat could be a normal happy couple—but she could also recall Nat's expression of misery and the apparent heaviness of his heart.

Her instinct assured her that there could be no lasting happiness if Janna and Nat attempted to change the rules of their relationship but she doubted Nat's ability to convince Janna that this was so. And now Monica was arriving amongst them again. Kate groaned aloud.

'What does Monica want?' she'd asked Roly curiously on the telephone last night.

'The best of both worlds,' he'd answered. 'She needs someone who will fill her life with pleasure, entertainment and love whilst demanding nothing from her in return. I disappointed her, let her down, so she chose someone who was stable, reliable and who loved her. I suspect that Jonathan has become less prepared to devote all his energy to her comfort, especially now he's writing this textbook, and she's looking around for distraction.

Nat disappoints her too. She can't brag about his job and he hasn't brought a daughter-in-law and grandchildren into the fold so, just at present, there's nobody to fill the terrible well of emptiness inside her. She's begun to think that I might now answer that need. Last time she was here she was very maudlin and sentimental, trying to rewrite the past to suit herself and to fit the present. It won't work.'

'I hope not,' Kate had answered fervently.

He'd laughed. 'Daisy will protect me.'

Kate smiled, drinking her coffee, thinking about him and Daisy and the dogs. She found that she was wishing that she had Floss for company and wondered if now was the time to make that decision at last.

The telephone rang: it was Michael.

'The Burnses have got the bit between their teeth,' he told her. 'They've raised the offer to the full asking price.'

'But you explained . . . ?'

'Oh, yes. I explained. Look, Kate, I don't want to put pressure on you, and if it weren't that you'd told me about needing some money for your pension I'd be leaving it alone, but I really think you should come in to the office right away and see if there's any other property that interests you. Surely it's worth giving it a go? If you're going to move anyway why not make every effort while this offer is on the table?'

'I suppose you're right. It's just such a big step.'

'Of course it is.' His voice was kind. 'Don't be afraid. I shan't pressure you into something that isn't right. I just want the best deal for you.'

'I know that,' she answered. 'OK. Give me

twenty minutes.'

She stood up and rinsed out the cup and saucer, wondering if she might telephone someone— Giles? Gemma? Roly?—for a quick word of advice and encouragement. Even as she contemplated it she knew that only she was able to decide her own future, only she could make this decision, and fighting a rising panic she went to get her keys.

*   *   *

She drove slowly into Tavistock, thinking about Michael's advice, wondering what she should do. The town was quiet on this early Monday morning and she was able to park the car in Policeman's Square. She crossed the road, cut through the churchyard to Church Lane and turned into West Street, still trying to make up her mind whether she should sell or stay. Michael was waiting for her and he showed her into his own office and closed the door.

'Kate,' he said, kissing her, 'this must be very difficult for you. I'm sorry if I sounded a bit unsympathetic earlier.'

'Oh, it's not you.' Kate sat down. 'I'm just being a fool. I've discovered that grieving disables you. It's rather similar to terrible depression; your mind feels paralysed and heavy so that any kind of decision-making is out of the question.'

'So why the cottage?'

'The cottage jolted me out of my apathy. I was still refusing to come to terms with losing David but the idea of buying the cottage made me believe I could bypass the whole grieving process by going back to the past and recreating a new life on the

329

basis of my memories. Once I'd been there a few times I realized that it was pure escapism. That sounds a bit confusing but I know what I mean.'

'But you're sure that the cottage couldn't still work?'

'Oh, Michael. The difficulty is that I'm not sure about anything—but, no, I don't think the cottage could work. It's odd actually, because I loved it so much when I first bought it. When I saw it was for sale all those feelings came back to me. I was convinced that living there had been one of the happiest times of my life and it could be like that again. I saw it as an answer to all my problems. It was only later that I remembered that it was whilst I was there my marriage finally broke up, my mother died and I had a disastrous love affair. I know that you don't necessarily love a place less for having suffered in it, but now I feel that in my present state having all my memories tied up in the cottage would be a negative influence. I'm sorry I made such a fuss about it.'

'Don't worry about that. I just wish we knew what the right thing is for you.'

'I have tried to be rational. I do need to add to my pension fund and the house is much too big for me. Those big, high-ceilinged rooms take a lot of heating and decoration. It's crazy to go on with it. I don't need five bedrooms. The family live near enough not to need to stay, except the grandchildren on occasional visits in the holidays, and I hope I can still find a place with enough room for that . . .'

'So does that mean we sell?'

She stared at him: tears suddenly rose in her eyes and she blinked, frowning angrily.

330

'Yes,' she said. 'Dammit. Yes. There, I've made the decision. Don't let me go back on it.'

Michael got up and opened the door; whilst she scraped at her cheeks with a tissue she could hear him asking his assistant for some coffee. He paused by her chair and she felt his hand on her shoulder.

'It's stupid,' she said, not looking at him. 'Now I've let go I can't stop myself. Anything can set me off: music, his paintings, his old coat hanging in the hall. It's embarrassing.'

'It's time, Kate; I think we all agree about that. Look, I've found a few cottages that might suit you. Just glance at them while we have some coffee and if any take your fancy I can drive you out to view them. If not we'll consider the renting option. The only ones we have are flats or modern houses in the town, which don't seem right for you at all, but we can go into that later if you decide not to buy.'

She took the sheaf of papers and stared at the photographs. There was a strange sense of unreality about the whole business but she tried to concentrate.

'The other disadvantage about the cottage,' Michael was saying, 'is that you'd have made very little money on the way through and you'd have wanted to do certain things to it. Maybe we can do better.'

She smiled at him, deliberately being cheerful, trying to will herself to enthusiasm.

'I'm sure we will. This place at Mary Tavy looks interesting.'

Coffee arrived and they drank it while compiling a short list of possibilities. Michael made a few

331

phone calls and two viewings were arranged for the afternoon.

'I'll come and collect you, shall I? We'll go together and then we can talk them through afterwards.'

She smiled at him, wondering why kindness was suddenly so unbearable, agreeing with everything. After all, nothing mattered much now she'd made the decision.

'By the way, Harriet said to say that you can always stay with us. You know, if you decide to sell but can't find anything at once. She said that with Cass so close you probably wouldn't need it but the offer's there. Just so you don't feel . . . worried.'

'Thanks.' She got up, turning away from him, pretending to be busy putting the papers into her bag. 'That's so sweet. Thank her for me, won't you? And you'll pick me up later. Half-past two? See you then. Thanks, Michael.'

She managed to get out of the office and into the street without breaking down and, as she took the path through the churchyard, she suddenly turned aside and went into the church. Someone was playing the organ, Brahms's chorale prelude *Es ist ein Ros'entsprungen*, and she took a seat at the back and listened with delight.

Here, at the end of each term, she'd sat with the twins amongst the other parents with their small boys, the church filled with an almost tangible atmosphere of excitement: expectation of the holidays ahead and the knowledge of tuck boxes and overnight cases waiting, packed and ready up at the school, to be collected after the service.

The music, interwoven with the memory, touched her heart and she remembered something she'd read earlier that morning in Dame Julian's *Showings*: 'I saw and I understood that our faith is our light in the darkness, and this light is God, our endless day.'

The music, infused with a calm, radiant joy at the coming of the Saviour, filled her with a strange, trembling happiness, and it was some while after the organist had packed up his music and disappeared that she picked up her own belongings and went out into the sunshine.

CHAPTER FORTY-THREE

Daisy took the Angelica Kauffmann postcard of Henrietta Laura Pulteney down from the shelf and stared at it. She turned it over and read the words Paul had written: 'I bought this especially for you.' His handwriting and the message no longer had the power to move her so painfully: she could look at it with little more than an aching sadness. She saw now that she'd never stood a chance with him. His heart had always belonged to his family, which is why he'd been so invulnerable, so cool, so much in charge of his relationship with her. He'd behaved selfishly in trying to hedge his bets. Trying to remember it truthfully, she guessed that he'd genuinely valued her as a friend and had convinced himself that it was possible to have the best of both worlds. After all, she reminded herself, he'd never gone beyond an affectionate friendliness and perhaps, with his own heart so safely guarded, he'd been unable to imagine that hers might be so vulnerable.

Daisy put the card back in its place, smiling wryly at this reluctance to think ill of him—or perhaps it was simply that she wanted to preserve a good opinion of her own judgement. Either way, it was a relief to wake up each morning without the twisting grind of misery in her gut and a sense of desperation at the prospect of the day ahead. Now, her work stretched and grew to fill every horizon; new ideas about the characters jostled with plans for dance routines and costumes. Gradually her memories of Paul were being squeezed out by the excitement of this wonderful project and she was ready to let them go without too much regret.

She liked to keep the card, though. It was a reminder of happy times, of the Nureyev exhibition and the trip on the river, of visits to cafés and to the theatre, of Henrietta Street and of Bath itself. The other postcard of Salcombe, with its connotations of deceit, she'd thrown away. As soon as she'd seen his children—Tom and the baby—she'd understood Paul's determination to hold his family together if he could. She remembered how Tom had shown her the football fashioned on the bottom of his shoe and how she'd held his small smooth leg between her hands and looked into his eyes: Paul's eyes.

Daisy deliberately closed her mind to the thought of the little scene—the baby so confident in her father's arms, the family group—and concentrated instead on her own new extended family: the stage school. Thinking of little Tom made her wonder who would be chosen for the part of Jimbo; which little girl would dance the role of Monkey and what about the older girl, Jane Anne? Was it possible that she and Cousin Henry might fall in love? Already Daisy could see the beginnings of a *pas de deux*. It was clear from the CD's sleeve that, in the play, Cousin Henry had been the same generation as the children's parents but Daisy could see no reason why this shouldn't be adapted to fit with her ideas for the ballet.

Then there were the parts of the sprites—the Dustman who carried the stardust, the Sweep who swept clean the hearts and minds of the wumbled humans so as to make way for it, the Lamplighter who touched people alive to the starlight of compassion and the Gardener who planted seeds of love and laughter, hope and courage. She'd decided that the role of the Gardener should be danced by a girl and that the Haystack Woman, who was the mother of all the sprites, should be a comic figure: large and cheerful and ungainly, rather in the tradition of the pantomime dame. She couldn't help but be influenced by those brilliant creations of Frederick Ashton: the Ugly Sisters from *Cinderella* and the Widow from *La Fille mal gardée*. Then there was the dance of the Little Night Winds who had to blow the Haystack Woman out of bed, whirling her canvas skirts over her head and driving her into the Star Cave where everyone had to go if they wished to accomplish anything useful. The music was already giving her plenty of ideas for the ballet of the four Little Night Winds.

It was the practice to invite one or two famous ex-students to perform at the Charity Matinée—it added a special excitement—and Daisy had begun to wonder whether to suggest to Mim that the roles of Mummy and Daddy should be danced by two well-known performers. Much more difficult

335

to cast, however, were the demanding singing roles of the Organ-Grinder and the Laugher: Daisy knew that even the oldest, most accomplished students would have difficulties with these.

Longing to see Mim and talk it through with her, all thoughts of Paul forgotten, Daisy went to the table where her notebooks lay and switched on the CD.

*   *   *

Roly, grooming Bevis in the yard, smiled to hear the music. Daisy was immersing herself in *The Starlight Express*. In fact she was listening to as much of Elgar's music as he, Roly, could find in his library: the *Cockaigne Overture*, the Cello Concerto, and the two Symphonies Elgar finished as well as some of the Oratorios. She already loved the *Sea Pictures* and was reading extensively on the subject of Frederick Ashton's ballet choreographed to the score of the *Enigma Variations*. It was clear to Roly that whilst Daisy's heart was mending her creative spirit was flowering.

Bevis whined a little, he hated having the tangled hair behind his ears teased out, but Roly was unmoved. He talked soothingly but firmly whilst Floss rolled a sympathetic eye, anxiously waiting her turn, and Uncle Bernard grunted contemptuously.

'It's all right for you,' said Roly in defence of Bevis. 'You don't have all this long fine hair to worry about.'

Uncle Bernard barked once or twice—he always had the last word—then yawned and turned his back on them, curling into a ball beside the wall in the sunshine. Roly picked up the scissors to clip out a particularly knotty piece of furze, combing the hair free and smooth of tangles, and all the while he was thinking about Nat. He was remembering how he'd run and jumped, calling to the dogs, his relief exploding in wild energy and his face unclamped from its habitual expression of wariness. His happiness had filled Roly with a generosity of spirit—a kind of magnanimity of purpose in response to such joy—that had made it easy to accept this new truth about his son and it was only much later, when Nat had gone, that misgivings and anxiety returned.

At one point he even wondered if a talk with Bruno might clear his mind and the sudden realization that he didn't want to tell Bruno about Nat shocked him almost as much as Daisy's revelation.

'I don't know how to deal with it,' he admitted to Daisy. 'I thought I did, I was fine when Nat was here, but afterwards I felt all the shock of it all over again.'

'Well, it is a shock,' she answered reasonably, 'and you need time to come to terms with it. That's OK. The important thing is that Nat knows you know and that it hasn't stopped you loving him. Take your time.'

'The odd thing is that I wonder now if some part of me *had* accepted it because I could never imagine Nat married, with a family. I always thought that he'd be better off on his own. I never analysed it but the thought was there. He's very self-sufficient, though he's got lots of friends.' He hesitated, almost fearing to ask the question that

337

had been nagging at him. 'How did you know?'

'It's difficult to put it into words. In my work, in the theatre world, I meet lots of gays. Some are in your face but with others there's nothing you'd notice except that there's none of the magnetism that usually exists between the sexes. Nat's like the second sort. It's as if something's been left out and you know that there's no point doing the flirty, female bit. I can't quite explain it but I always pick up on it quite quickly. I wouldn't be surprised if Nat isn't much interested in men, either, but he probably feels more comfortable in their company. I had the feeling that he's very wary of women, they have expectations he might not be able to fulfil, but I'd guess that most people wouldn't suspect anything at all. They'd put him down as the strong silent type who isn't into personal relationships.'

Roly felt relieved but, at the same time, he felt ashamed that he felt relieved. He wanted not to mind, not to care if people knew the truth, but he couldn't accept the situation quite so fully yet. He needed more time to adjust.

Giving Bevis a biscuit as a reward he called to Floss, who flattened her ears but advanced cautiously.

'Good girl,' he said encouragingly, picking up the brush again.

He was thinking about Kate now. On Sunday, before Daisy dropped her bombshell, he'd been certain that Kate was nearly ready to commit herself to Floss. Brushing her silky coat, Roly knew that he would miss her but deep down he was certain that Kate and Floss belonged together. Whilst Flynn had been with them she'd been anxious and unsettled and, though she might grow used to a procession of dogs passing through, she'd be happier with someone like Kate.

He'd phoned her later on Sunday, to tell her how it had been with Nat, and afterwards they'd talked about the cottage.

'I've made up my mind not to go ahead with it,' she'd told him. 'It was all rather foolish and romantic and I'm grateful that you made things clear for me. No, honestly, you were absolutely right. I can't go on pretending that the last fifteen years never happened. I shall phone Michael in the morning and tell him that it's off. Never mind about me. I'm much more interested in you and Nat.'

She'd telephoned in the middle of the week to say that she was looking at other properties, and that Monica was spending the weekend with Nat, but she sounded preoccupied and Roly had asked her to come to Sunday lunch. Mim would be home, he told her, and would love to see her. Now, he began to wonder if Monica might invite herself down again, and how Nat was managing, and found he was back full circle: thinking about Nat.

As he gave Floss a biscuit and collected up the grooming equipment, Daisy appeared on the stable steps carrying a tray.

'I've made some tea,' she said. 'I thought we both might need it after all our hard work. The dogs look so beautiful, don't they? Shall we sit out here in the sun? My head is reeling with ideas and if I don't stop thinking I shall go quite mad.'

'Your timing is perfect,' he said gratefully. 'We need distraction. Tell me one of your theatre stories while we drink our tea and then we'll drive the dogs down to Rock for a walk on the beach.'

CHAPTER FORTY-FOUR

Kate was ironing when Gemma telephoned. She'd
been reflecting on the process of grieving—how it
would strike so suddenly and violently but without
any apparent relevance, in Boots, buying face
cream, say, or whilst cleaning one's teeth—and at
other times it morphed into a flat, quiet
desperation that made every action such an effort.
Even lifting the iron seemed to require
superhuman strength. It was a welcome respite to
speak to Gemma. She'd already sent text
messages, first of all to report that she and Guy
were having very amicable and positive discussions
and, later, to say that Guy had begun to talk about
moving house; to suggest that a new start might be
the next best step forward.

Today, as soon as Gemma spoke, Kate could
hear that her voice held a kind of suppressed
excitement and was immediately alerted to the fact
that something new had happened.

'I know Guy will want to talk to you,' Gemma
said, 'but I thought I'd just . . . well, give you a bit
of warning. This plan he's got. He might not be
particularly tactful about it.'

'You're beginning to frighten me,' said Kate.
'What's happened? Do I gather that this move is
going to be a bit further afield than Dartmouth or
Fowey?'

'Just a bit.' Gemma sounded nervous now. 'The
truth is, Kate, that he's talking of us going to

Canada.'

Kate put a hand to her heart, as if she'd received a physical blow, and Gemma raised her voice as if she feared by the sudden silence that Kate could no longer hear her.

'Are you there, Kate? I'm sorry to be the one to break the news but there's simply no way of wrapping it up. Guy's been thinking of it for a little while, apparently, but didn't think I'd like the idea. Now he says that it will be a new start for us all and I don't think I can afford to argue with him. To be honest, now I'm getting used to it, I'm quite excited. Oh God, that sounds so heartless, doesn't it, and we shall miss you so much but it's a wonderful opportunity.'

'I'm sure it is.' Kate found her voice at last but she could hear that it sounded dull and flat. Canada seemed such a long way off. 'Is this something to do with Mark, by any chance?'

'Well, it is.' Gemma was clearly unhappy about explaining. 'You know that when he left the Navy he emigrated to Canada and joined a friend's boat-building business? Well, recently he's been suggesting that Guy should come out and take over the brokerage side. Mark wants to retire and he thinks it would be a very good opportunity for Guy. I'm not very clear on all the technical bits but it's much the same as Guy is doing here except that they actually build some of the boats they sell. It's a family-run boat-yard, rather fun by the sound of it, and Guy could actually incorporate his own business into it. We'd be living on Prince Edward Island.'

There was another silence whilst Kate struggled to control her feelings and Gemma searched about

341

for words. Kate got there first.

'I can't pretend to be thrilled that you're all going so far away, Gemma,' she said. 'You must know that this is a huge shock but if it's right for you and Guy and the twins'—oh, the thought of not seeing the twins!—'I'm very pleased for you. Of course I am.'

'This is bloody awful.' Gemma sounded exactly like Cass. 'I can imagine what you're feeling, I'm not so selfish that I can't tell that you're gutted, but Guy seems very set on it and I don't feel that I'm in such a strong position to fight it.'

Briefly Kate was overwhelmed with anger: if Gemma had behaved herself none of this might be happening. How could she bear for them to go so far away? She tried to calm her fast-beating heart and to maintain a sense of balance.

'The fact that it's all bound up with Mark doesn't help, does it?' Gemma was saying. 'This is why I wanted to speak to you first. I hoped to be able to come over but Guy really has the bit between his teeth and I was afraid that he might just phone up and tell you without thinking. He can be a bit single-minded and then he's not aware of the effect he's having on other people. It'll take ages to get organized, of course, but I thought you should be warned.'

'Do the twins know yet?'

'I'm afraid they do. Not that it's definite but that there's a possibility. Ben is very excited but Jules is more cautious about it.'

Yes, thought Kate. Jules would be. He'd be anxious about making new friends, going to a new school. Jules would miss his trips over the moor to see his grandparents . . .

'I suppose you haven't managed to be in touch with Cass?'

'No. It's not the sort of thing to bounce on her while she's away. But we'll come back to see you all and I know that she and Pa will come and visit us. And you too, of course. You'll all come over together. It'll be fun.'

'Of course.' Kate had no choice but to respond to Gemma's pleading. 'Of course we will. Look, I must go. I've left the iron switched on upstairs . . .'

'I'm sorry, Kate, I really am.'

'You mustn't be, my darling. If it's right for you all then it's wonderful. Let me know how things go. Give the twins a hug.'

She stumbled upstairs, crossed the landing and found herself standing in the doorway of the playroom. A memory jogged her mind. Once, years ago at the cottage, on the boys' first day at boarding school, she'd stood like this, looking at their tidy bedroom, at the toys placed neatly on the beds. Back then she'd felt a similar sense of emptiness and fear, of apprehension for her children going away from home for the first time. This time, however, she was conscious of some other emotion: an awareness of some source of strength that she might call upon if only she knew how to begin. Confused and anxious, she strove for some kind of understanding but it eluded her.

Closing the door she went into the laundry room and stared around her: it was impossible to stand calmly ironing with all these thoughts and fears jumbling in her mind. She switched off the iron and went downstairs, wondering what she should do next. Her instinct was to speak to Giles—how comforting it would be to hear his voice just at this

343

moment—but he might not have heard the news and, anyway, he would almost certainly be working. There was no answer from Roly's telephone—no doubt he was out with the dogs—and, once again, Kate longed for Cass to come dashing in to share the moment. After all, Cass and Tom would be just as gutted as she was to hear that Gemma and Guy and the twins were going so far away.

The usual answer to these moments of crisis was to go for a walk. Grieving was one thing, she reminded herself firmly, but self-pity was another and should be resisted. The moor, vast and unchanging, mysterious and magical, had never failed to bring a measure of comfort and peace, yet she longed for the company of a friend, someone who knew her and understood her, who loved her. She thought at once of the General, to whom she'd carried so many difficulties and fears, and wondered where he'd found his own particular brand of courage and wisdom.

She knew the answer, of course, and he'd left her his own source of comfort if only she would use it. The book opened easily at the well-read pages and her eyes jumped across the lines whilst she prayed for some kind of guidance and understanding.

No soul can have rest until it finds that created things are empty. When the soul gives up all for love, so that it can have Him that is all, then it finds true rest.

She let the tears come—'The whole point about grieving,' Roly had said, 'is that you mustn't resist it. Don't feel guilty, welcome it, tell yourself that it's OK to be doing this just now'—and she wondered, after all, how many people she was actually grieving for. She seemed to be letting go so much of her past along with her tears for David. When the telephone rang she blew her nose and scrubbed at her cheeks before answering it.

'Mum,' said Giles, 'I've just had a call from Gemma. I was wondering whether you'd like me to come over. Or would you rather come here? Tessa says whichever is best for you.'

'Oh, darling.' She could barely speak. 'That would be so . . . nice. Are you sure?'

'Quite sure. By the sounds of it I think I'd better come to you. I'll be over as soon as I can. Are you OK?'

'Yes. Yes, of course I am. It's just a bit of a shock.'

'That's one way of putting it. Henry wants a word. Can you manage or do you need an interpreter?'

'We manage very nicely. We just shout at one another and it works splendidly. Thanks, Giles. I can't tell you how grateful I am.'

'Not a problem. See you soon. Ready, Henry? Say hello to Grannie.'

*   *   *

The following morning, driving home from Tavistock, Kate found that some instinct took her through Whitchurch and on towards Horrabridge. She was still reliving Giles's visit, grateful for his understanding and insight.

'After all,' he'd said, 'it's not just that Guy's

345

decided to go out to Canada, is it? It's that he's going out to Dad. It's damaging to see it in terms of disloyalty but it's difficult to separate the emotions sometimes, isn't it?'

'I don't really mind,' she'd answered carefully. 'Much better that a relationship flowers late than it never flowers. Guy and Mark have always kept in touch and are very alike. My problem is seeing myself visiting them and meeting Mark again. How would that work?' She'd shaken her head. 'I don't suppose Guy has even given it a thought.'

Now, as she slowed down at the end of Nat's lane, she saw the flicker of scarlet and blue outside the cottage door, and she turned the car in and drove carefully past the row of cottages. Janna was tending to the pots of flowers and her face lit with pleasure when she saw Kate.

'Nat's off at work,' she said. 'Park over by the garage and come and have some coffee.'

'I just took a chance.' Kate stepped out of the car. 'I've been wondering how you are every time I use my lovely cup and saucer.'

It was easy to see how Janna was simply by looking at her. There were dark rings under her eyes, and her skin was like old parchment, papery and discoloured. The lion's-mane hair was dry and lifeless and even the pretty blue and scarlet cotton dress couldn't disguise the sharp birdlike quality of her bones.

' 'Tis good to be here,' Janna said as they sat together on a beanbag at the open door. 'I love the quiet and the smell of the lavender. 'Tis a little safe sort of haven.'

'I can believe that.' Kate stood her mug on the cobbles and ran her fingers through the lavender

346

flowers. 'Heavenly. But don't you get tired of the peace and quiet after a while? Feel the need to be on the move again?'

Janna folded her arms and let her head fall forward so that her chin rested on her chest. Her profile was etched sharp and brittle against the dark green leaves of the rosemary bush, and her face was sad.

'I do get like that,' she admitted. 'I don't want to but I can't seem to help it. That's why I wondered . . .'

'Wondered what?'

'Whether it would be different if I had ties. Something to hold me in one place. I'd begun to think we could make it work, Nat and me, but it's changed. *He's* changed,' she corrected herself. 'He's never really been happy about the idea of us living together as a couple and having a baby but I thought he was weakening.' She glanced at Kate, a quick sideways flick of the eyes. 'You didn't think it would work, did you?'

'No,' said Kate after a moment. 'No, I didn't think it would work. It's too big a risk, Janna, for both of you and especially for the baby. You're such good friends, you and Nat. Isn't that enough?'

'I could tell that night you came round to supper and told us about the cottage. You guessed, didn't you, that Nat and I had made love? You didn't say nothing but I could feel that you weren't happy about it.'

'Yes, I guessed. But Nat wasn't happy either, even then, was he? He didn't feel right with himself.'

Janna shook her head. 'He said he wasn't being honest about himself but even so I think he wasn't really sure it wouldn't work, not, like, real deep down. I still thought I could persuade him, I really did. But when I came back this time he told me he'd made up his mind. 'Twas all to do with Roly. Nat said that he's known the truth all along and I think 'twas realizing that Roly knew and it hadn't made any difference to the way he feels that made up Nat's mind. 'Tis silly really. He'd make a lovely dad.'

'But would he? Supposing he began to believe that he was living a lie and became resentful? Suppose that even after the baby you still wanted to go travelling? To do the markets with Teresa and go on having your spliffs or dope or whatever you call it these days?' Kate smiled at Janna's expression. 'Come off it, Janna. I'm not stupid. A baby should be a real commitment, something you both want more than anything in the world. It's not like buying a bottle of glue in the hope it'll keep you stuck together during difficult times. Good grief, there are enough hazards in the ordinary course of a relationship. Don't you think that Nat has the right of it?'

'Perhaps. 'Twas just that I could see myself. You know? Living here with Nat and being like everyone else.'

'Who wants to be like everyone else? What does that mean? It's an illusion. You and Nat have an amazing relationship. Why mess it up because of some biological urge? You love Nat, I know that, but are you *in love* with him?'

'I dunno. What's the difference?'

'Of loving and being in love? Oh, all the difference in the world. It's the difference between madness and peace. Between ecstasy and

348

contentment. If you have to ask you've never been in love.'

Janna laughed: she seemed faintly embarrassed. 'Maybe I haven't then.'

'Well, wait until you are and then think about babies. Meanwhile, enjoy what you have with Nat without complicating it. Sorry, Janna. I didn't come this morning to give you a lecture. After all, what do I know? I'm an interfering old bat and you've been very patient.'

' 'Tisn't interfering; 'tis caring. So what's happening about your cottage?'

'Ah!' Kate leaned her head back against the door jamb and closed her eyes. 'How long have you got?'

Janna grinned. 'As long as it takes. We can go up the pub for lunch. Come on, it's your turn now. What's been going on?'

CHAPTER FORTY-FIVE

Monica arrived in Horrabridge late on Friday morning. The top half of the stable door was open but nobody was around. She frowned at Janna's carelessness and went inside, looking about as usual, noticing the symbols of Janna's presence: the shawl on the chair, a small vase filled with wild flowers, a magazine on the table. She experienced the familiar twinge of irritation, suspecting that Janna didn't pull her weight financially and that Nat was being manipulated. She knew only too well how susceptible Nat could be to certain forms of feminine influence.

On the landing she paused, puzzled. The door to the small bedroom stood open and she could see that the bedclothes were rumpled and thrown back: Janna's tote bag stood beneath the window and her clothes were flung over the chair. Before she could check out the double bedroom she heard footsteps in the room below and then Janna was hurrying up the stairs. Monica saw the pale wedge of her face upturned towards her, noted the anxious expression and saw how her breast heaved.

'I didn't expect you just yet,' she said breathlessly, almost propitiatingly. 'Nat said you were coming some time late this afternoon. I was a couple of doors up with a friend, not far away.'

'I should hope not.' Monica didn't move. 'Not with the door left wide open. Anyone could have walked in.'

'We'd have seen anyone coming down the lane. We saw your car.'

Janna climbed the last few steps and looked beyond Monica into the bedroom.

'I'm just about to do the room. Shouldn't take very long. Shall I make you some coffee and you can sit and drink it while I'm getting the room ready?'

Monica watched her. She was aware that Janna was uneasy, that she was frightened of something, but she couldn't quite decide what it might be or how to approach the problem. However, it seemed important to hold this advantage she had somehow acquired and to use it carefully.

'I didn't know you used this room,' she said pleasantly.

Janna's eyes flicked away from Monica's steady gaze and she smiled anxiously. 'Just now and again.

Sometimes 'tis better like that, if you see what I mean.'

'I'm not sure that I do.' Monica laughed a little: inviting confidences. 'Have you two had a row?'

'Something like that.' Gratefully Janna seized the excuse held out to her. 'Nothing serious. Look, if you let me past I'll start clearing up.'

'I'm beginning to feel that I shall be in the way. I don't want to force you and Nat upon each other if you've fallen out.'

'Oh, 'tisn't that bad. Just a silly quarrel. Please . . .'

The girl's distress was palpable but Monica had no intention of backing down. She could sense something was seriously amiss here and she intended to pursue it.

'Perhaps I'd better have a word with Nat. He could sleep on the sofa and I'll have his room.'

'Please don't tell him. He'd be angry to think you didn't feel welcome. It's my own fault. I promised that I'd move my things out and get the room done. He's always the same when you're coming but this time I thought . . .'

'This time?'

'I usually make sure my stuff's cleared out and the sheets are changed for you the night before . . .'

Monica watched coolly as hot colour washed over the pale skin in a crimson tide. Janna bit her lips, trying to find a way back; her mind doubled and turned, thinking over what she'd said. The prospect of Nat's anger if his secret were to be guessed at by his mother made Janna even more nervous and clumsy.

'You know how 'tis. It's such a tiny cottage I

often keep my stuff in there.'

'And sleep in there too?'

'No. No, only sometimes. You know what it's like . . .'

'No, I don't know what it's like. It looks to me as if you do all the taking and Nat does all the giving. You use the place like a hotel, coming and going when it suits you or when Treesa'—she made the name a spiteful little sound—'clicks her fingers. You sit about, making no contribution whatever . . .'

'No!' cried Janna. ''Tisn't like that at all between me and Nat.'

'You aren't mature enough to know how to conduct a relationship.' Monica raised her voice above Janna's protests. 'I suppose he's in love with you, though God knows why, and you use him to suit yourself—'

'What the *hell* is going on?'

Nat's voice had the effect of a bucket of icy water. Monica fell silent and Janna began silently to weep. She turned her head away, trying to control herself, whilst Monica pushed past her and went down the stairs.

'Janna was explaining to me why my room isn't ready,' she said, very light, very brittle, her eyes bright with anger. 'And I was telling her what I think about it.'

'No, 'twasn't like that.' Janna descended with a rush. 'I haven't said nothing, Nat. Only that I was sleeping there for a night or two . . .' She pressed her lips tightly together, her face crimson with mortification. 'I was trying to explain.'

'She was trying to explain why she uses you the way she does.' Monica still felt in control, delighted at last to have been given this opportunity to make her feelings clear. 'I told her that I would hate to put her out. If she doesn't want to share your room then I'll use it. I'm sure you could cope with the sofa, Nat.'

'You don't have it quite right, Mother.' He stretched out an arm and pulled Janna to him, holding her close to his side. 'It is I who refuse to share a room with Janna. She's my very good friend and I love her dearly but I don't enjoy making love to women. There's no reason why you should know that I'm gay, Janna's allowed me to use her as a smokescreen for long enough, but I think that it's time the truth was told.'

Monica had put both hands to her mouth. She continued to stare at him with wide, horrified eyes whilst Janna sobbed silently with her face hidden in Nat's arm.

'I'm sorry.' He spoke more gently now. 'It's a shock, isn't it? But there's no way to break it more kindly.'

'A shock? It's disgusting.' Even the words seemed bitter to the taste and her mouth twisted as she spat them out as if she couldn't bear them on her tongue. 'Horrible.'

Janna broke free from Nat's hold and fled up the stairs; she reappeared in moments, clutching her tote bag, the tears still shooting from her eyes.

'I'll go,' she said. 'I'll go, Nat. I'm so sorry . . .'

She ran out of the door, tripping and stumbling on the cobbles, but Nat followed her, catching her before she'd reached the end of the lane.

'Don't go, Janna,' he said, holding her by both arms. 'Please don't go. Not now.'

' 'Twas all my fault,' she said. 'If I'd done the

bedroom first thing, like you said—'

'It was time,' he said. He shook her gently. 'Stop crying. It was the right time. Please come back with me.'

'I can't bear to hear her say those things, Nat.'

'We have to bear it. Come on.'

Monica was sitting at the table, her hands clasped in front of her. She stared at them as they came in.

'I'm waiting to hear what you have to say.' Her face was strangely altered: a mixture of shame and disgust made her mouth ugly but her eyes were fearful and shocked. 'I refuse to accept that you are one of *those*. A queer.' The word was a sneer. 'What have you to say?'

'I have to say this: the bedroom upstairs is Janna's room, not yours. This is her home. We may not have a conventional relationship but we value it. I suggest you find somewhere else to spend the night.'

Monica got to her feet, holding on to the table for support, but her expression rejected any help or compassion.

'I shall be glad to go.'

She picked up her overnight case and pushed past them, holding herself away slightly as if any contact might contaminate her. Nat stood quite still, his face white and strained, and Janna, looking at him anxiously, put her arms around him and held him tightly. They waited, close together, listening as Monica reversed her car up the lane and drove away.

CHAPTER FORTY-SIX

'I simply didn't know where else to turn,' said Monica, following Kate into the kitchen. 'He more or less threw me out.' She made a disbelieving sound. 'Of course, I was shocked and outspoken but, after all, what did he expect? Congratulations?'

Kate looked at the self-pitying face and realized that Monica, unlike Roly, only saw the situation as it related to her. It was clear that as far as Monica was concerned Nat was giving way to some kind of deliberate perversity simply so as to add to her burdens: how he felt or suffered was not important to her.

'Perhaps he hoped for understanding,' Kate suggested. 'After all, I imagine none of us chooses to be different from the herd and it can't be easy, even in this enlightened age, to come to terms with it.'

'Understanding!' Monica's lips curved in contempt. 'He knows very well how I feel about those kinds of people.'

'But this is Nat.' Kate sat down opposite. 'Not "those kinds of people". He's your son.'

She was seized with a great weariness: Monica's arrival was the last straw and Kate felt that her back might break beneath the weight of her emotional demands.

Monica looked at her, frowning. 'You don't seem terribly surprised,' she said slowly. 'Did you know he was queer?'

'Yes, I knew.' Kate struggled with a surge of great dislike. She found Monica's self-righteous

355

prejudice far more difficult to accept than the fact that Nat was gay. 'He didn't tell me but . . . I knew.'

'How did you know?' Monica's face was sharp-eyed and pointy-nosed: ferrety with fear. How many others, she was asking herself, how many of my friends know? 'How can you tell? He doesn't look like one.'

'If you mean he doesn't dress like Elton John, I agree. My daughter-in-law wondered about it. She's a very pretty girl who likes to flirt and after she'd met Nat a few times, and he didn't respond, she asked me if he was gay. It made me think about it. Look, would you like some lunch or something?'

'I couldn't eat anything. I feel quite sick. I think I might go down to Roly. I can't believe what he'll say when I tell him.'

Kate watched with distaste as Monica's expression changed to one of introspection, even to satisfied expectation, as she contemplated the possibilities of the situation that might force a more intimate connection between her and Roly.

'Mim's home for the weekend. And they've got Daisy staying. Anyway,' Kate simply couldn't prevent herself, 'I think you'll find that Roly already knows.'

'No.' Monica shook her head. 'No way. He'd have said something to me.'

'Are you sure? Knowing how you feel on the subject?'

'Anyway, how would you know he knows? Have you discussed it with him?'

Kate was silent for a moment, seeing the pitfalls: Nat's new confidence was built on his belief that Roly had known for a long time and nothing must shake that belief.

'Not in that way. It's just something that we've come to accept without finding it necessary to pick it to pieces. We love Nat and we want him to be happy. It's very simple really.'

'Roly *knows* and he never told me?'

'Well, now that you do know, and seeing how you've reacted to it, can you blame him?'

'And you. You knew and never hinted at it. That evening I came to supper and we talked about all those things . . .'

'But none of those things was to do with Nat. We talked about you and Roly. And we talked about Jonathan . . . and how you hated him.'

Monica's eyes grew dark and wide, her expression a mixture of anger and accusation. She stared fixedly at Kate, who felt that she was being willed into some kind of propitiatory response. The terrible needy emptiness behind the almost hypnotic stare demanded some kind of reaction that Kate was reluctant to give. She looked away, glanced at the kitchen clock and resorted to domestic platitude.

'Are you sure I can't get you something to eat?'

'Quite sure. I think the best thing I can do is to go home.'

'Home? But won't you try to see Nat again? I know he said hurtful things but try to imagine what he must be feeling. Don't do something you might regret. You could stay the night here and in the morning you might feel a little differently.' With great effort Kate called up a measure of sympathy. 'It's a great shock. I can see that it will need a lot of getting used to and a great deal of understanding on your part but don't go away in

357

anger.' She reached across the table to touch Monica's hands. 'Come on, Monica. This is Nat we're taking about.'

Monica shook her head, drawing back her hands; her martyred smile indicated that Kate had no idea either of the enormity of the favour she was asking or how much Monica was suffering.

'I'm beginning to remember why I was forced to flee to Jonathan in the first place,' she said bitterly. 'He was decent and kind and straightforward. It's clear that Roly's unreliability and weakness has manifested itself in different ways in his son.'

The telephone bell made them both jump. Kate got up to answer it whilst Monica reached for her bag.

'Hello, Nat,' said Kate. 'Are you OK? . . . Yes, Monica did come here. She's . . . fine. Hang on a moment.'

She held the instrument out to Monica with a look of hopeful entreaty. Monica gave a little sneering smile and turned her back. She went out and climbed into her car. Kate stood for a moment in silence, biting her lips. Presently she put the receiver to her ear.

'Sorry, Nat. You missed her by seconds. She's going back to London but I'm sure she'll be fine. More to the point, how are you and Janna? . . . Yes, of course I can come over. I'll be ten minutes.'

She grabbed her keys and ran out to the car. Afterwards she could never recall a single moment of the drive to Horrabridge.

Nat met her at the door of the cottage.

'I have to get back to work,' he said anxiously. 'The trouble is I don't like to leave Janna. She's in such a state. I'm sorry, Kate.'

'Don't be a twit,' she said cheerfully. 'Janna and I will be fine.'

'Was Mum very upset?'

She stared at his pale defenceless face, the troubled eyes, and savagely wished retribution on Monica.

'She's being typically Monica,' she answered. 'You have to accept that Monica is totally self-centred, Nat. Nothing in life matters except as to how much it affects her. She can't see people or their difficulties in any other light. She'll come round in time and, meanwhile, all the hiding and pretending is done with. That's great. It really is.'

'I know. It was just . . . I was a bit brutal.'

Kate laughed. 'Tough! Sorry, Nat, but it was her turn. Don't do the guilt thing. Let it settle a bit and then write to her. Where's Janna?'

They went inside together. Janna was sitting listlessly, huddled on the sofa in her shawl.

' 'Twas terrible,' she said to Kate, her lips trembling. 'Terrible. And 'twas all my fault.'

'No, my darling, it wasn't. Don't take it to yourself. This goes back years to long before Nat was even born. That's how life is. Tiny things—anger, resentment, selfishness, pride—all grow and mushroom out of control and when they finally explode lots of people are hurt by the fall-out. I think it's fantastic that Monica knows and, let's face it, this was the only way it was going to happen. Nat was never going to tell her.'

'It's true, Janna,' he said. 'I would never have had the courage.'

'But don't take that to yourself as some kind of weakness,' cried Kate. 'Your reaction to Monica is the outcome of the way she's behaved to you for the last thirty-odd years. What goes round comes round. Look, there's no time for this now. You must go or you'll be late. Janna and I will be fine. Is there anything you need? OK. Drive carefully and don't worry about us or Monica.'

She hustled him away and went back inside.

' 'Twas a mistake,' said Janna miserably. 'I was late doing my room and she suspected something. I got nervous because I knew Nat didn't want her to know and she kind of tripped me up.'

Kate sat down beside her and took hold of the thin cold hand.

'You did well,' she said gently. 'Honestly, Janna, don't you think it's better not to be pretending?'

'Nat stuck up for me. He said this was my home and that the bedroom was mine and that Moniker'd better find somewhere else to spend the night.'

'Did he?' said Kate, impressed. 'I should like to have seen that. Good for Nat.'

'He meant it.' Janna was clearly moved. 'He really meant it, Kate. I wanted to go but he wouldn't let me.'

'Of course he meant it. Good grief, you've been his friend for years, the best he's got. That's why I don't want to see you both cock it up with all this nonsense about babies. You have a right to be in Nat's life without resorting to conventional codes and behaviour. You've got something very special. Accept it and enjoy it.' She gave Janna a hug. 'Look, why don't you come back with me and I'll make us lunch.'

Janna scrambled to her feet. 'I can do lunch,' she said. Suddenly there was a new and touching pride in her voice. 'I made some soup in case

360

Moniker was hungry and there's rolls and some cheese.'

'Good. Got anything to drink with it? Moments of crisis make me thirsty.'

'Nat got some Merlot in for Moniker. 'Tis her favourite.'

'Well, she won't be needing it now, will she? Oh, good, he's uncorked it, clever fellow. Pass a couple of those glasses, Janna, and then you can tell me exactly what happened.'

CHAPTER FORTY-SEVEN

Roly and Daisy, with all the dogs, went to collect Mim from the train. It was a blowy evening with showers of rain, but nothing could dampen Daisy's high spirits. Mim was quite as excited, sitting with her head turned sideways whilst Daisy talked in her ear. There was so much to report, so many new ideas to convey and quite a few questions to ask. As far as Daisy was concerned, a discussion about her biggest problem simply couldn't be postponed for a moment longer though: before they'd been in the car ten minutes she brought up the subject she'd already talked through with Mim a few days earlier. She wanted to use the students to their full potential, of course she did, but she was now convinced that the roles of the Organ-Grinder and the Laugher should be sung by professional adult singers.

'Darling Daisy,' said Mim, when she could get a word in, 'I don't quite see your problem with this one. Nobody's arguing with you. After all, this is

361

not an end-of-term concert to show the parents how well their children are progressing. The Charity Matinée is a very different occasion. It's a showcase for the school. As you well know, we always invite guest artists to perform. I've already been thinking about this particular point since you talked to me on the telephone and I quite agree with you. I have a plan about whom I shall invite to sing the parts.'

The names of the two famous singers made Daisy gasp and stretch her eyes.

'I have to say that sometimes even I forget how very powerful you are, Mim,' she said humbly. 'Do you really think they'll accept?'

'My ex-students are very kind to me,' replied Mim contentedly. 'They'll probably manage to spare a few hours if I ask them nicely.'

For once Daisy was silenced: she sat staring out at the passing scene, seeing nothing but the images of her own creation, forming and re-forming in her mind's eye. Mim's suggestion made her suddenly fearful: how could her own puny efforts of creativity match the quality of such stars? Presently, however, she recovered her confidence and began to tell Mim about her ideas for one of the scenes outside the Star Cave where the children and Cousin Henry are waiting for the stars to appear in the night sky.

'They each have their particular constellation, you see. Jane Anne's is the Pleiades, Jimbo's is the Pole Star and Monkey's is the Great and Little Bear. When Cousin Henry arrives and they make him a member of their Star Society he tells them that his constellation is Orion. I love the idea that the Starlight Express is actually a Train of

Thought, don't you? I've been wondering if we might make something out of the constellation idea. Actually have children on flying equipment, like in *Peter Pan.* Did I tell you that I thought there might be a love interest with Jane Anne and Cousin Henry? I really think it would work but then I have this terror that I'm being rather too conventional.'

'This is a children's matinée,' Mim reminded her. 'It's not an avant-garde dance company performance.'

'That's the conclusion I'd come to,' agreed Daisy, relieved. 'And I know how you like to bring in one or two of the small ones if you can. Now, "The Waltz of the Blue-Eyes Fairy" absolutely lends itself to being used for that.'

'So,' said Mim to Roly, when they'd arrived home and Daisy had dashed away to find her notes, 'no more terrible, terrible love? She seems quite recovered.'

'I think she is,' answered Roly. 'Though I suspect she still has the odd painful twinge.'

'Oh, darling,' said Mim sadly, 'we all have those. Yes, please, I'd love a drink. And now tell me how Kate is. I see Floss is still with you.'

'Poor Kate is in a bad way.' Roly passed Mim her glass and poured some more wine for Daisy, who had just appeared, clutching her notebooks. 'She's finally decided against the cottage but her agent has persuaded her to sell the house anyway because the offer is so good and Kate needs the money. Apparently she's looked at several cottages this week but she simply can't find anywhere she likes so she's decided that, instead of being panicked into buying the wrong house, she'll

363

simply have to rent until the right place turns up. On top of that, she's just been told that Guy and Gemma and the twins are emigrating to Canada. So, as you can imagine, she's struggling a bit.'

'Poor Kate,' agreed Mim, shocked. 'She simply adores those children. Oh, what a blow for her. Have you offered her the stable flat, Roly?'

'Yes, of course. I knew you'd want me to do that. She was very grateful, and I think in the last resort she'd be glad of it, but for various reasons I think she'd rather be more independent. She likes to have friends and family to visit and it's a bit difficult here.'

'Yes, I can quite see that. There's not much privacy and Kate would be anxious that she might be intruding. How difficult it is.'

'If it were the autumn she'd pick up a winter let quite easily but in the middle of June it's a much more difficult proposition.'

'What about Bruno's cottage?' Daisy had been sitting quietly, listening to the interchange. 'Wasn't he telling us that the people are leaving and he's very anxious to find someone who fits in with everyone at St Meriadoc? It must be tricky, actually, when it's such a family community. He was wondering whether they ought to do summer lets.'

She realized that Mim and Roly were gazing at her as though she'd said something extraordinary and she looked anxious.

'What?' she asked defensively. 'What did I say?'

'You are amazing, Daisy,' Roly said at last. 'When did Bruno tell you all this?'

'You must remember, surely,' she answered impatiently. 'We were looking out of his big window and I asked who lived in the little row of cottages. They looked so pretty, right against the sea wall, and those great towering cliffs kind of sheltering them. He said that his cousins live in two of them—well, you both know that, of course—and then he was saying that the one on the end was rented out but that the couple were having to leave and he was wondering what to do with it. You *must* remember, Roly. I joked that if you got tired of me I'd go and live at St Meriadoc. Would Kate like it, do you think? Does she know Bruno?'

'Yes, she knows Bruno,' answered Mim thoughtfully. 'David and Bruno were very good friends and David loved the north coast. Go and telephone her, Roly. No. Wait. Speak to Bruno first to make certain that the cottage is still available.'

Roly went upstairs and into his study to look up Bruno's number, leaving the two women considering this new idea.

'Can you imagine Kate there?' Daisy asked Mim rather anxiously. 'She loves Dartmoor so much, doesn't she? Would she be happy by the sea?'

'There are the cliffs, so very wild and beautiful, and Bodmin moor is not far away.' Mim closed her eyes so as to see Kate in the setting. 'I think that this might be just what she needs: a complete change just for a while.'

'And she could have Floss there,' said Daisy, pleased at this new thought. 'Floss and Bruno's Nellie would be great friends.'

'The cottage is still available,' Roly was leaning over the gallery, 'and Bruno says that he'd be delighted to let it to Kate for as long as she needs it. I'm going to try her number now.'

He went back into his study and paused for a moment, glancing down through the feathery branches of the cherry tree into the deep, dark waters of the pond, but there was no gleam or glint of gold. Half hidden by the tall yellow irises and green willow, the silver-grey form of the heron was barely distinguishable: he waited motionless in silent contemplation, one foot raised, the great spear of his beak poised in readiness. Roly watched, fascinated as always by this living symbol of paradox: beauty and violence. As he stared down into the shadowy garden he remembered his mother reading to him about the heron.

*   *   *

They sit beside the fire, listening to the wind in the chimney, watching the flames leap up, blue and orange and yellow, whilst Claire reads the books by 'B.B.' to them. They are on to the second book about the Little Grey Men now, and in this chapter the gnomes are sitting on the river bank when the heron arrives. Roly always imagines the scene is set in his own garden: the dark green shining water beneath the silvery tangle of willows, the low beams of sunshine gilding the feathery tops of the bushes, and the fish darting below the big flat leaves of the water lilies. It is nice to know that the Little Grey Men revere the heron, calling him Sir Herne, and he likes to hear how the old heron gives one of the gnomes, Dodder, a lift up the Folly stream on his back.

'Could the heron carry me on his back?' he asks, kneeling up to see if there is a picture of Sir

Herne.

'Oh, no.' His mother shakes her head. 'You're far too big. Gnomes are tiny people. Look at the picture on the front of the book. Baldmoney is hardly bigger than the owl, d'you see?'

'Could he carry Mim?'

They both look at Mim, who is engrossed in removing the jacket from her doll and humming to herself: she likes the stories but is easily distracted. The thought of Mim riding on Sir Herne's back makes them both laugh. They can imagine how she would wriggle and scream with fear and pleasure, her small hands gripping his feathers.

'I like Sir Herne,' says Roly. 'Even if he does sometimes catch one of the fish.'

'Clever old Mother Nature holds a balance between all the creatures. He has to feed his babies just as I have to feed you and Mim. Listen, is that Daddy coming home?'

They hear footsteps crossing the yard, stamping mud off at the door.

'It's Giant Grum the gamekeeper with his big boots,' grins Roly—and he runs to open the door for his father. 'We're reading about Sir Herne,' he tells him. 'You're just in time to hear the end of the chapter.'

*   *   *

Roly moved, so as to see the heron better, and he rose at once, long legs trailing, the feathered edges of the great wings stretched, fingerlike, as he climbed steadily, turning downstream where his fledgelings waited, perched amongst the tallest branches of the heronry high above the river.

*   *   *

Kate put down the telephone and stood for a moment, trying to put her thoughts into some semblance of order. All through this last week, whilst she'd been trying to come to terms with Gemma's news which had been followed so closely by Nat's crisis, she'd been viewing cottages in the hope of finding one that she might love. She'd trailed round with Michael, longing for both their sakes to find the one special place, only to return home each day, dispirited and frightened.

She knew that this was foolish: so many people—Giles, Harriet, Roly—had offered her a temporary roof over her head, and she knew that Cass would insist that she must move into the Rectory until she found somewhere of her own to live, but so far she'd been able to believe that something would turn up. Kate loved her family and friends but she couldn't quite imagine herself living with them. And then there was Floss. Ever since Roly and Daisy had come to lunch, and they'd been to see the cottage, she'd wished that she'd kept Floss with her. She'd begun to see that Floss was a perfect answer to her need and there were moments when she longed to jump into the car and drive down to fetch her. Each time, however, some instinct had warned her against this hasty action, cautioning her to wait just a little longer.

Could this be the answer for which she'd been waiting: the cottage by the sea wall in St Meriadoc? She remembered The Row, their sturdy stone backs turned to the Atlantic storms, and the impression that the high cliffs curved protectively round the cove so as to hold it in their rocky embrace.

'You'd be among friends,' Roly had said encouragingly, 'but you'd be self-sufficient with plenty of privacy.'

Kate thought that he'd sounded the least bit wistful—she knew that he'd hoped she might accept his offer of the stable flat once Daisy moved to London—but she knew too that he genuinely thought that it was a very sensible plan.

'And it isn't furnished,' he'd added, 'so you could have quite a lot of your own things with you. Not so much to put into store, which is another bonus.'

Kate stared around her wondering how on earth she would decide which of these pieces of her life, and her children's lives, she would keep: how did one begin to make such heart-breaking decisions? There were so many things that she'd hoped that Guy and Giles would be able to have in due course—books, furniture and even toys that would give a sense of continuum to their families, passing on to their children. Well, at least the twins wouldn't be worrying about their playroom any more: they were much too excited about their great new adventure and all the wonderful things that they would see and do.

She turned her thoughts quickly away from the twins, ignoring the sickening stab of misery, and instead considered the cottage in The Row. If it was about the size of house she was looking for then, once it was furnished, a lot of her furniture could be sold. As she brooded over what she couldn't bear to part with, and what she might be prepared to let go, it occurred to her that for the first time she would be choosing a house simply for herself. It was an odd idea and one to which she needed to give some thought.

David and she had never bought a house together. This house had remained very much the family base that she and her brother Chris had chosen and shared when the twins were growing up: David's flat too had retained the impression of his first wife and their daughter. After their marriage, each place had adapted slightly to accommodate the changes but neither she nor David had been inclined to stamp their own personalities particularly strongly so as to mark the new territories as their own. David had always been sensitive to the fact that the Whitchurch house was Guy and Giles's home and had seemed perfectly happy to fit in to the existing scenario. Whenever David had been here on Dartmoor, there'd been an air of cheerful impermanence, of holiday: London for work, the West Country for holidays, he'd say. He'd loved the moor but he'd equally loved the north coast and he'd often woken early with a desire to go dashing off to the sea. She remembered that once, after a lunch with Bruno, he'd taken her to see the house his family had once owned at Polzeath where, as a child, he'd spent his summer holidays; St Meriadoc wasn't far from Polzeath.

'How would you like to live by the sea?' Roly had asked her.

'Oh, I'm no stranger to the sea,' she'd answered. 'Apart from all those naval ports, my family moved to St Just when I was quite young and I was at school at St Audrey's, up on the north coast of Somerset. I love the sea. It's just so difficult to imagine leaving Dartmoor, especially just now. It's always been such a strength and comfort to me.'

'I know.' His voice was gentle. 'But it's not for ever, Kate. Just to give you a breathing space. Anyway, perhaps it will give you the opportunity to find another source of comfort and strength.'

She remembered that, all the while they'd been talking, she'd been fiddling with the book of *Showings*, turning it round and round, flipping through the pages. Now, some touch of grace, a new hope and confidence, unexpectedly sprang up in her heart. With a kind of wordless supplication, she opened the book, turning the pages as if seeking for guidance.

'God of your goodness, give me Yourself, for You are enough for me.'

To Kate the words were surprisingly apt. Julian's simple little prayer seemed like a starting place: a point from which she might begin a new and exciting journey.

EPILOGUE

It was December. Backstage at the Adelphi Theatre the atmosphere fizzed with an almost tangible sensation of overwhelming relief and excitement: *The Starlight Express* was a success. Performers and members of the audience mingled with the lighting crew and scene-shifters whilst the younger students carried round tall fluted glasses of champagne on trays and plates of delicious food for their guests. Mim and Daisy stood together, talking with a rising young choreographer, their expansive gestures and beaming faces indicating their feelings of heartfelt satisfaction. Janna, Kate and Nat were laughing in a group that included Jane West and the Haystack Woman—a very promising young male dancer whose performance had the audience raising the roof with cheers and laughter, and who was still dressed in padded canvas skirts and immense black boots. Bruno was in conversation with the reviewers from *The Times* and the *Evening Standard.*

Half hidden in the wings Roly studied the scene with contentment. He and Kate and Bruno had driven up together, staying with Mim in the flat, whilst Nat and Janna had travelled by train and were staying with Daisy. Kate was looking so relaxed as she talked to the pretty Gardener about her performance and watching with amused sympathy whilst the young male dancer showed them the extent of the padding under his Haystack Woman's skirts. Roly knew just how much Kate was already missing Guy and his small family, although the move to St Meriadoc, and the settling in of Floss, had done much to keep her thoughts occupied.

'I'm just so lucky to have Giles and Tessa and the babes,' she'd said to him earlier. 'They are such a comfort and they love coming over to the north coast. Tessa thinks that Henry's old enough to do his first sleepover on his own so you can imagine how excited I am about that. I'm getting his room ready. And Bruno and his family are unbelievably kind. I feel I've known them for ever. You know we were talking about whether I'd ever find anywhere to buy? Well, I've decided to renew the lease on the cottage for another six months. I haven't seen anything I really like and Floss and I are very happy at St Meriadoc for the time being. It's rather like being on an extended holiday. And I can't tell you what comfort it is to have you near at hand.'

Now Roly watched affectionately as Kate slipped an arm through Nat's and he smiled down at her. Nat too looked happier: less wary and more serene, he had the air of someone who was slowly coming to terms with himself. Janna, bright as a peacock in Indian silks, with her lion hair like a golden aureole about her small face, seemed in her element and utterly at home amongst these people of the stage. Nat and Kate had had great difficulty in persuading her to come—she'd feared that she might be out of her depth—but she looked more in keeping here than Roly had ever seen her in any other setting.

As for Daisy . . . as if she guessed his thoughts she turned and looked at him. With a word to Mim she began to thread her way through the crowds until she reached him. Her face was radiant with joy and Roly grinned at her.

'Happy?' he asked.

She closed her eyes, as if in blissful contemplation of her exalted state, drawing a deep contented breath.

'I don't think I can put it into words. Happy is inadequate for the way I feel. I was so nervous I was sick with it; somehow, it was even worse than performing. When you're dancing, on the night you can only give as much as you are, but when it's your own work on the line, and you're watching other dancers out there performing it, you feel much more vulnerable to criticism.' She looked at him, clenching both fists and punching the air. 'It worked, Roly. I can't describe to you the feeling of seeing all my visions coming true.'

'I can understand a bit of it,' he told her. 'I am so proud of you.'

She hugged him, holding him tightly for a moment. 'You were the great unwumbler. Right from the very first moment I saw you, it was you who began the process.'

Mim joined them before he could think of a suitable reply. Elegant in supple soft silky wool of charcoal grey she smiled with tenderness upon them both.

'What a triumph,' she said, deftly taking a glass of champagne from a passing tray. 'We've just been talking about it with the choreographer, Daniel Malpass, and he's been saying some very nice things about Daisy. It all went perfectly.' She took a little sip, her eyes regarding Roly thoughtfully above the rim of the glass. 'Whom did it remind you of, Roly?'

He looked at her sharply and they exchanged a

long, nostalgic glance of remembrance: a shared and distant past of fun and laughter and loss.

'It reminded me of Mother,' he answered. 'The music and the dancing and especially that last scene; I couldn't help thinking how much she would have loved it.'

'I thought that, too,' agreed Mim. 'And in an odd way I felt that it was a tribute to her. Don't you agree? It was the sum of all her parts, the culmination of everything that she bequeathed to us, the echoes of the dance. Daisy gathered it all up and breathed life into it.' She shook her head, smiling at her foolishness. 'Take no notice, I'm being fanciful. Mad Madame Mim! Come, Daisy. There's someone I want you to meet.'

Roly watched them go, thinking about what Mim had said and knowing that she was right. In some strange way *The Starlight Express* had embodied all the joy and love and faith that their young mother had spilled so generously into their lives. Standing quiet and at peace he remembered how scene had followed magical scene, just as Daisy and Mim had planned through all those long weeks of summer, building inevitably to the final brilliant conclusion: the glorious voices of the Organ-Grinder and the Laugher joining together in the last duet and then that quite unexpected, heart-jumping orchestral slide into the first bars of the carol. And finally, whilst the carillon of bells heralded the rising of the gauzy backdrop, fully revealing the night sky with its shining web of stars, the whole cast had turned to welcome the rising of the most mysterious and wonderful Star of all: the Star of Bethlehem.